ONE LAST WISH

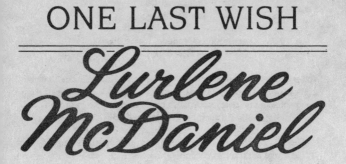

Lurlene McDaniel

I0639318

LAUREL-LEAF BOOKS

Published by
Dell Laurel-Leaf
an imprint of
Random House Children's Books
a division of Random House, Inc.
New York

This edition contains the complete and unabridged texts of the
original editions. This omnibus was originally published in
separate volumes under the titles:

Mother Help Me Live copyright © 1992 by Lurlene McDaniel
Let Him Live copyright © 1993 by Lurlene McDaniel
Sixteen and Dying copyright © 1992 by Lurlene McDaniel

Visit us on the Web! www.randomhouse.com/teens

Educators and librarians, for a variety of teaching tools, visit us at
www.randomhouse.com/teachers

ISBN: 0-553-57142-7

RL: 5, age 10 and up

Printed in the United States of America

Bantam Starfire edition November 1998
First Laurel-Leaf edition October 2003

20 19 18 17 16 15

OPM

ONE LAST WISH:
Three Novels

From *Mother, Help Me Live*

What could be more important than finding her birth mother? What could be more important than discovering whether she had siblings with compatible bone marrow? Her very *life* could depend on finding these people. Sarah practically jumped from the sofa. "I've got to go," she said.

From *Let Him Live*

She looked into his eyes and saw quiet desperation. *He needed her*. His appeal sliced deep into her heart. She needed him too. Needed him in her life even though she couldn't explain why to either one of them. Meg didn't feel confident at all, but she knew she would try her best for his sake.

From *Sixteen and Dying*

"I can't believe this is happening to me," she said suddenly, and her tears flowed freely. Blood—the very thing that once saved her life—was now turning her body against her. . . .

Doctor Stevenson took a deep breath and in a soft, troubled voice said, "I'm sorry. We'll do everything we can possibly do, but there is no cure for AIDS."

CONTENTS

Mother, Help Me Live

One

SARAH McGREGGOR SAT cross-legged on the hospital bed, staring at the handful of light brown hair in the palm of her hand. "It's starting all over again, isn't it, Mom?" she asked.

Her mother, a short, plump woman with a sleek cap of black hair, nodded sympathetically. "I'm afraid so, honey. But we both know it's temporary. Hair grows back."

"Sure," Sarah said miserably. "But it wasn't supposed to happen to me again. Not after two years of being well."

"Honey, I'd give anything to make it go away for you. Maybe this time the chemo will knock it out once and for all."

Sarah knew her mother was trying to make her feel better, and give her a ray of hope, but holding the wad of hair—hair she'd lovingly groomed since the last time it fell out from chemotherapy—made hope seem like an illusion. Not since she'd been ten and learned she had leukemia had Sarah felt so hopeless.

She'd endured treatments for three years. At first, the medications had made her deathly ill. Some had felt like fire as they'd dripped into her veins. She'd been sick, had lost all her hair, and had gotten painfully thin, then puffy and fat when her drug protocol had been changed. Yet, her leukemia had responded, and when she'd been thirteen, Dr. Hernandez had taken her off all therapy. "If you continue in remission for five years, Sarah," Dr. Hernandez had said at the time, "I'll consider you cured."

"And if I don't?"

"Let's not borrow trouble. Relapses can be tricky, because obtaining a second remission is much more difficult. For now, you're fine, and we want you to stay that way. Come in for blood work every six months, and as for your everyday life, go have fun."

For two years, she'd been happy and healthy. Then, three weeks ago, her routine blood work had shown abnormalities. Dr. Hernandez had sent her to the hospital and put her back on chemo.

"Dad says he'll bring Tina and Richie when he comes to visit this weekend," Sarah heard her mom say, and suddenly remembered that she was still in the room.

"Good. Don't tell them, but I miss them a lot."

Her mother smiled. "Richie is driving me crazy asking when you're coming home, and Tina's had her suitcase packed since Tuesday, according to your father."

As if it weren't bad enough being hospitalized,

Sarah was also three hundred miles from home. The big Memphis hospital might be one of the foremost cancer treatment centers in the country, but for Sarah, it was too far away from all that was familiar back in Ringgold, Georgia. She looked out the window and saw puffy clouds in a bright blue April sky. She wondered about her friends. She pictured Cammie, Natalie, and JoEllen in the school's cafeteria eating lunch without her.

Ninth grade was supposed to have been *their* year. All of them had made the JV cheerleading squad, which meant that they'd have a good chance of making the varsity squad when they entered high school in the fall. Now, all Sarah had to look forward to was three more weeks of intensive treatment in Memphis and then a new regime of medications and clinic visits for the next few years.

"Is Dad bringing my schoolwork?" Sarah asked. "I'm already behind, and I want to pass. Mom, I can't stand the idea of being held back."

"Don't panic." Her mother patted her arm reassuringly. "Your teachers all understand. What you don't get done before the end of the year, you can finish up over the summer. You're a good enough student that you'll be able to stay with your class. You did before."

"What a way to spend summer vacation," Sarah grumbled. "Why did this have to happen to me? It's not fair."

"None of it's fair, Sarah. But your dad and I never gave up hope of having you, so don't you give up hope now."

Sarah had heard the story a hundred times as she was growing up. Her parents had tried for years to have a baby, and just as they'd given up, Sarah had been born. Two years later, Tina had come along, and nine years after that, Richie. "Once we got the hang of it, there was no stopping us," Dad had often joked.

Sarah rolled her wad of hair into a fuzzy ball. "Would you ask the nurses for some scissors, please," she said. "I'd rather cut it off now than watch it fall out in clumps." She looked at the hair sadly. Somehow, when she'd been ten, it hadn't seemed as horrible. But now that she was fifteen, it felt as if she were losing her best friend.

"Maybe it'll grow some over the summer. I don't want to start high school looking like a freak," Sarah said.

"Honey, you're beautiful with or without hair."

Sarah sniffed. How could her mother think that would comfort her? "Mom, most guys like their girls with all their body parts—including hair."

"If it's going to make such a difference to them, then they can't be worth your time in the first place. Goodness, I hope Richie doesn't grow up to be that shallow."

Sarah bit back a retort. Arguing with her mother wasn't going to make her feel better, and it certainly wasn't going to keep her hair from falling out. "Just ask the nurse for some scissors, all right? And let's get it over with."

Her mother left the room, and Sarah shoved the clump of hair into a paper sack and flung it across the floor.

"You sure got a big room, Sarah." Four-year-old Richie crawled up on Sarah's bed and gave her a wet, sloppy kiss.

Sarah hugged him tightly. "I'd rather be in my room back home. Are you guarding it for me?"

Richie nodded. His fly-away hair was the color of dark chocolate, and his big brown eyes looked solemn. "I put a Keep Out sign on it. I made it myself." He glanced toward Tina, who was touring the room and reading the names on every bouquet of flowers Sarah had been sent. "Tina tried to borrow your green sweater, but I told Dad, and he made her put it back."

Richie's self-satisfied grin made Sarah smile. She remembered when he'd been born. She'd been eleven and had just completed her first year of cancer treatment. Richie had brightened her days. He'd been so adorable, so tiny and sweet with his little button nose and bow-shaped mouth. She and Tina used to fight over who would push him in his stroller.

"You sure got a lot of flowers," Tina remarked, ambling over to the bed.

Sarah didn't like her tone. Did Tina think Sarah had purposely relapsed so that she could collect flower arrangements? "They cheer up the place," Sarah replied.

"Doesn't look too awful to me," Tina countered, peering around. "Private room, your own TV, all this new stuff to read . . ." Tina flipped through a pile of the latest teen magazines their mother had bought. Her parents had gone down to the hospital coffee shop, so the three of them were alone in Sarah's room.

"The days are pretty long and boring," Sarah said. "Not to mention the chemo treatments." She knew Tina didn't understand. Sarah was never sure why she and her sister didn't get along too well. Maybe it was because they were only two years apart, but she always felt as if she and Tina were in some kind of competition.

"I know." Tina shrugged. "I didn't mean to make it sound like you were on vacation. I know this is a real drag."

Sarah felt her attitude toward her sister soften. Tina did have her moments. "How're my friends?"

"People call every night to ask about you. I give them a full report. JoEllen says that she's writing you a long letter with all the latest news." Tina flopped on the bed. "And this is from Scott." Tina handed Sarah an envelope. "He says to tell you that he's hurting in track this year because you're not there to time his workouts."

Sarah smiled as she took the envelope. Scott Michaels had lived next door to her all her life. They'd been friends since their sandbox days and had announced their "engagement" when they'd been three. Of course, then they'd been children, and now Scott dated other girls, but Sarah still felt a deep affection for him. "Tell him I'll write," Sarah said.

"When are you coming home, Sarah?" Richie asked. "I miss you."

"I miss you, too. But I can't come home until they give me a bunch of medicine."

"I don't like it when you're not home."

"I don't like it much, either."

Richie reached up and toyed with the scarf she'd tied around her head to hide her baldness. "Why are you wearing that?"

Tina caught her eye and gave a knowing nod. Of

course, Dad would have told Tina. "I have a new haircut," she explained.

"Can I see?"

"It's real different."

"I want to see."

Sarah slowly untied the scarf and let it slide to her shoulders. Richie's eyes grew wide, and his mouth dropped open. "Where's your hair?"

"The medicine I take makes it fall out."

Richie stared at her head from different angles. "I think I like your old haircut better."

Sarah laughed. "I do, too."

Tina looked self-consciously down at the floor. Sarah realized that Tina felt embarrassed and uncomfortable. It irked Sarah. How could Tina act so childish? Did she think Sarah enjoyed showing off her slick, shorn head?

Richie's face broke out in a sudden grin. "I know!" he exclaimed. "You can be on *Star Trek*. They like bald ladies."

Sarah laughed and hugged him. Tina laughed, too. Richie looked puzzled, trying to figure out what was so funny about his suggestion.

Sarah retied the scarf, glad they were all laughing. It beat crying.

Two

"DON'T BE NERVOUS. This is only a meeting to discuss our options," Dr. Hernandez began.

Sarah and her parents were sitting in one of the hospital's small consultation rooms with Dr. Hernandez and Dr. Gill, another oncologist. Her father had brought her down from her room in a wheelchair, and despite both doctors' reassuring smiles, Sarah was nervous. She glanced at her parents, who looked worried and uncomfortable, too.

"Sarah, you're almost finished with the induction phase of your treatment," Dr. Hernandez said, her brown eyes serious and compassionate. "Before we put you onto a maintenance protocol and send you home, Dr. Gill and I want to discuss some other possibilities with you."

Sarah had been given a chemo treatment that morning, and she was feeling queasy. Sores had formed in her mouth, and her gums throbbed, but she listened attentively.

"You know, Sarah, forty years ago, most kids with cancer died. Today, we have sixty percent surviving five years and more," Dr. Gill said. "The main reason we don't have a one-hundred-percent cure rate, especially with leukemia, is that no matter what kinds of chemo we throw at a malignancy, some cancerous cells survive. The cancer may stay dormant for years, but eventually it recurs, and even though we might obtain a second and third remission, the time between remissions shortens."

"That doesn't sound hopeful," Sarah's mother declared. "Isn't this therapy going to help Sarah?"

Dr. Hernandez held up her hand. "Please, Mrs. McGreggor. We don't want to alarm you. Yes, she will obtain another remission, but the best way to fight Sarah's type of leukemia is with a bone marrow transplant. Have you ever heard of this?"

Sarah's father said, "Of course, but isn't that risky?"

"It can be, but let me explain." Dr. Hernandez drew shapes on a yellow pad and turned it toward Sarah. "Once transplanted marrow takes a foothold in a leukemia patient, it has a good chance of knocking out leukemic cells and curing the disease. A much better chance than chemo or radiation alone."

"Then why don't I get one of these transplants?" Sarah was eager to learn about anything that might destroy her cancer forever.

"What are the risks?" her father asked.

"We get noncancerous marrow from donors," Dr. Hernandez explained, "and there's very little risk to them. The donor is given a general anesthesia, then we insert a special syringe into the pelvic bone and draw out a cup or so of marrow. Since the donor's healthy, new marrow is manufactured, and except for some achiness in the hips, the donor's up and around in no time."

"But what about me?" Sarah asked.

"The marrow is hung in a bag and dripped into the recipient's veins just like chemo. It migrates to the bone cavities and begins reproducing healthy blood cells."

Sarah pondered the idea while studying the drawings. "So, what's the catch? What's the bad news?"

Both doctors laughed. "You're right, Sarah—that's the good news, a best-case scenario. The bad news is that before the recipient can receive the donor marrow, she has to have all her marrow destroyed. We do that with chemo and radiation."

"Sounds creepy," Sarah said.

"Isn't it dangerous?" Sarah's mother asked.

"The threat of infection is very real and very life-threatening, but we take every precaution. We isolate the potential recipient in a germ-free environment before and after the process and until the new marrow starts growing. We put her on immunosuppressant drugs, which are eventually dispensed with as the healthy marrow takes hold."

"What about rejection?" Sarah's father asked. "I've heard about transplants that don't take because they're rejected by the body."

Dr. Hernandez nodded. "Graft versus host disease is medicine's biggest problem in the area of transplantation."

Sarah thought it was a big problem for her, too.

How could they promise something so wonderful as a cure, then snatch it away with a series of medical enigmas? "So, are you going to transplant my bone marrow or not?" she asked. There was a sour taste in her mouth, and the sores were starting to sting. Her mother poured her a glass of water, and Sarah sipped it slowly.

Dr. Gill thumped on the tabletop with a pencil. "Frankly, we believe that a transplant is necessary for you. We think it's your best chance of winning this battle."

The words hit Sarah hard. This was no scrimmage with a nagging illness she was fighting. This was all-out war, and in order to win, she needed a bone marrow transplant. "How do I get one of these transplants? Can we do it while I'm here now?"

Dr. Hernandez leaned back in her chair and folded her arms. "First, we need to find a suitable donor."

"What we look for in matching donor and recipient is HLA compatibility." Dr. Gill drew busily on the legal pad. "Remember that rejection factor?" Sarah nodded. "Well, we've discovered that if six proteins found on the surface of white blood cells match the proteins of your cells, we have an optimum, six-antigen match. Identical twins have identical HLA."

"But I'm not a twin."

"True, but you have siblings, which increases your chances of an antigen match."

"I could use my sister's or brother's marrow?" Sarah asked.

"What about my wife's or mine?" Sarah's father

blurted out, startling Sarah. He looked disturbed. Her mother looked pale.

"You are long shots," Dr. Gill explained. "You see, each of your children received chromosomes from both of you. That gives them a higher probability of matching Sarah. We can screen them with a simple blood test. I assure you, it only means drawing out a vial of blood from each for testing."

Her parents looked upset, and Sarah sensed something was wrong. Didn't they want Tina and Richie to be checked out? It didn't make sense to her. As a family, they'd fought her cancer for years, and she couldn't imagine having more caring, loving parents than hers. Her nausea was increasing, and a fine film of perspiration had broken out on her face.

Her mother rose to her feet. "I can tell that Sarah's not feeling well. I think I should take her back to her room."

"But, Mom, this is important."

Both doctors stood. "Don't worry, Sarah. You won't be left out of the process. You get some rest, and we'll pick up this discussion later," Dr. Hernandez assured her.

Sarah struggled against her rising nausea, angry that it was affecting her at this moment. "All right ... later." She noticed that her father didn't stand, nor did he offer to help return her to her room. He looked shaken and grim. The doctors sat back down.

"I'm okay. Really. I'm just sick from the chemo," Sarah said while her mother helped her into bed in her room. "Is everything all right with you and Dad?"

"Things are fine."

The expression on her face told Sarah differently. "Don't you think the transplant is a good idea? It seems all right to me."

"There are a lot of risks."

"But—"

"Sarah, let's not discuss this now, please. You get some rest, and your father and I will be in later."

Sarah was tired and ill, but her mother's distracted, serious expression worried her. Usually, both her parents were eager to discuss any approaches to combat her cancer, but ever since the doctors had mentioned the bone marrow transplant, both of them seemed different.

Sarah told her mother good-bye and watched her hurry from the room. Instinctively, Sarah knew she was returning to the meeting room and a discussion with the doctors Sarah wouldn't be able to hear. She swallowed her fear and fell into an exhausted sleep.

When she awoke hours later, both her parents were in her room with her. Her dad had the TV turned low, and her mother was flipping through a magazine aimlessly. "Hi," Sarah said. Her voice sounded hoarse, and she ached all over.

Her father quickly turned off the TV, and both he and her mother came to her bedside. "We need to talk," he said without preamble.

Her mother gave her a drink of water and helped her sit upright. Sarah fought to clear her groggy brain from sleep. "What's wrong?" She saw them glance at each other. "It's the bone marrow transplant, isn't it?" Sarah asked. "You don't want me to have it, do you?"

"That's not it," her father replied.

Sarah glanced anxiously from face to face. Had

the doctors told them something really serious about her condition? "Please, Mom, Dad, you're scaring me. Am I going to die?" Her heart began to pound.

"Oh, honey, it's nothing like that." Her mother put her arms around Sarah and stroked her lovingly. "But it does involve the bone marrow business and Tina and Richie."

"You don't want them to be my donors?" Sarah pulled away.

"Sarah, we love you so much," her mother said. Tears had formed in her eyes.

Her father stepped forward and took her hand. "Baby, there's no need for Tina or Richie to be typed for compatibility. They're not going to match you."

Sarah stared at them, confused and dumbfounded. "How can you be sure? They're my sister and brother."

Her mother shook her head. Tears trickled down her cheeks. "No, Sarah, they're not. When you were three days old, we adopted you."

Three

SARAH FELT AS if a bomb had exploded. She could not ever remember being taken so completely off guard, not even when she'd first been told she had leukemia. At that time, leukemia meant nothing to her, and besides, her mom and dad had been with her, holding her hand and supporting her. "What did you say?" Sarah asked, assuming she'd heard incorrectly.

"We adopted you, Sarah. It was privately arranged, through an attorney," her father said quietly.

"It was legal," her mother added.

The implication that it might not have been fell like another blow to Sarah. "How can that be? Why?"

"I couldn't have children," her mother explained. "We had tried everything, gone to all kinds of doctors, but I couldn't conceive. The doctors didn't know why, and none of them could help me. I was a medical mystery."

Sarah remembered her mother's being pregnant with Richie; she remembered feeling the baby kick from inside her mom's womb. "How about Tina and Richie? I saw Richie in the hospital right after he was born."

"That's another of those medical mysteries," her father said. "We adopted you, and right after your first birthday, your mom discovered she was pregnant. Sometimes it happens that way. Adoption leads to pregnancy. No one knows why."

"Once we got the hang of it, there was no stopping us." Sarah had heard him say those words many times, but now they took on a whole new meaning. Tina was the breakthrough, not Sarah.

"Sarah, listen to me," her mother said. Sarah turned toward the sound of her voice, feeling like a robot without a will of her own. Her mother's plump face looked sad and tormented. "We have always thought of you as our own, Sarah. I couldn't love you more if you'd come out of my body."

"Except I didn't," Sarah replied. She looked at her father. His brown eyes were misty. "I don't belong to either of you."

"Yes, you do," her father insisted. "You've been ours since you were three days old."

"You mean I was a legal transaction," Sarah said matter-of-factly. "Like when you bought our house." In her mind's eye, Sarah saw her father signing papers and handing them over to a nameless man, who handed a baby over to her mother.

"You were our joy," her mother said fiercely. "We tried for six years to conceive a baby. I thought I would *die* from wanting a baby to hold and love. I couldn't even watch TV commercials with babies in them, because it hurt too bad. It made me want a baby all the more. I got depressed. I couldn't eat or sleep." She looked to her husband.

"We went to adoption agencies, but the wait for a newborn was five years! Then a fellow in my office said he knew a lawyer who arranged adoptions, and the wait wasn't nearly so long," her father explained.

Sarah felt distanced from them, captivated by the story of two people who wanted a baby. She felt as though it wasn't her they were talking about—just some baby somewhere in time. Her mother continued, "We contacted the attorney, and after about six months, he called to say he had a pregnant girl who wanted to put her baby up for adoption. All we had to do was pay her medical expenses."

A pregnant girl. My mother, thought Sarah. She exhaled slowly and glanced from face to face of the two people she'd loved so unconditionally all her life. Dad and Mom. No. Two strangers. "Why didn't you tell me sooner? Why did you wait all these years?"

"It was a condition of the adoption. The birth mother insisted on absolute secrecy."

"Why, was she a criminal or something?"

"We never asked why." Her father brushed over Sarah's sarcasm. "We never met her, of course. The lawyer handled everything, but he let us know that if we broke the trust, we could lose you."

"Did everyone know I was adopted? Grandma McGreggor and Grandma and Papaw Douglas?" Sarah mentioned both sets of grandparents, then realized they weren't her grandparents, either. Not really.

"They swore to keep it a secret, and they have," her mother answered. "As for everybody else, we bought the house and moved to Ringgold when you were a few weeks old, and no one else ever knew."

"My birth certificate ... I saw it," Sarah announced, recalling the time she'd had to show proof of her age to join a summer softball league.

"You saw an amended copy of the original. It was issued at the time of the adoption," her mother told her. "The original was sealed by the courts. As far as the law is concerned, you are our daughter."

Sarah felt caught in some bizarre nightmare. Maybe she'd wake up and discover that all she was hearing and experiencing was some weird side effect of her chemotherapy. "But the promise you made was for when I was a baby. I'm not a baby now."

Her mother shook her head. "We couldn't take that chance. Besides, then Tina came along, and it was so simple to just keep it to ourselves. It wasn't anybody's business."

"It was *my* business," Sarah exclaimed.

"When you were ten, you got leukemia, Sarah," her father said as if that explanation would appease her. "We couldn't have told you then. It wouldn't have been fair. We were both scared for you. And you were so sick with the treatments and all. We didn't want to add anything more to your suffering."

"And if it weren't for this relapse, for the bone marrow transplant, you would never have told me, would you?" Sarah realized that her voice was quivering and rising in pitch. "I would never have found out if it weren't for this."

Her mother reached for her, but Sarah turned away. "We would have told you when you were older."

"When would I have been old enough? When I graduated from high school? When I started college? You should have told me when I was little." Sarah heard her voice crack and hated being unable to hold back tears. She buried her face in her hands.

"Honey, there was nothing malicious on our part for keeping your adoption a secret," her father said. His voice sounded as if it were coming from a long way off. "We love you, Sarah. We've always loved you. You've been ours for fifteen years, and you'll be ours until we all die. This shouldn't make a difference."

Sarah refused to raise her head. He was wrong. It made a difference. It mattered that all her life she'd been part of a lie. Regardless of its intent, keeping the truth from her was indefensible. "I—I want to be alone," Sarah said. "I want to think about all this."

"We should be with you—" her mother started.

Sarah's head flew up, and she clenched her fists around the bed covers. "Well, I don't want you with me."

She saw her mother step backward, as if she'd been struck. Her father put his arm around her protectively. "Don't speak to your mother that way," he said.

"You just told me she's not my mother. You are not my parents." Sarah knew she sounded hateful and mean, but she couldn't stop herself. She wanted to hurt them the way they had hurt her.

"We *are* your parents, young lady, and I won't have you treating us like garbage."

Sarah recoiled at her father's tone of voice. He'd never spoken to her so harshly before. Her mother pulled him closer to her side. "Patrick, this isn't helping. Sarah needs some space. I understand." She looked at Sarah, her expression wounded. "We'll go down to the coffee shop for a little while and give you some time alone. Tina and Richie will be back from the movie in an hour. We need to decide what to tell them."

Sarah remembered that the social services division of the hospital had organized an outing for the siblings of the patients on the oncology floor. It was part of an overall effort to reach out to what the psychologists called "the forgotten ones"—the healthy family members who often got lost in the shuffle because all attention was focused on the sick child. The mention of Tina and Richie caused Sarah to have a new thought. If her parents weren't really her parents, then Tina and Richie weren't really her sister and brother.

An image of Richie as a baby floated into her memory and caused a cry to escape. Everything was a lie! Her whole life, everything she'd ever believed, was founded on lies. She curled up in a ball and slunk under the covers. She didn't see her parents leave, but sensed she was alone in the room. When she was certain of that, she started to cry. She muffled her sobs with a pillow, not wanting a nurse to hear her and come into the room and ask a lot of questions.

How would she answer them? What would she say to Tina and Richie, to Scott and all her friends back home? Would she tell them at all? Yet, even as she considered the question, she knew she would never be able to keep it a secret. It was too big, too shattering.

Dr. Hernandez's explanation of the bone marrow transplant procedure crept back into her mind. According to the doctor, she needed a transplant from a sibling for optimum success. Now she knew there were no siblings. She was alone. Utterly alone.

Four

Propped on the tray table that stretched across her bed, Sarah sat and stared at her reflection in a mirror. Chemo had taken its toll on her looks, but that wasn't what she was seeing. She was seeing "eyes of such a pale, clear shade of blue as to resemble light streaming through a window." Scott Michaels had described them that way when she'd been eleven, and it had made her blush. "That was a compliment," he'd added. "I've never seen eyes the color of yours before."

Sarah reached up and tugged off the scarf. When she had hair, it was a peculiar shade of light, golden brown. Her forehead was high and wide, her cheekbones defined, her chin pointed with a cleft. Why had she never before seen that she didn't look like anyone in her family? Everyone had brown eyes except her. Tina and Richie both had their mom's black hair, and although her father was partially bald, his hair was dark brown. How could she have been so blind to the obvious physical differences between her family and herself all these years?

She'd spent the night in a fitful sleep. Her parents had returned to her room last night, but she'd felt stiff and awkward around them. Tina had kept giving her baffled looks and at one point blurted, "So, what's *your* problem?"

"Don't yell at your sister," her mother had told Tina. "Sarah's had a bad day."

"I can speak for myself," Sarah had said testily. Fortunately, they hadn't stayed long. Her anger had burned until Richie had thrown his small arms around her when their father had announced it was time to leave.

"I want to stay with Sarah!" he'd cried, his dark eyes filling with tears.

She'd held him, knowing she couldn't take out her frustrations on Richie. "I'll be out of here soon."

"Don't be a baby," Tina had ordered.

"Stop bickering," her father had snapped. "We have to hit the road tomorrow morning. Sarah will be home in a couple of weeks."

Their mother would stay with Sarah until Dr. Hernandez released her, but suddenly Sarah wished her mother was leaving, too. She didn't want to be around her parents. "Not my parents," Sarah reminded herself. She shoved the mirror aside and hunkered down in the bed.

Dr. Hernandez came into her room, but Sarah ignored her. She didn't feel like socializing. She wanted to fall into a deep sleep, like Rip Van Winkle. And maybe if she woke up in a hundred years, her life would be different.

The doctor pulled a chair alongside of Sarah's bed. "We have to talk, Sarah," she said.

"I don't want to talk." Sarah slid under the bed covers.

"No choice," Dr. Hernandez replied. "I'm going to sit here until you come out from under the covers, even if it takes all day."

Sarah knew she wasn't bluffing. With a sigh, she raised herself up. "What do you want?"

"First, I want to tell you how sorry I am that you learned about your adoption the way you did."

"It isn't your fault."

"And it's not your fault, either. Or your parents'."

Sarah glared at the doctor. "Yes, it is their fault. They should have told me sooner. It wasn't right to hide it from me all this time."

"Most adoptive parents do tell their children. They often start telling them from the time they're very small, but your parents explained their reasons to me. I'm sure they thought they were doing the best thing by not telling you. They can't go back and undo the past."

"Why did you come? To tell me not to be mad? Well, I am mad." Sarah crossed her arms and fought to hold back tears.

"I'm your doctor. And even though you've been hit hard emotionally, it doesn't change the dynamics of your cancer. You still need a bone marrow transplant."

Sarah felt overwhelmed and buried her face in her hands. "I can't think about that now."

"You must, my dear." Silent sobs made Sarah's shoulders heave. Dr. Hernandez gave her a few moments, then handed her some tissue. "Sarah, I'm not

trying to ignore your hurt," the doctor said kindly.
"I'm not telling you to forget and get on with the
program. I care about you, Sarah, and I want to see
you well—free of cancer. We have to discuss our
next strategy . . . all right?"

Sarah took a deep breath and nodded. "What do
you want me to do?"

"Dr. Gill and I had a long talk with your parents
yesterday to outline your options."

"You said I needed a sibling to be a donor. Well,
I don't have any siblings."

Dr. Hernandez leaned forward in the chair, her
dark eyes serious. "I said your *best* chance was with
a sibling donor. But it's not your only chance. We
can put you and your HLA compatibility factors into
the National Marrow Donor Program registry and
see if we can locate a match."

"What's this donor registry?"

"It's a nationwide network of transplant and donor centers, linked by computers, that medical professionals use to make genetic matches between
donors and recipients for organs and bone marrow.
Whenever a person volunteers to be a donor, we enter the blood factors into the system."

"You said someone needed to match me in six
ways."

"Very good," the doctor said with a smile. "You
were paying close attention yesterday." Her smile
faded. "Yes, a six-antigen match is ideal. Research
has shown us that with bone marrow, the chance of
finding someone outside of your family with compatible HLA is one in twenty-thousand."

Sarah gasped. "What kind of chance is that?"

"Actually, not bad—especially if more people are

willing to become donors. Imagine, if every eligible donor in the United States were entered into the registry, we'd be able to do numerous HLA matches. We'd have a constant source of marrow donors at our disposal if for some reason a patient's family situation didn't work out. Like in your case."

"So, why don't you have it?"

Dr. Hernandez shook her head. "Sadly, we simply don't have enough volunteers. People are pretty good about donating blood, but most don't know about the bone marrow program. Also, marrow donating is a little more complicated and, therefore, more trouble."

"So, I lose. Is that it?"

"Maybe not. We are going to go ahead and start a computer search on your behalf. Who knows— maybe we already have marrow to match yours."

Sarah wasn't very optimistic. "Sure. Maybe."

"We've put up quite a fight against your cancer so far. We can't give up now," Dr. Hernandez insisted. "Don't be discouraged."

"What happens in the meantime?"

"We continue with conventional treatments while looking for a compatible donor."

"Then I can go home?" For the first time, Sarah dreaded the thought. At least, here in the hospital she didn't have to face her friends and the life she'd left back home. What would they think when they found out she was adopted?

"Yes, you can go home. You'll still be taking medications, and you'll have to come back for blood work, but you'll be able to resume a normal life while we hunt for a match."

A *normal life.* Sarah felt like laughing in the doctor's face. Her life would never be normal again. She shut her eyes.

Dr. Hernandez patted her arm. "Sarah, your parents understand the risks. For your sake, for your health, you all need to pull together."

Sarah forced a tentative smile to assure the doctor she understood. How could they pull as a team when she felt fragmented into a hundred pieces? How?

Sarah woke with a start. Her room was in semi-darkness, and she was alone. She heard the dinner cart rattling down the hospital corridor and realized that she'd slept most of the day. At first, she felt disoriented and confused, but then reality started bombarding her. She remembered Dr. Hernandez's visit. She remembered her mother's coming in and trying to talk to her. She recalled asking her to please go away.

With a groan, Sarah sat up in bed. Her sheets were drenched in perspiration. She needed to ring for a nurse. There was a time when her mother would have changed her sheets and had dinner in the room with her. Sarah guessed her mother was down in the cafeteria. She flipped on the light over her bed and blinked from the glare.

She reached for the buzzer to summon a nurse and saw a long white envelope on her bedside table. She picked it up. Her name was written across it in a beautiful script. She turned the envelope over and discovered it had been sealed with red sealing wax, imprinted with the monogram OLW. "Pretty," Sarah said aloud. "I wonder who . . ." She shrugged her shoulders and broke the seal. After all, it was addressed to her. Sarah reached in and pulled out two sheets of paper. One was a letter. Lifting the pale parchment paper to the lamplight, she began to read.

Five

∽

DEAR SARAH,

You don't know me, but I know about you, and because I do, I want to give you a special gift. Accompanying this letter is a certified check, my gift to you with no strings attached to spend on anything you want. No one knows about this gift except you, and you are free to tell anyone you want.

Who I am isn't really important, only that you and I have much in common. Through no fault of our own, we have endured pain and isolation and have spent many days in a hospital feeling lonely and scared. I hoped for a miracle, but most of all, I hoped for someone to truly understand what I was going through.

I can't make you live longer. I can't stop you from hurting, but I can give you one wish, as someone did for me. My wish helped me find purpose, faith, and courage.

Friendship reaches beyond time, and the true miracle is in giving, not receiving. Use my gift to fulfill your wish.

Your Forever Friend,
JWC

Sarah reread the letter. She turned it over. The back was blank. Who in the world could have sent it? She racked her brain to think of anybody she knew with the initials JWC and drew a blank. She had no friend, knew no one, with those initials. "It must be a joke," she told herself.

She fumbled for the second piece of paper, held it up to the light, and saw that it was, indeed, a check. It was made out to her in the amount of one-hundred-thousand dollars! Sarah's eyes grew wide, and she went hot and cold all over. She dug inside the envelope for other clues. She found nothing. She had only the letter and a check from the One Last Wish Foundation. Neither one made sense to her. Who was JWC? Why was this foundation choosing Sarah to receive such a large sum of money?

The letter said it was a gift with no strings and that she was free to spend it on anything she wanted. "Wow . . ." Sarah whispered, dumbstruck. "Double wow." Her mind raced over hundreds of things she would like to buy, but nothing seemed important enough for such a generous gift.

"Slow down," she told herself. "No need to rush." The letter didn't put any time restrictions on her spending the money, so if the money really and truly was hers, then she could spend it whenever she felt like it.

With her thoughts spinning, Sarah decided to keep the gift a secret for the time being. She slowly got out of bed and tucked the envelope into an inner side pocket of her tote bag, which she shut securely in the closet. She smiled over the enormousness of her secret. Just knowing she had so much money at her fingertips picked her spirits up considerably. This money would really make a difference. Sarah didn't know how, but she knew most definitely that it would.

Sarah was released when the induction phase of her chemotherapy was completed. During the drive home, Sarah sensed that her mother wanted to discuss all that had happened, but the heavy doses of chemo that had put her into remission had also left her sick and weak, without much energy. Sarah didn't feel like discussing anything.

When they arrived at the house, her father carried her inside. A huge banner was stretched across the living room. It read, "Welcome Home, Sarah!" in letters that sparkled. Streamers and balloons were hung everywhere.

"Do you like it?" Richie asked, pointing to the banner. "I put the glitter on the letters all by myself."

"It's nice. Thank you," Sarah told Richie. She remembered the time she'd returned home after her first hospitalization. She'd hugged all of her family and actually bent down and kissed the floor. Somehow, now the house looked different to her, smaller and less homey.

Up in her room, her father settled her in her bed. She told her family she was tired and asked to be left alone.

"What do you want me to tell your friends?" Tina asked. "They keep calling and want to come over."

"Tell them to give me a few days. I'll let them know when I want visitors."

Tina looked puzzled. She obviously remembered Sarah's previous homecoming, when Sarah had demanded that every friend she had in the world rush right over to see her. "If you say so," Tina said.

"Let's give Sarah some time to settle in," her dad suggested. Minutes later, he cleared everyone out of her room and left, too, closing the door. Sarah lay still, listening to the murmur of voices. She knew that she was hurting her parents by pointedly ignoring them and their efforts to make her feel comfortable. She didn't care. They had hurt her.

There were gardenia bushes planted in front of the house, and a soft April breeze lifted their scent through her open window. From the kitchen below, Sarah caught the aroma of chocolate chip cookies—her favorites—baking in the oven. She also caught the smell of her mother's favorite perfume, and her father's aftershave. She'd grown up with these scents. Once, they had represented security and contentment. Now, they seemed foreign, part of the conspiracy to conceal from her the truth of who she was.

Sarah felt tears fill her eyes. Who *was* she? To whom did she belong? She wadded sheets of tissue in her fists and bit her lip as the sounds and scents of home and family settled around her. A family she'd never really been a child of in the first place.

* * *

"Welcome back, Sarah. How're you doing?"

Sarah was sitting in a lawn chair on the wooden deck at the back of her house, thinking of ways to spend a hundred thousand dollars when the sound of Scott's voice startled her from her semidrowsy state. Her eyes popped open. "Scott! I didn't hear you come over."

"When I saw you out here, I hopped the hedge. How's it going for you?" He sat down on the deck next to her chair.

"It's going," she replied without much enthusiasm.

"I was planning to come over last week when you came home, but Tina said you didn't want to have visitors."

"The ban didn't include you," Sarah said. "I should have told her that. Thanks for the cards you sent while I was in the hospital," Sarah told him. "They really perked me up."

He cocked his head. "You look as if you could use a little perk-up right now. What's the matter?"

She told him about needing the bone marrow transplant. She concentrated on the medical particulars, explaining it in as much detail as possible. "They've programmed my information into a computer bank," she said. "If they can match me with a donor, I'll go for it."

"How long will it take to find a donor?"

"They don't know. They search until they find someone." She had purposely left out the part about siblings being the best donors, because she couldn't tell anyone about being adopted. For some reason, she felt ashamed of it.

"When can you come back to school?" he asked.

"In a couple of weeks. As soon as my resistance builds back up."

"Are you telling me everything, Sarah?"

"What do you mean?"

"Look, we've been friends all our lives. You get a funny little expression in your eyes whenever you're fibbing." Scott grinned, and Sarah felt a hot flush sweep over her.

"That's not true," she protested. "I'm not fibbing about any of this. Why would I?"

"I believe you about the transplant, but are you sure there's nothing else going on?"

"Of course not!" It bothered her that he'd picked up on what she was trying to hide.

"This is your 'bestest-ever friend,'" Scott joked, using the words she had used when they'd been three. "And your fiancé," he added. "I know you like a book, and I think you're not telling me everything."

Caught in the web of her confused feelings, Sarah glanced away. "If there is something else, I can't talk about it now."

Scott's smile faded. "Hey, this is serious, isn't it?"

"Yes."

"It's more than the bone marrow transplant, isn't it?"

She nodded.

"You can tell me," he said.

She shook her head. "Not now."

"But you will?"

"Maybe." Sarah felt doubly uncomfortable, not only because she wasn't leveling with Scott, but because she still couldn't put all her emotions into words. "It's hard, Scott. Can you understand?"

He reached out and took her hand. "I know it must be hard enough to think about going through a bone marrow transplant. Whatever else is bothering you must be pretty grim, too, or you'd be able to tell me about it. Listen, I understand. If you feel like talking about it, call me, all right?"

"All right." She watched him stand. He looked lean and tall, hardened from weeks of training for track. "How's Susan?" she asked, mentioning the name of the girl he'd been dating before Sarah had gone off to the hospital.

"We're history," Scott told her with a casual shrug. "There's no one special right now."

"Too bad," Sarah said. But deep down, she wasn't very sorry at all. Not one bit sorry.

Six

SARAH'S MOTHER CAME into her room that afternoon holding a hatbox. "I bought this for you. What do you think?"

Sarah opened the box and removed a Styrofoam wig stand holding a cascade of golden brown hair. The wig was as close to her own hair color as she'd ever seen. "It's nice," Sarah said, but she felt awkward. They hadn't discussed getting it.

"I had it specially made up. I brought them photographs and a sample of your hair I saved from when we cut it. The wig makers are experts. They do a lot of their business with theater people and for cancer patients, too."

"It looks expensive," Sara remarked.

"It doesn't matter. We wanted you to have the best."

The expense part bothered Sarah. She knew her cancer treatments were costly and her father's insurance didn't cover everything. She felt guilty, too, because she knew she had the certified check still hidden away. She could have easily afforded the wig. "You should have asked me before buying it," Sarah said.

"Your father and I wanted to surprise you."

"I'm tired of surprises." Sarah saw her mother flinch and realized that her comment had stung.

Her mother sat down on the edge of Sarah's bed, her expression somber. "We need to talk about your adoption, Sarah."

Sarah recoiled. Talking about it made her feel angry, as if she'd been victimized. "I don't want to."

"You've got to forgive us for not telling you sooner. Your attitude is putting a strain on the rest of the family. Most of all, it's not good for your health to have this thing eating at you."

"I don't have health. I don't have a family. I don't have anything right now."

"Of course you have a family," her mother insisted in a rare display of temper. "We've raised you since you were an infant. You're as much mine as Tina and Richie are."

"No, I'm not! I don't even look like the rest of you. I was just some kid you ordered, *paid* for, and brought home."

"How can you say such a thing? I told you how badly we wanted a baby. You were a blessing, Sarah. You were special, an answer to our prayers."

"Well, I don't feel very special. I feel lied to and cheated."

"We never lied. We simply didn't tell you the whole truth."

"Excuse me. I didn't know there was a difference." Sarah's tone sounded harsh.

"There's a big difference, Sarah." Her mother stood abruptly, and Sarah could tell she was quite upset. "Sometimes, the whole truth hurts. It hurts because it isn't what we want to hear or need to hear. Dad and I tried to protect you. Maybe that was wrong. It's obvious you think so right now. Hurting you was never our intent. What we did, we did because we loved you. When you feel like discussing it, let me know." Her mother swept out of the room.

In the silence that followed, Sarah felt pangs of regret. She knew she was being unreasonable and unforgiving, but she couldn't seem to help herself. She wanted her parents to pay for hurting her, for deceiving her. Why couldn't they appreciate the depth of her hurt? Someone *had* to pay for all the lies. Sarah started trembling, then she wept.

Sarah returned to school on Monday. She wasn't feeling recovered from her chemo treatments, but just sitting around her house and waging a silent war with her parents was making her feel worse. She put on plenty of makeup, a new outfit, and the wig. Except for being thin, she thought she looked fairly normal.

As she came down the hallway at school, her friends squealed and ran over to her. "You're back!" JoEllen cried. "When we talked on the phone last night, you didn't say you were coming back today."

"I wasn't sure I would feel like it."

"Honestly, I'd have stayed out the rest of the year, if I were you," Cammie insisted.

"I like school," Sarah said as she fumbled with the combination lock on her locker.

"Only you, Sarah," Natalie joked. "How about lunch today? Can we sit together in the cafeteria, like always?"

"Sure," Sarah replied.

"And how about cheerleading? Are you coming back on the squad?" JoEllen asked.

"I can't handle that much exercise right now. Maybe in another month."

The three girls glanced at each other guiltily, and Sarah realized they were keeping something from her. Was the whole world conspiring against her? "What is it?" she asked. "What's wrong?"

"Um—Miss Connors sort of replaced you," Natalie told her.

"How was I 'sort of' replaced?"

"You shouldn't have found out this way, Sarah." JoEllen gave Natalie a scathing look. "*Some* people have no sensitivity." JoEllen turned to face Sarah squarely. "The truth is, the squad needs six girls to perform the routines. Miss Connors had to choose someone to take your place. I'm sorry."

"You should have told me. Someone should have told me." Sarah could barely contain her anger as she glared at her three friends.

"We just wanted you to get well. We didn't want you to be thinking about something you couldn't change."

JoEllen's words hit Sarah like cold water. *Something she couldn't change.* That was her problem with everything in her life—her leukemia, her adoption, being bumped from the squad. She couldn't change any of it. She had no control over her life, no choices about anything. She felt her anger ebb and depression settle in its place.

"Are you all right?" Cammie asked. "We didn't mean to ruin your day."

Sarah shrugged wearily. "It doesn't matter. I guess Miss Connors had to replace me. I'm really in no shape to do the workouts, and I don't know if I will be before school's out. It's no big deal. Forget it."

JoEllen looked as if she didn't quite believe her. "There's always next year," she offered cheerily.

Sarah could barely bring herself to think about next week, much less next year. "Right." She forced a smile. "I'd better get to homeroom . . . or has Mr. Parker taken me off his permanent rolls, too?"

Natalie giggled nervously. "Of course not, silly. No such luck—all your teachers have saved your place, along with all your work."

Sarah smiled in order to smooth things over, but inside, she felt numb and beyond caring.

Sarah was lying on her bed, staring up at the ceiling, when Tina asked to come in. "What do you want?" Sarah asked.

Tina opened the door a crack. "I want to borrow your green sweater." Without waiting to be invited, she came inside the room.

"I didn't say you could come in," Sarah said crossly.

"Don't have a cow." Tina crossed to Sarah's closet and started digging through it.

"What are you doing?"

"Looking for your sweater."

"You can't barge in here and take my things."

"But I need it for tomorrow. I'm giving a report in government class, and I have to look my best."

Sarah struggled off her bed. "How you look has nothing to do with how you speak."

"But if I feel good because I look good, then I know I'll do better." Tina turned back toward the closet. "Come on—don't be selfish."

Her sister's logic defied her, but Sarah was not in the mood for Tina's antics. "Leave my sweater alone, and please get out of my room."

"Why? Why are you being so mean to me?"

"Just leave, Tina."

Tina crossed her arms and jutted out her lower lip. "What's wrong with you, Sarah? Ever since you came home from the hospital, you've been as mean as a snake."

Sarah leaned into Tina's face. "Snakes bite," she hissed. "Please go away."

"I'm so scared," Tina replied, rolling her eyes. "You know what your problem is? You're mad at me because I'm the only person in this family who doesn't fall all over you. I'm the only one who treats you like a regular person instead of someone who's sick."

Sarah shook her head in exasperation. She didn't want to lose her temper, but Tina was acting like such a brat. "You don't know what you're talking about."

Sarah started to walk away, but Tina grabbed her arm. "Everyone around here treats you as if you're some kind of fragile doll. As if you're going to break or something. Well, I'm sorry you're sick, Sarah, but I'm not one bit sorry I'm well. That's the real reason you don't like me, isn't it? Because I'm healthy and you're not."

Sarah stared at Tina in disbelief. The hateful things she was saying must have been brewing in her for a long time. Sarah felt fury boiling inside her. "Go away."

"I won't. What are you going to do? Go tattle to Mom? Well, I don't care. You're mean and selfish, and I'll tell Mom so to her face. I'm tired of your getting all the special treatment around here. Everybody acts as if I don't exist. As if I don't have feelings, too. I'm sick of it, do you hear? You have no right to be so mean to me. I'm your sister!"

"No, you're not." The words were out of Sarah's mouth before she could stop them.

They halted Tina's tirade cold, and a look of utter confusion crossed her face. "What did you say?"

Sarah clenched her fists and looked Tina straight in the eye. "I said, we're not sisters. I was adopted, Tina. So cheer up—we're not related at all."

Seven

"THAT'S A LIE!" Tina shouted. "Take it back."

"Why should I?" Sarah felt her heart hammering, knowing she couldn't take back what she'd said in anger. She pretended indifference and plunged ahead with her story. "I really am adopted, which explains why you and I have nothing in common. We aren't sisters and never will be. If you don't believe me, just ask Mom."

"What's going on in here?" her mother asked as she barged into the room. "Why is Tina crying?"

Tina flung herself into her mother's arms. "Sarah is being so mean to me. And she's lying, too. She said you adopted her."

Color drained from her mother's face. She glared at Sarah. "Why did you tell her? Your father and I should have been with you when you told her."

"It's my life," Sarah said.

"It's true?" Tina blurted out, pulling away from her mother. "What she said is *true*?"

Sarah was shaken, caught completely off guard by Tina's distress. She'd thought it was something Tina would be glad to know. They'd never been super close, as sisters should be. "Tell her it's true," Sarah insisted.

Their mother lifted Tina's chin and gazed deeply into her tear-stained eyes. "Yes. Sarah was adopted."

Tina gasped, covered her ears, and ran out of the room.

Their mother turned on Sarah. "Now, see what you've done! Why, Sarah? Why couldn't you have waited?"

"Waited until when? Until she was grown?" Sarah was frightened. Everything seemed to be spiraling out of control.

"I'm going to try and calm your sister down," her mom said. "Will you *please* not say anything to Richie. Don't hurt him, too. He's too young to understand."

Her mother left the room, and Sarah felt sick to her stomach. Of course, she wouldn't tell Richie. She hadn't meant to tell Tina, but after weeks of being bottled up inside of her, the awful truth had just spilled out. All at once, Sarah felt as if the walls were closing in on her. Sarah hurried down the stairs and out the front door.

Outside, the night was cool and dark and tinged with the scent of blooming dogwood trees. She stood in the yard, wringing her hands, unsure of what to do, where to go. She saw a light on next door at Scott's and jogged around to the front porch of his house. His family car wasn't in the driveway.

Please be home, Scott, she begged silently. She rang the bell. A minute later, Scott opened the door.

"Hi, Sarah," he said, sounding surprised. He smiled, but the smile faded as he flipped on the porch light and took a good look at her. "What's wrong?"

"Everything's ruined, Scott, and I don't know what to do."

"Tell me what happened," he said, bringing her inside and settling her on his sofa.

Suddenly, Sarah felt foolish and shy. What had possessed her to run next door to Scott's? He must think she's crazy.

"My folks are out," he assured her when she hesitated. "Come on. Tell me. I'd like to help, if I can." The soft light of the lamp behind Scott threw shadows on the wall, and from across the room, the TV flickered. Scott had pushed the mute button on the remote control, and no sound came from the set.

Sarah struggled to put her thoughts and feelings into words. She told him everything, half crying as she spoke. The only thing she held back was about the letter and check, but the burden of them weighed heavily on her. Why hadn't this mysterious JWC considered what effect such a large amount of money might have on someone her age? Didn't JWC realize what a responsibility it was to be a guardian of so much money? To be responsible for doing the right things with it?

"Tina took it hard when you told her you were adopted?" Scott asked once Sarah had completed her story. Sarah nodded, and Scott said, "I'm not surprised. She worships the ground you walk on."

Sarah found that impossible to believe, yet didn't

want to debate it with Scott just then. "I guess I shouldn't have told her," Sarah acknowledged, her voice small and miserable. "What if my parents are so mad at me that they throw me out? How can I make it on my own?"

Scott put his hand on her shoulder. "That's never going to happen. Your folks love you. Still, that's some story, Sarah. What a way to find out you were adopted. No wonder you didn't feel like discussing it with me the other day."

"I didn't know how to tell you. I feel so—so— weird about it. As if my brain might fall out from thinking about it so much."

"It's nothing to be ashamed of. There's this guy on my track team who's adopted, and he's pretty cool about it. He says his parents used to tell him he'd been chosen, and when he was little, he thought they'd gone to the supermarket and picked him out like a head of cabbage."

The image of babies lined up in the produce section of the grocery store made Sarah smile momentarily. "But he's known all his life. I found out just a few weeks ago. How could my parents have lied to me all these years? It's the worst thing that's ever happened to me."

"Was it worse than finding out you had leukemia?"

"In some ways, yes," she replied. "I was younger when leukemia hit me, and it was a shock, but no one ever lied to me about my cancer. From the first, the doctors helped me understand what was happening to me. They'd say, 'Sarah, we're going to draw blood' or 'Sarah, we've got to do a bone marrow aspiration. It may hurt, but you have to lie perfectly still until it's over. Then you can scream all you want.' " Sarah remembered the painful days of treatment, and how her mother had held her hand and whispered words of encouragement throughout the procedures. *She's not my mother,* Sarah reminded herself stubbornly.

"I always thought you were brave," Scott told her. "I admired you."

"You did?"

"I still do. I couldn't believe it when you told me about needing the bone marrow transplant."

"That's another thing," Sarah admitted. "I can't even look to my family to help me with the transplant. My parents lied to me, Scott. My whole, entire life is a big, fat lie. My parents are not my parents, and Tina and Richie aren't my sister and brother."

Scott moved closer to her on the sofa and smiled. She felt herself softening. How was it possible for Scott to make her feel good when minutes before she'd felt so horrible? "I wish I weren't me," she said. "Every time I look in the mirror, I wonder, Who am I? Where did I come from? Why was I given away?"

"Ted, the guy on my track team, says he wonders the same thing, and he's known all his life he was adopted. I guess that part wouldn't be different whether you'd known all along or not."

"The not knowing is getting to me, Scott. I find myself thinking about my mother and wondering who my real parents are, where they are. I wonder if my real mother ever thinks about me."

"Ted wonders the same thing, but he says there's a difference between wanting to know and wanting to search."

"Search?" Sarah asked, suddenly interested in Ted in a new light. "You mean go find his real parents?"

"His birth parents," Scott corrected. "That's the term he uses. He says he's curious, but not enough to hurt his adoptive parents. They've really been good to him, and he doesn't want them to think he's ungrateful."

"It's natural to want to know," Sarah said slowly, turning the matter over in her mind. She identified with Scott's friend, Ted, completely. "There's nothing disloyal in wanting to know."

"Who knows," Scott speculated, "maybe you have blood brothers and sisters somewhere whose bone marrow would match yours."

Sarah bolted upright on the sofa. "Do you suppose Ted could find his birth mother if he really wanted to?"

Scott tipped his head thoughtfully. "In the first place, Ted doesn't want to, but even if he did, it might be tricky."

"Why?"

"Well, you have to figure that if a mother gives up her baby for adoption, she must have some good reasons."

"A person has a right to know where he or she comes from," Sarah argued.

"What if the mother doesn't want to be found?" Scott asked. "Doesn't she have a right to her privacy?"

Not when someone's life depends on finding her, Sarah thought. "Your friend may change his mind someday," Sarah said. "Then you'll feel differently about her right to privacy."

Scott gave her a level look. "I'm not arguing for or

against it. I'm just repeating what he and I've talked about. Don't forget, it might cost a lot of money to dig up the past," Scott added.

Sarah stared at him open-mouthed. "A lot of money?"

"Sure. Everything costs money—not that it should stop a person, but it's a consideration."

Sarah chewed on her bottom lip, her mind racing with possibilities. Why hadn't she thought about this before? She had money now. Plenty of money. Didn't the wish letter from JWC say she could spend it on anything she wanted? What could be more important than finding her birth mother? What could be more important than discovering if she had siblings with compatible bone marrow? Her very *life* could depend on finding these people. Sarah practically jumped up from the sofa. "I've got to go," she said.

Scott stood beside her. "You can stay longer. You can call your mom and tell her you're over here—"

Sarah interrupted him. "I have to talk to my parents right away."

"About searching for your birth mother? I can tell you've decided you have a right to do that," Scott said quietly.

"Why not?" Sarah challenged. "Maybe your friend feels comfortable in his home, but I don't in mine."

She rushed to the door, and he followed. On the front porch, she turned and looked at Scott. "Thank you for telling me what you did. You may have helped me save my life."

As she darted back toward her house, she realized that Scott had asked her to stay longer with him. It made her happy, but now the magnitude of the task that lay ahead of her was all she could think about.

Eight

WHEN SARAH WALKED into the kitchen, her parents were waiting for her. As she came inside, her father rose. "Where were you?"

"Next door, at Scott's," Sarah answered. "I needed to talk to someone."

"Sit down," her father said. "It's past time that *we* talked."

Sarah knew there would be no escaping a confrontation. It didn't matter. She wanted everything out in the open. She sat at the table and thought about the hundreds of meals they'd eaten there as a family. It seemed like only yesterday that Richie's high chair had been in use.

Her father's voice interrupted her thoughts. "First of all, your mother and I are very disappointed in the way you handled telling Tina about your adoption. We agree that she should know, but it was something we should have sat down and discussed as a family."

Sarah felt words of defense rise up in her mouth, but her father cut off her response with a look of warning. "We *are* a family, Sarah. Whether you like it or not right now, we're the only parents you've ever known, and you are our daughter—in both the legal and the moral sense of the word."

"I know finding out the way you did hasn't been easy on you," her mother added. "Sarah, when the doctors told us about the bone marrow transplant, we were heartsick in more ways than one."

"I bet," Sarah challenged.

"We knew we couldn't help you. You can't imagine how we feel. We've raised you, loved you, been through all your medical treatments with you, and now that you need us—need us in a life-and-death matter—we can't help you."

Her mother wiped away a tear that had slid down her cheek. Sarah felt a lump rise in her throat and quickly glanced away. "You are my daughter, Sarah," her mother said. "If you needed a kidney and I could give you one of mine, I would do so in a heartbeat. If my bone marrow, or our father's would work, we'd donate it to you tomorrow. We'd let Tina or Richie do the same without ever thinking twice, if it would help."

"But you can't," Sarah replied dully. "No one here can help me."

Her father came quickly to her side, stooped down, and put his arm around her shoulders. "We can't donate bone marrow, but we can see you through the next few, uncertain months while the hospital searches for a suitable donor. We'll always be here for you, through the good times and the bad."

Her father's gentle touch made Sarah's hostility vanish like water down a drain. The burden of her hurt and anger had grown heavy and made her miserable. Sarah turned her face into her dad's chest and allowed herself to cry. Surrounded by his embrace, she felt comforted, much as she had when she'd been a small child, running to him when she got hurt. After a few moments, she pulled away and looked at him, then turned to her mother. She knew that now was the time to tell them about the One Last Wish letter and check. "I have something to show you both," she said. "It's up in my room. I'll bring it down for you to see."

As she went to her room, she passed Tina's closed door. Sarah hesitated. For a moment, Sarah wanted to go inside and apologize. Tina had thought she had a sister, and now she knew she didn't.

Sarah shook her head, feeling overwhelmed by the complications the truth had brought. She realized that now wasn't the time to talk to Tina. Sarah went to her room, pulled the envelope containing the letter and check out from its hiding place, and went downstairs. She handed it over to her father. "When I was in the hospital, I found this on my bedside table one evening. I don't know who left it, but I think you'd better read it."

Her mother moved her chair next to her dad's. Sarah watched their faces. "Is it for real?" Sarah asked them.

"It looks real," her father said, holding the check up to the light. " 'Richard Holloway, Esq., Administrator,' " he read off the bottom of the check. "Evidently, he's in charge of this foundation, so he should be easy enough to check out. I'll take this to a bank to determine its authenticity. It's a lot of money for a complete stranger to have handed out with no strings," He sounded skeptical.

"Who could have done such a thing?" her mother asked, flabbergasted. "Who's this JWC? Someone at the hospital?"

Sarah shook her head. "Believe me, I've racked my brain trying to figure it out. I don't know—I wondered if it might be my birth mother."

"I don't think so," Sarah's mother said.

"I think we should call Dr. Hernandez and see if she knows anything about this foundation," her father suggested.

A spasm of fear squeezed Sarah's heart. "Can Dr. Hernandez take it away?"

"It's a certified check, made out to you. If it's legitimate, it's yours."

"And if it's not?"

"Then Dr. Hernandez and the hospital administrators need to know that some nut case is running around the hospital handing out bogus checks."

"That would be so cruel," Sarah's mother said. "Why would someone do such a hateful thing to a sick child?"

Could the letter and money be a cruel hoax? Sarah wondered. The letter sounded so sincere. JWC truly seemed to understand what it was like to endure pain and to feel scared and alone.

Please let it be real, she prayed silently. If it was, and the money was truly hers, Sarah knew exactly how she was going to spend it. She needed to feel in control of her life again, and the money was the key to giving her back such control. "Let's call Dr. Hernandez first thing in the morning," Sarah said.

"All right," her father agreed. He stared at the check. "Don't get your hopes up, honey. It looks real, but we must verify it."

Sarah nodded, afraid that her hopes for the money might be in vain. "I'll wait," she promised. An awkward silence fell, and her parents appeared preoccupied. Sarah took a deep breath. "I'm sorry about Tina."

Her mother folded the letter. "She's pretty shaken up."

"I'll go talk to her."

"Take it easy," her father admonished. "We love you both, Sarah. We don't want to see either of you hurt."

Sarah rapped lightly on Tina's door and heard her muffled voice say, "Go away." Sarah ignored the request and entered the room. Tina was lying on her bed amid a heap of stuffed animals and frilly pillows.

"Here. You can borrow this for that speech tomorrow," Sarah said, holding out the green sweater.

"I don't want it. I'm not going to school tomorrow," Tina replied, barely audible.

Sarah found herself feeling sympathetic and exasperated. "Tina, you can't let what's happened affect you so much. It's my problem."

"How can you say that? You've been my sister all my life, and now—and now—" Tina dissolved into another crying jag.

"I can't change it, Tina," Sarah said.

"How will I face everybody?" Tina asked. "All the dumb questions that people will ask?"

"Nobody knows except us," Sarah told her.

"Nobody?" Tina sounded hopeful.

"Scott knows," Sarah answered. "I told him tonight."

"Scott knows?" Tina flopped over on the bed and buried her face in a pillow. "How can I look him in the face?"

For a moment, Sarah was completely mystified by Tina's reaction. Then she reminded herself that Tina was only thirteen. When she'd been thirteen, nothing had been more important to her than what her friends felt and thought about her. But what exactly would her friends think?

Sarah sighed and sat down on Tina's bed. "Scott knows, but he won't say anything to anyone. And neither will I."

"You won't?"

"Why should I? It's nobody's business."

"Not even Cammie, JoEllen, or Natalie?"

Sarah realized that by discussing it with Scott, she'd lost the urge to tell anybody else. Besides, telling it around would simply make people ask a lot of questions she couldn't answer. "Not even them," Sarah declared. "I don't think anyone should know."

Tina rummaged around on the bed until she found a clean tissue. "All right," she agreed, blowing her nose. "If you don't say anything, neither will I. We'll keep it a secret."

Sarah was feeling weak and tired. Tonight had taken much physical stamina, and she still felt sick from the chemo medications. "Wear the sweater," she urged as she stood. "You'll look great. Good-night."

Tina mumbled, "Thanks. Good-night."

Sarah glanced over her shoulder to see Tina sitting in the middle of her bed, clutching the green sweater to her cheek, her eyes red-rimmed and swollen. Tina was the rightful daughter, while she was the daughter of a stranger. Without another word, Sarah left the room.

Nine

SARAH FOUND IT difficult to concentrate in school the next day. All she thought about was the check from the One Last Wish Foundation and whether or not it was for real. Scott cornered her in the hall between classes while students hurried past them. "How are you doing today?"

"I'm all right."

"Tina's acting strange," he commented. "She won't even look at me."

Sarah shook her head. "She has some strange idea that when her friends find out about my being adopted, she'll be ostracized. It's my problem, but she's acting as though it's hers."

"She'll get over it. School will be out in another month, and she'll have the whole summer to deal with her feelings."

Sarah thought about the end of school. As soon as it was out, she would have to return to Memphis for more tests and treatments. If she was lucky, the leukemia would be in remission. She wasn't looking forward to the confinement. "It's going to be a long summer," Sarah said with a sigh.

"Maybe they'll find you a donor," Scott offered.

"They haven't yet."

"Sarah, don't get discouraged."

"I can't help it. Nothing's going right for me. Nothing."

Scott touched her hair, and she drew back. The gesture was harmless and was meant in affection, but Sarah knew that her hair, a wig, was like the rest of her life—an illusion, a facsimile of the real thing. "I've got to go," she told him. Without waiting for a response, Sarah turned and walked swiftly down the hall.

When she arrived home that day and came into the kitchen, Richie was sitting at the table with a plate of cookies and a glass of milk. He was coloring a paper filled with line drawings of tulips. "Hi, Sarah. This is my homework," he said proudly.

Richie attended preschool every morning and was looking forward to what he called "big school" in the fall. He took his schoolwork seriously and showed off every assignment. She had to smile, watching him bend intently over the page, his pudgy fingers wrapped around a crayon. "You're doing a nice job," Sarah observed, peering down at the page. "I don't believe I've ever seen a black tulip."

"Everyone colors them red and yellow," Richie explained. "I want to make mine different."

"They're different, all right." Sarah patted his head and felt a wave of sadness. It was hard to think they weren't related to one another and never had been.

Her mother came into the kitchen and beckoned Sarah to join her in the living room. "I have something to tell you. The letter and the money are on the level," she said once they were alone. "Your father sent a fax of both to Dr. Hernandez this morning. She's called him back and said that there are several philanthropic organizations that do this kind of thing. The chief administrator at the hospital couldn't give details, but the One Last Wish Foundation is legitimate."

Sarah's heart thudded. The hundred thousand dollars was really hers. Her mother's face broke into a smile, and she hugged Sarah. "Honey, this is wonderful. I'm thrilled for you and very grateful to the mysterious JWC. I don't know how this person knows about you, but I'm delighted someone wants to give you so much money. You are special. Do you know what you want to do with it?"

The time had come for Sarah to tell her mother what she planned to use the money for. Sarah knew it was going to upset her, but she was determined. "Maybe we should talk about it after supper, when Dad's here," she said.

"Oh, you can give me a little preview, can't you? Come on, just a hint?"

"I'm sure I'll spend some of it on new clothes."

"Naturally. It's your money." Her mother's brown eyes were bright with anticipation. "But perhaps I could offer some suggestions, what with summer coming up—vacations and all—"

"Mom, I know what I'm going to be spending most of it on." Sarah interrupted her mother's sentence. She looked her directly in the eyes, took a deep breath, and calmly said, "I'm going to use it to find my birth mother."

Sarah's mom's eager smile faded, and her face looked sad. "Your father told me that's what he thought you'd want to do. I said no, you wouldn't. I thought you'd be able to put the adoption behind you. I thought we could do something wonderful as a family."

"It's not just for curiosity, Mom. I need the bone marrow. Maybe there are compatible donors in my other family."

At the words "other family," her mother winced. "I know it needs to be checked out, Sarah. I've been trying to prepare myself for this moment. I didn't do a very good job, did I?"

Sarah had wanted to hurt her mother for lying to her, but now that she was actually confronted by the look of pain on her mother's face, Sarah couldn't stand it. "I'm not trying to hurt you, Mom."

"I know. It would be unbelievably selfish of me if I tried to prevent you from finding your birth mother. Your father and I both realize that your life's at stake and that you have to pursue every available avenue. I guess I've known since that moment in the conference room when Dr. Hernandez explained the necessity of locating a compatible bone marrow donor that we would eventually be facing this moment—searching for your birth mother.

"I hoped and prayed that they would find a donor through the national registry, but that's not happening. I must admit that my hopes for finding an anonymous donor were purely selfish. I thought that if one was found, you wouldn't have any need to look for your birth mother. That's not true, is it?"

"I have to admit, I'm really curious about who she is and where I come from. It's been on my mind a lot since you told me the truth."

Her mother nodded. "Your father and I have discussed this also. We knew we had to help you find her, no matter what."

"The One Last Wish money will make it easier," Sarah said. "At least it won't cost you all anything."

Her mother smiled wistfully. "Oh, Sarah, it will cost us. I assure you, it will cost us plenty emotionally."

"But not in money," she insisted stubbornly.

Her mother turned toward the open window and gazed out. "I must confess, I've always been curious about her, too."

"You have?"

"Certainly. I wanted a baby so badly, and well, if you must know, she didn't want hers at all. I couldn't imagine such a thing."

Sarah felt wounded, thinking that her birth mother wouldn't have wanted her. "How do you know she didn't want me? Maybe it was just impossible for her to keep me."

Her mother turned back around. "The lawyer swore us to secrecy. He made it very clear that the mother wanted nothing to do with her baby. I found it unbelievable, but I was delighted. Deep down, I feared the adoption process, because I thought she might try to come back and claim you someday. I've read about that happening."

Sarah's emotions were in a jumble. How could a mother not want her own baby? She watched her mother carefully, looking for a sign of deception. Maybe she wasn't being totally truthful even now. Of course, for medical reasons, she had to locate her birth mother, but neither of her parents was happy about it. It was in their best interests for Sarah not to like the woman. "She hasn't tried to reclaim me," Sarah pointed out. "Maybe that's just because she doesn't know where to find me."

"I was there, Sarah. You weren't. The lawyer was very explicit."

Sarah refused to accept her mother's story. Even if there were a grain of truth in it, perhaps her birth mother had had a change of heart over the years. Maybe by reuniting now, Sarah would be bringing her happiness. Surely she must have wondered about the baby she gave up for adoption years before. A new thought occurred to Sarah. She asked, "How do we start looking for her? How will we find her?"

"Your father's researching the process. I understand it can be rather involved. The first thing he has to do is try to locate the lawyer who handled the adoption. If necessary, we may have to get a court order to unseal the original birth certificate. It could take some time, so it's a good thing we're still using the donor registry."

Sarah needed a bone marrow transplant, and she didn't have a lot of time. The One Last Wish money could help, but the thing it couldn't buy was time. "I'm scared," Sarah admitted.

Her mom came over and put her arms around her. "That makes two of us," she said. "I'm scared, too."

Ten

HER PARENTS SET up a special savings account for Sarah at the local bank. "It's your money," her father told her. "The letter made it very clear it was to be spent on something you want. Your mother and I feel the same way. Regardless of how the search for your birth mother turns out, I can't imagine it's costing the full hundred thousand. You should have plenty left over for college, or for anything else you might want to do."

No one said a word about the worst-case scenario, what Sarah knew was in their minds: If they couldn't find a bone marrow donor, there would be no college, no *life* for Sarah. She forced herself not to think about that possibility and concentrated on the last weeks of school and on her hopes of finding her birth mother.

Sarah's father was trying to locate the attorney who had handled her adoption; the lawyer, they'd learned, had retired and moved to Florida. "I'm hoping that once I reach him, he'll give us the woman's name without our having to go through the courts," he explained to Sarah.

"Her name?" Sarah asked.

"Obviously, we need her name before we can begin to search for her. The lawyer, Mr. Dodkin, knows her name, but he's under no obligation to divulge it without a court order. He can also help get a copy of your original birth certificate, which contains her name.

"There's an organization called Independent Search Consultants, and I've learned a lot from them. They are trained professionals who help adoptees find their birth parents. One of the women there, Mrs. Kolelin, has been very helpful. She told me that once we get your birth mother's name, we can begin the search in earnest. It won't be easy. No telling what's happened to her over the years or where she might be living."

"Can these people help us?" Sarah asked, eager for the search to start.

"There are records searchers, who tell me that no matter how obscure the trail is, there's always a clue in the paperwork left behind—physicians' records, social security registrations, tax records, information like that. Once we have a name, we hire a private investigator, one who's handled cases like this before, and the PI will find a current address on her."

"What if the lawyer won't tell us her name?" she asked. The entire situation felt like a TV movie, from the One Last Wish Foundation's mysterious check to hiring a private detective. She didn't say anything to her father and just kept listening.

"Fortunately, in Arkansas, the courts are fairly lenient about opening records for medical reasons."

"Why Arkansas when we live in Georgia?" Sarah asked, confused.

"That's where you were born, Sarah—in Little Rock, Arkansas."

It took Sarah days to adjust to the information that she hadn't been born in Georgia. All her life, she'd believed she had been born in Ringgold, at the same hospital as Tina and Richie. Now, she discovered another lie that had been fabricated to "protect her."

"What're you doing?" JoEllen asked when she found Sarah in the library one day after school.

"A report," Sarah fibbed.

"About what?"

"Arkansas."

JoEllen made a face. "Don't you ever quit? School's out in two weeks. Why work so hard now?"

"It's personal. It's a report just for me."

"Tell me what it's about." JoEllen's interest was real.

Sarah was tempted to spill all. Keeping her past a secret was taking its toll on her, but she remembered her promise to Tina. It still mattered to Tina that kids not know that she and Sarah weren't blood sisters. Sarah flipped the encyclopedia shut and turned to JoEllen. "Actually, it's for extra credit. I missed so many tests when I was hospitalized."

"Is that all?" JoEllen looked disappointed.

"That's all," Sarah replied, flashing a bright smile to discourage any further questions.

*   *   *

On Memorial Day, Scott's family hosted the neighborhood's annual picnic and barbecue. Every family on the block showed up and brought a dish to share. By late afternoon, both Scott's and Sarah's yards were overrun with people. The aroma of sizzling hamburgers and hot dogs saturated the air, and music blasted from outdoor speakers.

Sarah heaped her plate with food from a picnic table and made her way to the back corner of her yard. She ducked a flying Frisbee and slipped through a break in the hedge to a small clearing sheltered by a canopy of leaves. This spot had served as a hideaway she'd shared with Tina when they'd been younger. The ground was bare dirt except for two weathered tree stumps. Sarah sat on one of the stumps, balancing her paper plate on her knees.

"Are you in there, Sarah?" Scott's head poked through the hole in the hedge. "I thought I saw you sneak back here," he said with an easy grin.

"Too much racket out there. I wanted to eat in peace and quiet," Sarah explained.

"Want some company?"

"Sure. Pull up a stump."

Juggling a plate and a large slice of watermelon, he settled on the other stump. "I'd forgotten about this place," he remarked. "I haven't been back here in ages."

"I was just thinking about the tea parties Tina and I used to give for our dolls. We sat the dolls in circles around these stumps and served them tap water and cookies."

Scott smiled impishly. "I remember the talent show you gave for your teddy bears, too."

"You saw that?" Sarah gasped. Tina and she had

been six and eight years old, respectively, when they'd put on that particular show in the clearing. "We thought no one knew about it."

"I crawled on my stomach and peeked through the hedge. You did a tap dance, and Tina sang a song."

Sarah laughed as the memory flowed over her. "Weren't we awful!"

"I thought you were very talented. And the teddy bears didn't seem to object."

"They had no choice. I told them no supper if they weren't a good audience."

"Isn't this where I proposed to you?" Scott asked, glancing around the clearing.

How could Sarah forget that day? He'd given her a ring from a box of Cracker Jack and kissed her. It had been her first kiss, even though it wasn't a serious one. "We were just kids," she said. "That seems as if it happened a million years ago."

Sitting in the twilight with Scott, with the sounds of laughing children coming from the far side of the hedge, Sarah felt an eerie sadness creep over her as her childhood memories returned. "Sometimes, I wish I could go back in time and be a kid again—to the time before I got leukemia, when my life wasn't so complicated."

"Any news on your search?" he asked.

"Nothing yet. I really hope we find her soon."

"Because of the bone marrow?"

"Not only that. I want to meet her. I want to see somebody who looks like me. Did you know I was born in Arkansas? I've been reading everything I can about that state."

"Why? What difference does it make where you were born?"

"Don't you see? Everything I've been told about myself hasn't been true. I'm not really a McGreggor. All the things I believed to be true, all the people I've ever thought were 'mine,' really aren't. Somewhere out there—" Sarah gestured, "is my real family, whose blood and genes have been passed along to me. I don't know them, but I want to know them.

"I went to the library to read about Arkansas. I felt more connected knowing about that place. I felt like, 'Here's the place where the real Sarah comes from.' I want to know all about it, because it helps me know a little more about *me*." Sarah glanced over at Scott. Shadows covered his face. "I'm talking too much and not making any sense—sorry," she said with a shake of her head.

"Ted, the guy on the track team, wonders about those things, too."

"He does?"

"He says that when he gets ticked off at his parents, he imagines his real ones. They wouldn't hassle him. They'd be understanding. They'd be perfect." Scott chuckled. "I tell him, 'Get serious. All parents hassle their kids. It's their role in life.' "

"Does he believe you?"

"Sure." Scott's voice came out of the dark. "He knows that these fantasy people, these perfect parents, are all in his imagination. He knows that some kids pretend they were adopted when they are mad at their parents. Nobody's perfect, for sure."

Sarah felt a twinge of guilt. She had spent hours imagining what her birth mother could be like. Sarah hoped she was pretty. Maybe even rich. Or famous. "I guess imaginations have a way of taking over," Sarah admitted. "In a way, that's what makes me all the more anxious to meet my real mother. Then, I'll know for certain what she's like, and I won't have to make up things anymore."

From the far side of the hedge, Sarah heard her mom calling her name. "I guess we'd better get back before they send out a posse."

Scott tossed the rind of his melon into the darkness, wiped his hands on his jeans, and helped Sarah to her feet. She was close enough to feel his breath on her cheek. She wondered what it would be like to have him kiss her again. This time, for real.

"Sarah," he said, "don't get all your hopes pinned on your birth mother."

"What do you mean?" In the darkness, his presence felt warm and comforting.

"Sometimes, *wondering* about something is a whole lot more exciting than *knowing* about it."

She thought about what he'd said. "It isn't excitement that I'm after, Scott. It's truth. Don't you see? No matter what the truth is, it's better than lies or fantasy."

"I hope you're right. I hope your birth mother is worth the effort to find her. After all, both financially and emotionally—for you and everyone—this is going to cost a lot." Scott edged closer and lifted her chin. But the spell was broken when she heard Richie calling, "Sarah! Where are you, Sarah?"

Scott sighed. "Come on, my dad's made his own ice cream. I'll grab us a dish."

She followed him through the hole in the hedge.

She almost couldn't bear to fantasize about what might happen with Scott. He was not the usual guy; she knew that. He wasn't afraid of her because she had cancer. He wasn't turned off because she had problems. Maybe her luck was changing.

Eleven

TWO DAYS AFTER school ended, Sarah returned to the hospital in Memphis. Dr. Hernandez began new treatments. A Broviac catheter was inserted into a vein in Sarah's chest. The semipermanent plastic tubing made it possible for her to receive her chemo without having to be constantly stuck with needles. Sarah knew it was better than having her veins collapsing from constant jabbing, but she disliked the catheter. It required constant care so that the site didn't get infected. When she finally could go home, she wouldn't be able to go swimming all summer.

Dr. Hernandez listened thoughtfully as Sarah confided about searching for her birth mother. "The best we could get with blood siblings or even your natural mother would be a two-antigen match," the doctor explained.

"That's better than nothing, isn't it?" Sarah asked.

"I'd settle for it. Perhaps your birth mother might

know the whereabouts of your natural father—he and any children he might have fathered are also potential donors, you know."

Although Sarah had wondered about the identity of her father since she'd learned of her adoption, he seemed far more inaccessible than her birth mother. After all, the lawyer had informed Sarah's parents that she'd been born out of wedlock. And, Sarah reasoned, if her natural parents had married, she would never have been given up for adoption. "First, we have to find *her*," Sarah said.

"The sooner, the better," Dr. Hernandez said as she left the room.

Sarah's mother did not stay with her at the hospital in Memphis. "With no school for Tina and Richie, and with your father's work schedule, I have to be at home," her mom had explained. "Will you be all right without me? We'll drive up for the weekend."

"I'm fifteen, Mom. Of course I'll be all right," Sarah had assured her mother in a firm tone of voice. Now, Sarah missed her presence and companionship. The nights in the hospital seemed endless.

Sometimes, she pulled out the incredible letter and read it for the millionth time. She had brought it with her because she found the now familiar words comforting. She longed to talk to JWC face-to-face and had half hoped that while she was in the hospital, JWC might attempt to meet with her. She knew that JWC wasn't her mother; she only wished she knew who it was. "My wish helped me find purpose, faith, and courage." The words of the letter echoed in her mind. Sarah longed for courage to face what lay ahead of her.

When her family came that weekend, Sarah sat with Richie while her parents were talking to the doctors and Tina had gone for some snacks. "What're you doing this summer?" she asked him.

"Playing," he said, then added, "I miss you. Aren't you ever going to get well, Sarah?"

His question tugged at her heart. "I'm trying to," she told him. "It's hard."

"I don't like cancer. When I say my prayers at night, I ask God to make it go away from you."

Sarah pulled Richie closer and kissed his cheek. "Thank you, Richie. I pray for the same thing."

"When I grow up, I'll be a doctor and help all the people who have cancer. If you're not all better by then, I'll help you, too. You can live with me, and I'll take care of you."

His innocence brought a lump to her throat. "I think you'll be a great doctor. You grow up and be the best doctor in the world, all right?"

"All right. I'll do it for you, Sarah." His small face broke into a grin. "Guess what? I have a secret clubhouse in our backyard."

"You do? Where?"

He peeked around the empty room, leaned closer, and whispered, "Through a hole in the hedge. Now you know, too, but don't tell," Richie begged. "When you come home, I'll show it to you. It's a secret, okay?"

"Our secret," Sarah assured him, glad that Richie had found what she hadn't had time to show him.

"I learned a new song. Want to hear it?" Sarah nodded, and he began to sing in a high, warbling voice. Just as he finished, Tina swooped into the room, carrying treats.

"I bought you some ice cream, Richie, but you have to eat it over there." She pointed to a small table in front of a TV set.

"I want to stay here with Sarah," he said, jutting his lower lip.

"You know the rules," Tina insisted in her bossiest voice. "No eating on sofas. Besides, it's my turn to talk to Sarah. Don't hog her."

Sarah was surprised by Tina's wanting to talk to her alone. The ice cream was an obvious ploy to remove Richie from earshot. "Go on," Sarah urged him. "Eat it before it melts. You can come sit with me once you're finished."

Richie carried the bag to the table. Tina turned on the TV for him, then returned and flopped down next to Sarah. "What's up?" Sarah asked.

"Dad and Mom are helping you look for your other mother, aren't they? I can't believe you're really trying to find her."

Tina's accusatory, angry tone caught Sarah off guard. "So, what if I am?"

"I don't think it's very nice of you, that's all."

"Not *nice* of me? What's that supposed to mean?"

"Well, they've been your parents all your life, and now you're treating them as if their feelings don't matter. I know you're making them help you look for her."

Sarah got angry. "You don't know what you're talking about. Mom and Dad are helping me because they want to, not because I'm making them."

"You're not at home now, Sarah, so you don't

know, but I see Mom crying, and I know it's because she thinks you're trying to trade her in."

Flabbergasted, Sarah stared at Tina. "You're wrong," Sara declared, trying to register Tina's words. "If she cries, it's because I have cancer."

"And that's another thing—this bone marrow transplant."

"You know I need compatible bone marrow," Sarah blurted out. "I might have brothers and sisters somewhere who can help me."

"What about me?" Two bright spots of color had appeared on Tina's cheeks.

"What about you?"

"How come you never asked me for my bone marrow?"

"Because we're not compatible." Sarah felt exasperated and confused. Why was Tina behaving like this? Mom and Dad had explained the medical facts to her.

"How do you know we're not? Nobody ever checked me."

"I'm sure we're not."

"But how do you *know*?" Tina's voice wavered, and Sarah saw hurt in her eyes.

"Since we don't have the same parents, it isn't likely that you are," she explained patiently, suddenly aware that Tina cared.

"Everybody in this family treats me like a baby or worse, like I'm nonexistent. Nobody takes into account *my* feelings."

"No one meant to—"

"I should be tested. Maybe we are compatible and just don't know it. And how will we ever know if I'm not tested?"

Seeing how passionate Tina felt about being tested upset Sarah. "Nobody meant to ignore you, Tina. I guess since medically you're not a match, we didn't ask you to be tested. I never thought you might want to be tested."

"Why shouldn't I? I know we're not really blood sisters, but I'm a person close to you, and I'd like to help."

"It's great of you to want to be tested, Tina. I appreciate it." Sara felt overwhelmed by her sister's offer. "We'll talk to Mom and Dad about it, and they can ask Dr. Hernandez."

Tina sat back on the couch, looking mollified. "Sometimes, answers are right in your own backyard," she said.

Sarah caught the subtle message: So, why go looking for them elsewhere? It hadn't occurred to her that the search for her birth mother would be so troubling for Tina. *Why was it Tina's problem*, she wondered.

By the middle of the week, Sarah was totally bored. She was the only teenager on the floor undergoing treatment, so she visited the younger patients and played games with them. But she still wished for something else to do.

One afternoon, her father arrived unexpectedly. "Dad, you aren't supposed to be here until the weekend. Is anything wrong?"

"Everything's fine," he answered quietly. "I have business here in Memphis, and I have some news that couldn't wait."

Sarah's heart raced. "What?"

"The lawyer came through for us, honey. It seems

he has a granddaughter about your age, and he was sympathetic when I told him about your condition. He went through his files and sent me a copy of your surrender agreement."

"What's that?"

Her father was smiling, looking excited and boyish. "It's the legal paper your natural mother signed when she gave you up for adoption."

Sarah's mouth went dry, and for a moment she was afraid she might throw up, not from her medications, but from tension. "So, what does that mean?"

"It means we have a name. We have *her* name."

Twelve

SARAH'S FATHER HELPED her into bed, reached into the inside pocket of his coat jacket, and pulled out a sheet of white paper.

Her fingers trembled as she took it. She was almost afraid to open it, overwhelmed by the knowledge that the mysterious woman who had borne her was about to take on a name.

"Go on, honey," her dad said. "It's all right. This is what we've been waiting for so we can find a donor."

Sarah unfolded the paper. It was typed and looked neat and formal. At the top were the words "Agreement for the Surrender of My Child for Adoption." The first sentence began, "I, Janelle Warren . . ." Her gaze flew up to her father's. "Janelle's a pretty name, isn't it?"

"Yes," he agreed.

Sarah read further, ". . . being the mother of a female child named (Baby Girl) Warren . . ." She stopped reading. Was that all Sarah had been to her—Baby Girl Warren? Hadn't Janelle even bothered to give her baby a name? Sarah's vision blurred, but she continued to read, ". . . and having sole right to custody and control of said child, said child having been born out of wedlock . . ."

Sarah winced. Of course, she'd known for some time that her natural mother and father had never married, but seeing the words in black and white cut through her like a knife. The remainder of the document was full of dates and places and legal phrases about relinquishing all rights to "said child."

At the bottom, Janelle Warren had signed her name. Sarah studied the signature. The writing was small and neat, as orderly as the document giving her up for adoption. She ran her fingertips over the black letters, as if the act of touching them might bring the person of Janelle Warren closer to her.

"Are you all right?" her father asked.

"Sure," Sarah answered with a shrug. "It's just weird, that's all."

"It's weird for me, too," he told her. "I never thought we'd have to go back to the past in order to give you a future."

Sarah knew she should be happy about the discovery, and in a way, she was. She now knew her birth mother's name. They'd moved closer toward her ultimate goal of finding her. Still, it was scary for Sarah. She'd taken a first step down what seemed an endless road, and good or bad, there would be no turning back.

*   *   *

Sarah returned home ill and demoralized. Every period of intensive chemo left her sicker and weaker, and each recovery period was more difficult and took longer. She struggled to overcome the side effects, wanting to be ready to meet her birth mother if the records searcher was able to turn up anything. When she was strong enough, her father brought her and her mom to his office downtown. "I want you to meet the detective we've hired," her father said.

Sarah felt fidgety. Her mom obviously was upset. Tina had been right about that much. Sitting in her dad's sun-warmed office and watching her mother toy nervously with her rings made Sarah feel sorry for her parents. Yet, they had been the ones to keep the truth from her all these years. She hadn't asked to be born, or adopted, or lied to, and she certainly had never asked to be stricken with leukemia.

Her dad brought in a man, who smiled and offered Sarah his hand. "Hi. I'm Mike Lions," he said. He was a short, slim man with thinning hair, glasses, and a quiet voice. Sarah's surprise must have shown on her face, because Mike said, "I know I don't fulfill most people's expectations about PIs, but all those macho types on TV and in the movies give hardworking, ordinary guys like me a false image." He grinned. "So, I don't look like a movie star private eye. I've learned to live with it. I assure you, I'm very good at what I do in spite of it."

Sarah flushed and returned his smile. "I need to find my birth mother," she told him.

"Your father's told me. And he's told me about your special circumstances," Mike replied. "Therefore, your case gets top priority. While I can't promise you that I'll find her, I will tell you this—if I can't, no one else can, either."

His confidence in his ability made Sarah feel confident, too. He acted as if he understood the urgency of her search. "What do I do now?" Sarah asked.

"You wait to hear from me."

It seemed too simple. Sarah was still curious. "Once you find her, what happens?"

Mike's expression grew serious. "I want to be honest with you and your folks, Sarah. Birth parents don't always want to be found. If that's the case, when they are located, they can panic."

Sarah saw her mom shift forward in her chair. Hadn't she been telling Sarah the same thing all along? Sarah hated giving her the satisfaction of thinking she was correct.

"How do they panic?" Mrs. McGreggor asked. "Sarah won't be in any danger, will she?"

"Of course not," Mike assured her. "Once I find the natural mother, I use caution in establishing actual contact. Usually, I approach the subject on the phone. I say something like, 'Someone wants to meet you who was born on—,' and I give the searcher's birth date. Believe me, that special date is engraved in the birth mother's memory forever. No one ever forgets it."

"It must come as quite a shock," Sarah's dad said.

"Yes, it usually does. Some birth parents are overjoyed. They've wondered for years about the baby they gave up. Others say they can't talk now, but will call me back, so I leave them a number. Sometimes, when I call again, they hang up and refuse to take my calls."

"What if that happens? What if she won't talk to

me? I need her, you know." Sarah fought down anxiety.

Mike studied her kindly. "All I can do is locate her for you, Sarah. I can't force her to meet with you."

"What if you locate her, but don't call her?" Sarah asked. "What if you just tell me where she is and I call her." She was thinking that it might be harder for Janelle to hang up on her own daughter.

"You're the client, and I'll handle it however you want me to."

Somehow, that made Sarah feel better, as if she had more control over the situation. "That's what I want you to do," she said. "Once you find her"—she didn't even think *if* you find her—"please call me. I want to be the first one to contact her."

Her mom grew rigid. "Sarah, that may not be possible. You may be back in the hospital, or—"

"I want to meet my mother face-to-face," Sarah interrupted.

Mike leaned back and jotted in a small black notebook. "No telling where she might live," he said. "It could be expensive for you to go confront her yourself."

"I have money," Sarah said stubbornly, again grateful to the faceless JWC for the gift.

"I don't think you should make those kinds of plans," Sarah's mother advised.

"I *have* to," Sarah countered, feeling her temper rising. "She's my mother. I need her."

Her father reached over and took his wife's hands. "Carol, honey, you know we agreed to help Sarah all we could. First, Mike has to locate the woman. Then, we can decide how best to handle it. Let's cross that bridge when we get to it."

Sarah's mom pressed her lips together and nodded without glancing at Sarah.

Mike flipped his notebook shut and clipped his silver ballpoint pen to his shirt pocket. "Don't be discouraged. Many times, these jobs of reconnecting birth families with adoptees turn out pretty good. Mine did."

"You were adopted?" Sarah asked. Except for Scott's friend, whom she only had heard about, she had never met anybody who actually had been adopted.

"I was," Mike said. "The people who adopted me were great parents, who told me all along I'd been adopted. I loved the Lions very much—I've even kept their name—but all my life, I wanted to meet the person who had given birth to me. I wanted brothers and sisters, blood relatives. Even after I married and had kids, I couldn't stop wanting to know who I was."

"So you searched?" Sarah asked.

He nodded. "That's how I got into this business. It used to be much more difficult to get information. Records of adoptions were closed and sealed. It took court orders and years of waiting to find out anything. As more and more people started searching, they became organized, formed support groups and organizations. These groups started applying political pressure and eventually loosened up the system. It's still not easy in some states, but people are recognizing adoptees' rights to have basic information about their genetic heritage."

He pushed his glasses up on his nose and studied Sarah thoughtfully. "For me, the search was a bonanza. I had six brothers and sisters on my natural mother's side and four on my father's. All of them were ecstatic to meet me, my wife, and my kids. We get together every two years for a huge family reunion.

"Now, I spend my life helping others find their birth families, because I know what it feels like to want to be connected by blood. The search can be frustrating. But every time you obtain information—a name, an address—it's like a small victory. And every time you hit a brick wall, it's like a small death."

Sarah felt as if a light had gone on inside her heart. Mike *did* understand—as only one who'd been adopted could understand. She was certain that her birth mother, Janelle Warren, had wondered about the daughter she'd given away fifteen years before. Once Sarah contacted her, Janelle might be shocked, but she would want to meet Sarah. And once she was tested for bone marrow compatibility, Janelle would be a match and would feel compelled to help Sarah.

No one could convince Sarah otherwise. Mothers and their children belonged to each other, no matter what had happened to separate them. The bond, the link could never be completely severed, regardless of time and circumstances. "I'll be at home waiting for your phone call," Sarah told the detective. "I know you'll find my mother. You must."

Thirteen

SARAH FOUND THAT the chemo treatments had taken their toll on her. She felt so weak and exhausted that she spent a great deal of time curled up on the sofa. It was hard to wait for Mike to contact them with more news. She wanted to conserve her energy for when she needed it to meet with her birth mother, so she didn't mind doing nothing much at all.

The waiting seemed longer since most of her friends had gone off on vacation. She was glad to get postcards, but felt sad to be reminded that while everyone was off having a good time, she was housebound and bedridden.

"Mail call," Tina said, breezing toward her one morning.

"Anything important?" Sarah asked. For a moment, her heart hammered in anticipation, as it did every day when the mail arrived. Maybe this would be the day Mike would contact them.

"There's a package from New Mexico." Tina stared at a small box. "The address doesn't look familiar. Who do we know from there?"

Eagerly, Sarah took the box. It couldn't be from Mike. "It's from Scott," she said, feeling her disappointment dissolve immediately. "Remember, he went with his family to look at colleges and visit relatives in Santa Fe."

"Lucky him," Tina said.

Sarah felt a momentary stab of guilt. If it hadn't been for her search effort, the One Last Wish money could have been used for her family to go on a fabulous, luxurious vacation. Perhaps she was being selfish in not offering her parents some of the money to have a good time. "It's your money," her mom had told her. "Use it the way you must." Sarah hadn't offered any money because she honestly didn't know how long it would take to find her birth mother, or how expensive the search might be. Maybe when the search was over, maybe after her transplant, she could offer to take everyone on a trip.

"Aren't you going to open it?" Tina asked.

With a start, Sarah realized she'd been lost in thought. "Sure, I'm going to open it. Want to watch?" She could tell that Tina was interested.

Tina sat on the edge of the sofa and asked, "What do you think it is?"

Sarah shook the box. "Maybe it's some Indian beads. That's very popular stuff in Santa Fe."

"Open it already!"

Sarah pulled off the wrapping. Inside the small box was a bracelet of hammered silver, set with turquoise stones. "It's lovely," she said, thrilled that

Scott had not only thought of her, but sent her something so beautiful.

"I'll say," Tina declared, checking the bracelet over carefully. "Wish some guy as cute as Scott would send me a present."

"Someday, some guy will be falling all over you," Sarah told her, trying to be kind.

"Sure, if I stick my foot out and trip him."

Sarah laughed. She read Scott's note: "To the wonderful girl with eyes as blue as these stones. Scott." Sarah felt so happy, she blushed. Then, looking thoughtfully at her sister, she said, "Tina, you're pretty."

"Do you think so? I think my nose is too big."

"It looks like Mom's nose."

Tina rolled her eyes. "Oh, great. Why couldn't I have gotten one that looked more like yours?"

The comment was innocent enough, but their gazes tangled. Of course, there could never be a way for them to look alike—they weren't related. Tina dropped her gaze and shrugged. "You know what I mean."

"Sure," Sarah agreed hastily, not wanting the sisterly camaraderie to evaporate between them. It had been a while since they'd felt at ease around one another. "I know what you mean."

Tina stood. "I've got to split. I promised Mrs. Marcus I'd baby-sit Danny this morning."

Sarah felt a momentary twinge of jealousy. Baby-sitting Danny had always been her job. Now, she was too sick.

"Thanks for putting in a good word for me," Tina added. "If it hadn't been for you, she wouldn't have hired me. I'm saving my money for new school clothes."

"No problem," Sarah replied, with more cheerfulness than she felt. "Have fun." She watched Tina leave and settled back on the sofa with a sigh. She felt that life was passing her by, that everyone and everything was moving ahead.

She had little in common with her friends anymore. Cammie, Natalie, and JoEllen were a tight threesome, doing things together when they were home, and making plans for another year. Even Tina was thinking about the future. Sarah hardly let herself dwell on thoughts of tomorrow. Now, with the realization that she was adopted, she wondered if she'd ever had an honest past.

She thought about the enormous sum of money the anonymous JWC had given her. If only it could help her discover her past, then maybe she would have a future. She closed her eyes and prayed she'd hear from Mike soon.

Fourteen

SARAH SLOWLY BEGAN to regain her strength. She hoped they would get more information from Mike while she was feeling better, because she'd have to return to the hospital soon for additional chemo, and she knew she'd be sick afterward. She was finding it more difficult to rally between treatments, and she wanted to be well and strong when she met her mother for the first time.

Dr. Hernandez called, concerned about Sarah's latest lab work. In spite of the treatments, cancer cells had reappeared in her bone marrow. "We're continuing to scan the registry in Sarah's behalf," Dr. Hernandez told Sarah's parents. "I'm afraid, however, we're not having any luck."

Sarah tried not to think that time was running out on her. Once they found her mother, things would be different. Her chances would be better. All she had to do was hold on until then. Sarah was half asleep when the phone rang late one night. Her father came into her room, bringing the cordless receiver to her. "It's Mike Lions," he said.

Instantly awake, Sarah took the phone while her father went downstairs and picked up the extension in the family room. "Hi," Sarah said, her voice breathless.

"I hope it's not too late for me to call."

"It's all right."

"I found Janelle Warren."

For a moment, Sarah couldn't speak. Her voice jammed in her throat, and her hands began to tremble. "Where are you, Mike?" she heard her father ask.

"Los Angeles. I found her living in one of the little beach communities near LA. She has a home and a well-established reputation in the town. It looks as if she'll be running for mayor in the fall elections."

Sarah felt a wave of delight spreading through her. Her mother might be famous. "You haven't said anything to her, have you?" Sarah asked suddenly.

"I've merely been observing her, checking on her discreetly," Mike assured Sarah. "I've spent hours in the local library's newspaper archives. What I've learned is, she's been a resident here since the early eighties—very successful in real estate and influential in local politics."

"Does she have a family?" Sarah's father asked.

"She's never married, although she's dating a rather prominent attorney at this time."

Sarah felt a sinking sensation in the pit of her stomach. She had no blood brothers or sisters, which meant that bone marrow compatibility had to depend entirely on her mother. Unless, of course, her mother could help her find her natural father.

"What do you want me to do?" Mike's question brought Sarah back to the present.

Her dad said, "My wife and Sarah and I will talk it over and get back to you tomorrow. Tell me how to reach you out there."

Sarah half heard the remainder of the conversation as her mind raced ahead with possibilities. When both her parents came into her room, she was waiting for them, sitting up in bed with her chin resting on her drawn-up knees. Her mom sat on the bed; her dad crossed his arms and leaned against the wall. Without giving them an opportunity to speak, Sarah blurted out, "I want to go to Los Angeles."

"Sarah, I don't think you should—" her mother began.

Sarah interrupted her. "I want to go."

"Your mother's right, honey. Maybe we should let Mike handle it. He's a professional, and he's best prepared to deal with this kind of situation."

"No. I want to meet her ... talk to her face-to-face," Sarah insisted. She wanted to know why she'd been given away, but thought it best not to mention it.

Her mom glanced nervously toward her dad. "I would have to go with you. It would be a big expense."

Sarah waved her objection aside. "I have the money, remember? And it's all right if you come with me." Sarah realized she could never make the trip on her own. She would need help, especially if she got sick while she was out there. Her mom had dealt with her cancer for years and could handle anything that might occur. "But you can't get in the way of my meeting my mother," Sarah warned. "I know you don't want me to do this, but promise me you won't interfere."

Her mom looked stricken. "Sarah, this may be hard on my feelings, but I'm well aware it's your *life* we're trying to save. Of course, I won't get in the way."

Sarah felt agitated and restless. "How soon can we leave?" she asked.

"I-I don't know. . . . There's so much I'll have to do to prepare," her mother said. "I'll have to get someone to come in and watch Tina and Richie."

"Tina can handle it," Sarah replied.

"I don't think—"

"Stop treating her like a baby, Mom. You let her baby-sit for other people. She can look out for herself and Richie. She can cope in an emergency. You should let her do it. You can pay her with some of my One Last Wish money."

Her mother looked undecided as she nibbled on her bottom lip. "What do you think, Patrick?"

"Sarah's right. Tina's pretty capable." He thought a moment before continuing. "I'm right in the middle of some merger plans down at the office, but maybe I can put things on hold for a few days and come with you," he mused out loud.

"No," her mom protested. "I might be willing to let Tina manage during the daytime, but not nights. I don't want both of us out in California and the kids here alone."

He nodded in agreement. "Maybe you're right.

Mike will be out there with you, and if you need me, I can come."

Sarah listened while they made plans, barely able to contain her excitement. She was going to meet the woman who'd given birth to her, her *real* mother. Janelle might be surprised at Sarah's entrance into her life—maybe shocked by it—but after they met, after they talked, Sarah felt sure Janelle would be glad Sarah had contacted her. Perhaps she'd even want Sarah to become a permanent part of her life.

Tina's eyes were wide as saucers as, early the next morning, her mother explained what was about to happen. Sarah sat at the kitchen table, listening and toying with a spoon in a bowl of soggy cereal.

"You're going all the way out to California?" Tina asked her mother.

"It seems the only thing for us to do. Sarah needs to contact her—" she interrupted herself, "Ms. Warren as soon as possible. It may save time if Sarah goes to her personally."

Tina looked over at Sarah. "Gosh, I don't know what to say."

"Say you'll be all right here with Dad and Richie while we're gone," Sarah replied.

"I can take care of the three of us. I can cook— some. I can keep Richie entertained."

"I'll make up some casseroles and put them in the freezer," Mom said. "You can microwave them for suppers."

"How long will you be gone?"

"We're not sure."

Sarah kept her eyes on her cereal bowl. All the details were frustrating her. She simply wanted to get on a plane and leave. Tina asked, "What will you tell Richie?"

"I'll tell him we have to go away because of Sarah's illness. That's the basic truth."

"I'll talk to him," Sarah added. "I'll promise to bring him back a special surprise."

As their mom opened pantry doors and started making a grocery list, Tina turned to Sarah. "Are you nervous about meeting her?"

"Some." Actually, Sarah was extremely nervous.

"I hope she's nice to you."

"She'll be nice," Sarah said with more confidence than she felt.

"I wish there were something I could do to help."

"You're helping by taking care of Richie."

"I wish I could go with you."

"It's not exactly a vacation, Tina."

"I know, but I'd still like to go along. It seems exciting . . . going to Los Angeles."

Sarah stood, walked her bowl to the sink, and washed it out. Through the kitchen window, she saw the sloping backyard, bathed in sunlight that made the dew sparkle on the grass.

Later that day, Sarah told Richie about the trip. Immediately, he began to cry. "No! No, Sarah! Don't go."

"It's just for a little while," she assured him. She hugged him tightly and promised him toys and T-shirts. "Now, don't cry. We'll be back soon."

He clung to her and let go only when she took him to her room to sit on her bed while she packed. He watched her as she moved around the room, selecting outfits, discarding others. What did a person wear to meet one's mother for the first time, she wondered.

Richie lay his favorite stuffed bear on top of her things. "He wants to go, too," Richie said.

"I shouldn't take him. He might miss you."

Richie shook his head. "He wants to go."

A lump rose in Sarah's throat as she gazed down at the scuffed-up, well-loved bear. "Sing me a song," she asked Richie, forcing cheeriness. "One of your favorites."

His voice trembled as he sang, "There was a farmer had a dog, and Bingo was his name-o . . ."

Sarah continued to pack for the reunion of her life.

Fifteen

THE PLANE KNIFED through a bank of white clouds as Sarah stared out the window. Below, the city of Los Angeles sprawled in a haphazard maze of neighborhoods and buildings, broken by dark lines of roads and freeways as far as she could see.

"Are you feeling better?" her mother asked from the seat beside Sarah.

"A little," Sarah said. She had felt nauseated most of the trip, partly because of anxiety. Her wig was making her scalp itch, and there was now a small drop of blood staining the front of her blouse where the Broviac catheter, still implanted in her chest, had caught on her bra. "I'll be glad when we're on the ground."

"Me, too. Four hours on an airplane is quite enough for me."

Mike Lions was waiting at the gate as Sarah and her mother deplaned. He shook their hands and eased Sarah's duffel bag off her shoulder. "Let me take this."

"We have more."

Mike grinned. "I'm not surprised. My wife can't travel across the street without two pieces of luggage."

It took another two hours for them to gather their luggage, get to Mike's rental car, and drive to the hotel where he'd reserved Sarah and her mom a room. Once there, he ordered a platter of fresh fruit and cold drinks from room service. Sarah stretched out on the bed and sipped her cola, grateful for the relief the air-conditioning provided from the relentless California summer heat.

"Let me tell you what I've got," Mike said without preamble. "Janelle Warren is the head of a small real estate agency that's been very successful. As I told you on the phone, she's planning to run for mayor, and from what I hear, it's going to be a really tough fight. The man she's trying to unseat has been mayor for twelve years."

"You said she has no family," Mrs. McGreggor said. She and Mike sat at a small round table across from Sarah's bed.

"She lives quietly, in a modest house, with two cats and a parrot," Mike replied.

Suddenly, Sarah spoke up. "I want to see her."

"You will," her mom promised. "You should get some rest before we go out in this heat again."

"That's not what I mean. I want to *see* her before I meet her. Before I introduce myself to her, I just want to look at her." Sarah couldn't explain why it was important to her, but it was. Somehow, she had to reconcile her fantasies with the flesh-and-blood person before she actually met her.

Mike tapped the tabletop while he considered Sarah's request. "I've been shadowing her, so I'm pretty familiar with her habits. We could have lunch tomorrow at the place where she usually eats. That way, you could get a good look at her without her knowing."

"You mean spy on her?" her mom asked sharply.

"Observe," Mike corrected.

"That's what I'd like to do," Sarah said. "I'd like to observe her." She preferred Mike's choice of words.

"If that's what you want, then that's what we'll do." Mike stood up. "Why don't the two of you get some rest, and I'll phone you in the morning. If we leave here by nine, we can drive down the coast and be at the restaurant before she arrives."

Without waiting for her mom's approval of the plan, Sarah agreed. She fell asleep before the door clicked shut behind Mike.

The next morning, Mike drove them along a road that hugged the shoreline of the Pacific Ocean. Individual communities blended into one another, but finally, he pulled into a parking lot in a small downtown area. "Feel up to walking some?" he asked. "You might like to look around the city a bit. The restaurant we're going to is a few blocks over."

By the time the three of them had entered the restaurant for lunch, Sarah was so nervous that her stomach felt tied in knots. Her mom ordered her some crackers, which Sarah nibbled on halfheartedly. Mike scanned the menu and made suggestions, but Sarah was in no mood to eat. As it got closer to noon, the restaurant began to fill up. Sarah asked, "What if she decides not to come here today?"

"Then we'll go by her office," Mike said. "Relax. She'll be here." He was looking toward the doorway when Sarah saw his eyes narrow.

Quickly, she looked up. In the doorway stood a tall, slim woman with stylish, short blond hair. Mike didn't have to tell Sarah she was seeing Janelle Warren. She would have known her mother anywhere. Sarah's heart thudded, and her mouth went perfectly dry. "There she is," Sarah whispered.

Mike nodded confirmation.

Sarah watched as a waiter led Janelle to a table, where a distinguished-looking man with steel gray hair stood and pulled out a chair for her. "The boyfriend," Mike explained. Sarah thought Mike's term an odd one to use for people who were adults. Teenagers were boyfriend and girlfriend—not grown-ups.

Sarah couldn't take her eyes off her mother. She seemed so elegant and poised. Back in Sarah's hometown, the women were so ordinary. Her mom's friends wore sweats and sneakers, jeans and casual shirts to the grocery store and to PTA meetings. Women like Janelle, who dressed in silk and linen suits were glamorous and exciting. For a moment, Sarah felt dazzled.

"You should eat something," Carol McGreggor said when the waiter brought their lunch.

Sarah ate automatically, hardly tasting the soup and salad placed in front of her. She couldn't take her eyes off her birth mother. Every move Janelle made, the way she held her fork, the way she tossed her head when she laughed, seemed magical to Sarah. A part of her wanted to rush over and throw her arms around Janelle's neck. She wanted to shout, "I'm your daughter! Your only daughter."

Another part of her trembled in fear. What would her mother's reaction be? Would she be pleased to see her? Would she embrace her? Had she ever missed having Sarah in her life? "I'm not sure what to do," Sarah confessed to Mike. "What should I do?"

"It would be best to approach her when she's alone," Mike replied.

"When will she be alone?"

"Maybe when she goes home tonight. Are you sure you don't want to contact her by phone first? It might be less awkward."

Sarah shook her head emphatically. After having seen Janelle, she couldn't resort to the impersonal use of the telephone. "Can we follow her when she leaves?" Sarah asked, feeling a peculiar need to be near her birth mother.

"That's not a good idea," Mrs. McGreggor said. "It seems sneaky to me. Besides, you should get some rest this afternoon."

"I don't want to rest. I want to be with my mother," she insisted.

Her mom looked as if she'd been slapped. "It was only a suggestion."

Before anything else could be said, Sarah saw Janelle and her lunch companion rise. "Look. They're leaving." Sarah felt an edge of panic. "I don't want to lose her."

"It's all right," Mike assured her. "We'll keep pace behind her."

Sarah could tell her mom didn't want to do such a thing. Still, Mrs. McGreggor rose and tagged along when Sarah and Mike stepped out onto the sidewalk.

"Don't crowd her," Mike cautioned.

Sarah kept her eyes on Janelle as she ambled along the sidewalk. Janelle walked with confidence, greeting people along the way. The walk to her office was short, and when Janelle stepped inside, Sarah felt disoriented. She didn't want to lose sight of her.

"Her habits are regular as clockwork," Mike said. "She'll head home about six o'clock, and we can be there waiting for her."

"Perhaps we can take in a movie," Mrs. McGreggor offered. "It will pass the time and get Sarah out of the heat of the day."

Reluctantly, Sarah agreed. The three of them sat through a film, and as soon as it was over, Sarah headed for Mike's car. He drove her and her mom into a quiet neighborhood where palm trees lined the streets and exotic tropical flowers bloomed on bushes and trellises. Sarah scarcely saw the lush scenery, she was so preoccupied.

Mike parked across the street from a white stucco house with a red Spanish tile roof and a red tile porch. "That's it," he told them.

Minutes later, Sarah watched as a car swung into the driveway and Janelle emerged from the driver's side. "I guess this is it," Sarah remarked, after giving Janelle a little time to get inside. Now that the time had come to meet her mother, Sarah grew apprehensive. She struggled to find courage to approach the house.

"I could go with you," her mom ventured.

"I want to go alone."

"If you need me . . ."

"I won't." Sarah stepped away from the car and walked slowly across the street, up the walk, and onto the porch. The scent of gardenias and summer roses mingled in the humid air. Her finger trembled as she poked the doorbell. From within, she heard a chime. Moments later, the door opened and she was looking into the face of Janelle Warren—the face of her biological mother.

Sixteen

SARAH'S KNEES SHOOK, and her tongue felt stuck to the roof of her mouth. Janelle gazed at her expectantly. "Is it Girl Scout cookie time already?" she asked with a smile.

Sarah experienced a sinking sensation in the pit of her stomach. Janelle didn't even recognize her own flesh and blood! "No," Sarah managed to say.

"Are you lost?" Janelle frowned.

"I'm S-Sarah," Sarah stammered.

"Yes?"

Sarah silently scolded herself. Of course, the name *Sarah* wouldn't mean anything. Desperately, she searched for a way to express who she was. "You knew me as 'Baby Girl Warren' when I was born."

The color drained from Janelle Warren's face. Her eyes darted nervously over Sarah's head and she blurted out, "Go away!"

"But I want—"

"Get out of here. I don't know you. I don't know what you're talking about. Go away!" Janelle slammed the door in Sarah's face.

Stunned, Sarah stood on the porch, unable to move. She felt as if someone had hurled a brick at her. Her knees buckled, and she grabbed for the door for support. Suddenly, Mike and her mom were beside her, leading her away from the porch.

"What happened?" her mom demanded.

"She told me to go away. She said she didn't know me and didn't want to, either. Sarah felt like a robot—her emotions were frozen.

"I was afraid of this. The shock was too much," Mike said. "Maybe if I explain things to Janelle Warren . . ."

"No! We're going back to the hotel," Carol McGreggor said forcefully. "Now, we do it my way, not Sarah's."

Sarah didn't argue. She felt foolish. The sound of a slamming door reverberated in her ears, the hostile, fearful look on Janelle's face indelibly stamped in her memory. *Go away!* she'd been ordered. *Go away!* Sarah got into the backseat of Mike's car, and her mom climbed in next to her. Even though the evening air was warm, her teeth began to chatter and she felt chilly.

Back in their hotel room, Sarah crossed to the window and opened the heavy drape. She heard Mike and her mom talking quietly. Then the door closed, and Mike was gone. "You tried to warn me, but I wouldn't listen," Sarah said bitterly. "Go ahead and say, 'I told you so.' "

"I'm sorry, Sarah."

A tear trickled down Sarah's cheek, and she

reached up and wiped it away. "She said she didn't know me."

"Sarah, I'm not defending her, but your showing up on her doorstep after fifteen years must have been quite a shock for her."

"She hates me. My real mother hates me."

Her mom touched her shoulder and turned her around, her face dark with anger. "Stop talking like that, Sarah, and listen to me. Your *real* mother loves you. I know that's true, because I'm your *real* mother. I'm tired of your pretending otherwise. Why wasn't I enough for you, Sarah? What's wrong with me?"

Sarah blinked, caught off guard by the heat in her mom's voice. "Nothing's wrong with you."

"Then stop treating me like a second-class person. As if I'm somehow inferior because you didn't drop out of my body." Her voice rose with intensity. "*I'm* your real mother. I was the one who held your hand when you took your first steps. I was the one who took you to your first day of school and held you when you cried. I was the one who was with you when the doctors diagnosed leukemia. I sat through the tests with you. I wept with you, prayed with you, stayed nights in the hospital with you. It was *me*, Sarah. Not Janelle Warren. It was *me*—I am your mother."

As she listened, a jumble of childhood memories tumbled through Sarah's mind, as if she were watching a speeded-up video. She saw herself in the hospital with lab technicians jabbing her with long syringes while her mother held her hand and stroked her cheek.

"I didn't mean to be ungrateful." Sarah hoped desperately that her mother knew she meant it.

"Ungrateful!" Mrs. McGreggor fairly shouted. "Is that what you think I want from you? Your gratitude? Grow up, Sarah. We are *family*. All of us—your dad, Tina, Richie, me. You belong to us, not by virtue of some piece of legal paper, but because we chose you, raised you, loved you."

Suddenly, Sarah felt herself growing angry. "You never wanted me to look for Janelle. You would never have even told me that I was adopted if it wasn't for the bone marrow transplant."

"You bet I didn't want you to look for her. I was afraid of her, Sarah. Afraid that she was better than I am, more interesting and exciting. Look at me. I'm short and fat and boring. I've been a housewife and a mother all my life. My family *is* my life and is all I ever wanted. Until today. I saw Janelle in that restaurant, too, you know. I saw how your eyes lit up. And it made me feel so . . . inadequate."

Her mom's confession surprised Sarah. She hadn't expected jealousy and envy. "I don't think you're inferior to her. That's not it at all. It's just . . . I've told you before . . . I'm curious about her," Sarah insisted.

"Curious is one thing, but this fascination you've carried around has been unfair. It's hateful and punishing." Her mom turned and walked to the far side of the hotel room. "All these months, I've felt so threatened by her."

"How could you? You didn't even know her."

"I had this idea that she'd steal you away. What right did she have to you?"

"Steal me? She won't even talk to me."

"She's stolen you, all right," her mom countered. "You've spent the last three months consumed with locating her—and not just because of the bone marrow, either."

"I need to know who I am."

"I'll tell you who you are. You're Sarah Louise McGreggor, and have been since you were three days old."

"No . . . Maybe my name is Sarah McGreggor, but *I* am part of Janelle Warren and my natural father. There's a difference. I'm different from Tina and Richie, from you and Dad. Why can't you understand what I've been going through?"

"Why can't you understand what *I've* been going through?"

As they stood glaring at each other, Sarah realized how deeply her preoccupation with her birth mother had wounded her mom. While she had fantasized about her birth mother, her mom had felt rejected. Sarah recalled Tina's trying to tell her as much. "I'm sorry if I've hurt you. It's just that the One Last Wish money seemed to give me a way to have everything—my birth mother, the bone marrow, you, Dad, Tina and Richie . . ." Sarah's voice trailed, thick with unshed tears.

Her mother gripped the back of a chair. "That Wish money could have given our family wonderful things. But now, as far as I'm concerned, it was a curse."

"How can you say that? It's a ton of money, and it's paid for all of this."

"Contrary to popular belief, Sarah, money doesn't buy everything. In this case, for me, it's bought a boatload of unhappiness."

Sarah remembered what she'd explained to Scott—that she wanted to know the truth, she wanted to trade lies and fantasy for reality. He had tried to caution her that sometimes the truth hurt and might be better left undisturbed. Now, she understood what he was trying to tell her, but it was too late.

Her mom shrugged. "At the time, we thought we were doing the right thing by respecting your birth mother's wishes and keeping your adoption a secret. If I had known it would cause so much pain on both our sides, I would have never agreed to secrecy." She crossed the room and flipped the wall switch on. "Regardless of how things were handled, we're here now," her mom said. "Sadly, despite the way Janelle treated you today, you still need her. Get your purse. I'm calling Mike, and you and I are going back to see her."

"She won't talk to us."

"Yes, she will," her mom said. Her eyes looked steely hard, and her voice sounded determined. "Whether Janelle Warren likes it or not, fifteen years ago she gave birth to a baby. Now, that child needs her. She won't walk away from you this time, Sarah—I won't let her. You need her bone marrow, and I'm going to tell her so."

Seventeen

SARAH WASN'T NEARLY as afraid the second time she stood on Janelle Warren's porch as she'd been the first time. This time, her mom and Mike were standing shoulder-to-shoulder with her. The worst had already happened—she'd been rejected by her birth mother.

When the door opened, Janelle stared at them incredulously. Light from her living room flooded through the doorway. "I told you I don't want to be bothered," Janelle said. "Please go away."

"We can't do that," Sarah heard her mom reply. "We must talk to you."

"If you don't go away, I'll call the police," Janelle insisted.

Sarah watched Janelle's knuckles turn white as she gripped the door frame. "Ms. Warren," Mike began to explain, "We're not here to harm you or make trouble for you. I'm a private investigator, and these people want to talk to you . . . *need* to talk to you."

"Your standing here is harming me," Janelle replied.

"Ms. Warren," Sarah's mom said, "believe me, this is very difficult on all of us. I can assure you, we'll be going just as soon as we talk to you. Sarah doesn't really have a choice about this. Without your help, she may die."

Janelle didn't say anything. She gazed at Sarah, who felt insignificant by the inspection. "All right." Janelle spoke in a suspicious voice. "Come in, but make it brief. I'm expecting company." She opened the door wider.

"I'll wait out in the car," Mike told Sarah and her mom. "You don't need me anymore."

Sarah stayed close to her mom as Janelle led them inside the house. Sarah looked around. She noticed wall-to-wall white carpeting. Janelle led them into a beautifully decorated room, filled with expensive objects arranged on polished wood tables and sparkling glass shelves. She motioned for them to sit, and Sarah noted the lush, elegant cream-color sofa. Janelle took a chair opposite them. "What do you want?" she asked stiffly.

I want you to look at me, Sarah felt like saying. *I want you to tell me who I am and where I came from.* "This is as awkward for me as it is for you," Carol McGreggor began. "I never dreamed I'd ever have to meet you, face you."

"I believe not meeting me was a condition of the adoption," Janelle said coolly.

"My parents never told me I was adopted," Sarah said, somehow feeling defensive toward her mom and dad. "I just found out when I was told about my medical problem."

"Then you understood that I didn't want to be found? Yet, you came looking for me, anyway."

"We told her your wishes, too," Carol assured Janelle. "We understood them from the day we signed the papers, and we respected them until we had no choice."

Janelle sat forward on the edge of the chair. "You had no right to come here." She turned toward Sarah. "I had my reasons for giving you up. Very good reasons. It wasn't easy, you know. But what's done is done. There's no turning back."

Sarah didn't believe what she was hearing. Janelle made it sound as if it had been easy and final. "What were your reasons? I deserve to know."

Janelle looked startled. Abruptly, she stood. "I don't have to defend my choices to anyone. Giving you up was *my* choice. Believe me, the Supreme Court had already legalized abortion, and I was certainly free to take that route. An abortion doesn't show on a woman's body the way a pregnancy does, you know."

Sarah wondered if she was supposed to feel grateful because Janelle had elected to have her instead of getting an abortion. "I'm sorry I was such an inconvenience," Sarah snapped. She couldn't hide her anger. Maybe it was better for her to feel angry, so it hurt less.

"I have a very good life now," Janelle told them.

"And you don't need me complicating it," Sarah finished.

"I don't mean to sound cruel or heartless. I'm sure you've been curious about your background. I just don't think I can help you. I have a high profile in this community. The man I'm seeing seriously is being considered for a judgeship. Even a hint of scandal could be ruinous to both of us, even in this day and age. Certainly, for him it would change things. I can't do that to myself. I don't want to."

Sarah felt as if she'd been spat on. Janelle was worried about her reputation? If she didn't feel so heartbroken, she might have laughed.

"We didn't come here to ruin your reputation," Carol insisted. "I told you we're here for Sarah's sake, and that's the truth. Perhaps she looks healthy to you, but Sarah has leukemia."

Janelle sat forward, her eyes wide, but she didn't soften. She held her body rigid. "I am sorry."

Carol waved her comment aside. "I'll get to the point. Sarah has been in remission, but now she's had a relapse. Her doctors have told us that her best hope is a bone marrow transplant, and the best donor would be a blood relative—preferably a brother or sister."

"There are none." Janelle's voice was barely a whisper.

"That's what Mike Lions, our detective, has told us. Therefore, the only candidate left is you."

"Or my natural father," Sarah added hopefully. "Maybe he has children."

Janelle's face looked bloodless, and for a moment, Sarah thought she might crumble. "He doesn't," she said tersely.

Sarah waited for some other word about the man who had fathered her, but none was forthcoming. Carol said, "Then that leaves you. The test to check for compatibility is a simple one. A lab draws blood—"

"I can't help you," Janelle interrupted.

"What?"

Janelle turned and walked to a large picture window and toyed with the drapery cord. The curtains were already shut, *just like Janelle Warren's heart*, Sarah thought.

"I'm very sorry for you, but there's nothing I can do," Janelle said. "It's quite impossible. Really."

"I see," Sarah's mom said, and stood up.

Sarah didn't "see" at all. All she knew was that the woman who'd opted to bear her fifteen years before was now refusing to have a blood test for bone marrow compatibility. Sarah felt sick to her stomach. How could Janelle hate Sarah so much that she didn't want to know her or help her? Perhaps it would have been more merciful if she had had an abortion. Sarah's sense of rejection was unbearable.

An awkward silence hung in the air, broken only by the ticking of a grandfather clock. "Well, we've taken enough of your time," Carol said finally. "I know you're expecting company."

Janelle nervously glanced at the clock. "Yes. He should be here soon."

"And we wouldn't want to have to explain who we are, would we?" Carol's tone was cutting.

Two bright spots of color appeared on Janelle's cheeks, but she said nothing. Sarah rose beside her mom and watched as she opened her purse. She put a piece of paper atop the coffee table. "This is the hotel where we're staying. I've also written down the name and phone number of Sarah's doctor in Memphis. If you want to discuss anything with her, feel free to call."

She snapped her purse closed and started to the door. Janelle didn't move, and neither did Sarah. They gazed at each other across the beautifully furnished living room. Janelle's eyes looked pained, but she made no move to stop Sarah and Carol from leaving. Sarah's knees felt rubbery and weak, yet she crossed to the door, her head held high. From there, she followed her mom out into the night.

Sarah's tears didn't start until they got back to the hotel room. She climbed into the shower stall, turned on the water, and let them flow. *Janelle honestly didn't want her.* She had cut Sarah out of her life and offered no hope for a future. When she came out of the bathroom, her mom rose from a chair and opened her arms. Without a second's hesitation, Sarah rushed to them. Her mom held her, rocked her, and told her, "It'll be all right, honey. I love you. Dad loves you. We've told you, we are your true family."

Sarah needed the words, soaking them up like a sponge. Through her sobs, she said, "What now, Mom? Without Janelle, I'll die. Mom, please help me. I don't want to die."

Eighteen

THE NEXT MORNING, there was nothing left to do but pack to go home. Sarah felt weighted down, her legs so heavy that she could barely lift them to move around the room. Her mother kept trying to be cheerful, supportive, just as she'd been the night before. Her mom had insisted, "You're not going to die, honey. You're just disappointed about your birth mother. After a good night's sleep, you'll feel better. Things will look better in the morning."

Sarah was so distraught, she didn't know what to feel. Nothing could ever take away the sense of abandonment and rejection she felt. As her mom packed, she told Sarah, "Your father will meet our plane in Atlanta and drive us home. Tina and Richie are excited about seeing you. They've all missed you terribly, Sarah. I think Tina's planning a party for you with some of your friends."

"I really don't want a party. I don't want to explain things to people."

"As far as everyone knows, Sarah, we took a trip to California for medical reasons. No one knows about your adoption."

Now that things had turned out the way they had, Sarah was glad she'd decided to keep her adoption a secret. At the time, she'd thought she'd done it for Tina. As it turned out, she'd done it for herself.

There was a knock on the door. Her mother glanced at her watch. "Mike's early. Sarah, tell him we're not ready and to come back in about an hour."

Sarah opened the door, but it wasn't Mike standing in the hall. It was Janelle Warren. "Can I come in?" Janelle asked.

"What do you want?" Sarah's mom swooped alongside of Sarah protectively.

"To talk."

Reluctantly, Sarah backed away from the door so that Janelle could enter. "What do you want to talk about?" Sarah asked as Janelle walked to the large window and turned to face her.

"I was up most of the night thinking about our meeting. I feel that I owe you some kind of explanation," Janelle said.

"We're leaving pretty soon, so you don't have to worry about me spoiling your life. I'm sorry I bothered you," Sarah said sharply.

"I'm sorry I wasn't more cordial to you. It was such a shock seeing you, knowing who you were."

"Especially since you'd always thought I was out of your life forever." Sarah's tone was challenging.

Janelle carefully set her expensive-looking handbag on the table. "You may have been out of my life, Sarah, but you were never forgotten."

"It didn't seem that way yesterday."

"A woman doesn't give birth to a baby and erase the experience from her mind—or her heart. It's especially difficult every year on your birthday. I carried you for nine months. I was in labor with you for twelve hours. I held you for ten minutes before they took you away. I walked out of the hospital with empty arms, while other women took their newborns home. It was one of the hardest things I have ever had to do."

Sarah was skeptical. "But you did it."

"I thought it best that you have a good home, with *two* parents. I couldn't give you that." Janelle glanced toward Carol. "You did go to a good home, Sarah. I'm sure of it."

Carol moved closer to Sarah. "I love Sarah very much."

Janelle studied the two of them. "It shows."

"I have a good home," Sarah confirmed. "Is that all you want to say?"

Janelle opened her purse and pulled out some photographs. "Since I know you've come a long way, and I understand your desire to know something of your heritage, I've brought some things to show you." She laid the photos on the table.

Sarah edged closer and peered at the black-and-white photos. The first was of a run-down shack with old junk cars sitting on the barren ground of the yard. "This is where I grew up, in the heart of the Ozarks," Janelle explained. "Mom and Pop had eight children. Two died from scarlet fever when they were babies—something that can be easily cured with penicillin, but my folks had no money for medicine, and the nearest doctor lived in the next county."

Sarah was shocked at the condition of the house, unable to picture the elegant woman in front of her growing up in such poverty. Neither could she imagine not being able to afford medicine for a sick child. "You lived there?"

"Until I was sixteen. We didn't even have indoor plumbing. We got along by farming a garden, and sometimes my dad got work as a hired hand. My parents were good people, Sarah, but ignorant and uneducated. I loved school from the first day I walked into a classroom. It didn't take me long to figure out that if I didn't want to end up like my parents, I had to get a good education. Fortunately, I was bright and really did well in the classroom."

Janelle showed Sarah another picture. It was a blurred group shot of a man and a woman standing on the porch with a cluster of blond-headed kids around them. "My kinfolk," Janelle continued. Her fine, cultured speech had taken on a hint of her Ozark roots.

"I was the only Warren up to that time to graduate from high school. All the others quit school as soon as they were old enough, so they could work. It was a proud moment for me. An even prouder moment when I learned I'd been awarded a full four-year academic scholarship to the University of Arkansas.

"I remember how the whole family came down to the bus depot and sent me off. I cried all the way to Little Rock, but I never looked back. I was doing the only thing I could to make something out of my life."

"You were happy?" Sarah asked.

"I was happy. I did well in college. Earned top grades, special honors. I wanted to be an attorney, and after I graduated, I was accepted to law school on scholarship."

"But you didn't become a lawyer?"

"No. I wanted that scholarship in the worst way, but . . ." Janelle's voice trailed off.

"But instead, you had me," Sarah finished.

"I had you," Janelle confirmed. She stared at another photo for a moment, then placed it on the table. It was of a handsome, brown-haired man with a cocky smile. "This is your father. His name was Trevor Benedict. He was training to be a navy pilot when I met him on a spring break trip to Pensacola, Florida. I'd never been in love before, and I'll tell you now, I've never been in love like that since then."

Carol had leaned over to peer at the picture. "Sarah looks like him through the eyes," she commented. "And she has the same kind of cleft in her chin."

Sarah was too mesmerized to see the resemblance herself. Merely being able to look on the face of the man who had fathered her was making her heart hammer wildly. "Didn't he want to marry you when you told him about me?" she asked. It was a bold question, but she wanted to know all she could about him.

"I never told him," Janelle said. Sarah looked up quickly and saw that Janelle's eyes were shimmering with tears. "He was killed in a flight training accident before I could tell him. His fighter jet hit the ground and exploded."

Horrified, Sarah felt her own eyes well up with tears. She heard her mom gasp. Janelle pushed the photo aside. "I was devastated. If I hadn't been pregnant, I might have killed myself. At the time, my options were very few. I couldn't not have you—you were all that was left of him. I couldn't go back home—my folks had such pride in me. They didn't know I was pregnant, and I didn't want them to know. In those days, there was a certain amount of shame in being an unwed mother. Women didn't wear illegitimate pregnancies like badges of pride, as they do today. Adoption seemed like the best solution."

"Yet, your instructions about anonymity were so explicit," Sarah's mom said. "I believed that you didn't want anything to do with your baby."

"I knew it had to be a clean break. I assumed that if I sounded threatening about it, she would never come searching for me." Janelle's voice took on a softness. "I see I was wrong. It didn't deter you at all."

Sarah felt sad and a bit overwhelmed by what she'd heard. Perhaps her mom had been right: Using the One Last Wish money to search for her roots had upset the lives of many people—and it had all come to nothing.

"As you know, Sarah didn't initiate this search frivolously," Carol McGreggor said. "Her father and I wouldn't have helped her if she hadn't had a very pressing reason for finding you."

Janelle nodded with understanding. "Yes . . . the

bone marrow. I called and spoke with your doctor, Sarah. She explained more fully about the transplant."

"Will you take the test for compatibility then?" Sarah felt a resurgence of hope.

"It won't matter if I am compatible, Sarah. Dr. Hernandez can't use my marrow. I'm not a suitable candidate."

"Why not?" The hope seemed to be slipping through her fingers like sand.

"Several years ago, I had a lump removed from my breast. It was cancerous. I underwent chemo and radiation, and even though I've been cancer-free for the past three years, I can never be a bone marrow donor. Not for you, not for anyone."

To Sarah, it seemed as if a giant iron door had closed and locked her in a cage. "Breast cancer?" she asked, thunderstruck.

Janelle gave Sarah a long, sad look. "My doctors told me the disease has a tendency to run in families—my mother, your grandmother, died from uterine cancer. I hoped the tendency would stop with me. I never dreamed it had been passed on to you. I'm so very, very sorry, Sarah."

Sarah could think of nothing to say. As she stood in the room with her mother and her mom, she felt as if she'd come to the end of a long journey, a journey that had brought her to the edge of a future she couldn't navigate.

"I'm sorry, too. For you and for Sarah," Carol said, stepping to Sarah's side. She put her arm protectively around Sarah's shoulders. "Thank you for taking the time to come by and tell us all of this. It was kind of you, and I know it means a great deal to Sarah."

Janelle picked up her purse and draped the strap over her shoulder. "As I told you, I felt you both deserved some kind of explanation. I didn't want you to leave thinking I hated you."

Sarah's throat felt swollen shut as she nodded her understanding.

Janelle walked to the door, where she turned and gazed longingly at Sarah. "Could you . . . would you mind terribly if I hugged you good-bye?" she asked.

Sarah glanced at her mom, who dropped her arm from Sarah's shoulders. Slowly, Sarah stepped forward to face the woman who had borne her, and who had given her up for adoption. Janelle's arms slipped around her, and Sarah felt herself pulled closer. The scent of Janelle's lovely perfume filled Sarah's senses as she closed her eyes and slowly wound her arms around her mother. They stood motionless in the quiet of the room while Sarah searched inside herself for something to link them. She could not find one memory of this woman to whom she was bound by blood.

Janelle released her, letting her hands slide along Sarah's arms until she was holding Sarah's hands. Tears glistened in her eyes as she studied Sarah's face. "I haven't held you since you were a tiny baby. Since the nurse brought you to me and laid you in my arms," Janelle whispered. "Now, you're all grown up."

She dropped Sarah's hands. "I'll leave you the photos, Sarah. They're your birthright, you know. When I put you up for adoption, I was certain I'd never see you again. In the long run, I'm glad I was able to meet you, and I truly regret not being able to help you. You're a lovely young woman, and I know your parents are very proud of you."

Sarah watched her open the door and, without a backward glance, slip silently into the hall and out of her life.

Nineteen

SARAH AND HER mom arrived home to a party arranged by Tina. Scott threw his arms around Sarah and talked excitedly. She listened to their chatter, but felt as if she weren't a part of their world anymore.

She was sitting on the steps of the front porch, moodily watching a sprinkler spew water on the front lawn, when Scott brought her a piece of Tina's homemade chocolate cake. She thanked him for the cake and for the bracelet he'd sent. "I thought about you a lot this summer, and about what you were going through," he said, lowering himself to the front stoop. "I guess things didn't work out between you and your birth mother."

"Not really. I'm glad I met her, even though, at first, she wasn't too thrilled about my arrival on her doorstep."

Tina stole quietly up beside Sarah and sat on the

porch step below Scott. There was a time when Sarah would have resented her intrusion, but now she didn't care. She wanted Tina to hear, uncertain that she was up to telling the story more than once. She was feeling hot and achy all over, and a headache pounded behind her eyes.

"What's she like?" Tina asked.

Sarah gave the highlights of her trip and of the conversations with her birth mother. "The big reunion wasn't easy on any of us," Sarah said.

"I can't believe she can't be a bone marrow donor for you."

"That was the hardest part of all. I have to admit, I was really counting on her helping me out in that department."

"What happens now?" Tina asked, looking worried.

"I don't know." Sarah felt defeated, as if time was running out on her. "I guess they have to keep trying that bone marrow registry."

"I wish I could help," Tina said.

"Me, too," Scott said.

The screen door flew open, and Richie bounded out onto the porch. He had chocolate frosting still smeared on his face. "Sarah," he said with a beaming smile, "come and see what I made for you."

Sarah held him at arm's length. "Slow down, buster. You didn't tell me how you liked having Tina for a mommy while Mom and I were gone."

Richie sneaked a peek at Tina. "She was bossy. She made me pick up my toys every night."

"That doesn't sound so terrible."

Richie shrugged. "She read me stories before bed and let me help her fix breakfast."

Sarah glanced at her sister, who grinned. Tina looked older to her, more mature, not so much the thirteen-year-old pain in the neck she'd been months before. Sarah wondered if it was Tina who'd changed, or she herself. She turned back to Richie. "What did you make for me?"

"A necklace out of clay." His small face broke into a giant grin.

"Show me." Sarah stood, but she felt woozy.

Richie grabbed her hand, then dropped it. "You're *hot*, Sarah."

Her mother was just coming out on the porch. Concern replaced the smile on her face. "Are you all right?" she asked, feeling Sarah's forehead.

Sarah swayed and grabbed the porch rail. She noticed how cool her mother's hand felt on her skin. "Why, you're burning up!" her mother exclaimed. "You get into bed right this minute. I'm calling the doctor."

Scott and Tina helped her up to her room. She heard Richie ask, "Is Sarah sick again?"

The noises of the afternoon faded in and out as Sarah shivered under the covers. No matter how many blankets they put on her, she couldn't get warm. By nightfall, her mother came into her room and began to pack a suitcase. "Dr. Hernandez wants us to bring you to Memphis right away."

"We haven't even unpacked from California yet," Sarah protested through chattering teeth.

"You're sick, honey, and she wants you in the hospital. Dad's fixing the backseat of the car with pillows so that you'll be more comfortable for the trip."

Sarah felt like crying. She didn't want to go back

to the lonely days and nights of the hospital. She wanted to stay home. She wanted to start school on the first day of classes. She wanted to be well. She thought about the money and JWC's letter and the part that said JWC's granted wish had brought purpose, faith, and courage. The fulfillment of Sarah's wish had brought only a bittersweet reunion, frustration, and fear. She still had no bone marrow to save her. No amount of money could buy that.

Scott poked his head through the doorway, concern written all over his face. "You going to be all right?"

"Sure," Sarah lied. "Can't keep me down."

He crouched next to her bed and ran the back of his hand across her cheek. "You'd better be all right. Who's going to be my personal trainer when school starts?"

"Maybe you'd better start looking for someone else."

"No way. You're my fiancée, remember?"

She smiled, but the effort hurt. "I release you to choose another."

"Maybe I don't want to be released."

She reached up and touched his hair. "Don't hold me to a promise I can't keep."

Scott's eyes clouded. He kissed her cheek and stood stiffly. "No deal," he said. "A promise is a promise."

How wonderful it would have been to grow up and marry Scott Michaels. How wonderful—and now, how impossible.

When Scott had gone, Tina came in to see her, looking scared.

"Thanks for the party," Sarah said.

Tina's eyes filled with tears. "It wasn't supposed to end this way. It was supposed to be a happy homecoming."

Home. For Sarah, the word had a whole new meaning. Home was here, and now that she'd found it again, she didn't want to leave it. "You keep my green sweater, okay?" she told Tina.

Tina looked startled. "I don't want—"

"Wear it on the first day of school."

"What if you want to wear it?"

Sarah knew she was going to miss the start of school this year. "Just wear it," Sarah insisted, squeezing Tina's hand with what little strength she had left.

After Sarah had hugged a sobbing Richie, her mother helped her out of bed. As they started for the door, a sense of urgency came over Sarah. There were so many things left undone. She said, "Please, wait. Listen—I don't want the One Last Wish money to go to waste. Make sure it goes to Tina and Richie . . . in case . . ."

"We can discuss that later. Right now, I want to get you out of here," her mother said, holding Sarah firmly around the waist.

Sarah refused to be sidetracked. "The family can use the money, Mom."

"That's thoughtful of you, but you'll be back to spend the money with us."

"Will you just promise me?" Sarah pleaded.

Her mother nodded. "I'll take care of it as soon as possible. Don't look so frantic—Dr. Hernandez will fix you up, and you can help me shop for whatever you want to buy."

"I'm scared," Sarah confessed. "This time, it's different." Whenever she'd gone to the hospital before, it had been for treatments. This time, she was sick, and not from any chemo. She was flushed with fever and felt as if she were melting from the inside. She had been warned that her leukemia was active again. After five years of fighting it, Sarah was battle-weary.

"Don't be frightened. We're family, and we'll be with you all the way. We're going to stop this thing somehow."

There was so much Sarah wanted to do, to say. "I forgot to tell you thank you," she whispered to her mom.

"For what?"

"For putting up with me all summer. For letting me search for my birth mother, even though you didn't want me to."

"Now that it's over and done, I'm glad you did it. I'm glad I was able to meet her for myself."

"Why?"

"Because it took the mystery out of her. It helped me see her as a flesh-and-blood person. I'm grateful to her for giving you up."

Sarah understood. Janelle Warren had done what she'd had to do at the time of Sarah's birth, and Sarah no longer held it against her—or her parents for keeping it from her. "She has a nice life. We're better off without each other," Sarah said.

Her mom squeezed her hand. "All I know, Sarah, is that while I may not have carried you beneath my heart for nine months, I've always carried you *in* my heart. That will never change. You'll live in my heart forever. I love you, Sarah."

"I love you too, Mom." They held one another,

until Sarah, too weak to stand, glanced longingly around her room and said, "I'm ready."

Once her dad settled her in the car, Sarah asked, "Will you bring Tina and Richie to see me this weekend?"

"I couldn't keep them away." He tucked the blanket under her chin, and Sarah saw that his eyes were misty.

"You'll take good care of them, won't you?"

"Yes."

"And Mom, too?"

"And Mom, too. You were my firstborn, Sarah. Don't forget that. I'm so proud of you."

"Although I was grafted onto the McGreggor family tree?" she asked.

"Grafts have a way of turning out an entirely different blossom—unique and special."

"I love you, Daddy."

"I love you, baby."

Numb and feverish, Sarah lay back on the seat while her mom and dad climbed into the front. Tina held Richie, and they gazed anxiously through the car window. Richie clung to Tina, tears smudging his face.

"Hurry home," Tina called as the car backed out of the driveway.

Sarah didn't answer, so certain she was that she'd never see her home again.

Twenty

~❦~

IN THE HOSPITAL in Memphis, Sarah was immediately placed in an isolation unit. No one came into her room without donning sterile paper gowns, head coverings, and masks. "It's a massive infection," Dr. Hernandez told Sarah and her parents. "And you have no resistance to fight it off."

"What will you do?" Sarah heard her dad ask.

"Keep her isolated, pump her full of antibiotics, and pray that we find a bone marrow donor for her," Dr. Hernandez answered.

For Sarah, time passed, but she couldn't keep track of days and nights. All around her, people came and went dressed in masks and rubber gloves. An IV line was hooked to her arm, and a heart monitor to her chest. She knew her parents took turns staying with her, for she'd wake in the night and see one of them sitting by her bedside. It comforted her, knowing they were within arm's reach.

As some signs of improvement came, Dr. Hernandez warned that the antibiotic treatment was only a stopgap. Although they had stemmed the infection, her white blood count was alarmingly high—her leukemia was active and destructive.

One evening, Dr. Hernandez came rushing into Sarah's room. "You and your mother must see this," she said, still tying on her mask.

She turned on the TV monitor that hung from the wall in the corner of the room. The face of one of the network's evening newscasters filled the screen. Midsentence, he was saying, ". . . final story from Ringgold, Georgia, where a young girl walked into our affiliate station to make this eloquent plea for her sister's life."

Sarah almost choked as Tina's face came onto the monitor. Staring straight into the camera, Tina said, "My sister has leukemia, and if she had a bone marrow transplant, she could probably be cured. But she can't get one because her doctors can't find a compatible donor. It's not that there aren't compatible donors, you see . . . it's just that one hasn't been discovered yet.

"That's because not enough people are willing to become donors. It's real simple to be one. If you're between eighteen and fifty-five and in good health, you can be a donor. And maybe you'll be the one to help Sarah. She's only fifteen. She's too young to die."

The camera zoomed in on a very tight shot of Tina's face. "All you have to do is have a little blood drawn, sign a consent form, and become a part of the National Marrow Donor Program. And someday, if you're lucky, you'll get a call telling you that you're a preliminary match. The doctors do some more blood work on you, and then if you're still a match, they take some of your healthy marrow and transplant it into the person who needs it—like my sister."

Slowly, a big smile spread across Tina's face. "I know lots of people watch this news show every night, so I hope all of you will go to your doctor tomorrow and get your blood checked. Maybe you'll be the person who saves Sarah."

The camera zoomed out, and a reporter recapped the story and added some details. Then she turned to the camera and said, "Thank you, Tina. And good-night, Sarah. God bless."

Dr. Hernandez flipped off the set and came over to Sarah's bed. "That was a gutsy thing for your sister to do," she said. "Totally amazing that she got on national news."

Sarah felt a surge of exhilaration that almost carried her off the bed. "Tina did it for me, Mom," she said. "And millions of people saw it."

Her mother threaded her way through the maze of tubes and wires and hugged Sarah tightly.

"There's more," Dr. Hernandez said. "One of the wire services picked up the story. It's being carried in newspapers all over the country. Just think about it, Sarah, people will read about you, and hundreds will respond. I know they will."

"Maybe one of them will be a match," her mother said.

Dr. Hernandez smiled. "Maybe. The bigger the number of volunteers, the better the odds."

When Tina came that weekend, Sarah held her

and wept, overcome with gratitude. "How did you come up with the idea?" she asked.

"It was a brainstorm I had right after Mom and Dad took you to the hospital," Tina admitted sheepishly. "I told Scott, and he helped me."

"How?"

"He drove me to the TV station, and we talked our way into seeing one of those consumer advocate reporters. She was really nice, and once I told her what we wanted to do—tell people about the donor registry—she did an interview for the local evening news. She called later to say that the people at the network liked the interview so much, they would run it on the evening news for the whole country to see." Tina adjusted her paper mask, and Sarah could tell that behind it, she was grinning. "I'll bet everybody in the country saw me and knows about you by now."

Sarah wondered if her birth mother had seen it, then knew it didn't matter. "Thank you, Tina."

"I hope it helps. The reporter said that it would be nice to run full-page ads in newspapers, or order up billboards in some of the bigger cities. That way, even more people could get the message." She puckered her brow thoughtfully. "It's a good idea, but I know those things cost a lot of money."

Sarah *had* a lot of money. Her eyes grew wide with revelation, and her gaze locked onto her father and mother. Her father read her thoughts instantly and, barely able to contain the excitement in his voice said, "I'll get right on it."

The drama of the moment was lost on Tina, who continued talking. "I also wanted to do it for you because I was feeling kind of guilty about something."

"About what?" Sarah returned her attention to her sister.

"I was glad when you found out you didn't have any other sisters. Even though it meant you couldn't have the bone marrow you needed. That was selfish of me, but I didn't want you to like any sister better than you like me." She peeked over the top of her mask. "Are you mad at me?"

"There's only one of you, Tina. No one could ever take your place." Sarah knew that was true. She saw that even if she had a hundred sisters, Tina would be number one. Of course, they'd had their differences, but they were sisters, bound more tightly than ever. Sarah cleared her throat, afraid she'd break down and cry. "Where's Richie?"

"Still getting all that gear on," Tina said.

Richie came through the double doors in a burst with Dr. Hernandez. The long paper gown trailed behind him, and the mask almost covered his face. He crawled up on a chair beside Sarah's bed and stared down into her face. "I feel like it's Halloween," he said.

Everyone laughed. Looking around at them, Sarah felt so deeply moved, she choked back her emotions. Here, in a hospital ICU room, were the people whom she loved most in the world. Her family was with her—her real family. All the money in the world couldn't buy what she already had—a family who cared for her, loved her, fought for her, worked for her. At that moment, she felt as if her heart would burst with love for them.

"What now?" Sarah asked Dr. Hernandez, who stood at the foot of her bed, looking on.

"Now, we wait," the doctor said, "and we hope that lots of people volunteer to become donors."

Sarah hoped it wouldn't be too long a wait. Waiting could be so tedious. "Do I have to stay in isolation?"

"Yes. You're too vulnerable to infection."

Sarah felt exhaustion creeping over her, and sleep reaching out for her. She gazed up at the cherubic face of her brother. "Sing me a song, Richie. One of your favorites."

His head bobbed in assent, then his little child's voice began chanting, "There was a farmer had a dog, and Bingo was his name-o . . ."

As Richie continued singing, Sarah closed her eyes. "Faith, courage, and hope"—that was what JWC had given her, more than the money. She knew she had so much to be grateful for, no matter what happened tomorrow.

Let Him Live

One

⸙

MEGAN CHARNELL WHIPPED her red convertible into the only empty parking space in the crowded parking garage at Washington Memorial Hospital. She screeched to a halt, grabbed her purse and notebook, and ran inside the glass doors. When she reached the elevator, she impatiently punched the button.

"Late, late, late," she muttered. Her first day on the job, and she was missing orientation. Her father wouldn't be pleased. She'd hit an unexpected traffic snarl. Usually, it didn't take this much time to come from her Virginia suburb to downtown Washington. If her car had wings she would have made it in plenty of time.

Meg pounded the elevator button until the door slid open. She barreled inside and hit the button for the fourth floor. It was her father's idea, not hers. She didn't want to become a candy striper for the summer. "Your therapist thinks getting involved will help you come to terms with what happened to Cindy. Maybe a job will be helpful," her father had insisted. Meg knew that her last choice would have been to work at the hospital, but here she was anyway. Part of her wanted to move on and connect to people, and yet she still grieved for her lost friend.

Meg had been overcome with grief at the news that her best friend had been killed in a car accident. She'd seen Cindy only weeks before the fatal crash. After Cindy and her family had moved away, Meg had been afraid their best friendship might end. But Cindy had promised, and so had Meg— "forever friends"—and they'd managed to stay as close as ever, even though they were no longer neighbors.

When Cindy's parents called Meg, she couldn't accept the reality of Cindy's death. Now, a year later, the therapist Meg had talked with felt she was ready to face new relationships with trust and courage. *Easy for everyone to say*, Meg thought, but she was nervous.

On the fourth floor, Meg raced out of the elevator and into the auditorium, grimacing as the door banged open. She was sure every person in the room looked up at her, including her father. He was standing on the stage, giving his opening remarks. Meg slunk into an empty seat in the shadowed depths and heaved a sigh. She mopped sweat from her forehead and wished with all her heart that she could be anyplace but here.

"As I was saying," Dr. Charnell continued, "volunteers like you, along with our faithful Pink Ladies, are a vital link to the welfare of our patients here at Memorial. The nurses are already overloaded with duties, so volunteers are necessary to enhance patient comfort. Without your helping hands and smiling faces, this place would be dreary indeed.

"For those who participated in our Saturday training program, you already know Mrs. Stanton, our volunteer coordinator." A woman with dark hair in a French knot waved from her chair beside the podium. "She'll have a few words to say, then she'll pass out floor assignments."

Others from the hospital staff spoke. When, at last, Mrs. Stanton wrapped up the orientation with an invitation for refreshments, Meg halfheartedly walked to a table piled with doughnuts and juice. Because she'd missed breakfast, she loaded a paper plate, then went to check for her name on the assignment sheet posted on the auditorium bulletin board.

"Hi. I remember you from the training sessions," said a tall, slim girl who was standing beside Meg. "I'm assigned to pediatrics. How about you?"

Meg found her name on the list. "Looks like I am too."

"I'm Alana Humphries." The girl smiled and

Meg felt she could like this person who seemed so friendly.

Meg smiled back. "Megan Charnell—but I prefer just plain Meg." She wiped powder-sugared fingers on her wrinkled pink-and-white pinafore, the uniform of the candy striper. "These stripes make me look like an overripe candy cane," Meg complained.

Alana laughed. "Charnell . . . Are you related to Dr. Charnell?"

Meg reddened. "My father." She hated people's knowing. She was certain they would think she was going to be given special favor, when in reality she loathed the whole idea.

Alana's eyes grew wide. "I think Dr. Charnell is the most wonderful man in the world."

"You do?"

"He helped save my brother's life."

"He did?"

"My brother, Lonnie, had a disease that was destroying his kidneys. He was on dialysis for years. Your father put Lonnie in Memorial's transplant program, and two years ago, Lonnie got a donor kidney. He's twenty now and doing fine. I guess my brother was really lucky. He got a transplant right away, which according to your dad, is highly unusual for African-Americans. It seems that organs are most compatible when the donor and recipient are of the same race, but not enough black people are signing up to be donors. That's really hurting black people who need organs." Meg had never really thought about such things.

Her dad was an accomplished surgeon who had taken over as head of the organ transplant unit at Memorial five years before. Meg couldn't count the times she'd heard the phone ring in the middle of the night for him. Neither could she recall one single holiday, one special family occasion that hadn't been interrupted by a call from the hospital because Dr. Franklin Charnell was needed to handle some emergency. For years, she believed that the hospital was his true home, and that his patients were his preferred family.

"I'm glad for your brother," Meg replied.

"That's why I signed up to be a candy striper," Alana explained. "To give something back. I mean, money couldn't buy Lonnie's life, so there's nothing I could give even if I was rich, which I'm not. The least I can do is volunteer to help out, try and make things easier for people who are sick like Lonnie used to be." She paused. "Did you sign up to work with your father?"

Meg couldn't admit the truth—she'd been made to sign up to help her pull out of a progressive depression. "Dad suggested it," she said, "and it sounded like an okay idea for the summer."

"Well, I think it's going to be fun work. And it's really cool to know I'll be working with you. I mean, Dr. Charnell's daughter . . ."

Meg squirmed under Alana's generous smile. How long before Alana discovered she was a fraud?

Her father came over, and Meg hoped he wouldn't mention her tardy entrance. "Hello,

Alana," he said. "Lonnie told me you'd be here. I see you've met Megan."

"We were just discussing our assignments."

Meg nodded vigorously. "Pediatrics."

"I know. I asked Mrs. Stanton to put you there."

A warning bell sounded in Meg's head.

"Super," Alana said. "I really like kids."

"The floor's divided into units," Dr. Charnell explained. "One for kids under twelve, one for older kids. Both sections need extra hands."

"We'll do our best," Alana promised.

Meg only nodded.

"My office is in the same general area." His motives became clear to Meg. He wanted to keep an eye on her, and she resented it. All at once, his beeper went off. "That's me," he said. "I've got to run."

Meg watched him hurry toward a house phone.

"He's so busy," Alana said.

"You've got that right," Meg replied, without elaborating. She and Alana headed toward the elevator that would take them to pediatrics.

"I'd like to be a doctor someday," Alana told her as they rode up to the seventh floor. "How about you?"

"No way."

"You're kidding? I thought medicine would be in your blood."

"I prefer doughnuts in my blood."

Alana giggled. "Honestly, girl, you're such a comedian."

They emerged onto the pediatric floor. A huge

painted picture of a clown holding a sign that said "Kids World" adorned the wall. Meg paused to study the cute artwork.

"Get out of the way. You're in the middle of the drag strip!" a boy's voice called.

Meg flattened herself against the wall, turning in time to see a teenage boy pushing an IV stand with lines attached to the inside of his arm. He loped beside a very young boy who was rolling his wheelchair as hard as he could down the length of the hall.

Astounded, Meg watched them fly past with a clatter of metal and a cascade of laughter. *What have I gotten myself into?* she wondered. *What does Dad think he's doing?*

Two

At the end of the hall, the boy with the IV stand halted. "You beat me, Mark," he said to the boy in the wheelchair.

The child grinned up at him. "I told you I could."

"How about best two out of three? Give me a day to rest, and we'll try it again tomorrow."

"You got it."

The older boy ruffled Mark's hair, and Meg watched him approach her, pushing his IV stand. "Sorry I yelled at you," he said. "I didn't want you to get mowed down. I'm Donovan Jacoby."

"Meg."

He glanced at Alana, and his eyes danced mischievously. "You two look like twins."

"Maybe it's the uniforms," Alana joked.

Donovan was tall and thin, with curling brown hair, gorgeous blue eyes, and a fabulous smile, but Meg saw that his skin had a yellow cast and that he appeared slightly stooped. He leaned against his IV stand. "Excuse my friend here, but we're very attached."

"Maybe you should be in your bed," Meg suggested nervously, after a quick smile at his joke.

"That's where I'm supposed to be, but it's pretty boring in my room. I was walking the hall looking for action when I saw Mark. Now, I've met you two, and things are really looking up."

"This is Dr. Charnell's daughter," Alana announced proudly.

Meg cringed inwardly.

"No lie?" Donovan asked. "He's awesome."

My father? Meg thought. "We're working here this summer," she said hastily, "and according to our training, we're supposed to help patients. Why don't I help you back to bed?"

"You do sound like your father," Donovan said. Yet, he didn't protest returning to his room.

Meg followed as he led the way, half afraid he'd keel over and she wouldn't know what to do.

"I'll meet you at the nurses' station," Alana called.

Donovan's room was sunny and bright. Although it contained two beds, only one looked as if it had been occupied. "Yours?" she asked.

"How did you guess? I lost my roommate last Friday."

Meg's heart squeezed. "Lost?"

Donovan saw her look of distress. "He went home."

She realized she'd been a doctor's daughter too long. In her father's world, "lost" meant died. "Can I help you?" she asked as Donovan climbed in the bed, trying to keep his IV lines from tangling.

"Can you hold the stand steady for me?"

She gripped the cold metal and parked it beside his bed. He lay back on the pillow, and she saw a flash of pain cross his face. "Should I call a nurse?"

"No. It'll pass. I—um—guess I overdid things."

Meg's training had taught her to be helpful and polite, but not personally involved. "Now that you're settled, I think I should be going," she said. "I haven't even officially reported in yet."

His hand reached out for hers. "Can you visit just a minute?"

"Maybe for just a minute." She found it difficult to say no. She glanced around at the bed, desk, windowsill, and curtain that separated his bed from the other one. She saw a child's drawings pinned to the curtain and taped to the bottom of the sill. There was a photo on the bedside table of a gap-toothed, brown-haired boy and a pretty woman with green eyes. "Your family?" she asked.

"My mom and my brother, Brett. Those are Brett's drawings all over the place. He's six and draws me a new picture for every day I'm in here." Meg's eyes grew wide. She began to quickly count the drawings. "Fifteen," Donovan said, as if reading her mind. "Where do you go to school?" he asked.

"Davis Academy. I just finished my sophomore year. And you?"

"Actually, I'm not from the Washington area. Mom and Brett and I lived in a small town on the border of Virginia and North Carolina. When I got sick last March, Mom was determined to find the best doctors possible for me. She sold our home and moved us here because Memorial has one of the best liver specialists in the country on staff. She's rented an apartment, but it's miles away, and she has to ride the bus just to visit me."

"You have something wrong with your liver?"

"You could say that. I had to drop out of school, but I would have been a senior if we'd stayed."

"Can't you be a senior here when school starts in the fall?"

"Maybe." He shrugged. "So, tell me, what's it like living with a doctor?"

It took Meg a moment to adjust to his shift in subjects. "It's like living with a god. Occasionally, Zeus comes down from Mount Olympus to mingle with us mere mortals." Her own candor shocked her. Why was she saying such a thing to a guy she didn't even know? She giggled nervously. "Just kidding. Dad's a pretty busy man, so sometimes it seems like he's hardly at home. How about your dad?" she asked. "Did he come with you?"

"My dad skipped out five years ago. Address unknown. There's only the three of us."

"He doesn't know you're sick?"

"No, but so what? Mom, Brett, and I are making out fine by ourselves. When this is all over with, maybe I'll look him up and tell him we made it without his help."

"I think I'd better go check in at the nurses' desk," she said, glancing at her watch.

"Sorry. I didn't mean to keep you so long."

"Want me to turn on the TV?"

"No, there's nothing worth watching."

Meg felt sorry for him and felt a silent tug-of-war with her conscience. "I'm scheduled to work until three. Maybe I can stop by later and see how you're doing," she finally told him.

"I'd like that. Mom doesn't come by with Brett until after six because she has to work."

She thought his eyes looked tired, and in the sunlight, his skin, as well as the whites of his eyes, looked quite yellow. "I'm not going to see you in the hall racing any more wheelchairs, am I?"

"Not today." A grimace of pain crossed his face, but he still managed one of his illuminating smiles. "No promises about tomorrow though."

Meg left Donovan and found her way to the nurses' station. At the desk, an older nurse, Mrs. Vasquez, said, "So, there you are. I've sent your partner on an errand, but I need both of you to help with activity time in the playroom for the children under age ten."

"I was with a patient named Donovan," Meg explained even though Mrs. Vasquez hadn't asked for an explanation.

"Alana told me. He's one nice kid. Has a friendly word for everybody and a special affinity for the smaller kids. We don't get many as nice as him."

Meg itched to ask more about him, but just then Alana came down the hall. "Mission accomplished," she told Mrs. Vasquez.

"Then it's to the playroom for both of you."

Inside the playroom, Meg discovered twelve kids ranging in ages from four to ten preparing for a session with an art therapist. Some were in wheelchairs, others were in casts, a few were bald. "From chemotherapy, I'll bet," Alana whispered.

Meg felt overwhelmed. She realized how isolated she'd been from her father's world. The hospital was like a separate city, with a hierarchy of people in charge. But in this city, people were sick, some of them sick enough to die. Seeing the children, small and vulnerable, carrying around basins in case they had to vomit, and with apparatuses attached to their arms or protruding from their chests, made Meg queasy. And it brought back the memory of Cindy much too vividly. Meg didn't see how she was going to last the summer in such an environment.

"You all right?" Alana asked. "You look a little green."

"Too many doughnuts," Meg mumbled. "Doesn't this bother you?" she asked.

"Lonnie was on dialysis so long, I got used to coming to the hospital. I saw lots of sick people. Now, I want to help them."

Meg wished she could feel the same way, but all she really wanted to do was go home. She began to think she'd made a mistake by agreeing to work at the hospital. She really wasn't up to the task. She made up her mind that at the end of the day, she'd tell her father that she couldn't manage it. That it was too painful for her emotionally.

At the end of her shift, she stopped by Donovan's room. He was sound asleep, and she didn't wake him. She studied his drawings from his brother carefully. There were many of a house with the words "Our Home" and "Where the Jacobys Live."

Nervously, she approached her father's office, where she discovered him hunched over his desk, doing paperwork. He looked up and beckoned her inside. "How was the first day?"

"I'm not so sure this is such a good idea for me," she said.

"Sit and tell me about it."

"I tried to help with activity time, but I didn't do a very good job. The art therapist had to help me more than the kids."

"You'll catch on."

She felt cowardly, wishing she could simply come out and tell him the truth. "I also met a boy named Donovan."

Her father nodded. "He's one sick kid."

"What's wrong with him? I know it's something to do with his liver."

"I'm afraid his liver's shot. That's really why he's here. His physician referred him to me because our program is his only hope."

Meg felt her hands turn clammy. "Your program?"

"Donovan needs a liver transplant. Without one, I'd say he has less than six months to live."

Three

❧

"Donovan's going to die? But he's not much older than me."

"He's almost eighteen, but age has nothing to do with it. He's in advanced stages of cirrhosis brought on by a non-A, non-B strain of hepatitis. Cirrhosis is deadly."

"How did he get such a thing?"

"His hepatitis is idiopathic." She looked perplexed, and her father added, "That's medical talk for 'We don't know how he got it.' Frankly, at this late stage, it doesn't matter."

"There must be some kind of medicine for it."

"I'm afraid not. And the virus has all but destroyed his liver. Sometimes, cirrhosis can be reversed, but not in Donovan's case. The liver filters out toxins—poisons. Once it begins to fail, toxins build up. Eventually, the liver atrophies altogether and the victim dies. The only hope is a transplant."

"Will he be able to get one?"

"Only if we can locate a compatible donor."

"What's that mean?" Meg's head began to swim with the complexity of Donovan's circumstances.

"A donor has to match in blood type, plus be about the same weight and height as the intended recipient. The liver is a large organ and can't be expected to function properly if it's mismatched. And there simply are not enough donor organs to go around to all the patients needing them."

"Why not?" Meg recalled how her dad would hurry off to perform surgery whenever an organ would be specially flown in for one of his patients. He was on virtual twenty-four-hour call.

"Ah, Meg," her father said with a sigh. "That's a complicated issue. To be of any use for transplantation, organs need to be free of disease and injury, so donors are most often healthy individuals who die unexpectedly and traumatically—often with a massive head injury. Anyway, families have to be approached about donation when their loved one is on life support, when he or she is declared brain dead. It's a very trying time for everybody, and families are in shock.

"It's not always easy for them to accept what's happened, much less agree to donate organs. Yet, people working with transplant services attempt to help families see that organ donation is sometimes the only positive thing to come out of such tragedies as premature death. The best way for a family to deal with the issue is to know how members of the family feel about donating their organs. That requires discussing it *before* a tragedy happens."

"Does Donovan know how sick he is?" Meg asked.

"His mother's aware of the gravity of his condition, but even though I've had several talks with him, I'm not sure he's totally accepting it. Kids, especially you teens, believe you're invincible, bigger than death. Also, the condition itself often brings on bouts of confusion and extreme fatigue that dulls a victim's perceptions about his illness."

Had Cindy thought she was invincible? Meg wondered. *Didn't everyone have the right to grow up and grow old?* "So, once you find him a donor, he'll be all right, won't he?"

Again, her father shook his head. "It doesn't always work that way. The transplantation operation and recovery period aside, he's not the only person here at Memorial awaiting a liver transplant. I have a list of patients."

"But you said he'd die without one."

"They'll all die without one."

Meg felt as if she'd wandered into a maze. "Still, there's hope, isn't there?"

"There's always hope. That's what keeps us going." His beeper sounded. "Excuse me." He picked up his phone and dialed his exchange.

Meg had grown to hate the sound of the beeper, and she felt particularly irritated now that she had so many questions about Donovan and his necessary liver transplant. She waited while her father carried on a clipped conversation and hung up. He stood. "Meg, tell your mom I won't be home this evening."

"What's wrong?" She looked up at him, watched as he removed his lab coat and slipped on his suit jacket.

"That was a colleague in Baltimore. He's got a donor heart for us, and I've got a thirty-three-year-old mother of two who desperately needs it. According to the National Network for Organ Sharing, the two of them are a match."

"Can't someone else go get it?"

"Time is critical, and I want the retrieval done properly. Nothing's more frustrating than having a perfectly suitable organ go bad because of improper surgical procedures or storage conditions. It's best if I use the hospital's private jet to go retrieve it myself."

"I'll tell Mom," she said. He was already out the door. Meg stood and shook off a chill. Images of her father, Donovan, and the hospital bombarded her, but the sound of the beeper took on a new meaning. One day, it might sound for Donovan. One day, it might mean medical science had located a donor liver for him. Still, she kept seeing the image of Cindy's face. For Cindy, there had been no hope, not with an organ transplant, not with hospitalization, not with any assortment of new and experimental drugs.

Meg hurried to the parking garage. All she

wanted to do was go home and put the entire day behind her. And also to forget what had happened to her very best friend.

At dinner that night, Meg shoved green beans and broiled chicken around on her plate. She didn't have much of an appetite. Her sister, Tracy, kept jabbering about her upcoming stay at gymnastic camp for the summer. Meg listened, half-heartedly, still brooding about Donovan.

"How was your first day as a volunteer? Do you like it?" Meg heard her mother ask.

"I'm around sick kids all day. What's fun about that?"

"Honey, it's good for you to be active, remember? You were getting too introspective, and your father and I were concerned about you."

That's why it's called depression, Mom, Meg felt like saying. The phone rang, and Tracy hopped up to answer it. She returned, saying, "Mom, it's Mrs. Hotchkiss from the Junior League."

Meg was relieved, knowing that her mother would get involved with her Junior League responsibilities and forget about delving into Meg's day.

Later, in her room, Meg flopped across the bed. She wondered if her father's effort to retrieve a donor heart and save a patient under his care had gone well. She thought about Donovan's need for someone to die so that he could live.

Meg got a sense that she was viewing some kind of low-budget horror film. Maintaining human parts and flying them around the country for use in dying people sounded so bizarre. But she was able to see the necessity for the process in a new light because a stranger named Donovan had become a real person, not a case.

Sadness engulfed her, and she tried to recall the last time she'd felt happy. Somehow, since the accident, she didn't feel right about being happy because Cindy could no longer be happy. Her therapist had helped her see that she had to overcome that feeling. She remembered the night Cindy had been with her for a sleep-over and it had been great.

"So, what do you think, Meg? Will I always be the tallest girl in our class, or will my hormones give up and leave me in peace for a while?"

Meg sat upright and looked around her room, half expecting Cindy to be sitting on the floor, complaining about her height. The room was empty. Of course, she'd imagined her friend's voice. "You're going to have sporadic periods of renewed grieving," Dr. Miller, her therapist, had often explained and tried to reassure her. "We call them 'grieving pangs,' and they're normal. It's when a person can't rise up out of the spiral and go on with everyday life that he or she gets into trouble."

Suddenly, Meg realized she was tired of feeling grieving pangs. Agitated, she circled her room. She didn't want to think about the loss of Cindy. She wanted to forget the pain. What could her father and Dr. Miller have been thinking to suggest that she work around sick people at the hospital? This wasn't going to help her. It was harming her.

Meg went to her desk and picked up Cindy's class photo. The image grinned out at her—a slim girl with a head of wild, frizzy brown hair and freckles on her face. "I wish you could meet this guy I saw today. Even though he's sick, he's cute. You'd probably think he was too thin, but that's not his fault. I wish . . ." Meg's voice trailed.

She carefully set down the photograph. It was stupid to be talking to a picture. She glanced at the bedside clock. It was only nine o'clock, but she suddenly felt overwhelmed by exhaustion. "Excessive sleeping is a sign of depression," the therapist had informed Meg when she'd first started seeing her in April.

"So what?" Meg said to the memory of Dr. Miller's face. Without a second thought, she flipped off the light and crawled beneath the covers, into the blessed arms of a deep, forgetful sleep.

Four

WHEN MEG ARRIVED at the hospital the next morning, she headed straight to Donovan's room. Once there, she skidded to a halt, seeing a woman and a young boy beside Donovan's bed. "Meg," Donovan greeted her. "Come meet my mom and brother."

"Donovan's been talking about you," said the woman with hair the same color as her son's.

"He said you were pretty," the young boy blurted out. "You are, but I don't like girls very much. I think they're mean. Bonnie Oakland's mean. She's in my class, and she always butts in line and my teacher doesn't do anything about it."

"Brett, that's not polite," his mother scolded. "Excuse Mr. Chatterbox here. Today's teacher conference at his day school. I asked my boss if I could come in late so that I could meet with Brett's teacher." She patted Donovan's arm. "And on our way home, we stopped to see Donovan."

"Nice to meet you," Meg said, her mind still dwelling on Brett's comment about Donovan's thinking she was pretty. She'd struggled with her weight most of her life, and boys had never seemed to notice her the way they did slimmer girls.

"I'm glad you didn't go right home," Donovan told Meg. "I wanted you to meet each other."

"It's *not* home," Brett interrupted. "It's an apartment. And I hate it."

"It's home for now, big guy," Donovan said. "Come on and climb up on the bed with me. I've got something for you."

Eagerly, Brett scrambled up on the bed. Meg knew she should say something about its being against the rules for anyone other than a patient to be in the bed, but she couldn't bring herself to spoil the look of delight on Brett's face.

Donovan reached under his pillow and pulled out a toy laser gun. Brett's eyes grew large. "Wow. Thanks."

"Where'd you get that?" his mother asked.

"I coaxed one of the night-shift nurses into buying it for me." He offered his melting smile, and Meg realized that he could probably coax Eskimos into buying ice cubes. "Don't worry—I paid for it."

"But the money—"

"I've been saving what you give me." He ruffled Brett's hair, while the younger boy busily removed the packaging from the bright plastic pistol.

Meg noted that Mrs. Jacoby seemed genuinely concerned about the expense. Meg couldn't imagine not having enough money to buy a small toy.

"I only want you to have enough for the things you want and need for yourself," Mrs. Jacoby said.

"What I need, I can't buy," Donovan replied.

The expression on his mother's face tore at Meg's heart, and after Meg's conversation with her father, she understood exactly what Donovan meant. "Let me see that," Meg said, lifting Brett off the bed and bending down to examine the gun.

While she kept Brett occupied, Donovan and his mother had a low, quiet discussion. Minutes later, Mrs. Jacoby said, "We need to be going, Brett. They're expecting you at the day-care center."

"I *hate* that place."

"What's worse? The center or school?" Donovan asked, distracting Brett.

"School," the boy answered glumly.

"Then lucky you," Meg inserted. "No school today."

Brett looked thoughtful, and Mrs. Jacoby smiled warmly at Meg. "We can't get back until Sunday," Mrs. Jacoby told Donovan. "I get paid time and a half if I work on Saturday."

"No problem," Donovan assured her, but Meg could see he disliked being alone.

Once they were gone, even Meg felt the hollowness in the room. She could go to work, but Donovan was stuck with another long day to face by himself. "Do you like to read?" she asked. "I'm supposed to go to the hospital library and pick out books for the patients. Maybe I could choose something just for you."

"Reading's all right, but what I'd really like to do is get outside on the grounds."

"You can do that?"

"If someone takes me in a wheelchair." He made a face. "I hate being pushed around, but if it's the only way to get outdoors . . ."

"I could take you down after I finish my shift today."

"What happened to you yesterday? I thought you were coming by to see me?"

"I did, but you were asleep."

"You should have awakened me. Really. I hate sleeping in the daytime. That means I'm awake half the night. You know how long the nights can be around this place?"

"Twelve hours—same as the daytime?"

"Technically, that's true, but it feels like a hundred hours when you're alone with nothing to do and no one to talk to."

She didn't dare admit that she knew exactly what he was talking about. Her periods of excessive sleeping were often followed by bouts of sleeplessness. "I guess the nights can seem pretty long in this place."

A lab technician strolled through the doorway.

"Time for my bloodletting," Donovan said with a grimace.

Meg backed away as the tech put down the basket filled with syringes, swabs, and glass tubes for blood samples. "Doctor's orders," the tech said.

"I'll see you later," Meg promised, and slipped out of the room. She didn't want to watch needles poked into him.

At the nurses' station, Alana greeted her, and together they went over the schedule for the day's activities. "I'll do the bookmobile," Meg said. "I already know my way around the library downstairs."

"And I already promised Mrs. Vasquez I'd handle the afternoon reading time in the activity room," Alana said. "See you for lunch?"

"Sure thing," Meg said. But she never made it to lunch. The hospital library was so devoid of appealing books for kids that Meg called her mother and asked if she could go through some of the Junior League book donations stored in their basement.

At noon, Meg rushed home, rummaged through boxes and sacks earmarked for the store the Junior League ran to raise money for charity, and chose an armful of new reading material. She came across a set of *The Chronicles of Narnia* by C. S. Lewis and decided to offer them to Donovan. By the time she returned to the hospital, lunch was a memory.

The hospital librarian seemed delighted with the new books, but Meg had to promise to help

her catalog them on Saturday before she'd put
them out on loan.

The afternoon passed so quickly, Meg could
scarcely believe it when Alana told her good-bye
for the day. Meg remembered her promise to
Donovan, checked out a wheelchair, and was on
her way to his room when she met her father in
the hall. He looked tired, but was freshly shaven,
and she knew he'd probably ducked into the upstairs doctors' lounge for a shower and a change
of clothes. "How's your heart patient?" she asked.

"The transplant went smoothly, and she's in intensive care now. The next forty-eight hours are
critical. If she hangs on and doesn't have a serious
rejection episode, I think she'll make it. I'm hoping we'll hit on the best combination of immune-
suppressant drugs right off the bat." For the first
time, he noticed the wheelchair. "Going for a
stroll?"

"I promised Donovan I'd take him outside."

"That's nice of you. The nurses are so busy,
we're always shorthanded. And the patients need
these extra touches."

His approval pleased Meg more than she cared
to admit. "Will he ever be well enough to go
home and wait for his transplant?" she asked.

"We're trying to stabilize him. He's much better
than he was when he checked in a week ago. Even
if he does leave, he must stay close to the hospital. He'll wear a beeper so that we can page him
if a suitable donor is found. Dr. Rosenthal, his

primary physician, and I aren't ready to release him quite yet, but I will give him a pass."

"A pass?"

"I'll let him check out of the hospital for a few hours to go have some fun. Unfortunately, there's not too much for kids his age to do up here. Too bad his mother doesn't have a car. I'd release him for an afternoon to her care."

"I met her and Brett this morning." Meg hesitated, then asked what had been on her mind most of the day. "They don't have much money, do they?"

"No."

"Then how can they afford a liver transplant?"

"Money, or lack of it, isn't a criterion for transplant consideration. Need is. There're federal funding programs for those who can't afford a transplant. It's complicated, and the paperwork's a headache, but I saw to it that Donovan would be covered financially."

"*You* did?"

Her father gave her a tired smile. "Don't look so shocked. I do it frequently. I want to save him, Meg. I want him to get the transplant and live a long time. I want to save everybody who needs a new organ. Unfortunately, sometimes the money's easier to get than the organ." He squeezed her shoulder. "You'd better get going. I know Donovan well enough to know he's sitting on his bed, dressed and ready to get outdoors."

Megan hurried off to Donovan's room and went right in. "Notice anything different?" he asked. Donovan was wearing jeans, a shirt, and a baseball cap.

"You're a Braves fan?"

His smile lit up. "True, but also I've lost my lingering attachment to my IV." He held up his arms. "See—no lines." He scooted off the bed, but even though he tried to act as if all was well, she could see his unhealthy, sallow coloring and the slow, painful way he bent over. "Let's get out of here," he said. "This place depresses me."

Meg couldn't agree with him more.

Five

WASHINGTON MEMORIAL HOSPITAL was a large complex, located near the Beltway, an expressway that circled DC. Gardens with winding paths had been created off a patio area next to the cafeteria in an attempt to build a more restful environment for patients and personnel. Shrubs, flowers, and gurgling fountains lent the area a serene, peaceful atmosphere, in spite of rush-hour traffic that moved beyond the complex.

As Meg pushed Donovan's wheelchair along one of the paths, she recalled how the gardens had been one of her mother's Junior League projects. Meg had been only ten at the time the League had raised the money to create them, but she could still remember the day the gardens had been dedicated. She and Cindy had raced throughout the looping trails, pretending they were lost in Alice's wonderland.

"You're quiet," Donovan said, interrupting her thoughts.

"Sorry. I was thinking how pretty it is here." She pushed aside memories of Cindy. "Do you like it?"

"Yes. There was a park near the house where I grew up in southern Virginia. When Brett was a baby, Mom and I would take him and have picnics on the grass in the summer. I used to play on a Little League team there. Why, that park was sort of the social center of our town. Everyone spent time there."

"You sound like you miss it."

"I miss everything about home."

"Brett sounds as if he misses it a lot too."

"The apartment is really small, and it's up on the fifth floor, so he can't just run outside and play with his friends the way he used to. Plus, Mom works such long hours. It's usually dark before her bus gets to our stop." He sighed and stretched back in the chair. "Everything's changed because of me."

Meg stopped pushing and walked around to the front of the chair. "It's not your fault you got sick," she said.

"I know that up here." He tapped the side of his head. "But why does it bother me so much down here?" He put his hand over his heart. "I used to get boiling mad about it, but I don't have the energy to be angry anymore."

Meg understood just what he was saying. Hadn't she been angry about what happened to Cindy after the shock had worn off? She still got angry sometimes. It was so unfair! "So, if you're not mad anymore, what are you?" she asked.

"Tired. And scared."

Meg remembered what her father had told her about Donovan's not realizing that he was dying. Had he figured it out? "Scared that I'll bump you into a tree while I'm pushing you?"

"You're not that bad a driver. No . . . I'm scared because I don't know what will become of Mom and Brett if something happens to me. All we have is each other. It's especially hard for Brett. He was just a baby when Dad left, and he looks to me to be his dad as well as his brother. Mom depends on me too."

Meg thought Donovan seemed too young to have so much responsibility on his shoulders. Although she had often resented her circumstances because of her dad's medical obligations, she had had two parents and a beautiful home to grow up in. And she'd been basically happy until Cindy . . . "What about your friends back home? Do you hear from them?" she asked abruptly.

"Not much. When I first got sick, in high school, kids were pretty sympathetic, but the sicker I got and the more school I missed, the harder it was to keep up with the old crowd. Some of them tried to understand what I was going through, but unless you've been really sick . . ." He didn't finish the sentence.

"I've never been sick," Meg said, "but I really do know what you're talking about."

He tipped his head and stared deeply into her eyes. "I believe you do."

She felt her face flush. Except for Dr. Miller, this was the closest she'd come to discussing her feelings of loneliness and of being outside life's mainstream. "I guess people get so involved with their own lives, they sometimes forget there's a whole world of people who don't quite fit in for one reason or another."

Donovan nodded. "You said it. Even my girl dumped me."

Meg felt a pinprick of jealousy over the girl he'd liked, whoever she was. "That was nasty of her."

He shrugged. "I guess it wasn't all her fault. I was pretty hard to live with when the doctors told me my liver was shot. I was rude and mean. I helped push her away."

Meg could remember acting hateful herself during the past several months. She even had stopped studying, and for the first time in her life, her grades plummeted. That had been another reason her parents had insisted she see a therapist. "What's the old saying? You only hurt the ones you love?" Meg said.

Donovan grinned. "I've heard that before. Truthfully, Lauren is better off without me. She started dating another guy right away, so I guess she thought so too."

"Maybe things will get back to normal for you after you have your transplant," Meg suggested.

"Maybe. Listen, I didn't mean to sit here having a pity party. I really appreciate your taking time to bring me outside."

"I don't mind listening, and besides, it's been fun seeing the gardens again. For the record, I don't think you're feeling overly sorry for yourself. What's happened to you hasn't been any picnic."

He reached out and plucked a flower from a nearby bush. "Don't ever have your liver crash. It leads to weirdness."

"Why do I get the feeling that you'd be weird even if your liver was healthy?"

"I guess I can't fool you." His eyes glowed, and for a moment, Meg saw him as he must have looked before he got sick. *A real heartbreaker*, she thought. "Here." He handed her the flower. "A token of my gratitude."

She accepted the flower and tucked it into a buttonhole on her uniform. "Do you know we've been out here for an hour?" she asked, glancing at her watch. "I'll bet they're bringing the supper trays to your floor by now. I'll take you back to your room."

"Are you trying to punish me?"

Meg laughed. "The food's not that bad."

"Why don't you try it sometime."

"Like when?"

"Like tonight."

Meg felt her heart beat a little faster. He seemed to like being with her. The notion pleased her immensely. "I can't tonight. My kid sister is leaving for gymnastic camp, and Mom wants me to come to the airport to see her off. Dad can't make it."

"No problem." He looked away, and Meg realized that he thought she was making up an excuse to put him off.

"How about Saturday?" She remembered that his mom couldn't come for a visit on Saturday.

"I thought you didn't work on Saturdays."

"I don't, but I promised the hospital librarian I'd help catalog some books. I could come see you when I finish. Maybe I could bring along some videos and we could order in a pizza. I have a car. I could pick one up and bring it back to the hospital whenever we get hungry. Can you eat pizza?"

"My doctor says there are no restrictions on my diet right now. I think he'd like me to gain some weight."

"You can have some of my weight," she said. "I've been looking for a place to dump it for years."

"I think you look terrific."

"I wasn't fishing for a compliment. Honest. It's just that being overweight is something I've always struggled with." Meg wished she hadn't brought it up. She didn't want him knowing how inadequate and inept she felt around guys her own age.

"You don't have to fish," he said. "I wouldn't have told you so if I didn't mean it."

Feeling inordinately pleased, Meg pushed him back to his room, chattering enthusiastically all the way. After making sure he was settled and comfortable, she gave him the C. S. Lewis books. "Until Saturday," she said, and hurried home to put her sister on a plane for gymnastic camp. More than ever, she wished she could call Cindy and talk to her, but of course, that was impossible.

"You're certainly dressed up just to help in the hospital library," Meg's mother said as Megan started out the door early Saturday morning.

Meg felt her cheeks turning red. "I'm sick of wearing my uniform. Can't I wear something different for a change?"

"I'm not complaining," her mother added hastily. "I think you look nice. It's good to see you take an interest in your looks again."

Meg wondered if she should go change. If her mother thought she looked nice, maybe she had overdressed. She had wanted to look good for Donovan, wanted his approval. "I'll be at the hospital until tonight if you want me," Meg told her mother, then hurried out the door.

At the hospital library, Meg worked quickly while the librarian talked about how much she appreciated Meg's extra effort. She seemed so grateful that Meg promised to bring in more books and help on other Saturdays. Meg began to realize just how valuable volunteer help was to the place, and was sorry she'd resisted the idea of volunteering when her father had first mentioned it.

It was noon when she got to Donovan's room. He was dressed and sitting in a chair, flipping through TV channels. "I've got two games, a deck of cards, and a video for us," she said, breezing into his room. "What's your pleasure?"

He clicked off the set with the remote control device and turned toward her. "Can you get me a wheelchair and take me outside?" He sounded distracted and preoccupied.

"Sure, if that's what you want. Why?"

"Please, just do it. Do it right now."

Six

MEG GOT THE wheelchair, and Donovan climbed in it, clutching a small leather shaving kit in his lap. "Am I taking you out for a shave and a haircut?" she asked, trying to joke with him. He looked tense and nervous.

"We'll talk outside," he said.

Bewildered, she pushed him down the corridor, into the elevator, and out into the garden area. The sun beat down, wrapping the afternoon in a blanket of humid summer heat. Many other patients and their visitors were out too, and finding a spot alone was difficult, but Meg finally parked the wheelchair beneath a willow tree that was off the beaten path. The tree's filmy leaves grazed a pond, where dragonflies flitted above the motionless water.

"I think this is as alone as we can get today," Meg said. She settled herself at the foot of his chair and gazed up at him anxiously. "Want to tell me what's going on?"

Donovan fingered the leather kit and glanced about. "I . . . um . . . guess I must be acting pretty strange."

"Not at all. How exciting can games and a video movie be to a guy who has a death grip on his shaving kit?"

For the first time since she'd seen him that day, a smile appeared at the corners of his mouth. "Now that we're out here, I'm not sure where to start."

"Start at the beginning. Take your time, we're in no hurry."

"I admit I've been hogging your time," Donovan said. "I'll bet you've got other things to do on Saturdays. I don't mean to crowd you or put something on you you might not want."

"I don't mind," Meg said, suddenly realizing that it was true. How had she become so involved with him in so brief a time? Yet, she knew that she had. "I feel like I've known you for ages."

"It's a phenomenon," he remarked.

"What is?"

"The way sickness makes you close to people you'd never meet or be with in the regular world."

Had Donovan felt the uniqueness of their relationship too? Had he sensed the curious bonding that had seemed to sweep away barriers of awkwardness that usually accompanied the initial stages getting to know someone?

"Your dad calls the phenomenon 'intimate strangers,' " Donovan said. "He says that people will tell a stranger sitting next to them on an airplane the secrets of their soul, when they won't tell their closest family member the same thing."

" 'Intimate strangers' . . . interesting," Meg said.

"It explained some things to me. You see, I had a roommate in the hospital back in my hometown, and I talked to him about everything. He was what the guys in my school would classify as a nerd, but he was sick also, and we got real close over the weeks we were hospitalized together."

"What happened to him?"

"He got well and left the hospital. He came to visit me, but over time, the bond between us weakened. Maybe I was jealous because he got well and I didn't. Maybe it was because we never had a true friendship, just the intimate stranger business." Donovan shook his head, as if to clear out the memories.

"So, is that what we are?" Meg asked. "Intimate strangers? When you're well, will you forget all about me?" Meg couldn't believe she'd ever forget him.

"I think we're friends, don't you?" A smile lit up his face, causing Meg's heart to skip. She hadn't had a really close friend since Cindy. "Because if we're friends—and not strangers—I can tell you something and make it our secret."

"Is it something to do with your transplant?"

Meg was genuinely puzzled by the odd direction of his conversation.

"In a way."

"What is it? Have they found you a donor?"

"If they had, I'd be throwing a party. No . . . it's something else." He chewed his bottom lip. "It has something to do with your father in a round-about way."

"My father?"

"I'm confusing you." He raked his hand through his hair. "It's just that I want to tell you something . . . show something to you . . . that might affect our friendship. I mean, once you see it, you might have to tell your father about it."

"I won't if you don't want me to. Doctors are asked to keep confidences all the time. My dad will understand."

Donovan appeared hesitant for a moment longer, then he zipped open his shaving kit and pulled out a folded envelope. "I can't keep this a secret any longer. If I do, I'll bust. I'm going to trust you to keep it between us." He thrust the envelope at her. "Read this. I woke up yesterday morning with it on my pillow and not a clue as to how it got there."

Gingerly, Meg took the envelope. Donovan's name had been written on the front in beautiful, flowing calligraphy. Red sealing wax, stamped with the initials OLW and broken when the envelope had been opened, covered the flap. She pulled out a handsome calligraphed letter and began to read.

Dear Donovan,

You don't know me, but I know about you, and because I do, I want to give you a special gift. Accompanying this letter is a certified check, my gift to you with no strings attached to spend on anything you want. No one knows about this gift except you, and you are free to tell anyone you want.

Who I am isn't really important, only that you and I have much in common. Through no fault of our own, we have endured pain and isolation and have spent many days in a hospital feeling lonely and scared. I hoped for a miracle, but most of all, I hoped for someone to truly understand what I was going through.

I can't make you live longer. I can't stop you from hurting, but I can give you one wish, as someone did for me. My wish helped me find purpose, faith, and courage.

Friendship reaches beyond time, and the true miracle is in giving, not receiving. Use my gift to fulfill your wish.

> *Your Forever Friend,*
>
> *JWC*

Meg didn't know what to say. Blankly, she looked up at him.

"There's more," he said, reaching into the kit

again. He pulled out another piece of folded paper and handed it to Meg.

She unfolded it and saw that it was a check made out to Donovan Jacoby in the sum of one hundred thousand dollars. It was signed, "Richard Holloway, Esq., Administrator, One Last Wish Foundation." Meg gaped.

"Do you think it's legit?" Donovan asked. "Do you know anything at all about this foundation?"

"I've never heard of it." Meg racked her brain for the names of the charitable organizations that supported the hospital. "Money usually comes to the hospital, not to any individual in the hospital. Especially not a patient." She held the check up to the sun, but saw only a watermark for a bank in Boston, Massachusetts. "Do you know anyone with the initials JWC?"

"I've been thinking all morning, and the only person that comes to mind is a guy in my school named Jed Calloway—I don't know his middle initial. But it couldn't be him. He's poor as dirt and not very charitable either. No, it can't be Jed."

"How about this Richard Holloway?"

"Never heard of the guy. What's that E-s-q mean? Do you know?"

Meg puckered her brow. "I've seen it in old books. It's an abbreviation for 'esquire,' an old-fashioned term for a lawyer. I guess he's in charge of this foundation. Maybe he's in the phone book—we could look and see."

Donovan moistened his lips. "It's a lot of money, isn't it?"

"We both know that it is. Why would someone give it to you?"

"I don't know. All the letter says is that this JWC understands what I'm going through and wants me to spend it on something I really want."

"So, what do you want?"

"A new liver." He gave a mirthless laugh. "But we both know I can't buy one of those."

"There must be something else."

"There're lots of something elses. I have to think about it. I can't blow this much cash on myself."

"I think that's what JWC wants you to do with it."

He glanced off toward the willow tree. "There's another problem," he said slowly.

"Tell me."

"It—it's hard for me to say it."

"You can tell me." Meg felt her pulse throbbing in her throat.

"It's the part that involves your father," he said.

"How is my dad involved?"

"I'm afraid if he knows about the money, he'll take it away from me."

Seven

〜✦〜

"TAKE IT AWAY? My dad wouldn't do that!" Meg was both startled and hurt by Donovan's suggestion.

"I don't mean he'd take it away on purpose. But he might *have* to take it away."

"But why? Obviously, JWC wants *you* to have it." Donovan shrugged, and Meg could tell he was having trouble putting what he wanted to say into words. She tried to make it easier by rising up on her knees and clasping his hand. "It's *your* money. Why would my dad want it?"

He touched his other hand to her hair, smoothing it back. Her scalp tingled from his touch. "My family's poor, Meg. I know we're a charity case for this hospital. Mom explained how your father got us on Medicare in order to help pay for all of this."

"Money's not supposed to decide who gets organs." She recalled her conversation with her father, and how he assured her that need was the main factor in determining who got organs for transplantation.

"I know that, but now that I have money, will I have to use it for the operation?"

Meg couldn't answer his question. "What if you did? Would it mean you'd give up the chance to get the transplant?"

He stared down at the check. "It's a lot of money, and my family could use it for lots of things."

"How can you consider using it on anything else? I know your mother would spend every cent on keeping you alive. What difference does it make if it has to be spent on your transplant?"

"It makes a difference to me," Donovan said quietly. "That's why I'm holding you to your promise to keep it a secret from your father. If it's really my money, I should decide on how I spend it."

"But—"

"You promised," Donovan interrupted. He softened his words by stroking her cheek. "Friends keep promises to friends. That's a fact." He tugged her upward. "Come on. I think I can beat you in Monopoly. Want to give me a chance?"

Meg wanted to discuss the One Last Wish money some more. "But, Donovan—"

"Maybe I shouldn't have told you. I don't mean to put you in a tough place. I just need some time to think it through."

"I'm glad you told me, but I don't know how to help you with it."

"Then let's go inside and talk about it later. Right now, I want to have some of that fun you promised me."

Meg spent the rest of the afternoon and evening with Donovan, playing board games and watching the video movie in the recreation room. Several of the younger kids joined them, and Meg saw how fond they were of Donovan. He had a way with them, a friendly, open manner that put people at ease. She knew she felt comfortable with him.

By the end of the day, Donovan was completely worn out and couldn't eat the pizza Meg brought to his room. "You don't mind?" he asked as he crawled into his bed.

"Who needs the calories?" She kept her question light, as she shoved the unopened box to the side and fluffed his pillow. His coloring, which looked more yellow than it had that morning, bothered her. "Maybe you pushed too hard today," she observed.

"I wouldn't have traded today for anything. I really appreciate your spending your free time with me. It meant a lot."

"I had fun." Meg meant it. The time she'd spent with him had seemed to fly. "Your mom and Brett will come by tomorrow, and then it'll be Monday again and the start of a brand-new week."

"Another week in paradise," he mumbled cynically. His eyelids looked heavy, and Meg watched them close. "Don't forget your promise," he whispered.

"I won't forget," she said. He was asleep instantly, but Meg couldn't bring herself to leave. His breathing sounded shallow, and she was concerned about him. She wished her father were there to assure her that Donovan was all right. She fiddled with the bedcovers, smoothing them the way she'd been taught during her candy striper training. She kept thinking about the letter he had received, and the check.

Meg realized that she had been raised quite differently from Donovan. She'd been given many material things and had never truly wanted for anything. At sixteen, she attended a top private school, wore expensive clothes, had her own car. Not that her parents hadn't taught her values. Many a time, her mother had lectured, "We have a duty to help others who are less fortunate. Your father's profession is aimed toward helping and healing. I work hard with my charities because it gives me a deep sense of satisfaction to know I'm doing something useful for others."

Until now, Meg hadn't paid much attention. But JWC's generous gift to a person he or she claimed to not even know, caused Meg to pause and reevaluate her parents' philosophy of life. Why would a complete stranger give Donovan so much money? Who was this JWC anyway? Meg found herself not only curious, but also a little jealous. Not that she didn't want Donovan to have the money—she did. The money didn't threaten Meg at all. It was the caring, the concern, from an anonymous, faceless person that intimidated her.

"Don't pout. It won't help." Meg heard Cindy's voice in the back of her mind.

"But you don't understand. My dad thinks more of his patients than he does of me!" Meg recalled wailing to her friend the day she'd graduated from eighth grade and an emergency had made him miss the ceremony.

"Doctors don't belong to just their families, Meggie. They belong to everybody," Cindy commented. "Sort of like the President, I think. I'll bet he feels he owes something to the people he takes care of."

"Then why did my father even bother to have a family? Why didn't he just devote himself to humanity and forget about having us?"

"Probably because he wanted you," Cindy answered. "Who says you can't have both?"

Now, years later, standing next to Donovan's hospital bed, watching his chest rise and fall with labored breathing, Meg recalled the conversation with vivid clarity. Did JWC feel he or she *owed* something to the sick and dying? Was that the motivation behind the One Last Wish Foundation? And if so, where did that kind of compassion come from? Did Meg have it within herself to feel the same way? The way her parents did?

She longed to talk it over with Cindy. Her best friend would have helped her make sense of it. But, of course, there was no Cindy. Stricken, feeling more depressed than she had in weeks, Meg pushed away from Donovan's bed and quickly left the hospital.

"Your father and I are going to run out to the country club and play a few rounds of golf. Want to come along?" Meg's mother asked her Sunday afternoon.

"Not really." Meg felt listless, as if her energy had been drained away. "I'd rather lie here by the pool."

"If that's what you want." She saw her mother hesitate. "Is everything okay with you?"

"Things are fine."

"You seem to be a little down today. And last week, you seemed so much more animated. Did something happen at the hospital yesterday?"

"Nothing happened. I had a good time with one of the patients. I'm concerned about him."

"The Jacoby boy—your father's told me about him."

Meg sat upright. "Has Dad said how Donovan's doing today?"

"I'm trying to get him off for a little relaxation. I asked him not to even call in today. If he's needed, he'll be paged."

Meg had seen her mother's efforts to protect

her father from overwork before. She planned frequent getaways and weekend minitrips. Still, most jaunts were interrupted by calls from the hospital, moreso now that he was head of the transplant unit. "Go on to the golf course," Meg said. "I'm perfectly fine by myself."

Once they were gone, Meg tried to lounge by the pool and read a book, but she couldn't concentrate on the story. Her thoughts kept returning to Donovan, his medical prognosis, JWC, and the One Last Wish Foundation. Around five o'clock, she gave up, dressed, and left her parents a note: "Went for a drive to buy some frozen yogurt. Don't worry, Mom. I'll get the low-fat. Honest."

She hoped the note's levity would keep them from being concerned about her. She was in the pits emotionally and was attempting to take her therapist's advice—"stay busy, stay involved."

Meg wasn't sure how she ended up near the hospital, but before she knew it, she was pulling her car off the exit ramp that would take her to Memorial. The neighborhood around the complex was well kept. Older houses, once the homes of Washington's elite, dominated the area to the north, away from the expressway. To the west side of the hospital, signs announced the construction of sleek new medical office buildings. Meg saw the whole area as an odd mixture of the old and the new, with a sturdy median strip lined with cherry trees separating the past from the present.

As she neared the entrance of Memorial, Meg recognized Mrs. Jacoby and Brett waiting at the bus stop. She pulled to a halt in front of them. "How are you?" she asked.

Brett waved. "Hi," he said. "I remember you."

Mrs. Jacoby's face looked lined and drawn, and Meg's heart went out to her. "Come on," Meg urged, throwing open her car door. "Let me give you a ride home."

"We live too far," Mrs. Jacoby said.

"No problem. I'd love to take you."

"Are you sure?"

"Positive," Meg replied, knowing instantly it was the truth. She wanted to know Donovan's family better, and she wanted to help. She couldn't change the past, but she could affect the future. "Hop in and tell me all about Donovan. I have a ton of questions for you."

Eight

⤜⤏❦⤎⤛

Brett bounded into the backseat, and Donovan's mother wearily got into the front. "This is very nice of you. For some reason, the bus doesn't seem to run on schedule on Sundays."

"Hey, this car is neat!" Brett blurted, bouncing on the leather seat. "Is it yours?"

"It's mine," Meg said.

"Put on your seat belt," his mother insisted.

"That's the rule in my car," Meg told him as he began to protest. When she heard the buckle snap into place, she asked, "So, how was Donovan today?"

"Crabby," Brett announced.

"He wasn't feeling well," Mrs. Jacoby explained. "Dr. Rosenthal said his electrolytes were imbalanced and his potassium levels were elevated. It's happened before, and it always makes Donovan spacey and incoherent. The doctor says it's hard on his heart too."

"He kept talking like we were back home," Brett chimed in. "He kept telling me to call Lauren for him and tell her he was picking her up for their date. That's dumb."

"I explained it was because his blood was messed up," Mrs. Jacoby said over her shoulder. "He didn't know what he was saying."

"He didn't even listen when I told him about the fort I'm making in my bedroom."

"Please, Brett, he couldn't help it."

Meg thought Mrs. Jacoby sounded on the verge of tears. "I have an idea," Meg said. "Before I take you home, how'd you like some ice cream? My treat."

"Yeah!" Brett's voice filled the car. "Chocolate."

"Don't go out of your way for us."

"I was going to get some for myself when I saw you. There's a minimall not too far from here."

"It's kind of you," Mrs. Jacoby said. "I don't want any, but Brett will follow you anywhere if you feed him."

Meg laughed. When she reached a small strip center, she parked and the three of them went inside an ice-cream parlor decorated like an old-time country store. They ordered, and while they waited, Mrs. Jacoby handed Brett two quarters for a game machine tucked back in a corner. While he was preoccupied, Mrs. Jacoby leaned against the booth and shut her eyes. "I'm exhausted. Thanks again for offering us a ride."

"Too bad you live so far away from the hospital."

"Believe me, I tried to get closer, but the immediate vicinity had no rental apartments. I'm afraid the homes there are out of my league."

"Donovan told me about your home in Virginia. He misses it."

"So do I, but once we were told he had to have a liver transplant, I knew we had to be closer to the transplant center. The call could come anytime, day or night. The closer we are, the sooner we can get here. I'm sure you understand how critical timing is for something like this."

Meg nodded. "Maybe the call will come soon."

"Maybe. I have mixed feelings, however."

"You do?"

"Think about it. His life, the liver he so desperately needs, depends on someone else's dying. I think about that. I think about some mother losing her child, and it makes my heart ache. But my son is living on borrowed time—every day is one less that he has to live. And every day brings him closer to either dying or surviving with a part of another mother's child inside his body. These days, medical science gives us strange choices."

"Sometimes it seems like doctors play God, doesn't it?" Meg asked.

"Don't get me wrong . . . I'm grateful for the technology, grateful for men like your father who've devoted their lives to bringing recovery and longevity to the dying. Organ transplantation is a wonderful thing, but human beings are always involved, and that makes it complex, not simple at all. Life and death never is." Mrs. Jacoby studied Meg and smiled sheepishly. "I'm sorry. I didn't mean to get so philosophical. It's been a long day."

"Now that you've moved to the city, will you stay even after Donovan's transplant?"

"I assume so. He'll need to be checked regularly, and of course, his dosage of immune-suppressant drugs will have to be carefully regulated. Washington's not such a bad place to raise two sons. There's plenty of history here. And the suburbs really are lovely, although I'm positive I couldn't afford anything too grand. Still, there must be some nice neighborhoods I'll be able to afford someday." She laughed wryly and added, "Tonight, I'd trade a mansion in the boondocks for a room with a view nearer the hospital. This commute is the pits."

Once again, Meg realized how sheltered her own life had been. She'd lived in the same house since she was a baby, and she took her life-style for granted. "If you had a car—" she started.

"I couldn't afford the insurance. No, for now, this is simply the way things have to be. I'm resigned to it."

The ice cream arrived, and Brett bolted over to the table and dug in. Meg enjoyed his enthusiasm, and soon the three of them were laughing over his stories about taking his laser gun to school. Yet, subconsciously, Meg kept mulling over Mrs. Jacoby's dilemma. How terrible it would be to have someone in the hospital and no way to get to him quickly. She wondered if Donovan would want to spend a portion of his Wish money on transportation for his mom. She decided that as soon as he was feeling better, she would ask him.

When Meg arrived for work Monday morning, she went by the nurses' station in order to get an update on Donovan's medical status. "His blood work hasn't come up from the lab yet," Mrs. Vasquez said. "But he seems more coherent this morning."

"My brother would get the same way when his blood chemistry got out of whack. Once Donovan's balanced, he'll be back in his right mind," Alana told Meg.

Meg tried to feel encouraged, but she didn't want to see Donovan not in control of his facilities. Something cautioned her that he wouldn't want her to see him that way either. Around lunchtime, she overcame her inhibitions and went to his room anyway. He lay on his side, staring into space.

"Hello," she said cautiously. His eyes slowly focused on her face. He attempted to sit up, but she put her hand on his shoulder to keep him down. "I can't stay but a minute."

He nodded and held his arm slightly aloft. An IV line led to a pole beside his bed where clear plastic bags hung. "As you can tell, my friend and I are reattached." Donovan's voice sounded hoarse.

"That's what friends are for."

"I hate this one," he whispered. "He cramps my style."

"I'm sure you won't need him in a couple of days." She told him about taking his mom and Brett for ice cream and then home to their apartment.

"What did you think of our castle?"

She couldn't tell him that she found the place small and depressing. "It was interesting. Your Mom's fixed it up pretty nice." His gaze never left her face, and soon she felt her cheeks burning. "You should call Brett later. He thought you were being mean to him yesterday because you were so out of it. He can't quite catch on to what's happening."

"Me either," Donovan said glumly.

"Brett said you kept asking for Lauren. Do you miss her?" Meg wasn't sure why she was asking. It wasn't any of her business, but she wanted to know, needed to know.

"No. I miss what she represents—freedom from this place. The life I used to have before I got sick."

"After your transplant, you'll be able to have your old life back."

"How can a person go back after he's been through something like this? How can I ever feel normal again?"

She wanted to tell him she understood perfectly what he was saying. She wanted to tell him about what she had been through during the past year. Instead, she asked, "What's normal anyhow, and who decides? Let's make our own 'normal.'"

"I need a favor," he said after a moment.

"Name it."

"I need you to find out if the money from the Wish Foundation is really mine to spend on whatever I want. When I got sick, I started thinking I could die and never spend the money, and that wouldn't be right. My family needs the money."

"I'll see what I can find out," Meg assured him, even though she hadn't a clue as to how to go about it.

"You have to figure out a way of getting the information without telling anyone I received it."

"I'll take care of it." She hoped with every fiber of her being that the money would be his completely. Donovan deserved it. JWC must think so too, or why else would Donovan have been chosen?

Meg returned to work, determined to find out what she could. She hung around the hospital after her shift ended, until she knew that her father was alone in his office. Meg hurried to corner him before some medical emergency called him away.

"Are you busy?" she asked, stepping into his office and closing the door.

"Not at the moment. Come on in."

He was all smiles, obviously in a good mood,

and she didn't want to ruin it. "You look happy," she said.

"My heart transplant patient is doing so splendidly that I'm going to release her at the end of the week. I love it when things go off without a hitch."

"That's super." Meg felt her heart hammering against her ribs as she struggled with a way to phrase her questions on Donovan's behalf. "I was wondering if you could tell me something."

"I'll try."

Meg took a deep breath. "Can someone who's been accepted for your transplant program be kicked out of it?"

Nine

"Kicked out?" Meg's father sounded puzzled. "It's not a social club, Meg. We don't admit people into the program lightly. We conduct medical as well as psychological tests—interviews with psychiatrists and other doctors to determine if a person can handle undergoing a transplant. Not everyone is a candidate, but once a patient is admitted, he stays until either we find a matching donor or he dies waiting for one."

"And so if the money part's already handled, it won't matter if someone waiting to get a transplant gets rich all of a sudden? What I mean is, what if someone needs a transplant and he's accepted and the cost is already covered and then that person wins the lottery or something. Will he have to pay for his own transplant just because he's gotten filthy rich?"

"Once funds have been allocated for a patient, his medical procedures are covered, no matter how rich he gets. But there are many costs following the transplant that the patient will incur," her father replied.

"Such as?"

"A changed life-style. The immune-suppressant drugs. They can run upward of ten thousand dollars annually."

"That's a lot of money." Meg's elation over Donovan's being able to keep his Wish money quickly vanished.

"But those drugs allow a patient years more of life. How can you put a price on that?" He steepled his fingers together and eyed her quizzically. "Why all this interest in finances?"

Meg thought quickly, then replied, "I've been noticing things this hospital could use."

"Such as?"

"For instance, why isn't there a hotel nearby for a patient's family to stay at while they wait around for a transplant?"

"I admit it would be very helpful, but land around here is at a premium. This area was all residential until Memorial was built, but slowly, over the years, people have moved to the suburbs. Ever since the transplant program's come in, Memorial's grown even more."

"It bothers me that people like Mrs. Jacoby have to live so far away. I'll bet Donovan would like to have her closer. And it must really be hard on littler kids. I see their parents sleeping in their rooms in chairs, or even on the couches in the waiting rooms. They don't look very comfortable."

"You're right. I wish we had a special house for patients' families. A big corporation talked about building one years ago, but then they thought the need was greater for one near the children's cancer facility in Maryland, so they built one up there. Without their financial backing, our project never got off the ground."

"But Memorial still needs one—especially now, for people waiting for transplants."

"It would take a couple of years to get such a project going."

"Why?"

"I remember when we looked into it before. All monies had to be raised from scratch. An architect was needed to draw up plans, building materials had to be bought or donated, furnishings acquired, not to mention kitchen and bathroom fixtures, recreational areas for leisure time, people to manage the facility, volunteers to help out—I'm telling you, Meg, it's a mammoth undertaking."

"But it seems to me as if you need it now more than ever." She tried not to be dismayed over the length of his list.

"I agree, but even if we had the land and the money, the actual building of this kind of facility could take close to a year of construction work."

"You have to start sometime." Meg wasn't sure why she felt so strongly in favor of the idea. She'd never been a crusader. Maybe it was seeing how Donovan's mother was struggling to keep her family together. Or having to comfort some of the kids on the pediatric floor when they were sobbing because they missed their mothers. Or maybe it was knowing what Cindy's family had gone through. All the things together caused her to imagine such a house vividly. "I can't believe this hospital can't spare some of its land to build a home away from home for patients' families."

Her father eyed her thoughtfully. "The land's only one hurdle. What about the rest of it? Money doesn't grow on trees."

"What if some group took it on as a project?"

"That would be nice. Any ideas?"

"A couple."

"Then go for it."

"What?" His answer drew her up short. "*Me* do something?"

"You're the one with the ideas. And I know how determined you can get once you set your mind on something." She opened her mouth to argue, but he continued, saying, "Aren't you the girl who staged a sit-down strike in the school cafeteria in the eighth grade to protest the quality of the food?"

Of course she remembered the event, but Cindy had been her cohort, and together they had masterminded the demonstration.

"And *won*?" her father added.

"That was different. This is serious."

"I know it's serious. I'm not telling you to raise the money yourself, only to find a group to spearhead such a project. I have faith in you. I think you can do it."

Meg wanted to argue against the idea. She wanted to tell her father that all she'd agreed to do this summer was be a volunteer. But even as she silently listed her reasons for not tackling such a project, she knew it intrigued her. And all because of someone whose initials were JWC. If this anonymous person could calmly drop one hundred thousand dollars into Donovan Jacoby's lap, then why couldn't Meg do something of equal or even greater value for him?

All the way home, Meg warred with herself about such an undertaking. A part of her said, "You're sixteen. You can't do this." But another part of her argued, "Why not? All you have to do is discuss it with Mom and ask how one of her Junior League projects gets going. Maybe the League could be the spearhead group that Dad mentioned. The worst that can happen is the idea won't work."

That evening, she broached the idea with her mother. "We have many worthwhile projects," her mother told Meg after she'd listened carefully.

"Don't you think this one is worthwhile?"

"Yes, I do. However, I'm only one board member. There are others who'll need convincing."

"Can't you convince them?"

Her mother put her hand on Meg's shoulder. "I

could never do it as well as you. Perhaps you can speak to them at our next board meeting."

Meg groaned. What had she gotten herself into?

A week later, Meg found herself standing in front of the Junior League's board of directors in her own living room, her heart hammering as she made her case.

"I have a friend at Memorial who's dying. He needs a transplant, and he needs his family near him while he waits for one. You probably can't help him with his transplant, but you can help his family get closer than an hour's ride away from him."

Meg had prepared for the presentation. She had statistics and logical arguments. She made a strong case for an immediate and concentrated fund-raising effort. Appealing to the emotions of those women in the room, she spoke of a mother's love for her child, a family's need to be involved with their loved one's care, a patient's longing to have someone he loves near him to ease emotional and physical suffering.

When Meg wrapped up her talk, she knew by the women's expressions that she had had an impact. She silently hoped it had been strong enough to persuade the board to take up the project of building a special guest house.

"Thank you, Meg," Mrs. Hotchkiss, the president, said. "We'll discuss your suggestion and get back to you."

Meg was disappointed. She had hoped they'd

say yes on the spot. The next day over lunch, she confided in Alana, who'd become a pal.

"I think it's a dynamite idea," Alana said. "My brother will too. In fact, I'll bet if we get endorsements from all the people who've gotten transplants at this place, we could make one *fine* fund-raising letter."

"I'll bet you're right," Meg agreed, warming to the suggestion. "Maybe we could ask local reporters to feature stories about former patients. Would Lonnie volunteer for an interview?"

"Of course. Especially if his sister strong-arms him." Alana giggled. "Lonnie's working for a big company in Washington. Maybe they will cough up some big bucks. Maybe we can talk folks into being Santa in July."

"Why not? For every gift Santa leaves, he could take up a donation for our cause."

"We'll be Santa's special elves."

Meg laughed. The home away from home for the families of sick people was no laughing matter, but somehow the joking made the task seem less insurmountable. Laughing with Alana about grandiose plans such as building a place was just plain fun.

Fun. Wasn't that what had been missing in her life for over a year? What an odd place to get it, Meg thought. Through the lives of people she hadn't even known six weeks before.

Ten

By THE END of the week, Meg had no news about her project, but good news about Donovan. His blood chemistry had stabilized, his IV had been removed, and he was in good spirits. "It's a six-hour pass for Saturday from your father," he said, waving a piece of paper under Meg's nose. "Where do you want to take me?"

"Where do you want to go?"

"Besides Alaska? I'd like to go home." His expression grew wistful, then he said, "Mom wants us over for dinner at the apartment. Would you come with me?"

"I'd love to," Meg said, realizing she was his sole means of transportation and that without her, it would cost him a fortune in cab fare to get to his mother's apartment. "I'll bet your Mom's a good cook."

"Even the dying get a final meal."

"Don't joke about that."

Donovan took her hand. "Sorry. Being cooped up for so long has blackened my sense of humor. Promise me something."

"What?"

"Before we go to my mom's, let's have some fun on our own."

She smiled. "You're on."

Donovan checked out of the hospital on Saturday afternoon, and Meg started their outing with a drive down Pennsylvania Avenue, past the White House. "Think we should stop in and say hello to the Prez?" Donovan asked. "I think he should allocate more funding for transplants. There's not enough money for people who need them."

"He's out of the city—too hot this time of the year."

"Great. Where's government in action when I need it?"

"Have you seen the Washington Monument? How about the Lincoln Memorial?" She tried to think of things that didn't require much walking, since Donovan was still recovering.

"I've never seen them," he admitted. "The most I've seen is the inside of Memorial Hospital."

Meg took him to the Washington Monument first. The great obelisk soared upward from the green grass into the bright blue sky. People had spread blankets on the grass, and children ran squealing and trailing kites. Meg thought the air humid and muggy, but Donovan insisted the warmth felt good. "I've been cooped up so long in the hospital, I feel like a mushroom," he told her.

They walked toward the Lincoln Memorial, along the rectangular Reflecting Pool, then sat beside the cool water, where Meg watched reflections of clouds float on the water's surface. She hoped Donovan wasn't overly exerting himself.

"Do you know how tired I am of being sick?" Donovan asked with a sigh. "Sometimes I don't think they'll ever find a donor for me."

"Sure they will." Meg tried to sound confident. "You've come this far."

"Far?" He gave a sarcastic chuckle. "Far from what? My home? My friends? Look what my mother's had to sacrifice for me. I think about all she's had to give up because I'm sick."

"Don't think about it. Think about all the things you'll get to do once your transplant is over."

"Like what?"

"Like spend your Wish money. You could buy your mom a car." Meg had already told him how she had talked to her father and confirmed that Donovan's medical expenses would be covered regardless of his personal finances. The One Last Wish check was his to keep and spend as he wanted.

"No . . . I want to get her something really awesome. She could use a new house." Donovan sat up straighter the moment the words were out of his mouth. He turned and looked at Meg with an expression of total revelation. "That's it. That's what I can buy her. I haven't told her anything yet."

"A house is a big deal, all right. Don't you think your mother might like to pick out her own?"

"But then it won't be a surprise. That's the part that would make it special. She'd be surprised— the way I was surprised when I discovered the Wish money and decided it was for real. I can't tell you how it felt to open that letter and see that check. And then to know it was mine—all mine—to do anything I wanted with. Well, what I *want* is to buy my mother a house."

"Houses cost lots of money."

"I have a ton of money."

"But it still may not be enough."

"I won't know until I start looking." Donovan took her by her shoulders. "You can help me."

Meg blinked. "How? I don't know the first thing about looking for a house."

"How hard can it be? When we sold ours in Virginia, Mom hired a real estate agent. She showed the house to a bunch of people, and one of them bought it. That seems simple enough to me."

"I know how the process works," Meg said. "I just don't know what I can do to help."

"You can help me find an agent. You can tell her how much money I have to work with. And about how I need to be near the hospital. It needs to be a nice neighborhood, one with good schools for Brett."

Meg noticed that Donovan had excluded himself from the school agenda. "Gee, I don't know . . ."

"Meg, please, I need you. I need you to be my arms and legs while I'm stuck at Memorial."

She looked into his eyes and saw quiet desperation. *He needed her.* His appeal sliced deep into her heart. She needed him too. Needed him in her life, even though she couldn't explain why to either one of them. "Well, I guess I could ask around for you."

"I knew I could count on you."

She wanted to tell him not to get his hopes up. "I'm not even positive I can persuade a real estate agent to talk to me. I mean, I don't look old enough to have the kind of money it takes for a house. An agent will think I'm a fraud."

"So tell her you're a rock star." He grinned. "Everybody knows rock stars are young, rich, and weird."

"A rock star! Who would believe that?"

"You'll think of something. I have complete confidence in you."

Meg didn't feel confident at all, but she knew she would try her best for his sake. "Listen, Mr. Moneybags, if I somehow manage to bamboozle some agent and get her to take me, *you*, on as a client, and I line up some houses for you to see, then you have to do your part, understand?"

"What's that?"

"You have to stay well."

He cupped her chin in his palm. "I'm doing my best. With my luck, I'll find the perfect house and just before I close the deal, my beeper will go off and your father will want to give me a transplant."

Meg gazed deeply into his eyes. "May you have such good luck," she said. "May you have such good luck."

The meal Donovan's mother prepared for them that evening was simple, but tasty. "It's terrific, Mom," he told her.

Meg agreed, looking around the apartment at Mrs. Jacoby's meager belongings and well-worn furniture. Through the walls, Meg could hear a baby crying and a television blaring in neighboring apartments.

Brett bounced enthusiastically in his chair. "We can spend the night together," he said. His face fell when Donovan told him that he had to return to the hospital. "But that's not fair. Why can't you stay?"

"Because I'm still sick. I don't want to go back, but I have to."

"You've been gone a long time. I want you to come home."

"I can't, Brett."

Brett pushed away from the table. "You could if you wanted. Me and Mom can take care of you."

"I have to leave."

"I hate you!" Brett shouted, his eyes filling with

tears. "I don't want you to come home. Stay at your stupid hospital forever."

"Brett—" Mrs. Jacoby called as he ran down the hall and slammed into his bedroom. "I'll go get him."

Donovan stood. "No. Let me talk to him. It's me he's mad at."

"He doesn't mean it, you know."

"I know." Donovan disappeared down the hall.

Meg understood perfectly how Brett felt. Hadn't she been angry—*furious*—about Cindy? In her pain, hadn't she wanted to strike out at everybody? "He'll get over it," Meg said in the awkward silence that remained in the room. "He'll feel sorry for being mean to Donovan and will want to see him as soon as possible, just to make sure his anger didn't harm Donovan in some way."

Mrs. Jacoby looked at Meg. "You're right. It's happened before. He cries and worries that his brother will get sicker. How did you know?"

Meg averted her eyes. "I'm a doctor's daughter, remember? I could call him later, after I check Donovan back in to the hospital, and let him know that all's well."

"You'd do that?"

"Sure. Brett feels left out, and that makes him feel worse because he knows Donovan's really sick and he can't make it go away."

"You're a smart and tenderhearted girl, Meg. I appreciate all you're doing. For both my sons."

Meg shrugged. She liked Mrs. Jacoby and Brett. And she liked Donovan too. Liked him more than she knew she should, given his circumstances. *He's going to beat the odds*, she told herself. The Network for Organ Sharing would find him a liver, and he'd have the transplant, recover, and be all right. He had to be.

Meg checked Donovan back in to the hospital that evening. "Don't forget to help find my mother a house," he said as he crawled into bed.

He looked awfully exhausted to Meg. "I won't," she promised. She drove home and went to bed, but couldn't fall asleep. She was still tossing when she heard the phone ring at two A.M. She realized it would be for her father, and felt a vague sense of foreboding she couldn't explain. When she heard his footsteps in the hall, she got out of bed and met him at the top of the stairs.

"I'm sorry if the phone woke you," he said, startled by her appearance. "Go back to bed."

Something in the way he averted his eyes made her ask, "What's wrong? Is there something wrong with someone I know? With Donovan?"

Her father looked at her fully, hesitated, then said, "That was a call from a hospital in Bethesda, Maryland. I'm driving over there now because they have an accident victim on the verge of brain death, and his blood type is the same as Donovan's."

Eleven

"Are you saying they've found a donor for Donovan?" Meg's heart began to race in anticipation.

"Don't jump to that conclusion. All I know is that the victim meets several criteria that *could* make him a match. I'm going over there to be available for organ retrieval, just in case."

"I want to come with you." The words jumped from Meg's throat.

"Meg, that's not necessary. The family hasn't even been approached about donating yet, and there would be nothing for you to do but hang around the waiting room."

She caught his arm. "Please, Dad, let me come along. I-I've never asked for anything like this before. Don't say no. It's really important to me."

Her father studied her intently, as if weighing

his medical professionalism and his role as her father. "I need to leave now."

"Five minutes," she pleaded. "I can be dressed to go in five minutes." Her heart hammered as she waited for his reply.

"All right," he said, jangling the keys in his pocket. "I'll leave your mother a note. Meet me in the garage."

Meg spun, ran to her room, tugged on clothes, grabbed her purse, and raced down the stairs. They rode in silence along the Beltway through sparse traffic, toward the Maryland exit. She watched her father pick up his car phone and call Memorial. "I want you to prep Donovan Jacoby for surgery," she heard him tell an assistant on his transplant team. "Start him on the donor protocol, and I'll let you know as soon as possible if I'm able to retrieve."

"Will Donovan know he may get the transplant tonight?" she asked when her father hung up the receiver.

"He'll know. We'll do blood work, an EKG, and X rays. Then we'll start him on antibiotics and antirejection drugs right away."

"What if he doesn't get the organ?"

"We have to prepare as if he will. We have to lower his risk for postoperative infection and give him a head start on organ acceptance. As for the other—well, the specter of disappointment, of not getting the new organ, is something all potential transplant recipients have to learn to live with."

Meg watched the lampposts flash past the car window as her father sped along the expressway. She felt events were hurtling by just as fast. She pictured Donovan's face as he heard that he might get his new liver. She knew how he longed for the waiting to be over. "I hope this is it for him."

"I hope so too."

At the Bethesda hospital, Meg followed her father up stairwells and through a maze of long corridors. He paused in front of a set of double doors marked "Personnel Only Beyond This Point." He glanced about. "There'll be a waiting room nearby. Go there and wait for me while I check with the trauma team. The patient's on life support, but I want to make sure he's being well oxygenated."

Meg found her way to a cubbyhole of a room, where six people were gathered together in a small huddle. Their grief hit her like a wall the moment she walked inside the room. She wanted to back out slowly, but realized they had taken no notice of her, so she slunk to a chair. Her palms felt clammy and her mouth dry. She fumbled in her purse for a mint.

"We can't lose him," Meg heard a woman sob.

"They're doing all they can, Peggy. We just have to wait," the man beside her said.

Meg sucked in her breath. This had to be the potential donor's family. Meg lowered her gaze, trying to make herself as small and as inconspicuous as possible, wishing she'd chosen any room but this one to wait for her father.

"He's still alive," another woman said. "The police said he was alive when the ambulance left the accident."

Meg experienced a wave of horror. The person they were talking about wasn't alive. She'd heard her father mention brain death on his car phone. She felt guilty withholding the information, but knew there was nothing she could do or say.

"Remember when Blake was little?" the woman asked. "Remember how he'd drive his trike to the end of the driveway for hours on end? Then, when he got his driver's license, he was happy. So full of life."

"Don't do this to yourself, Mama," a young woman said.

"Do I remember? How could I not remember? He was my baby." She broke into quiet sobs, and the man beside her put his arms around her.

Meg felt desperately sorry for them. Death meant going away forever. It meant leaving families and friends behind. It meant leaving a hole in time and space that only that one special person could fill up. She understood that part— understood it very well. She began to grow queasy.

Two men and a woman entered the waiting room. Meg could tell at a glance that they were medical personnel. "Dr. Burnside!" the woman cried. "How's Blake? How's my son?"

The doctor took her hands and pulled her to

her feet. "Peggy, I want you and your family to come into the conference room with me. I want my colleagues to talk to all of you." He nodded toward the other man and the woman.

"Are they surgeons? Does my Blake need some special kind of operation? Whatever he needs, doctor, do it."

"Come, let's go where there's more privacy." Dr. Burnside's gaze flicked over Meg.

Her cheeks burned, and she stared stonily into space. Once they all left the room, Meg released her breath, startled that she'd been holding it all this time. The room seemed too quiet, and she wished her father would come. Maybe she should have stayed home after all. She had no idea how long the operation to remove the boy's—she couldn't bring herself to say his name—organs would take. Not long, she figured. She knew how critical a factor time was in transplantation. *Just a little bit longer, Donovan*, she told herself. His wait was practically over.

Meg lost track of time, but when her father appeared at the doorway, she was surprised. Somehow, it didn't seem long enough for him to have completed his tasks. There was no liveliness about him either, no undercurrent of raw energy, as she often saw when he was facing a transplant surgery. "Are you finished?" she asked haltingly.

He came over and sat heavily in the chair beside her. For the first time, she noticed lines of fatigue around his eyes and mouth. "There isn't going to be any surgery," he said.

"There isn't? Why not?"

"The family refused to grant permission."

His words hit her like stones. "B-but they have to. Don't they know Donovan's dying?"

Her father took her hand. "Honey, they don't know Donovan. All they know is their eighteen-year-old son is dead."

"Didn't you try to change their minds? Didn't you tell them how important it was?"

"Organ donation is voluntary, Meg. People can't be forced."

She felt panic well up inside her. "So, what will they do with him? Just shove him into the ground? Just let his organs go to waste when they could be put into someone else and help him live longer?"

"You can't think about it that way. You have to understand and respect their feelings."

"Well, I don't!" Meg tore her hand from her father's and stood. Her legs felt rubbery, but she began to pace. "It's not fair. Why wouldn't they? Why wouldn't they say yes?"

"People have a hundred reasons." He shook his head. "They're afraid of disfiguring their loved one—which we don't. They feel it's freakish to transfer body parts from one person to another. Too many Frankenstein movies," he added. "Whatever their reasons, we can't intervene. We can't ever force anyone to agree to donation. It's a tough thing to even broach with grieving relatives. I told you that once before."

She remembered, recalling her own feelings

about transplantation. Hadn't she herself once been turned off to the whole idea? Yet, now that she knew Donovan, her feelings had completely changed. "So, why do you even bother to ask at all? Why get somebody's hopes up for nothing?"

"First of all, we ask because it's the law. We *have* to ask. Second, because there are many people who realize that this is the ultimate gift to others and an opportunity to do something good and kind. This is a way for their loved one to continue living."

"But not these people," Meg said. "These people don't care about others at all."

Her father came quickly alongside her. He took her arms and turned her to face him. "Don't ever say that, Meg. These people just had their son die, and they are inconsolable."

Meg began to tremble, understanding exactly what inconsolable felt like. It was a deep, black hole. A bottomless well of tears and anguish. A place without sunlight or even air. Her lip began to quiver. "I don't want Donovan to die, Daddy."

Her father drew her into his arms. "I'm doing all I can, Meg. There'll be another donor for him. You have to believe that."

She nodded, forcing down the tears that were trying to burst free. "I thought this was it for him. I thought his waiting was over."

He looked down into her face with troubled eyes. "Meg, medicine is a strange business. It's life and death. Sometimes it's making choices that no one but God should have to make. I know what you're feeling because I've felt that way myself. I want to tell you something, and I want you to listen closely."

"I'm listening."

"The only way to treat patients and not go crazy is to distance yourself from them. You can't allow yourself to become so personally involved that you lose your professional perspective. Do you understand what I'm telling you?"

"Yes. You think I'm overreacting."

"No, your concern is all too human. But you can't become too personally involved in any one case or in any one patient's life. It's the first rule of the doctor-patient relationship."

She took a deep breath, forcing down a retort. She wasn't a doctor. Nor did she ever want to be. Medicine was her father's world, and she was sorry she'd gotten mixed up in it at all. "Don't you ever get involved, Dad? Doesn't someone ever become special to you?"

He shrugged and glanced away. "It's a fine line to walk. I have to watch myself. My patients are just that—patients. No matter how hard I try, I can't save them all."

She tried to apply brakes to her runaway emotions. She took a deep breath and attempted to distance herself from the drama she had just witnessed. "I'm all right now," she said. "I-I'm sorry I got so angry."

"It's understandable." He ran his hand through his hair. "Now, I've got the tough job of telling Donovan."

"Will you tell him now?"

"I'll take you home first, then go check on him. My transplant team knows there won't be any surgery. Donovan will be fairly groggy for the next couple of days, but sooner or later, he'll figure out he didn't have the transplant. You're right about one thing—he's going to be a very disappointed young man."

Her heart squeezed as renewed concern for Donovan swept through her. She was going to have to face his disappointment also. Meg took a deep breath and followed her father out into the hall. If professional distance was one of her father's rules, she knew she was in trouble. She'd already broken it and could figure no way to turn the situation around.

Twelve

❧

"YOU'RE DRAGGING AROUND today, Meg. Did you have a hot date last night?" Alana asked.

Meg shook her head in response and sipped a soda, hoping the cola would revive her sagging energies. The lunch crowd in the hospital cafeteria seemed especially loud to her. "I wish it had been a hot date. No, I'm afraid last night was a real downer for me." Quickly, she recounted her and her father's false alarm run to Bethesda for Donovan. "I didn't get to bed until four A.M. and then I couldn't go to sleep. I feel like a zombie today. Sorry if I'm not carrying my share of the work on the floor."

"Forget it. I'm just sorry the donor didn't work out for Donovan. Have you been by to see him this morning?"

"Not yet. Frankly, I'm not looking forward to talking to him. I know how depressed he's going to be, and I feel so helpless. I don't know what to say to him. I mean, how do you go about consoling someone because he didn't get a transplant? Someone who's still living on borrowed time?"

Alana's expression was sympathetic. "You know I understand because of my brother's situation. I wish I could help people understand that."

"I wish I could help the whole *world* understand it," Meg countered. "The truth is, unless it happens to someone you care about, it isn't important to you."

Alana started stacking the empty plates from Meg's lunch tray onto her own. "You've got some free time. Why don't you go see Donovan now?"

"He's still in ICU and won't be brought back to his room until tomorrow. Maybe by tomorrow, I'll feel better myself. I don't want to make him even more depressed."

"He doesn't have to know about your going to the other hospital with your father. And all you have to do is hold his hand and listen to him. Don't feel you have to be responsible for making him cheerful. Sometimes, it's okay to let a person work through his anger by himself."

Meg thought Alana sounded very wise. "The voice of experience?" she asked.

Alana nodded. "Sometimes all I could do for my brother was listen. He needed to get it out, and I was the one person in our family who let him say anything he felt like saying." She smiled impishly. "And sometimes that boy had some pretty shocking things to say. I didn't know he knew such words."

Meg felt a flood of gratitude toward her friend. Maybe it would be best not to tell Donovan how upset she'd gotten over the family's refusal to donate their dead son's organs. "I'll remember what you said." She touched Alana's arm. "And thanks for the advice."

Alana smiled. "Anytime."

Two days later, Meg could visit with Donovan. Even after he was brought down from ICU, he was still incoherent. Meg spent time with Mrs. Jacoby during one of her visits to the hospital. They met in one of the pediatric playrooms, where Brett, well out of earshot, was building a spaceship with giant snap-together blocks.

"The night the hospital called me, I almost went delirious with joy," Donovan's mother told Meg, sighing. "I thought it was finally happening for him. I bundled up Brett and took a cab to the hospital. The two of us waited and waited. Brett fell asleep—thank heaven—but I couldn't think about anything except Donovan's surgery."

"And then there was no surgery," Meg commented. "You must have really felt cheated when you found out."

"I felt both disappointed and relieved at the same time."

"I don't understand."

"Disappointed for the obvious reasons. Relieved because the unknowns are so scary for me.

I mean, once he has the transplant, he has a long road of recovery ahead. Also, once it's done, there's no turning back. If his new liver rejects, or if something goes wrong, Donovan will certainly die. I know I shouldn't borrow trouble, but that fear always lurks in the back of my mind."

Meg swallowed her own taste of fear. "I guess you're right. Even though he's sick, even though his own liver's failing, at least he's alive."

Mrs. Jacoby patted Meg's hand. "I shouldn't dump my doubts and fears on you. Forgive me. There are people here at the hospital—psychologists—I should be talking to."

"I don't mind," Meg said quickly.

"No, it's not fair to you. My only excuse is that you're so genuinely concerned about my son."

"I am, Mrs. Jacoby. I care about him so much." Meg felt her cheeks redden after her impassioned words. Donovan's mother must think she sounded like a moonstruck child.

Mrs. Jacoby smiled with understanding. "He had a girlfriend back home. I wish she'd been half as caring and sensitive as you. I'm afraid she really hurt him."

"It was *her* loss," Meg said, realizing she wasn't Donovan's girlfriend in the sense Mrs. Jacoby meant. Still, she truly cared about him.

"I agree. Have you heard anything more about building that special house where parents can stay and be near their kids while they're being treated here at Memorial?" Donovan's mother changed the subject. "Believe me, I sure wished for one the other night. I think that cab ride back to the apartment after I learned there would be no transplant was the longest ride I've ever taken. All I wanted to do was tuck Brett in and curl up and go to sleep myself, but I couldn't. We had to traipse all the way back across town first."

Meg shook her head. "Sorry . . . I haven't heard anything yet."

"Oh, well . . . It is a big undertaking." She made a face. "Poor choice of words."

Undertaking. Meg caught the meaning. Undertaker. She shivered, even though the playroom was sunny and warm.

The next day, when Meg went to Donovan's room, he was sitting up in bed, flipping through TV channels. Seeing him upright and alert caused a rush of relief. "You must be better," she said, coming inside. "You're scanning the TV wasteland."

He flipped off the screen and held out his hand to her. "I'm better," he said. "Whatever that means."

She took his hand, noticing that his color looked strange—somewhere between yellow and pasty white. But his voice sounded strong and lucid once more. "It means that you'll be hanging around until another potential liver donor comes along," she said.

"I was pretty out of it, wasn't I?"

"Do you remember anything?"

"I remember being awakened in the middle of

the night by some nurse promising me a wild and crazy time."

Meg giggled. "She didn't lie, did she?"

"They put me on a gurney and wheeled me down to the operating room. They did a bunch of tests and forced a Krom's cocktail down me."

"What's that?"

"The most foul-tasting stuff ever invented by medical science. It's a decontaminant for your intestinal area, you know—to kill off all the nasty germs lurking inside the body. That way, once you have the transplant, your body has a better chance of accepting the new organ."

"Too bad it was for nothing," Meg said.

"Yeah . . . too bad. But, then, I never did have much good luck."

She braced herself against a wave of pity for him. She'd learned that patients don't want pity, they want understanding. "You've had some good luck. You met me," she quipped.

A smile softened Donovan's face, and in spite of his gauntness, she felt her pulse quicken. "Okay, so I'll give you that one."

"What else did they do to you?"

"They gave me a preop shot that sent me off to never-never land, so I was kind of spaced out. I remember my mom coming in to see me. Then I don't remember anything else for the next twenty-four hours. I just woke up in ICU. It took me a while to figure out that something had gone wrong with the transplant, because I knew I'd have big staples in my side from the operation and I didn't." He shook his head, as if clearing out the memory.

His grip had tightened on her hand. She wanted to say so many things to him, but recalled Alana's advice to simply listen. "I was disappointed in a *major* way," he said. "And mad. I was trapped in medical purgatory, and there was absolutely nothing I could do about it. There'd been no operation, and what was worse, I have to go through the whole thing all over again when they do find me a liver."

He glanced up at her, and his intense inner struggle with self-pity was written on his face. "Anyway, here I am. Still waiting."

"All of us felt bad for you," Meg said softly. "I talked to your mother, and now more than ever, I think we need that family guest house."

"Maybe so. But now more than ever, I think she needs a home of her own. How's your search coming along? Any prospects yet?"

Crossing her fingers and hoping he didn't see how she was hedging, she mumbled, "Not yet." In truth, she hadn't looked at all. So many things were going on that she'd not done a thing about her promise to him.

"I don't want this Wish Foundation money to go to waste," Donovan insisted. "If anything, this check from JWC is what's keeping me from going nuts."

"How do you mean?"

"Because I know it's there. Because I know it can buy my mom and Brett a future. It was all I thought about when my head started to clear in ICU. I kept telling myself to hang on so that I could get well enough to get out of this place and take my mother to the house I'm going to buy for her."

Meg swallowed guiltily. She was holding up his dream by not following through with her promise to find a realtor and go house hunting. "Well, you keep getting stronger, all right? I swear I'm going to find some houses for you to pick from."

"Just think, I don't have to recuperate from transplant surgery before I buy, do I? All I have to do is survive until the next time." He looked directly into Meg's eyes. "If there is a next time."

That evening, as Meg wearily let herself into her house, her mother hurried up to hug her. "I've been waiting for you to get home. Guess what, honey? The Junior League board has approved your project. We're going to work on raising money to build a home away from home for patients' families. Isn't that exciting?"

Thirteen

MEG SET DOWN her purse and car keys on the marble-topped table in the spacious foyer. "The project's been approved? That's great, Mom. We need the house so much." Meg kept thinking about Mrs. Jacoby and all the parents like her.

"I knew you'd be pleased. It was your brainchild." Her mother hooked her arm through Meg's. "We'll have a meeting Friday morning with an architect. He's a relative of Betty Hotchkiss's and is willing to donate his services. That's the key, you know—to get as much donated as possible. I think it would be nice if you could attend the meeting."

"I'll be working at the hospital."

"You're only a volunteer. You may have to reexamine your priorities now."

Meg didn't want to reexamine her priorities. She wanted to be around the hospital. Around Donovan. "People are counting on me up in pediatrics."

"This idea was yours, and your presentation to the Junior League board was so persuasive. I naturally assumed you'd want to be a big part of it. I'm proud of you, Meg. This is such a good idea, but it will require a lot of work. We can do it if we all pull together."

Meg had assumed that once the Junior League took it over, she wouldn't be involved. She remembered the ideas she and Alana had joked about regarding fund-raising. "I had thought about a fund-raising letter," she said tentatively.

"A letter! We'll do many of them. You know, a project of this scope needs the support of the entire community. We have to get everyone involved, from schoolchildren to high-level politicians. However, if you have an idea for such a letter, go ahead and work it up."

Meg felt a growing respect for her mother. All her life, Meg hadn't taken her mother's charity work seriously. Perhaps it was because she was always going off to some luncheon or party, hardly *work* to Meg's way of thinking, but now Meg saw how significant all her mother's contacts were. Without the help of important Washington people, the project would never materialize.

"You're needed at the planning stages also, Meg. Your ideas are important," her mother said.

My ideas? Meg thought. All she had been interested in was a place near the hospital where Mrs. Jacoby could stay close to Donovan.

Her mother continued, "We'll be having a brainstorming session Sunday afternoon. I've invited some of the hospital personnel, several community and business leaders, and some politicians. I'm certain we'll select a special board of directors from this group, since they'll be people with a vested interest in our project. Each one of them has a special link to Memorial—a few have lost someone they loved."

Meg thought of Cindy's parents. Too bad they lived so far away. "Will big foundations support us?" Meg was thinking about Donovan's Wish money and the "invisible" One Last Wish Foundation. Perhaps it could be flushed out into the open and asked for a major donation. Perhaps she could learn the identity of JWC, maybe even meet the person who had written Donovan's letter and been responsible for authorizing his check.

"There's lots of competition for charitable dollars, but we have a very valid project that will benefit the whole community. I don't see how foundations and corporations can refuse. They require a special touch, however. Fortunately, some of the people attending Sunday's meeting have experience in that area."

"And you want me to attend that meeting?"

"Absolutely."

"How about my friend Alana? Her brother had a transplant."

"Bring them both. Your father also thinks we should ask Mrs. Jacoby. She's got a son in need of a transplant. Who better to speak up about the project?"

"Mom, thanks for all your help." The words sounded inadequate.

Her mom smiled. "I think our family is extremely blessed, Meg. Your father, myself, our children. I truly believe that giving something back to show appreciation for our blessings is our duty. I know you've had a rough year, but it does my heart good to see you pulling out of it."

A rough year . . . you could say that, Meg thought. And yet, her mother was right. Whole days now passed by when she didn't think about Cindy. A momentary twinge left her feeling disloyal, then the feeling passed. She had others to think about now. She had Donovan, and she wanted to keep him. More than anything in the world, she wanted him to live.

"Two million dollars, Alana! Mom said the architect estimates that the house will cost close to two million dollars. How can we raise that much money?"

"It is a lot." Alana was sitting out on the hospital patio, licking an ice-cream cone. "More than in this girl's piggy bank."

"We'll be old ladies by the time this house gets built."

"At least out of high school."

"You're not taking this seriously."

"Yes, I am. I just know it won't help to get all worked up about that sum of money. You've got to think in bite-size pieces." She took another lick off her cone. "All we need is two million people to give one dollar. Or one million people to give two dollars apiece. Or four big corporations to give five hundred thousand dollars each. Two million doesn't seem so overwhelming when you think of it that way."

Meg opened her mouth to argue, but stopped. Alana's logic made sense. "The other thing Mom told me was that the architect was concerned about the site, the place to build the house."

"Do they have a site?"

"Right now, land's pretty scarce around the hospital. Most of it's already been bought by developers, and it really is expensive. There's a place here on the Memorial property, but it's been designated for a new parking lot."

Alana wrinkled her nose. "A house for parents is more important than a parking lot."

"We know it, but the hospital board has to approve the change. It'll go into a committee for study—I swear, this is going to take forever." Feeling glum, Meg slouched in her chair.

"But it *will* happen," Alana assured her. "It may seem like it's taking forever, but one day, you'll look out across the grounds," she gestured with her arm, "and you'll see this wonderful house full of parents with kids up on our floor. And you and I will say, 'We helped get this house off the ground.'"

"Okay. I won't get too discouraged this early in the project. Will you and Lonnie be at the meeting Sunday?"

"We'll be there. You want to go to the mall with me tomorrow? I need something new to wear if I'm going to be with all those important people."

Meg shook her head. "I can't. I've already made plans." She didn't explain, even though Alana was looking expectant. How could she tell her that she was going house shopping? Especially when it was Donovan's secret?

"May I help you?" asked the woman behind the front desk of the real estate office when Meg entered.

Nervously, Meg licked her lips and smiled. She had spent two hours trying to make herself appear older than sixteen. She had selected her finest designer clothing and accessories and donned her best gold jewelry. She was glad that her mother had taught her how to dress for a strong first impression. While she certainly felt more comfortable in jeans, she knew the best way to be believed was to appear believable. "I have an appointment with Ms. George."

The receptionist buzzed an inner office, and soon a tall woman with blond hair came out to greet Meg. If she was surprised by Meg's youth, she didn't show it. Stepping into Ms. George's office, Meg took a seat on a sofa.

"I'm positive I can find you just the right home, Miss Charnell. After our phone discussion, I've chosen several houses I think you will find satis-factory," Ms. George said.

Meg cleared her throat. "As I told you, I'm doing this for a friend. He trusts my judgment for the preliminaries, but he'll be making the final choice."

"Don't think a thing about it. I understand completely. I've done many real estate transac-tions via third parties. Just last month, a wealthy foreign businessman sent his daughter to me. It seems that she'll be starting at Georgetown Uni-versity in the fall, and he wanted her to buy her-self a house near the campus rather than live in the dorms. It's not only a place for her to live, but an investment for him."

Meg returned the agent's cheerful smile. "You understand that my friend needs to be around the Memorial Hospital area."

"So you said." The agent frowned thoughtfully. "I must tell you that it won't be easy. That area rarely has houses on the market." She brightened. "But I have many alternatives to show you. Lovely homes that are only minutes from Memorial via the Beltway."

"Let's take a look," Meg said. "My friend wanted to get this house business settled as quickly as possible." She didn't add her deepest concern: *"Because he might not have too much longer to live."*

They spent several hours looking at prospective homes. Meg liked some, yet found only two she wanted to show to Donovan, and they weren't perfect. Frankly, she thought the residences were too far from Memorial in spite of their proximity to bus routes.

When they arrived back at the real estate office, Ms. George told her, "Don't be discouraged. Finding the right home takes time. It's not like buying a dress you can take back if you don't like it."

Meg agreed. "Keep looking, please. And call me anytime you think you have something to show me."

"I shall. Your friend won't be disappointed. We'll find something that's just right for him."

Meg drove home, disappointed that she hadn't done better in her search. She was feeling the pressure of time more acutely than ever. Donovan was stable at the moment, but she knew that could change in the blink of an eye. She gripped the wheel and prayed his health would hold until his dream was accomplished to buy his mother a home with his One Last Wish money.

Fourteen

❧

"How can I help?" Donovan asked once Meg explained her idea to him.

"As soon as Alana gets here, I want the three of us to work on a fund-raising letter together."

"What kind of a letter?"

"It was an idea I had when I heard all those people sharing ideas at Sunday's meeting. Everyone agrees that we need some letters to get public support. Did I tell you that several of the TV stations are carrying the story on their six o'clock news shows throughout the week?"

"My mom told me. She's pretty excited about the project. It's all she talked about when she visited me last night."

"So about the letter . . . I thought, 'Why not do

a letter from an actual patient? Someone who knows about the problem firsthand?' "

"You mean me?"

"Of course, I mean you. I had this idea because I saw how difficult it was on your mother and Brett having to be so far away from you."

"You mean something like JWC's letter?"

"Something like it, only different." Meg admitted that the One Last Wish letter and its personalized, informal feeling had impressed her. Surely, they could do something similar, except using it to ask for money instead of giving away money.

"It's a good idea, but I'm not much of a letter writer," Donovan said.

"That's why Alana and I are volunteering to help. If the three of us write one terrific letter, the board will have no choice but to use it. It'll be our contribution."

"Sounds all right to me. Who will you mail it to?"

"The new board for the project has a big mailing list of people who've been patients at Memorial, or who are known to give contributions to worthy causes—especially medical ones. This whole project is going to take off like a rocket."

"You really think the place is going to get built?"

"I do. First of all, we're naming it the Wayfarer Inn, a home away from home. Do you like it?"

"It sounds like a hotel."

"Oh, it'll be more than a hotel. It'll have ten to twelve bedrooms, a central kitchen, a playroom, a

TV room, a game room, laundry facilities, a library—" She paused to catch her breath. "And any family who has a child over here in Memorial for long-term treatment, like an organ transplant, can stay at the inn for only five dollars a night."

"I'm impressed," Donovan said.

"You're impressed with what?" asked Alana, breezing through the doorway.

"I'm impressed with the plans for the Wayfarer Inn."

Alana pulled up a chair alongside Meg's and sat down. "I'm so excited about the whole thing that I was awake half the night. Lonnie has a great idea—a fund-raising marathon."

"It works for me," Donovan replied.

"And did Meg tell you our ideas for the schools next year?"

"I haven't had a chance yet."

"So, tell me."

Meg moved forward. "We'll get kids in the elementary schools to bring a penny a day for a whole month to plop in jars in each classroom. If every kid brings just a penny a day, we'll collect a fortune."

"We figure every kid can afford a penny," Alana inserted.

"For the middle schools, we'll have walkathons and bake sales. In the high schools, we'll have highway holdups."

"Never heard of them. Are they legal?" Donovan asked.

"Sure are," Alana said. "Certain kids get official

badges to stand at busy intersections and hold buckets for motorists to toss in their pocket change. Everytime the light changes, there's a new crop of cars and a new source of coins."

"What else?"

"Well, we don't want you to think Meg and I have *all* the good ideas," Alana said. "The others at the meeting had a few too. In two weeks, the Junior League is planning a Moonlight on the Potomac cruise."

Donovan rolled his eyes. "That sounds pretty romantic—you know, not like mud wrestling or bowling for charity."

"You got something against romance?" Alana chided.

"Romance with a purpose," Meg insisted, swatting his arm playfully. "We get all these rich people out on a riverboat on the Potomac River, feed them, let them dance, then put on a presentation for the Wayfarer Inn and ask each person how much he or she wants to give."

"Notice we said, *how much*, not *if* they want to give."

"Sort of a captive audience out there on the river," Donovan observed.

"Exactly. Either they give or they swim home."

They shared a laugh over Meg's reasoning.

"Will you two be going on the cruise?" Donovan asked.

"Sure," Alana said. "Someone has to keep a check on donations."

"Who are you going to take?" Donovan's question was for both of them, but his eyes were on Meg.

"She'd like to take you, boy, but she's too slow in asking."

Meg felt her face turn beet red, and she shot Alana a glance that could kill.

"Are you inviting me?" Donovan wanted to know.

Meg straightened. "I was planning on it, but in my own time." No one mentioned what was on all their minds: In two weeks, he could be too sick to go.

"I accept," Donovan said.

"You do?"

"He does," Alana replied, standing. She brushed her hands together, as if dusting them off. "That was an easy matchup. Now, I'd better get to it and find myself a date. First person I'm asking is Carl Douglas, one fine hunk of man."

"Now that we have your social life settled, how about that letter?" Meg hauled Alana back to her chair.

"I was getting to that." Alana sat down, and Meg passed her a pencil and paper. "How should we start?"

"Donovan, if you could tell people one thing about how you feel concerning the Wayfarer Inn, what would it be?"

Sobered, he contemplated Meg's question. When he spoke, the words came from deep inside him. "Waiting for an organ transplant is truly hard work. It's hard not to get discouraged. Even harder when you get psyched up to go through the surgery and have a possible donation fall through. But I have to say that the hardest part of this whole ordeal is not being able to have your family near you while you're waiting.

"I'm seventeen and thought I was beyond the stage of needing my family close by. But I'm not. Sometimes, when I feel so low, I think it would take a crane to boost me over a curb, I need the closeness of my mom and kid brother. It's not that the hospital people aren't good to me—they are. But sometimes, more than anything in the world, I want to hold my mother's hand."

Donovan's voice had grown thick with emotion. Meg felt a lump in her throat. She had thought she understood Donovan's situation, but she hadn't. Not truly. She realized that her simple ability to come and go as she pleased, to be with her parents in her home, was something that she'd taken for granted. Donovan had no home, and his family was not able to help much because there was no place nearby for them to stay.

"That was pretty real, Donovan," Alana said, her voice sounding whispery. "If we can put that kind of emotion into a letter, I know we'll raise a ton of money."

He glanced away, obviously self-conscious. "It's common for little kids to want their mommies," he said. "I thought it might be more effective if people understood that big kids need theirs too." He offered a sheepish smile. "So, that was from the bottom of my heart. Now, on the lighter side, you can say that another reason for building the inn is to have access to a kitchen where my mom can bake up a batch of her special chocolate chip cookies. This hospital food gets boring."

"That request alone should bring in plenty of contributions," Meg joked.

"I already want to donate to the cause," Alana added. "Anyone who can bake chocolate chip cookies deserves a place to do it."

They worked for another hour, each making suggestions, but allowing Donovan to put his unique perspective into the letter above all else. When they were finished, Meg felt satisfied with the results. "I'll show this to Mom and Dad and see what they think," she said. "If they like it, we can get it out soon."

"I hope it helps," Donovan said.

"I know it will, because it came from your heart."

"That's true," he said. "Straight from my heart."

Once Alana had gone, Donovan took Meg's hand and sank back onto his pillow. He looked tired. "I appreciate all you're doing for me," he told her.

"It's for every kid stuck in long-term hospitalization," she said, but knew that he sensed the truth—it was mostly for him she was doing it.

"I'm going to do everything I can to stay well so that I can go on that cruise with you."

"You'd better. I'm counting on you."

"Unless a new liver comes along, that is."

"It's the only excuse I'll accept," she said. Then, on impulse, Meg bent, quickly kissed his cheek, and bolted from the room.

Fifteen

"Meg, this is wonderful." Her mother put down the rough draft of Donovan's letter and wiped moisture from the corner of her eye. "It's so sensitive and heartfelt. I think you've done an excellent job. I'll present it to the board, and maybe we can get it mailed out before the cruise. I know it'll raise some money for our cause."

Her father took the letter and read it as he ate. They were having one of their rare dinners together, and Meg was actually appreciating their time with one another. "This is good," her father said. "I told you Donovan was a special kid."

"I'd like to take him on the cruise if you'll give him a pass from the hospital again," Meg said.

"To be honest, I'm planning on releasing him from Memorial."

"Is he well enough?"

"He's well enough to wait around his apartment as easily as at the hospital. Medically, Dr. Rosenthal has done all he can for him. Now, it's up to me and my team to find him a new liver. It's still his only recourse."

Meg felt nervous about having Donovan so far away from the hospital—and from her. "But what if you find a donor? Or what if he gets sick? His mother works all day—"

"He'll be on a beeper," her father interrupted gently. "If we get a compatible donor, he can be brought here by ambulance in no time at all. Same thing if he starts feeling bad. Calling for an ambulance is a decision he can make for himself if he gets sick and he's alone."

Meg was certain that Mrs. Jacoby wouldn't like leaving him alone day after day. "It just seems that he's safer in the hospital," she said.

"He's stable now, and there's nothing we can do for him at Memorial for the time being. Frankly, we need the beds for sicker patients." How sick did a person have to be? Meg wondered. Needing a new liver seemed to qualify in her mind. Her father reached over and squeezed her shoulder. "It'll be all right, Megan. It will be good for his morale to get out of the hospital for a while. I know what I'm doing."

Her father was right about the morale part. When she saw Donovan the next day, he was all smiles. "I'm blowing this place," he said. "Mom's coming to help me pack tonight after she gets off work."

"I'll drive you home."

"She was going to get us a cab."

"Why spend the money when I know the way?"

"You don't mind?"

"Of course not. Meg's Taxi, at your service."

"You'll come visit me?"

"Every chance I get." She watched him shuffle over to the dresser and remove clothing from the drawer. She realized how much she was going to miss stopping by his room every day. She told herself that this was good for him, but it was herself she was thinking about. "I'll call you during my breaks."

"I'd like that."

"And I can drive over this weekend."

"Mom'll fix us dinner."

"And in two weeks, we have the cruise."

"Don't worry. I'll be going." He came over to her and placed his hands on her shoulders. "Look, I'm scared about leaving Memorial too."

"I hope I'm not making you feel that way."

"You're not. According to Dr. Rosenthal, it's natural for me to be uneasy. As long as I'm here, I can ring for a nurse if I need anything. I know when I stay at home, I'll have to be on my own. Even though I'll have my medications and the phone close by, it's still scary. But I'd rather be scared than stuck here another day." He grinned down at her. "Besides, you should have heard Brett's voice when I told him on the phone I was coming home. He's planning some big surprise for me."

"I'll bet." She knew how much Brett had missed him. She was beginning to miss her sister, Tracy. Meg guessed that separation did make people long for each other. "Just stay well," she told Donovan.

"I'll do my best," he said. "Maybe next week, I can go see some of those houses you were telling me about."

"Maybe," Meg answered, wishing she had more choices to show him. "The agent's still working on it."

"Then, things are looking pretty bright, don't you think? We're helping to get contributions for the Wayfarer Inn, I'm shopping for a house for my mom—thanks to JWC—I'm getting out of Hotel Memorial, and I'll soon be going on a moonlight cruise with a pretty girl. Things don't look too bad at all to me."

Except for your health, Meg thought. She longed to share his enthusiasm, but she'd been with her father on that late-night run to Bethesda. She'd never told Donovan about it. But she had seen with her own eyes how quickly joy could turn into mourning.

"I didn't exaggerate one bit, did I? Isn't this place perfect?" Ms. George ushered Meg and Donovan through the front doorway of the old house. Her heels clicked across the hardwood floors, sending echoes off the walls. "I couldn't believe anything would actually become available in this neighborhood. As I told you on the phone, the elderly woman who owned it recently died in a nursing home. She had no relatives and left no will. She'd taken out a mortgage to help pay her nursing home bills, and when she died, the bank put the house up for sale."

Ms. George waved her hand. "I don't mean to rattle on about it, but when my friend at the bank called and told me about this house, I thought it sounded just perfect for you."

Meg glanced about the house with dismay. It looked run-down and smelled musty, of rooms too long closed up against fresh air and sunlight. "It's really old," she observed, filling in the silence.

"It was built in the 1890s. I know it needs work," Ms. George said hastily. "That's a big reason why the bank is selling it below market value. But its structure is sound, and you won't find craftsmanship like this anymore. Wallpaper, new paint, new appliances will fix the place up like new. I'm telling you, it's a real bargain."

Meg glanced at Donovan, who was taking his time touring the Victorian-era room. He stopped in front of the fireplace and ran his hand over the mantel. "This has been hand-carved," he said.

"There's another fireplace upstairs. Five bedrooms too." Ms. George chuckled. "I know that's far more space than you said you needed, but I figured I owed you right of first refusal on it."

Meg and Donovan exchanged glances. She

wished she could read his mind. Was he as disappointed in this house, as he'd been in the others she'd selected for him to see?

"The thing I thought you'd appreciate most was its proximity to Memorial Hospital," Ms. George continued. She turned toward the open front door with its beveled, stained-glass insets. "Only two blocks away."

"You said it's on a double lot?" Donovan asked.

"Yes, indeed." Ms. George fairly beamed. "Come through the kitchen."

Meg tagged behind the agent and Donovan through a swinging door. The kitchen looked bleak and cramped, in need of renovation. Ms. George led them out onto a back porch and pointed toward the backyard. "The bank hired a crew to mow and clear out the overgrowth, but see how generous the yard is?"

Meg saw that it sloped downward and a huge oak tree loomed in the back corner like a giant sentry. "Brett would have fun playing back there," she said, trying to sound upbeat.

"My mom loves Victorian houses," Donovan said. "She's always buying magazines about them. She wants a garden and lots of wildflowers on her lawn every spring."

"Come see the upstairs," Ms. George urged. "The staircase is solid cherry, and the newel post has a carved figurine—very unusual. There's a stained-glass window set over the stairwell too. It's a true antique."

As they climbed the stairs, the late-afternoon

sun slanted through the old window and peppered Donovan's shoulders and head with shades of red, yellow, and purple, making him look as if he'd stepped out of the past, from a time and place Meg had only read about. As they passed from room to room, Meg could see the beauty of the house beneath layers of grime and dust. Wainscoting, vaulted stenciled ceilings, rich old woods needing little more than lemon oil and buffing to make them gleam, caught her eye. "It is pretty," she whispered to Donovan as they circled the master bedroom.

"Our house in Virginia was an imitation of this," he said. "This is the real thing."

"Brett would be sliding down the banister every day."

"And I could have two rooms for myself. One to sleep in, one for my stereo gear." He walked around, touching the walls. "Mom could have an office of her very own, where she could help with the fund-raising effort for the Wayfarer Inn."

Meg thought that was a strong feature too. Mrs. Jacoby had become quite involved with the work of raising money for the inn. "Do you think you should look at some others?" Meg asked.

"No, this is the house I want for my mom," Donovan said, facing Ms. George. "How do I go about buying it?"

"I can have the paperwork started tomorrow. All I need is a down payment."

"I can write you a check right now. Tell me what else I have to do."

Meg was amazed that he'd made his decision so quickly. It was true that the house was in a perfect location, but she wanted it to be newer and more modern. While Donovan and the realtor discussed details, she formulated a plan to help spruce up the place. As she was driving him back to his apartment, she said, "We can paint it and clean it up. I know Alana will help if I ask her. There are others too up in pediatrics who will pitch in." She thought of all the nurses and technicians who cared about Donovan.

"I'd appreciate all the help I can get. I can do some of the work, but I know I can't do much. I don't have much energy these days."

Meg's heart constricted with his words. She wanted him to be well and healthy. "We can do it," she said cheerfully.

"I want my mom to see it at its best," he said. "But we can't take too much time fixing it up. I don't mean to sound ungrateful, but I have to think about getting it done quickly." He cut his eyes sideways. "Time is my enemy," he said softly.

Meg gripped the wheel, knowing what he said was true. "We'll get it done," she promised. If JWC could supply the money for fulfilling Donovan's dream, then the least she could do was help him present his dream in the best possible condition.

"It's a beautiful house, Meg and it's mine." He touched her hair, gently tucking it behind her ear. "All mine."

Sixteen

THUNDER RATTLED THE windows of the old house, and rain pelted the glass panes. "This is some storm," Alana exclaimed as she climbed down from a ladder with a bucket of paint. "I'm sure glad we're on the inside looking out."

Meg paused as she scraped peeling paint off of plaster walls. "Maybe we should take a break." The empty room amplified the sound of the pounding rain, making it difficult to hear the portable radio plugged in to the wall. She turned toward Donovan. He was sitting on a beanbag chair in the center of the room, watching them work. "Up for a snack?" Meg asked. "I've brought food in an ice chest I stashed in the kitchen."

"I'm okay," he insisted with a wave of his hand. "But you deserve a break."

"Thanks for the permission," Meg joked. She knew it was hard for him to sit and watch, even though it was all he had the strength to do. Meg had organized a crew, and over the past week, they had painted almost every room. Most of the day's volunteers had left before the heavy rain had started. Now the only ones left were Donovan; Alana; her boyfriend, Clark; Alana's brother, Lonnie; and Meg.

From upstairs, Meg heard the rumble of the floor polisher Lonnie was using. She hoped Lonnie's robust health encouraged Donovan. To look at Alana's well-muscled, broad-shouldered brother, it was difficult to believe he'd been in complete kidney failure. Surely, Donovan would rally physically in a similar way once he had his transplant, Meg told herself.

"I'll get the food," Clark said, taking the paint bucket from Alana. "Let's have an indoor picnic."

"Who cares if it's raining," Donovan said.

"No ants," Meg added.

Clark pushed aside the door separating the front room from the kitchen. "I'll help," Alana volunteered, tagging after him.

"It's not that heavy," Meg called.

"There's help, and there's help," Alana replied. "I'm thinking I should help with a kiss or two!"

"I understand." Meg laughed. She sat cross-legged on the floor beside Donovan and glanced about the partially painted room. "How's it look, boss?"

"You have paint chips stuck in your hair." Smiling, he picked off several. "And on your nose, your cheeks, your neck."

"I promise to get them all off before the cruise Saturday night. You are still coming, aren't you?"

"I rented a tux. Clark took me to the mall."

"That was nice of him."

"He's nice, that's true. And he and Alana really like each other."

His comment left Meg feeling uncomfortable. She wondered if he was remembering his former girlfriend and wishing he was with her. "They make a cute couple," Meg said.

"I'm looking forward to tomorrow night," he said.

"I found a great new dress," Meg told him.

"Just for me?" He grinned. "But then, I know how girls like to buy new clothes . . . any old excuse."

"Not 'just for you,' " she sniffed. "I needed something new." Ordinarily, she wouldn't have taken the time to go shopping. She'd tried on her best dress and discovered a lovely surprise—it was too large. When she'd gotten on the scale, she'd seen that she'd lost ten pounds since the beginning of the summer.

" 'Needed,' " he echoed with a lift of his eyebrows. "You mean the way Brett needs another laser water pistol?"

"What happened to the one you gave him?"

"He shot one too many girls at summer school, so it was confiscated."

"He's a cute kid. I really like him."

Donovan sighed and surveyed the room. "I hope he likes this place. I hope it helps make up for our having to leave our old house and for life's being so hard." He tipped his head and looked deeply into Meg's eyes. "I appreciate all you've done for me," Donovan said. "I know you've spent a lot of time on this."

"I don't mind." She hadn't realized how much work went into buying a house until she'd helped him spend his Wish money. She'd had the water and electricity turned on. She'd selected and lugged all the paint and supplies to the house. "I want your mother to like it. The realtor was right—it needed paint and cleaning up. It really is a great house."

"Keeping it a secret from my mom's been hard, but time's almost up, isn't it?"

"I figure we'll be finished next week."

"Good. I'll feel like I can rest easier after I give her the keys."

A loud clap of thunder shook the windows. The lights flickered and then went off altogether. From the kitchen, Alana gave a squeal. Overhead, the drone of the polisher stopped abruptly. "Uh-oh," Meg said. "Looks like we're alone in the dark."

"Scared of the dark?" Donovan asked.

"Not a bit. Unless this house is haunted."

"I'll bet it is haunted. Just think—a long time ago, some sweet young thing sat in this very room—and some guy—put the moves on her."

"Maybe guys weren't like that once upon a time."

"Don't bet on it." He chuckled.

She felt his hand cover hers in the dark. His nearness and the husky sound of his voice in her ear were causing her pulse to flutter. "I've read that back long ago, girls and guys were never without chaperons."

"If chaperons were needed, then that just proves my point."

"We don't have a chaperon."

"Do you wish we did?"

"Why would we need one?" Her heart beat faster as his hand covered hers in the dark.

"We don't, I guess. You know what I wish?" His breath against her forehead made goose bumps skitter across her skin.

"That the lights would come back on?" She tried to joke, but her heart was thudding hard against her rib cage. She wanted him to hold her.

"I wish you could have known me before I got sick. I wish we could have dated when I was well."

Meg considered his words, while the rain splattered on the windowpanes. She doubted he would have even noticed her; she was plain and, until very recently, plump. "If you hadn't been sick, we would have never met," she concluded softly. "Why else would you ever have come to Washington?"

He was silent, but his hand moved slowly up her arm, to her face, where his fingertips glided along her hair. "You're right. Funny how good things can come out of bad."

Meg's mouth went dry, and she felt lightheaded from his nearness. More than anything, she wanted him to kiss her. "Is that what I am? A good thing?"

"You're the *only* thing that makes this whole crazy experience worth anything at all."

Suddenly, a flash of lightning lit the room, and for an instant, Meg saw Donovan's face etched in eerie brightness. She wanted to grab hold of him. Wanted to keep him from joining any ghosts that might be hovering over the house.

"Alana and Clark to the rescue!" Alana's voice called from the kitchen. The beam of a flashlight cut through the darkness. "Guess what Clark found in his car?" She flicked the light over Meg and Donovan. "It looks like you two don't need rescuing."

Meg scrambled to her feet. "No problem," she said. Her hands were trembling. "We're fine. How about your brother?"

"Lonnie?" Alana called. "You all right up there?"

"Fine, sis. I'm just sitting here in the dark with my trusty machine waiting for the electricity to roll."

"You want Clark to come up with the flashlight and lead you down to us? It might be a long wait."

"That would be nice."

Alana handed the flashlight to Clark. He flipped the beam toward the staircase. "I think we should pack it in for the night. I'll bet the electricity will be off for quite a while."

"Suits me," Donovan said, rising. "I wouldn't mind hitting the bed early. It's been a long day, and I've got some cruise to go on tomorrow night. I don't want to miss it."

"We're almost through here. We can finish things up next week," Meg added, still quivery with emotion.

Later, when the rain had stopped, Clark and Lonnie loaded up the cars while Donovan waited in the front seat of Meg's car. Meg and Alana stood together on the front porch. The fury of the storm had left the night freshly washed and sweet-smelling. "Sorry I came into the room when I did. I didn't mean to interrupt anything. My timing stinks," Alana said.

"I don't know what you mean. Donovan and I were just waiting for the lights to come back on. Nothing was going on."

"Sure. And I'm the Queen of England."

"It's true."

"Why don't you just admit it, girl? You're crazy about that boy."

"Because I'm not—not in that way."

"Listen, you can deny it with your mouth, but not with your heart. The way you feel about him is stamped all over you."

"I don't want to talk about this."

"Denying it won't make it go away. I know what you're thinking. You're thinking that it's stupid to love somebody who might up and die on you."

"Stop it. That's not true." Yet, Meg knew it was true. She didn't want to be in love with Donovan.

"Friends don't fib to friends," Alana said. "Don't be so scared of what you're feeling. If he does die, you won't be able to tell him how you feel. Don't let this opportunity get away from you."

Meg kept thinking about the loss—so senseless—of her friend Cindy. It had made her empty and afraid when she'd learned that Cindy had died. She couldn't go through something like that again. Admitting to herself that she loved Donovan would reopen wounds that still weren't healed, even though she knew she felt better after therapy. Why hadn't she listened to her father when he'd told her not to get emotionally involved?

Because by the time he told me, it was too late. Meg answered her own question. "I know you think you're helping me," Meg told Alana. "But I know what I feel. It's concern. It's overinvolvement with a patient. It's more than I should be feeling. But it isn't love. And Donovan isn't going to die either. The hospital will find him a donor, and my father will save him. That's his job, you know. He's saved others, and he'll save Donovan too."

Alana shook her head slowly. "Your father's a wonderful doctor and a fine man, but don't put that on him. It's not fair. He's not God, and he can't perform miracles."

"Are you saying that you think Donovan's going to die?"

"Not me. I've seen a miracle happen with my own brother. All I'm saying to you is to go with what you're feeling toward him and don't waste the chance to have something special because you're afraid."

"I'm not afraid," Meg snapped.

"We're *all* afraid," Alana said.

Meg could think of nothing to say to blot out the searing honesty of Alana's words. She wrapped her arms around herself and shivered. The rain had cooled the night air, but she knew that her shiver had come from inside herself, and had nothing whatsoever to do with the temperature. Not a single thing.

Seventeen

MOONLIGHT CUT A wide swath across the peaceful, dark waters of the Potomac River. Standing on the deck of the huge riverboat, listening to the chug of the engine and watching moonbeams glitter on the water, Meg felt as if she'd been transported to another world. Behind her, from the ballroom, the music of an orchestra floated through the porthole.

"Having fun?" Donovan asked.

"The most. How about you?"

"I feel better tonight than I have in days. It's like I've been given a reprieve—you know, a delay in my sentence of sickness."

Alone with him in the moonlight, she felt as if his illness didn't exist. For just a little while, she could forget the real reason they were together on the boat. "I wish your mother had come," Meg said.

"I did everything to try and persuade her, but she didn't feel she belonged with these people. We're way out of this league financially. We're happy to get by, even though now the Wish money will help us. I've seen some people I recognize from newspapers and TV. I feel out of place myself."

"They're just people. And they all want to help build the Wayfarer Inn. We need them."

"I wonder if JWC is on this cruise. What do you think?"

Meg looked thoughtful. "I've seen the guest list, but no one with those initials stands out in my memory. Why does it matter?"

"Are you kidding? My mom will own a home because of JWC. I still can't get over being chosen to get all that money, so I'm really curious."

Meg straightened, feeling a slight prick of jealously because JWC had given Donovan something she could not. "No one I asked at the hospital ever heard of the One Last Wish Foundation," she said.

"I don't even know if JWC is a man or a woman."

"For that matter, you don't even know if that's the person's real initials. Maybe they're made up."

"But why?"

"Who knows?"

"Intimate strangers?" he offered.

She recalled their conversation—Donovan's ex-

planation about how strangers could become
linked by the intensity of a shared problem. She
had no illness to share with him, as JWC had.
"Maybe JWC only wants privacy. Rich people are
like that sometimes."

"But I keep asking myself, 'Why me?' I'm so ordinary."

He wasn't ordinary to Meg, but she didn't tell
him that. "If you ask me, I don't think JWC is
playing fair."

"What do you mean?"

"Remaining anonymous is a cop-out. I think
it's sort of cowardly to pass out money and then
hide in the shadows. What's it prove? I mean,
look at you. You'd like to say thank you, but how
can you? And if JWC has so much money, then
why not step forward and support our cause?"

Donovan shook his head slowly. "I don't know.
In a way, what you're saying makes sense. I would
like to meet the person who's been so good to
me, but JWC must have big reasons for staying
out of the spotlight. I'm not sure that if it were
me, I wouldn't choose to do the same thing."

"How so?"

Donovan thrust his hands into the pockets of
his tux and leaned against the ship's rail. "All
those people inside are rich, and everybody
knows it."

"That's one of the reasons they were invited."

"I know. They expect to be asked for charitable
donations. Maybe some of them get jollies out of
it because it makes them feel important. But

when you do something for someone and expect nothing in return, it makes you feel good inside. It makes you feel ..." he searched for a word, "fulfilled. Doing something nice for someone in secret has its own reward. Maybe JWC knows that too."

Meg remembered how nice Donovan was to everyone on the pediatric floor. Why, the first time she'd met him, he'd been racing a kid in a wheelchair in spite of being so sick himself. And she thought of how different she herself was. Hadn't she become a candy striper because her father had coerced her into it? Helping others hadn't been something she'd longed to do, as it was for Donovan, or Alana.

Hadn't she spent over six months in mourning for her loss of Cindy without much concern for Cindy's parents? Had she called them, written them recently? No, she had not. And how about her own parents? How worried they must have been about her when depression had all but taken over her life.

Losing Cindy hurt so much, she told herself. But at what point had Cindy's death become a crutch that she used for an excuse to insulate herself from friendships and relationships that might cause her hurt? *Intimate strangers.* Did she want to go through the rest of her life never making lasting friendships again because she was terrified of being hurt? Had Alana been right when she'd challenged her the night before?

She felt Donovan's nearness, like a comforting

embrace. She cared for him so much. How could she have not understood all of this before? How could a sick, possibly dying boy, and a stranger who donated money anonymously, have given her so much? Why had she become interested in the Wayfarer Inn in the first place? Of course, there was a need for one, but as long as she was being brutally honest with herself, she had to admit that it was also because she felt competitive with JWC and wanted Donovan to feel indebted to her the way he did to JWC.

"You sure got quiet all of a sudden, Meg. Did I say something to upset you?"

Donovan's question snapped Meg out of her soul-searching. Quickly, she looked up at him. His face was softened by moonlight, and she felt something stir deep inside. A sleeping part of her was awakening as if from a long drugged sleep. "No, Donovan. You said some things that made me think."

"I did? Like what?"

"Like friends. We are friends, aren't we?"

He straightened and took her by the shoulders. "Since you've asked, Megan Charnell, you're the best friend I've ever had."

A warm melting sensation went through her.

"Look at them, will you, Clark? The two of them stand under a perfectly gorgeous moon *talking*! I swear, I've never known two people who spend so much time flapping their lips."

Meg and Donovan turned in unison toward Alana and Clark, who had come up beside them.

Alana stood with her hands on her hips, a look of pure frustration on her face.

Donovan suppressed a smile. "And what have you two been doing?"

"Not talking, that's for sure," Alana said with a saucy flip of her head.

Donovan glanced at Clark. Clark shrugged, spun Alana around, and kissed her firmly. When he pulled away, he said, "It's the only way I can shut her up."

"Shut me up!" Alana squealed.

"See you guys," Clark called over his shoulder, and darted across the moonlit deck. Alana followed, promising dire repercussions.

Watching them flee, Meg felt a wave of sadness come over her. She didn't want to feel sad. No matter what happened tomorrow, what became of her and Donovan, now it was safe and lovely. She turned back toward Donovan. "Do you suppose it's okay for best friends to give each other a kiss?"

He put his arms around her and drew her close. "I think it's required," he said. "Only for the sake of making the friendship stronger."

She slid her arms around him. "And only because we're best friends," she whispered, lifting her mouth to his. "And only to get Alana off our case."

He ducked his head downward. "Absolutely. That Alana can be so testy." His lips brushed hers, soft as a summer breeze.

Eighteen

~∞~

"The final tally is in, and we raised a bundle on the cruise last Saturday night," Meg's mother said as she hung up the phone in the kitchen. "That was the treasurer of our board, and she's very pleased. This, coupled with the letter you helped write, is really going to get us off to a fantastic start."

On her way out, Meg paused to hear her mother's enthusiastic report. "I'm glad. I know I had a wonderful time on the cruise."

"We'll have other fund-raisers. Right now, we're discussing a possible charity softball game. Initial inquiries to several big-name stars have been encouraging." She eyed Meg, who stood jangling her car keys. "I thought you had the morning off."

"I do. I'm taking Donovan and his mother someplace."

"Oh." Meg's mother started clearing off the kitchen counter. "I was hoping we could do something together. Shopping, lunch—we haven't done that once this summer."

Momentarily surprised by the wistful tone in her mother's voice, Meg stepped closer to the counter. "I already promised them," she said. This was the day that Donovan had chosen to take his mom to the house and tell her about the Wish money and how he'd spent it. Meg felt an edge of excitement. People had worked hard to get it ready. She wanted to tell her mom what was going on, but thought it best to keep Donovan's secret for a little while longer. Besides, the news would bring a barrage of questions from her mother, and she didn't have time to answer them. "Maybe we can go shopping tomorrow after I get off work," Meg suggested.

"I'll look forward to it."

Meg came around the counter and kissed her mother's cheek, causing her mother to glance at her with surprise.

"I just felt like it." Ever since the night of the cruise, she'd felt an affection for her parents she'd not experienced in a long time, and she was determined to make up to them for the strain her personal problems had caused her family. Now more than ever, Meg appreciated how they'd stood by her over the past months since Cindy's death and her difficult adjustment to it.

"Well, thank you. Anytime you feel like it is fine with me." She reached out and touched Meg. "You're doing better, aren't you?"

"You mean about Cindy? Yes, I think the worst is over."

"I'm glad. I've missed having my daughter around."

Meg gave her a quick hug and hurried out the door.

By the time Meg stopped her car in front of the old Victorian house, her palms were damp with nervous perspiration. From the backseat, she heard Mrs. Jacoby ask, "Donovan, what *is* going on? The two of you have been acting strange all morning."

Meg and Donovan exchanged glances in the front seat. "Just a little surprise Meg and I cooked up for you." Meg couldn't help noticing how tired and thin Donovan looked. A slight yellow cast tinged his skin. This was a moment he had been looking forward to for weeks, and she didn't want anything to ruin it for him.

"Where are we anyway?" Mrs. Jacoby asked, peering out the window. "My, what a lovely old house."

Donovan went around to his mother's door and offered his hand. "Come on. I want to show you the inside."

"Do you have permission? Is the owner home?"

Meg walked with them up onto the porch, trying to see the house through Mrs. Jacoby's eyes.

The front door with its leaded-glass panels sparkled in the morning sunlight. She remembered polishing each pane.

Donovan put the key into the lock, turned it, and swung open the door. "Come on, Mom. Look around and tell me if you like it."

"Donovan, are you sure—"

He pulled her in. "I'm sure."

The smell of fresh paint and lemon oil hung in the air, and sunlight streamed through the freshly washed front windows. Echoes sounded when they walked across the floor to the fireplace, now clean and empty of old ashes. Donovan ran his hand over the ornately carved mantel. "What do you think?" he asked.

His mother's gaze darted everywhere. "I think it's the most beautiful house I've ever seen. Who owns it?"

Meg stepped back, lingering near the entrance. She wanted them to have this special moment, yet felt that she would burst if Donovan didn't tell his mom the truth right away.

He crossed to his mom and took both her hands in his. "I want you to know how much what you did means to me."

"What did I do?"

"You sold our house and moved us here just so I could be near Memorial and have the chance for a transplant."

She shook her head. "It was your best chance, and I never thought twice about it. You're my son, and I love you. It was much harder on Brett than on me, although I think even he's adjusted."

"Still, I know what our home meant to you."

"It was old and needed repairs." She was obviously flustered by his words.

"It was our home," Donovan insisted.

"Well, if you brought me here to show me how beautiful a house can be, you've succeeded. I think this one is exquisite."

"You haven't even seen the upstairs yet," Meg blurted out.

Mrs. Donovan turned to her and smiled. Her eyes narrowed. "What have you two cooked up?"

Meg gave Donovan a helpless shrug, and he held up the house keys, opened his mother's hand and settled them in her palm. "It's yours, Mom. This house is yours—ours really. It's a present."

Her bewildered expression turned skeptical. "Now, Donovan, you can't expect me to believe that someone *gave* us this house."

"Believe it. It's a long story, and I'm going to sit right here in the middle of the floor and tell you all about it, but first, look at this." He reached into his back pocket and pulled out a folded manila envelope. Meg knew that inside was the deed to the house.

As Mrs. Jacoby read the legal document, the expression on her face turned from doubt to shock to stunned disbelief. "But how—?" Her voice cracked.

Donovan said, "I bought it for you and Brett. I

want you to have a home again. To make up for the other one."

"But—"

He shook his head. "In a minute." He opened his arms. Meg watched as his mother slid into them. Sunlight washed over them, bright and golden like a soft embrace. Meg blinked back tears as she heard Mrs. Jacoby begin to weep softly in her son's arms. "I love you, Mom," he said. "I love you."

It took over an hour for Donovan and Meg to explain about the One Last Wish Foundation and for Mrs. Jacoby to begin to believe them. She had many questions, most of which neither of them could answer, but Donovan did have the original letter and a copy of the check that Meg had made on the hospital's copy machine. Those things and the deed to the house were the only proof they could offer. In the end, it was enough.

Mrs. Jacoby went over every inch of the house, exclaiming over details that had escaped Meg even though she'd helped paint the whole thing. The size of the house almost overwhelmed Mrs. Jacoby, but she made plans for each room. They might have stayed longer, but Donovan wasn't feeling well, so Meg drove them back to the apartment.

Mrs. Jacoby chattered nonstop all the way. "Maybe we can arrange to move next weekend. I'll give notice to the landlord. I can rent a trailer. Do you think some of the people who helped you fix the place up would help us move? I can't pay any-body, but I could make a big pot of chili ..."

Meg saw that Donovan was pleased, but also tired. He leaned back against the car seat on the long drive and closed his eyes. Meg let them off, promising to call later. "I have my own mother to tell," she told them. "Once she finds out I worked so hard on your house, she may put me to work on ours." She made a face that caused Mrs. Jacoby to laugh, and waved good-bye.

Once she returned home, she found her mother relaxing by the pool. "Back so soon?" her mom asked.

"Donovan wasn't feeling well, so we cut it short."

"Cut what short?"

Meg dragged a patio chair over and sat down and proceeded to tell her mother the whole story. When she finished, her mother stared at her in-credulously. "I can't believe it," she said.

"I'm sorry I couldn't mention the One Last Wish Foundation and the mysterious JWC before, but it was Donovan's money, and he asked me to keep it a secret until his mom got the house."

"Does your father know?"

"No, not even Daddy."

"And the two of you pulled this off all by your-selves?"

"Yes," Meg confessed. "Are you mad at me?"

"Mad? I'm impressed!" Her mother's face broke out in a generous smile.

"You are?"

"Your ingenuity is overwhelming."

"It is?"

"Meg, I think what you did is wonderful. I want you to start at the beginning and tell me the whole story all over again. Every detail—don't skip a thing. Then, I'm going to begin checking into this One Last Wish Foundation. I'd say they need to be approached for a *major* donation to the Wayfarer Inn."

Meg stared at her mother open-mouthed. "Why, that's exactly what I wanted to do!" she cried. "They should give to our cause."

Her mother smiled more broadly. "Like mother, like daughter," she quoted, then leaned forward, her eyes twinkling. "Scary, isn't it?"

They spent the afternoon talking and laughing as Meg told stories of her adventures as a candy striper. It was after six before her mother realized that they needed to start dinner. "Your father promised to be home tonight."

"Maybe we should go out to eat," Meg suggested. "Daddy hasn't taken the two of us out to eat in ages."

"Good idea. I think we should both dress and pounce on him the minute he comes in the door. I mean, how could he possibly refuse an invitation from two gorgeous women like us?"

The electronic ring of the phone interrupted Meg's reply. She tensed. Years of hearing the phone ring at dinnertime meant only one thing. Her father had an emergency and wouldn't be home for dinner. She tried not to feel resentful.

Her mother picked up the receiver. Her smile quickly faded as she spoke to Meg's father, and when she hung up, Meg braced herself for bad news.

"It's Donovan," her mother said. "He's just been brought into emergency, and he's unconscious."

Nineteen

❧

MEG FELT MISPLACED sitting in the familiar surroundings of Memorial. She wasn't a candy striper this time. She was a visitor. A watcher. One who waited for news about someone who was critically ill. She felt helpless.

Her mother sat in a corner with Mrs. Jacoby, holding her hand and consoling her. Brett was slumped in another chair, staring down at his lap; his legs dangled, still too short to touch the floor. The sight of him looking so small and lost in the ICU waiting room caused a lump to lodge in her throat. He looked over at her forlornly. "Donovan fell down on the floor," he said. "There was blood."

Meg slid over to sit next to the boy and put her arm around him. "I'm sorry, Brett. The doctors are trying to fix him up right now. Think about him getting better again."

"Is your daddy going to get him his new liver now?"

Sadness almost overwhelmed Meg. She knew that Donovan had been delegated a Status 9—the highest priority for transplantation—but she didn't know if the nationwide appeal for a liver had been answered. "I know my daddy's trying his very best," she told Donovan's sad little brother.

"The last time Donovan got real sick, Mommy told me that he might have to go to heaven. But he got better and got to come home. Will he have to go to heaven if your daddy can't find him a new liver?"

His questions, his innocence tore at her heart. Yet, his mother had discussed the possibility of Donovan's dying, so Meg figured that it would be cruel to gloss over the child's concerns. Still, she could hardly face the thought herself. "I-I don't know. Maybe." She turned her head and fought for control.

"He can have my liver," Brett said. "I never liked liver much anyway."

His cockeyed view of the situation brought Meg a brief smile. "Sorry, but one liver to a customer. You still need yours."

She heard someone rush into the room and looked up to see Alana, Clark, and Lonnie. They swiftly surrounded Meg and Brett. "Mrs. Vasquez called and told me. Oh, Meg, I'm so sorry."

"It stinks," Clark mumbled. "We just returned his tux on Monday. He didn't feel good, but I didn't think much about it. He never feels really good."

"I think he was holding on just so he could get the house finished," Meg said, realizing that was probably the truth. Any mention of being sick, and he would have been put back into the hospital immediately. "Turning over those keys to his mom was everything to him."

"Don't give up hope," Lonnie said. "I know what it's like to lie in a hospital bed and think life's over, then to get a reprieve. It can happen for Donovan too, if they only find him a donor."

Meg hung on to Lonnie's words as if they were a lifeline. *If they only find him a donor.* Suddenly, she wanted to see Donovan and touch him. Meg moistened her lips and stood. "Will you all wait here with Brett? I'll be back soon."

Clark eased into her vacated chair. "Hi, Brett, my man. I'm Clark, and I know your brother and we are pals."

Meg left the waiting room, went to the elevators, and punched the button that would take her to her dad's office. She had no reason to even hope that he was there, but she wanted him to be. She wanted to talk to him, wanted to hear straight from him how the search was going.

Because it was late, the halls were ghostly quiet. She walked swiftly down the long corridor and stopped in front of her dad's office door. She muttered a quick prayer, turned the knob, and stepped inside. "Daddy?" she said.

He swiveled the chair slowly to face her. "Hi, Meggie."

Again, she felt coldness clutch her heart. "Why aren't you down prepping for OR?"

"They just called me from the lab. Donovan's in kidney failure."

Meg's knees felt wobbly. She crouched in front of her father's chair and gazed up at him. "So, will you have to do a kidney transplant too?"

He didn't answer right away, but took a deep and shuddering breath. "There won't be any transplant. We've run out of time."

She heard the sharp intake of her own breath. "Is he—is he—?"

Her father shook his head. "Not yet. I was just sitting here figuring a way to go down and tell his family." He looked at her. "And you."

It dawned on her that her father was truly sad. What good was all the technology if it couldn't come through when it was needed? "Does Donovan know?"

"He's semiconscious, but I don't know if he's aware of what's happening. I don't think so. He'll go to sleep and slide from this world into the next. I can't stop him."

Meg had passed from acute pain into numbness. The pool of light from the lamp shone directly down on her father's hands, clasped in his lap. His fingers were long and tapered, spotlessly clean, smelling faintly of antiseptic soap. *Surgeon's hands. Hands that healed.* It was as if she were seeing them for the first time.

His hands were beautiful, and they had the power to transplant life from one human being into another. And yet, now, for all his knowledge, for all his ability and surgical skill, his hands could do nothing. He had the power to sustain life, but not to restore it.

She stared at her own hands too. Smaller than his, with a few stubborn flecks of paint embedded under her nails. She thought of Alana's hands, dark and nimble. She thought of all the hands that had reached out, that were still reaching out to Donovan and his family. Human hands, helping, healing, giving. Perhaps in the long run, that's what life was truly all about—helping one another.

Meg reached out and covered her father's hands with hers. "We broke the rules, didn't we, Daddy? We got too involved."

He nodded. "I'm afraid so, Meggie."

"Can I see him alone? Just for a minute while you go tell Brett and his mother?"

He answered by taking her hand and leading her out of his office.

ICU was quiet and dark except for the lonely vigil of beeping machines and glowing monitors. On the bed, Donovan twitched and tossed restlessly, as if struggling to remain in place. Tubes and wires protruded from every part of his body. Meg stared down at him, thinking, *He's tethered—*

these lines hold him to the bed. If they weren't in place, would he float away?

She felt detached, like an alien seeing something that made no sense in her world of health and wellness. Sickness she had seen, but death? Death wore a different face.

"Donovan, it's me, Meg. I-I want you to know I'm here with you." She had no way of knowing if he heard her, or even remembered her.

"Cold," he mumbled. "So cold."

His discomfort angered her, and she looked about for another blanket with which to cover him. There wasn't one. She could go to the nurses' station and ask for one, but she couldn't bear to leave him even for a minute. She had so little time as it was.

The curtain in front of the glass partition was pulled back, and she could see a nurse bent over a chart, dutifully filling it in. A glass wall and twenty yards separated them. It may as well have been a chasm. Meg couldn't catch her eye.

"Cold," Donovan mumbled through chattering teeth.

Making up her mind what to do, Meg reached over and jerked the curtain across the glass window, sealing herself and Donovan off from the main desk. Very carefully, she moved aside wires and tubes, and gently, she crawled into the bed beside him so that his back was resting against the front of her body.

She realized she was breaking all the rules, but it didn't matter. He needed her. With great care, she slipped her arms around him and held him close.

She willed the warmth of her body to seep into his, hoping he might somehow absorb a portion of her life into himself. She would gladly give a few of her years to him. "I'm here, Donovan," she whispered against his neck. "Right here."

His trembling seemed to stop, and after a few minutes, his body seemed more relaxed. She hugged him tighter, filling her arms with the weight of him, and her memory with his smile. Tears slipped down her cheeks.

With one hand, she stoked his hair. "When you get where you're going," she said into his ear, "please don't forget me. And once you're there, look for a friend of mine. Her name is Cindy, and you'll like her. Trust me."

She whispered his name like a prayer, "Oh, Donovan. Oh, Donovan. Oh, Donovan."

Twenty

~❦~

Meg stood at the top of the staircase and looked down at the whirlwind of activity below. Carpenters were hammering boards, putting the finishing touches on a sun deck and a doorway that had been added on to the old Victorian house. Painters and decorators hurried from room to room behind her, dragging bolts of cloths and cans of touch-up paint. She heard her mother's voice call out, "Hurry up! The reporters and TV people will be here in less than an hour."

"Where do you want this tray of hors d'oeuvres?" another voice yelled from the kitchen.

"Put it in the fridge, and don't forget to take the others out of the oven," Mrs. Jacoby answered. She was standing on a ladder, held steady by

Alana, and hanging a plaque above the mantel, next to an oversize rendering of the Wayfarer Inn.

Meg knew the inscription on the plaque by heart, for it had been a gift to Mrs. Jacoby from all the candy stripers who'd worked together the previous summer. It was dedicated to Donovan's memory. She still couldn't believe it had been eight months since he'd died. At the time, she didn't believe she'd ever get over it, but although she still missed him terribly, the sharp pain of loss gradually had turned into a dull ache over the months.

She was positive that her involvement in the renovation of the house had made the time pass more quickly. She remembered with perfect clarity the day Mrs. Jacoby had come to her and her mother and asked, "May I talk to you about something?"

Donovan's mother had looked pale and borne the marks of her grief. His final days in ICU had still been fresh. "It's about the house," Mrs. Jacoby had said once Meg's mother had served them tea by the pool.

"Is something wrong with it?" Meg had asked.

"I can't live there."

Meg had been dumfounded. "Why not? Donovan wanted you to have it. It meant so much to him."

"I can't live there knowing so many parents such as myself have no place to stay when their children are in Memorial waiting for transplants."

"We're working as fast as we can to raise funds

for the Wayfarer Inn," Meg's mother had said. "It's going well, but these things take time."

"That's just the point. So many of those kids don't have time to wait. I have an idea—a way to help out." That day, she had outlined a plan to renovate her house, add necessary rooms, and open the house up as a temporary inn until the other could be built. She'd said that she and Brett would live there and be a source of support for parents whose kids were facing transplantation. "It seems so logical," she had added, after presenting her plan. "Donovan chose that house because of its proximity to the hospital. Volunteers can help me. We can cook and keep the rooms neat and baby-sit younger siblings. I've thought about it very carefully, and it's what I want to do."

In the end, the board of the League had thought it an excellent idea. They had allocated money for the renovation and appointed Mrs. Jacoby coordinator of the Wayfarer Inn, with the offer of extending the job to the new house once it was built. Meg had been pleased for her. It was something Mrs. Jacoby obviously wanted to do, and it seemed to give her a new lease on life.

Now, in less than an hour, journalists and TV anchors from Washington and Virginia would be showing up for the formal dedication of Wayfarer One. Meg stepped aside as a decorator hustled past, juggling rolls of wallpaper.

"You must be very proud," she heard a familiar voice say.

Meg turned and saw Mrs. Vasquez standing

next to her. "I didn't have too much to do with all this. It was Mrs. Jacoby's idea."

"I know how you've helped," the nurse insisted. "And I've seen copies of the letter you and Alana helped Donovan write. It's raising a lot of money for the cause."

"We're still a long way from building the main house."

"I've heard about a year. That's not so long."

Meg shrugged. "I'll be a senior by then."

"Will you work at the hospital next summer?" Mrs. Vasquez asked.

"I'm not sure." Meg wasn't sure she could go through another summer like the last one. How did long-time nurses like Mrs. Vasquez manage it year after year, caring for people who sometimes didn't get well?

"You want to know something?" Mrs. Vasquez asked.

"What?"

"You've really got a knack for medicine."

Meg stared at her in amazement. "Who, me?"

"I didn't always think that," the nurse continued. "When you first appeared on the floor I thought, 'This one will be gone by the end of the week.' But you fooled me. You not only stayed, you exhibited a real gift for doctoring."

"A gift? Me?"

Mrs. Vasquez laughed. "Don't sound so shocked. I've been in this business for over twenty years, so I've seen plenty of professionals—and believe me, not all of them should be in the business. No, true medicine requires the gift of caring. Your father has it. And from what I've seen, you do too." The nurse patted her arm. "For what it's worth, you might think about becoming a doctor. I know you'd make a good one."

Meg let Mrs. Vasquez give her a quick hug, then watched her hurry away. She mulled over the conversation. A doctor? Impossible!

"Are you going to stand there gawking all day, or are you going to come down here and give us a hand?" Alana called up to Meg from below.

"I'm coming," Meg called back. She took one final look at the upstairs area and at the stained-glass window set in the stairwell. The beautiful colors spilled over the landing and brought back the memory of the first day she and Donovan had toured the house. She felt his presence. Certainly, he was with them this day. As was the secretive JWC, whose identity remained a mystery despite her mother's efforts to ferret out information.

Meg knew that Donovan would be proud of what was going on in his house. She bounded down the stairs, dodging a man tacking down new carpet. Meg knew she'd never be able to give large sums of money to people in need, but she did have other things to offer. "Hey, Alana," Meg shouted as she reached the floor. "I've been think-ing ... maybe we could go to med school to-gether? What do you think about a career in pediatrics?"

Sixteen and Dying

One

❧

"ANNE, DOES THE ranch measure up?" her father eagerly asked.

Anne Wingate stopped unpacking and smiled. "Give me a minute, Dad. We just got here an hour ago."

Her father leaned against the four-poster bed where Anne had opened her suitcase. "Is your room as large as mine?" she asked. "Why don't you go unpack?"

"My room's fine. I'll unpack, but I want to be sure you're happy with everything first. No use staying if you don't like it."

Anne shook her head, controlling her urge to tell him to stop worrying so much. "The Broken Arrow Ranch seems to be just what the brochures promised," she said. "Wide open spaces, terrific luxurious cabins, and plenty of horses. Did you see how blue the sky is out here? The Rocky Mountains in the distance are awesome."

"Sure it's great, but I miss New York's skyscrapers!"

"Oh, Daddy, New York City isn't the only place in the world. I'm actually tired of concrete and smog, and of never seeing the sky. I've wanted to come to a place like this all my life. Remember, now that we're here, you promised to forget about the city and the university and everything back home. Start having a good time."

She wasn't angry. She knew her father only wanted her to be happy. Taking the summer off from classes as a history professor at New York University, closing up their apartment in Brooklyn Heights, and traveling out to Colorado to a dude ranch simply because she asked him hadn't been easy for him. Especially under the circumstances.

"If you have a good time, I'll have a good time," her father assured her. "You know I've only seen and ridden horses in Central Park, but I'll do my best." He watched her a few minutes longer, then asked, "Do you want anything? Can I help?"

"Dad, I'm sixteen. I think I can manage to unpack a suitcase by myself."

"I know, but it's been a long trip. I don't want you getting tired out."

Anne paused, observing her father. He was the one who looked tired. They had flown out of La Guardia at seven A.M., changed planes in Chicago, and landed in Denver. Now they were on Mountain Standard Time, but it was six o'clock in New York. Then, they'd been greeted by Tom Green, a representative from the Broken Arrow, and driven another hundred miles out to the ranch. Anne walked over to her father and put her hands on his chest. "Stop worrying about me. I feel just fine," she said softly.

"I can't help it. I—"

"You promised me we could have these few weeks to have a good time—just you and me."

"I know what I promised." Wearily, he raked his hand through his crop of fuzzy brown hair. "I'm a man of my word. I won't ask you any more questions."

Anne dropped her hands, glancing away, unable to tolerate the look of sadness on his face. She didn't want to be sad. She only wanted to finish unpacking and take a tour of the ranch. "Did you see the corral when we drove in? I want to walk down and get a look at the horses."

"I thought you were unpacking."

"There's plenty of time for that."

"Mr. Green said that dinner would be at six. You don't want to miss out on dinner in the mess hall."

"I'm sure I'll hear the dinner bell," Anne said. "Right now, I'm changing into jeans and going down to that corral."

Once she had changed, Anne left the small cabin she would be sharing with her father and hurried outside. She breathed the fresh, sweet-smelling air. She thought it was both wonderful and intoxicating.

Quickly, she got her bearings. She jogged past the cluster of cabins where the guests stayed, past the main lodge where guests and ranch hands shared meals, to a barn and a large corral where several horses milled about. Their hooves kicked up dust, making her cough. Anne boosted herself up onto the railing and peered over the top at the animals. She'd always loved horses, always wanted one of her own, but keeping a horse in the city was impractical. Over the years, she'd read books and collected pictures and horse figurines. She'd gone riding around Central Park, but that was never satisfying enough.

Anne held out her hand toward one of the horses. "Hey, fella," she called softly. The bay's ears pricked forward as she cooed to him. "Come on over. I won't hurt you." Anne wished she'd brought along a lump of sugar to tempt the animal closer.

"What do you think you're doing?"

The harsh male voice startled Anne, and she almost lost her balance on the fence. She half jumped, half fell the few feet to the ground and whirled to face an angry-sounding young man with broad square shoulders, black hair, and cold blue eyes. "Don't you know these premises are off-limits to you tourists?" He pushed his Stetson hat back on his head and gave her a withering look.

"I was just looking," Anne stammered, completely intimidated. The angry voice belonged to a handsome face. His denim shirt was soaked with perspiration, and his jeans looked dusty and well worn. He wore brown boots, caked with dirt and mud.

"These are range ponies," he added sharply. "They've been out on the range for months and have just been brought in. They're mostly wild. You could get hurt."

She didn't like being yelled at by someone who looked close to her own age. "I was being careful," she insisted. "I wasn't going to crawl over the fence, you know."

His blue eyes swept over her arrogantly.

"My dad and I got here about an hour ago from New York." Anne wasn't sure why she explaining anything to him, he was acting so unfriendly.

"Well, New York, the Broken Arrow is still a working ranch. The tourists' horses—the tame ones—are over in the other direction, on the far side of the cabins. You'll be safer petting one of them."

He made it sound like she was foolish—looking for a puppy to play with. Anne lifted her chin. "Well, Colorado, I'll use my compass next time so I can navigate to the other side of this place."

She saw his mouth twitch at the corners. He crossed his arms and held her gaze. "The name's not Colorado," he said. "It's Morgan."

"Like the breed of horse?" she asked.

He looked surprised that she could name a particular breed of horse. "That's right."

"Name fits you," Anne snapped. "Like the back end of the same." She spun and trooped off toward the cabins before her insult had time to register.

She hadn't gone far when he caught up with her. "We're responsible for visitors' safety," Morgan said, stepping in front of her, blocking her retreat. "An accident could cost us plenty in insurance."

She noticed that his tone didn't sound quite so condescending and that she'd become a "visitor" instead of a "tourist." "I didn't mean to go into a restricted area. I just got here. I guess I'll hear the guidelines tonight, so I won't get into the wrong place at the wrong time again."

Morgan stared at her until she began to grow uncomfortable, then asked, "What's your name?"

Anne wanted to ignore him, step around him, and return to her cabin. She didn't have much experience with boys, and he seemed unpleasant. "Why? Are you going to report me?" she asked.

His curious expression gave way as he sarcastically added, "Forget it, New York. I really don't care who you are. Just be careful. This isn't some spa—it's a real ranch, where people work. I wouldn't want you to chip a fingernail or something."

Anne watched him turn and march back toward the corral. She wanted to slug him. He was arrogant and rude, and she hadn't come more than a thousand miles to be insulted by some cocky cowboy. This was supposed to be her special summer with her father. A summer with no thought of what lay ahead for her.

She had selected the Broken Arrow after poring over dozens of brochures about dude ranches. The place seemed perfect. Why should she let a rude ranch hand ruin it for her? Anne turned her face skyward and took several deep breaths to calm her seething anger. The smell of hay and dust made her throat feel dry and parched, but was strangely exhilarating.

With a sigh, Anne welcomed the warmth of the sun on her skin, the feel of the breeze in her long, brown hair. Then, with a start, she realized that the beauty surrounding her, the quiet of the June afternoon, even the encounter with Morgan, had distracted her completely. Just for a little while, she had completely forgotten that she was dying.

Two

❦

THE THOUGHT OF her problem left her shaken, as it always did, when it came upon her unexpectedly. *Dying.* That's what the doctors had told her in April. Anne walked slowly to the cabin but decided not to go inside yet. Her dad was probably taking a much needed rest. She sat down on the porch steps and watched the afternoon shadows grow longer, until shade covered her back and shoulders. Absently, she hooked her arms around her knees and allowed herself to remember. . . .

Nagging tiredness had drained Anne for months, no matter how much sleep she got. There were other problems too: her vision blurred while she was doing schoolwork, her appetite was poor, and she was losing weight. Eventually, her father noticed and insisted she get a checkup. A routine physical revealed nothing, but her family doctor suggested she have tests taken at the hospital.

Anne protested, but in the end, she spent spring break in St. Luke's Hospital while her friends went off on vacations. "We need to find out what's wrong," her father had said, trying to console her.

"But I'm missing all the fun!"

"We'll do something special this summer," he said.

Anne scoffed. "That's what you say every year, but then you end up teaching a summer course, and I end up taking enrichment classes."

"Anne, you should take extra classes. You're brilliant, and you'll qualify for a scholarship anywhere you want to go when the time comes. Don't worry about missing your break. I've already told the dean that you and I are going to be in Oxford next summer."

"Dad, England obviously has a lot to offer, but I'd prefer to go out West, someplace where there're horses and mountains and wide open spaces."

"Hang around smelly horses?" He feigned horror. "Wouldn't you rather walk along the Thames? Walk with Shakespeare, Wordsworth, Byron, and Shelley?"

Anne shared her father's love of books and had found comfort in poetry and novels ever since her mother's death, when she was ten. "You're not playing fair," Anne said, half pouting. "You know I look forward to going to England with you, but that's over a year from now. It seems like forever."

"The impatience of youth," her father kidded. "None of you kids can wait for anything. Trust me—next summer will be here before you know it."

Anne now looked back on that day and remembered it as the last carefree day of her life. That evening, Dr. Becksworth and Dr. Stevenson came into her room. She noticed their serious expressions. Her father, who was visiting with her, took her hand, as if to ward off their foreboding presence.

"Anne, we'd like to ask you some questions," Dr. Stevenson began without preamble. "They might sound odd, but it's important that you answer truthfully."

Wide-eyed, she glanced at her father, but nodded. "All right," she said, wondering why they'd think she might lie.

"Do you have a boyfriend?" Dr. Becksworth asked.

"No. I'm not really into dating." She felt color rise to her face. The question seemed completely off the subject. She didn't date at all. Not that she didn't want to, but the few boys who'd ever asked her out also attended her small private school, and she considered them boring and not really attractive. She'd rather not date at all than spend time with someone who didn't appeal to her.

"What's Anne's social life got to do with her medical problems?" her father asked. "Tell us the results of all those tests you've been running."

Dr. Becksworth gazed at Anne solemnly. "As a hematologist, I specialize in diseases of the blood."

Anne felt herself growing queasy. The idea that she might have some serious disease frightened her. "Do I have cancer?" she asked. She knew that leukemia was a blood disease.

"No," he said, giving her a momentary sense of

relief. "But according to your blood test results, you're HIV-positive."

Anne strained to make sense of his words and heard them echo in her head. "HIV-positive." She recalled that a famous athlete had announced that he was quitting pro basketball because he was HIV-positive. The announcement had shaken the country and caused a furor in her school. The administration and faculty had organized an awareness program about HIV and how it was transmitted, as if the kids didn't know already.

"Are you saying that my daughter has AIDS?" Anne's father demanded incredulously. "That's impossible! Absolutely impossible."

Anne was so taken aback that she couldn't speak.

"Please, Dr. Wingate," Dr. Becksworth said. "I'm not making any accusations. I'm simply trying to tell you what we've found and then figure out how Anne acquired the virus."

"I have AIDS?" Anne finally found her voice.

"No," Dr. Stevenson replied. "You have the virus that leads to AIDS." Anne couldn't sort out the distinction. The doctor continued, "I'm sure you know that AIDS is an immune-deficiency disease. The virus, HIV, attacks the body's T4 cells, which are the master programmers of the immune system. Without natural immunities, infections run rampant. Many illnesses are possible."

"According to your chart, you went to see a gynecologist a few weeks ago." Dr. Becksworth flipped through pages on a metal clipboard.

Anne felt her face redden. She gave her father a guilty, sidelong glance. "I didn't tell you, because it was . . . personal." Despite their closeness, there were some things Anne found difficult to share with her dad. If only her mother were still alive. She looked back at the doctor. "My gyn told me I had an infection and gave me some medicine."

"You still have the infection," Dr. Stevenson said. "The fact that it hasn't cleared up, combined with your other symptoms and blood results, is a signal of HIV."

"But Dr. Segal never said a word about that!"

"HIV is diagnosed only through a blood test. Very frankly, she would never have considered HIV in your case. There are other ways of getting this type of infection."

"I don't like your insinuations," Anne's father said quickly. "Your lab has messed up on my daughter's blood work. It's that simple."

Dr. Becksworth shook his head. "There's no mistake. I wish there were."

Anne felt tears stinging her eyes. "How could I have gotten HIV?" she asked. She felt trapped in some nightmare, caught in some awful, bad dream from which she couldn't wake up.

"That's what we must determine," Dr. Stevenson said kindly. "We need to figure this out, Anne, for everybody's sake."

"I don't know how," she cried. She felt her father's arm go around her protectively.

"You're not an intravenous drug user. Sharing contaminated needles is a major cause of transmission," Dr. Stevenson said. Anne shook her head emphatically. She never used drugs! "That's why I asked about your boyfriends," he said. "The virus is also sexually transmitted." Anne had a few friends who were having sexual relationships, but she certainly wasn't.

"Anne doesn't even date," her father said defensively.

Anne wished he'd keep quiet; he wasn't helping. The doctor put his hand on her shoulder. "If there was anyone, Anne, even if it was only once—"

Anne interrupted him. "No one. Not ever."

Dr. Becksworth cleared his throat. "The other most logical possibility is via a blood transfusion, but you said you haven't had one." He glanced back down at his chart.

"But, she has," Anne's father interrupted. "It was a long time ago, after the accident."

"When?"

The horror of the past flooded over Anne. "My mother and I were in an accident when I was ten. She died." Anne shook her head to dislodge the memories.

"Anne almost died too," her father added, holding her against his side. "They gave her a blood transfusion in the emergency room."

Anne scarcely remembered. She definitely recalled the long recuperation in the hospital. She and her dad, alone. Her mom, gone forever.

Dr. Becksworth nodded with understanding. "That was before eighty-five."

"It was in December. We were going Christmas shopping," Anne explained. The memory was extremely painful, even after almost seven years.

"It wasn't mandatory for labs to start screening blood for HIV until January eighty-five. All I can say is that it's very likely you received contaminated blood at that time."

Anne could scarcely absorb what the doctor was telling her. "But that was years ago!" her father exclaimed. "Why would it show up now?"

"One of the longest dormancy cases on record is almost ten years," Dr. Becksworth replied. "That's highly unusual, but Anne's young and healthy. Think back. Did she have any unusual complaints or symptoms in the first couple of weeks or even months after the transfusion?"

"My wife was dead, my daughter was in serious condition. How should I know?" her father snapped.

Anne touched his arm, stopping his explosion of temper. "Dad, I remember, I had a skin rash and my glands swelled up. The doctors thought I might be having a reaction to the antibiotic they were giving me."

"They should have caught it," her father stormed. "Why didn't they diagnose the virus then?"

"The test wasn't done routinely then," Dr. Stevenson explained. "There's no way that anyone would have guessed that someone in such a low-risk category as Anne might have contracted it. She was given the transfusion to save her life."

"I can't believe this is happening to me," she said suddenly, and her tears flowed freely. Blood—the very thing that once saved her life—was now turning her body against her.

"What are you going to do about it?" Her father challenged both doctors, balling his fist at his side.

"How are you going to keep my daughter from getting AIDS? How are you going to cure her?"

Dr. Stevenson took a deep breath and in a soft, troubled voice said, "I'm sorry. We'll do everything we can possibly do, but there is no cure for AIDS."

Three

"THERE ARE TREATMENTS —ways of delaying the onset, of stalling full-blown AIDS," Dr. Becksworth told them. "The drug AZT, especially combined with other drugs, is our most potent weapon in AIDS treatment at this time."

Anne wasn't concentrating on what he was saying. She felt as if she'd stepped out of her body and was standing at the side of the bed, hearing medical information about some stranger. It wasn't Anne they were discussing ... it *couldn't* be. She was only sixteen. She had her whole life ahead of her. This was some terrible mistake. She felt shocked pity for the girl on the bed.

"I want a second opinion," Anne heard her father command.

She looked up at his face. It was the color of white chalk. "I think I need to be by myself for a while," Anne said softly. "I need to think about what you've told me."

"We can talk about it in the morning," Dr. Becksworth said. "The important thing is to start you on medication and begin a regimen for you before you leave the hospital."

"What about her day-to-day life?" her father asked, still agitated. "Is she supposed to drop out of school, stop going places?"

The idea of returning to school seized Anne, frightening her. How could she go back? What would happen when everyone found out she was HIV-positive? They'd hate her, shun her. Why, the administration might not even allow her to return!

"Anne should resume a normal life," Dr. Stevenson replied. "Once she starts taking AZT, and adjusts to its side effects, she can do the things she used to do."

"But the people I'm around—"

The doctor interrupted her. "The virus can't be passed through casual contact. Touching, kissing, even sharing eating utensils and drinking glasses won't spread the virus. Caregivers of AIDS patients do not contract the illness unless they exchange body fluids with the patients. We know for a fact that the virus isn't very strong outside the body—a simple disinfectant like chlorine bleach can destroy it. Don't worry about passing it to anyone, Anne. So long as you don't have sexual contact or donate blood, the people in your life are perfectly safe."

Anne wanted to laugh at him. *Perfectly safe.* Who was he kidding? The illness held such a stigma that no one was safe from the ostracism it caused. She wiped a tear aside.

When the doctors left, her father took her in his arms. His grip was so tight that she could hardly breathe. "I'll talk to other doctors," he promised. "There have got to be better doctors, specialists. We'll find someone to help you."

She felt sorry for him. She couldn't picture her father living alone. He needed her. They planned things together, cleaned their apartment together, did laundry together on Saturdays. She chose his ties and made certain he was on time for his classes. "Sure, Daddy. Whatever you say."

She finally made him go home, telling him she was exhausted. He swore to return first thing in the morning with other news. Once she was alone, Anne turned off the lamp and lay in the darkness. Only that morning, she'd thought she'd be home by now. Only hours before, she'd been annoyed at having to spend spring break in the hospital. How different her world looked now.

Her tears came as if a floodgate had opened. Why was this happening to her? What had she done to deserve such a terrible sentence as AIDS? First the loss of her mother, now the loss of herself.

She drifted off to sleep, but woke with a start, late in the night. She had the sensation that someone was in the room with her. Her heart pounded, yet as she glanced around, she saw that she was alone. Taking deep breaths to calm her ragged breathing, Anne turned her head. She noticed that beside her cheek, on her pillow, lay an envelope.

Curiosity beat out her fear. Anne flipped on the

light over her bed and squinted at the envelope. It looked like parchment and was sealed with wax, stamped with the initials OLW. Carefully, she broke the seal and pulled out two pieces of paper. One was a letter. She held it up to the light and began to read.

Dear Anne,

You don't know me, but I know about you, and because I do, I want to give you a special gift. Accompanying this letter is a certified check, my gift to you, with no strings attached, to spend on anything you want. No one knows about this gift except you, and you are free to tell anyone you want.

Who I am isn't really important, only that you and I have much in common. Through no fault of our own, we have endured pain and isolation and have spent many days in a hospital feeling lonely and scared. I hoped for a miracle, but most of all I hoped for someone to truly understand what I was going through.

I can't make you live longer. I can't stop you from hurting, but I can give you one wish, as someone did for me. My wish helped me find purpose, faith, and courage.

Friendship reaches beyond time, and the true miracle is in giving, not receiving. Use my gift to fulfill your wish.

Your Forever Friend,
JWC

Mystified, Anne looked at the check. It was made out to her in the sum of one hundred thousand dollars! She gasped. What was the One Last Wish Foundation? The check was signed by Richard Halloway, Esquire. Who would have done such a thing? She didn't know anyone with the initials JWC. She certainly didn't know anyone with so much money. Anne read the letter again and again. It said she could spend it on anything she wanted. Was one hundred thousand dollars enough to cure AIDS? She knew it wasn't. What good was money if it couldn't buy a future? She'd give the money to her father, if this was for real, at least he'd be able to be secure.

One hundred thousand dollars. She turned the possibilities for its use over in her mind. College? Probably not. Health care? How much did it cost to take care of someone with AIDS? Her funeral? Anne shook her head, hating the macabre direction her thoughts had taken. She decided to try to sleep. She'd wait until the morning and think about it again—if the check didn't evaporate. She put it under her pillow for safekeeping, turned out the light, and lay still in the dark.

Her father arrived while the nurses were clearing away the breakfast trays. His eyes were red-rimmed. He bent and kissed her. "You should have shaved, Dad. You look awful," she told him.

"I was up most of the night."

"Me too." She slipped her hand under her pillow to feel for the letter, certain she had dreamed it. The tip of her finger touched the edge of the envelope.

Her father sat down heavily in the chair next to

her bed. "I spent the night using the computer library looking for information about AIDS and the AZT treatment."

Anne's father had a modem, a special phone, on his home computer that tied into the university's system, so he could call up a data bank of reference libraries. She'd used it often when researching papers for school reports. "What's the bad word?" she asked.

"AZT is currently the best drug there is for AIDS treatment. There's also a drug called DDL, but people use AZT first."

"Tell me everything, Dad. Remember, I know how to use your computer, and can look this up for myself as soon as I get home, so save me the time and trouble."

He rubbed his eyes and slouched. "AZT's a powerful chemical. You'll have to take it several times a day and put up with the side effects—nausea, vomiting, tremors, depression."

"Sounds like a real lifesaver, all right."

"Patients adjust," he said, not hiding his sadness. "If things get too bad, you can go on antidepressants and other drugs to counter the effects."

Anne felt a fresh wave of tears clog her throat. It wasn't how she wanted to spend the last days of her life. "Is AZT my only choice?"

"It's your best choice."

"What if I don't start taking it right away?"

"What do you mean?"

"What if I wait until I actually get AIDS?"

"Anne, that's not wise. All reports suggest the importance of immediate treatment." Her father straightened and looked at her. "Doctors agree, the sooner, the better."

"What could be 'better' about being sick and depressed?" Anne felt herself getting angry, wanting to lash out at the shapeless enemy that waited to kill her. "You said there might be other doctors, specialists."

"I have the names of several specialists in the city."

"Maybe we should talk to one of them first."

"You mean, not go on the AZT immediately?"

"That's right. What difference could a few days make?"

He frowned, and Anne could see that her logic didn't appeal to him. "You're only putting off the inevitable."

"I don't care. I don't want to have to deal with this now. I want to go home, I want to finish the school term, and I don't want anyone to know about the diagnosis." She reached out to him. "We can keep it a secret, can't we, Daddy?"

"It's nobody's business," he replied. "We won't tell anyone until we have to. But we do need to see a specialist immediately. I don't think you should delay starting treatment for long."

Anne appreciated him for respecting her wishes, but then, he'd always treated her as an adult, capable of making her own decisions. "Please get me out of here," she said.

The doctors agreed to have her released that morning. At home, Anne tried to believe that life was normal, that she could pick up where she'd left off before her hospitalization. When her father had to go teach his classes, she set to work on the computer searching for information on AIDS treatment. She knew she was running up a large phone bill but figured it didn't matter. If the Wish money was for real, she could certainly pay a phone bill.

The more she studied, the more depressed she felt about her situation. All the treatments indicated debilitating side-effects, at least for awhile. She felt overwhelmed and immobilized by her situation. To divert herself, she reread the letter from JWC. The check was such an irresistible lure. *To spend on anything you want,* her benefactor had written. *Anything.*

In a burst of inspiration she turned to the computer bank libraries for information about ranches and summer vacations. Sometimes the descriptions were so vivid, she could almost smell the fresh mountain air. Ranch vacations offered horses, trail rides, grassy plains, and sun-drenched skies. For Anne, the ranches represented freedom. Choices.

When she realized what she wanted to do, Anne went to her father.

"Are you all right?" he asked anxiously when she asked to speak to him late one night.

"I feel pretty good considering." She sat down across from him in his study. "While I'm feeling so good, there's something I want to do." She handed him the letter. "First, read this. I think you're going to be as surprised as I was."

She watched as he read, his expression turning to utter amazement. Next, she handed him the check, which he examined closely. "It looks real," he said incredulously.

"I'm hoping it is real. Do you have any idea who

JWC can be? Maybe someone you or Mom once knew?"

"I haven't a clue. But it won't take long for me to validate the check's authenticity. I'll take it to the bank in the morning."

"If it's real, then I know what I want to do with it." She told him and he started shaking his head before she finished talking.

"I can't allow you to go play at a dude ranch this summer. You must begin treatments."

"I will take them, just not right away. All I want is a slight postponement, a reprieve. Let me have a few weeks of fun, then I'll start right in on the medication. I promise."

"Don't you know what you're asking? Your delay can accelerate the onset of AIDS."

Anne reached out and covered her father's hand with hers. "You've always allowed me to make my own choices. Please, Dad, let me have this one last wish. Please."

She saw him warring with his emotions and felt the full brunt of his anguish over giving her what she wanted. "Are you sure?" he asked.

"Very sure," Anne said. "It's my life, and it's what I want to do with it."

Four

ANNE WAS STARTLED by her father's voice as he pulled open the cabin door and stepped onto the porch. "Why are you sitting out here all alone?" he asked.

"I didn't want to wake you. Besides, it's beautiful outside, don't you think? Look at the sun setting behind the mountains."

Her father sat next to her on the steps. "My lungs aren't used to all this fresh air! It's going to take some adjusting. Were you able to get close to those smelly horses you like so much?" he asked.

His innocent question reminded Anne of her encounter with Morgan, the cowboy who'd taken an obvious dislike to her. She decided against telling her father about the rude way she'd been treated. "The horses were fine. There was one, a big bay, that I really liked."

"I thought a bay was a body of water."

"Oh, Dad, you're impossible! You're going to have a good time out here in spite of yourself. Wait and see. And thanks again for allowing me the grace period on taking the medication. This trip together means a lot, more than you'll ever know."

His grin faded, and he smoothed back her hair. "All I care about is your having a good time. Whenever I think—"

"Don't," she said. "Let's not depress ourselves."

They heard the clang of the dinner bell. She hopped up and dusted off the seat of her jeans. "Saved by the bell. I'm hungry. How about you?"

"Starved." He stood up, and together they walked the distance to the rustic-looking lodge. They were joined by other guests in a huge main room, sectioned off into more intimate areas by the furniture arrangement. Along one wall there was a massive stone fireplace, which Anne imagined could be cozy when the winter wind howled outside. The scent of fresh pine mingled with the smells of pot roast and warm bread coming from a long wooden table set with dinner plates and steaming bowls of food at the opposite end of the room.

"Come on! Don't be shy," said a tall, brown-haired woman from the head of the table. "Welcome to the Broken Arrow. If you don't hustle up to the dinner table, my boys will clear it off like a plague of locusts."

Anne saw a line of cowboys standing behind chairs at the table. She could tell they were workers by the weathered look of their clothes. The guests stood out in their brand-new jeans and store-pressed shirts. Even though her own jeans weren't new, they had a designer chic about them.

"Take a chair anyplace," the woman said. "My name's Maggie Donaldson. My husband, Don, and I own this ranch, and we want you to have a fine old time while you're with us." A large man with sun-weathered features stepped up beside Maggie and waved.

Anne and her father chose chairs about midway down the table. She glanced about curiously, hoping to see girls her age, though many of the guests seemed to be couples with young children.

Anne shook out her dinner napkin and placed it across her lap as Maggie continued with introductions. "These kids will be our waiters." She motioned to a cluster of young people who emerged from the kitchen. "Many are college and high school kids from all over the country who've come here to work, earn some money, and have a taste of the West. They'll be responsible for cooking, clean-up, cabin clean-up—in short, whatever you need to make your visit to the Broken Arrow the best. And the ranch hands are here to work, but if you need anything, ask one of them. We all want to help."

Maggie gestured toward the food. "Right now, eat up. We'll have a meeting later tonight to tell you what's in the works for you all this week. The hands get up early, and you will too. There's too much to do for a body to lie abed all day."

Once Maggie had completed her speech, the bowls of hot foot were passed along the table. A girl who Anne guessed was close to her in age came alongside with a basket of hot rolls. Anne smiled, and she smiled back and moved on.

Morgan Lancaster watched Anne from the other side of the table, warily. He was convinced that he knew her type—pretty, rich, and pampered. It was the only part of life on the ranch he hated. Every summer, his Aunt Maggie and Uncle Don took in wealthy, often snobby guests who thought that a few weeks on a ranch made them experts on the West.

The spoiled teenage girls were the worst, to his way of thinking. Some of them had provided diverting summer fun for him over the years, but for the most part, he didn't like them. And he didn't like the girl across the table from New York City, either. The only thing that got to him about her was her large, expressive brown eyes, which appeared somehow sad. What could a rich girl from the East have to be sad about? He could tell her plenty about sadness, if he had a mind to. *Forget it*, he told himself. She wasn't worth his time.

Aunt Maggie stood up and clanged her spoon against the side of her water glass. "When you're finished, feel free to wander around the premises. Stables for the horses and ponies you'll be assigned to ride during your stay are open for you to tour. Our boys will be glad to show you around. There'll be a roping demonstration down at corral four—maps are available at the desk. Remember, the lodge never closes, so come over anytime, day or night. See you back here at eight for the general meeting."

"So, what do you think?" Anne asked as she and her father walked toward their cabin after dinner.

"I think the food's great, but I don't know about

all this fun stuff. Frankly, I'm glad I brought along my laptop computer."

"You're impossible!" Anne exclaimed, hooking her arm through his. "I'm going down to the stables to choose my horse for the trail ride tomorrow."

"You do that," her father said. "I'll see you back at the lodge for the meeting. I'm glad to see you smiling so much."

Anne threaded her way around the cabins. She heard the sound of children laughing. The softness of the summer night, the laughter and squeals, made her pause. She would never hear the sound of her own children. Melancholia stole over her. The thought jarred her. Until now, she'd never even thought about being married and having children.

Even if the AZT helped her body arrest the inevitable progress of AIDS, having children was out of the question. The virus could be passed to a pregnant woman's unborn baby. Anne knew she couldn't do that to an innocent baby. *No marriage. No babies. No sex.* Anne mentally went down the list of what HIV was denying her.

"Stop thinking about it," Anne told herself firmly. No sex didn't mean no love. She told herself there was a difference, but what man would want to love her, knowing he couldn't have a total relationship with her?

The Wish money had offered her a few weeks of uninterrupted happiness. She wanted to capture all the fun and good times she could for whatever time she had left. She forced herself to resist negative thoughts about tomorrow, and concentrate on the here and now.

She was just rounding the final cabin site when she heard the distinct sound of someone crying. Anne stopped and strained to catch the direction of the soft sobs, then started toward the source.

For a moment, Anne studied the girl who'd served the rolls at dinner. She tried to put herself in the girl's place. Would she want some nosy stranger to intrude on her sadness? Yet, even as she wondered, Anne knew she would speak. "Excuse me," Anne said. "Can I help?"

The girl started, wiped her eyes, and turned away. "*Nada*," she said in Spanish. "Nothing."

"I have a friend back in New York," Anne told her. "Whenever she says 'it's nothing, ' she means 'it's the end of the world. ' I won't pry, but if there's anything I can do . . . even just listen . . . I will."

With her back still turned, the girl said nothing. After a few awkward moments, Anne stepped backward. Admonishing herself for interfering, Anne started to leave.

She'd gone only a few steps when she heard the girl's quivering voice say, "Don't go . . . please. I need to talk to someone. I'm so unhappy, I could die. Just die."

Five

A SLIVER OF MOONLIGHT allowed Anne to see the girl's tear-streaked face. "I'm Anne Wingate. What's your name?"

"I'm Martes Rodriguez—my friends back home in Los Angeles call me Marti. You're obviously a guest here. I *have to* spend the summer out here working. My parents are forcing me."

"They're making you work here against your will?"

"It's really all my brother's fault. Luis is a cop in L.A. He's the one who arranged to have me sent out here. About ten years ago, he worked here for two summers in a row. He said it saved his life, because he was in a gang and now all the boys from that gang are dead. He'd be dead too, he said, if it hadn't been for this place and the Donaldsons' influence. According to him, this place turned his life around." Marti sounded angry.

"You're in a gang?" Anne could scarcely believe that the trim, raven-haired girl in front of her ran with a street gang.

"Not me. My boyfriend, Peter Manterra. My family thinks he's bad for me. What do they know? They don't remember what it's like to be in love."

Anne saw that Marti was hurting, but she couldn't imagine feeling such sorrow over being separated from a boyfriend. "It's only for a summer. Maybe time will pass more quickly if you're busy."

"I doubt it. Did you leave a guy back home?"

"Not me. I wanted to spend the summer here. I'm with my father. He's the only guy in my life! I thought a summer out West on a ranch sounded like fun."

Marti made a face. "I don't mind the work, but I miss Peter so much. What if he finds another girlfriend? What if he forgets about me?"

"But if he really loves you, why would he look for another girl?"

"You sound like my mother," Marti retorted.

Anne laughed. "I'm sorry. I guess that was a parent-type thing to say. But the way you're complaining about being here reminds me of my father. He gripes constantly about the fresh air and open spaces."

Marti smiled tentatively. "I didn't mean to complain about the ranch. Actually, I think it's a pretty nice place. I live in L.A. near the barrio, and summers are hot and mean. I guess that in some ways, this is a change for the better." She cut her eyes sideways. "*Un pocito*. That's Spanish for a '*very* little.'"

"You can write to your boyfriend, can't you? Every day if you want to."

"I guess, but it's hard being separated from him. I love him so much. You must know what it's like." Anne didn't want to admit that she had no idea what it felt like to be in love. "Why are you here just with your dad?" Marti asked, blowing her nose. "Are your parents divorced?"

"My mother died years ago. It's just me and my dad. I'm used to it, I guess." Then, changing the subject, she asked, "Will you get to go on any trail rides with us? Maybe riding horses can take your mind off your boyfriend."

"The workers are kept pretty busy. We got here over a week before you guests arrived. Our free time's our own whenever we can grab some of it. I hope to do a lot more riding. A couple of the hands, some of the younger guys, have offered to take me along. The owners' nephew, Morgan, works on the ranch like an ordinary hired hand, and he's been nice to me," Marti added.

Morgan's image sprang into Anne's mind. "What's so unusual about that?"

"You can bet that if I were related to the owner, I wouldn't be working like a hired hand." She paused thoughtfully. "But you know, he's a regular person, not bossy or mean one bit. He's kind of reckless though. He reminds me of my brother, Luis . . . kind of *loco*, you know, crazy." Marti made a face. "But if it weren't for Morgan and his friend, Skip, I'd have gone crazy last week."

Anne could hardly believe that Marti was describing the same guy she'd had words with at the corral. "You sure Morgan was really nice?" she said.

"What do you mean?"

"Nothing, forget it." Anne peered at Marti more closely. Her tears had completely dried. "Feeling better?"

Marti nodded. "Thanks. I guess I really did need to talk to someone—someone female and my age who'd understand."

"Since we're both going to be here for the summer, maybe we can do things together," Anne offered. Although Marti was different from Anne's friends in New York, Anne already liked her. She was open and honest about her feelings.

"I'd like that. The other girls working with me are older—sophomores and juniors in college. We don't have much in common. I could use a friend. My quarters are on the south side of the lodge, in cabins close by the kitchen. Maybe we could meet tomorrow afternoon. I have free time from two till four."

Anne gave Marti her cabin number and invited her to come by anytime. The crunch of boots on gravel made them both turn. Morgan ignored Anne and addressed Marti. "My aunt's looking for you. They've cranked some ice cream, and she wants you to help serve it after the meeting."

"Back to the salt mines." Marti sighed and shrugged. "See you around, okay? I'm glad we got to talk."

Anne watched her hurry off. Alone with Morgan, she felt unsure of herself. "I was headed to the stables, toward the *tame* horses," she said, unable to resist getting in a dig. "I heard Marti crying and investigated."

Morgan hooked his thumbs through the belt loops of his jeans. "Marti's all right—sort of lost out here, but she's getting used to it. My buddy, Skip, has taken a liking to her."

Anne wasn't sure why it pleased her to know that Skip, not Morgan, was interested in Marti. "I guess I'll get down to the stables before all the decent horses are snatched up."

"Would you like me to help you pick a mount?" Morgan's offer surprised Anne. He continued quickly, "I know the animals—all their idiosyncrasies. I could help you choose the right one."

"Yes, I'd appreciate your help," she said. His input could be valuable. She wanted a horse with some spirit.

As they walked to the stable in silence, Morgan wondered why he'd volunteered. Yesterday, he'd decided to steer clear of this particular girl, and now he was headed to the stables with her. Deep down, he felt Anne of New York City was trouble. She obviously had money and probably was spoiled. He thought back two summers before, when he'd been sixteen and fallen like a load of bricks for Stacy Donner, a rich debutante from San Francisco. She'd toyed with him. He learned from the experience. Rich girls were fickle and not to be trusted.

At the stable, Anne stopped in front of each stall and studied each horse. The horses were well cared for and content. "Most are quarter horses," Morgan explained. "They've worked on the range and earned the right to some leisure time."

"Not like the ones in the other corral," Anne said. "I liked them better."

"They're wild. Most of them are jugheads."

"Jugheads?"

"That's what we call a horse with no sense. They usually end up as broncos in rodeos."

"The bay seemed different."

Her natural eye for horseflesh impressed Morgan. "I'm going to cut him out and work with him. I'd like a new horse, but first I've got to see if it's worth the time and effort to train him."

"You mean you're going to break him yourself?" The idea of taming and training a wild horse fascinated her.

"It's no picnic. It's hard, time-consuming work," Morgan replied. He pushed back the brim of his hat and gazed down at Anne. "Before I make a recommendation about a horse, why don't you tell me which one you think is right for you."

Anne wandered back along the stalls. She stopped in front of a good-size palomino. "If I have a choice, I'll pick this one. He's got nice confirmation and bright eyes."

Morgan was pleased. Anne had chosen the horse he would have picked for her. "That's Golden Star, a nine-year-old gelding. He's yours while you're here."

Anne smiled. "I've always wanted to have my own horse—and now I will, even if it is only temporary." *Temporary.* Now, everything about her life was temporary. She wondered if JWC, her mysterious benefactor, had experienced this sense of impermanence.

"Making plans too far into the future is stupid,"

Morgan said. "You never know what's going to come along and blow them away."

Anne was surprised that he seemed to understand a person's life could be shot down, even when the person did nothing to bring it about.

"Look, I should get back to the lodge. Do you mind?" he asked.

"No problem. I'll stay here and admire my new horse, then head back for ice cream." She was glad he was being nicer.

Anne watched him walk away and tried not to feel so hopeless. This ranch represented everything she could never have, everything that had been stolen from her by an unalterable circumstance. Tears welled in her eyes and slid softly down her cheeks.

Six

ANNE AWOKE BEFORE dawn the next morning. She tossed restlessly, finally got up, dressed, and headed down to the main lodge. Maggie Donaldson glanced up. "Morning," Maggie said with a broad, friendly smile. "You're up early."

"Couldn't sleep."

"You'll be so tired by this time tomorrow, we'll have to shake you awake."

Anne saw some of the kitchen crew clearing away the table. "Did I miss breakfast?"

"The hands eat early so they can be about their chores. But you've got a few hours before the morning bell. Would you like a piece of fruit to hold you over?"

Anne plucked an apple from a fruit bowl on the table and waved at Marti, who offered a smile and exaggerated sigh. "Catch you later," Marti said.

Anne wandered over to where Maggie was working. "I already like the ranch," she told her. "I've lived in New York City all my life. It's so different out here."

"I'll bet." Maggie's kind green eyes looked up at Anne. "I grew up out here—my Pa, Frank Lancaster, owned the next spread over. I married Don, who owned this place, and when it became impossible to make ends meet ranching alone, we decided to open the place up in the summer. Guests get a taste of the West, and we get to keep working the ranch."

"You've never traveled out of Colorado?" she asked.

"Oh, I've been to other places, but no place I liked better."

"Do you have family here too?"

"Just Morgan, my brother's boy."

Anne was curious about why Morgan wasn't with his father. She would have thought the families would be working together. "Where's your brother?"

Maggie looked up, catching Anne's gaze and holding it. She said nothing, and Anne knew that she'd overstepped the boundary of small talk. Just as Anne began to feel self-conscious, Maggie said, "Why's a pretty little girl like you sitting around jawing with an old gal like me? You should go out into that fresh air and watch the sun come up. It's a pretty sight you'll never forget."

"Sometimes entire days go by and we don't see the sun in New York City." Anne laughed.

"Then all the more reason to see the sun come up over God's country. When you hear that morning bell, come back for flapjacks and bacon."

Anne walked outside. She realized Maggie had definitely changed the subject when she'd asked about Morgan's father. She shrugged. It wasn't any of her business anyway. Just as her life wasn't any of theirs.

Overhead, the sky was turning gray with faint streaks of yellow and pink. She heard the sounds of men's voices, hollering and whooping. Curious, she followed the noise and soon found herself near the corral she'd discovered the day before. A group of men hung over the fence watching. Anne edged closer, straining to see what the commotion was about.

"Come on, Morgan, show him who's boss," a dark-haired man called.

"He's ornery, but you can take him," another fellow shouted.

Anne unobtrusively slipped into an opening in the cluster of men. In the center of the corral, she saw Morgan standing in front of the big bay range horse. The horse was blindfolded and held by a taut rope around its neck. Morgan, holding the rope, was attempting to inch closer, all the while muttering soothing words to calm the frightened animal.

One of the men called out, "You can think of plenty of sweet things to say if you pretend it's a pretty woman."

The hands laughed, and Morgan retorted, "How would you know, Ben? The last pretty woman you talked to fainted dead away."

Catcalls followed. Anne grasped the fence and leaned against the rough wood. She saw Morgan gather the rope tighter, until he was almost nose to nose with the horse. He ran his gloved hand along the bay's tense neck and said, "Take it easy, boy. I won't hurt you."

Anne watched as Morgan retrieved a bridle that dangled from the back pocket of his jeans. Expertly, he slipped the bit between the animal's teeth. The horse protested, half rearing. Anne gasped, as she saw the hooves strike the air near Morgan's head. Morgan maintained control with the rope, using his strength to force the bay down. Dirt flew from the horse's hooves. The men shouted more encouragement.

Tossing the reins over the horse's shoulders, Morgan stepped to one side and, catlike, sprang onto the bay's broad bare back. A cheer went up. In the gathering light of dawn, Anne could make out the tenseness of the horse's muscles. They looked like springs waiting to uncoil.

"Here goes nothing," Morgan announced. He leaned forward and whipped the bandanna off the horse's eyes. The bay struggled to dip his head and then exploded into a bucking, twisting banshee.

Morgan stayed with the horse for what Anne thought was a long time. Then, the horse flung him off, and Morgan flipped through the air and hit the ground hard on the far side of the corral. She squealed in spite of herself.

The minute the horse was relieved of his burden, he stopped bucking and began to gallop around the ring. Morgan scrambled for safety. Hands reached through the bars of the fence as the horse thundered past, and Morgan was pulled to safety. "You all right?"

Gingerly, Morgan dusted himself off. "Sure. . . . That was some ride."

"What's going on?" A man's voice bellowed. Anne spun to see Morgan's uncle charging toward the corral like an angry bull. "You get to your chores!" he commanded. The men slunk away.

Anne tried to vanish but was trapped by the wall of the barn. She hid in its shadows while Morgan's uncle continued, "Not you, Morgan. You stay put."

Anne saw Morgan bend, pick up his hat, and stand to face his uncle, squaring his shoulders in defiance. "What is it, Uncle Don?"

"What do you think you're doing? Are you crazy?"

"Breaking in the horse. You said I could have my pick of the range ponies, and that's the one I want."

"You know how to break a horse proper. You break him to saddle first. *Then* you climb on. You could have gotten killed out there."

"So what?"

"Don't take that tone with me. Maggie would never get over it if anything happened to you."

"Something could happen to me no matter how careful I am. Her too. You know what I mean."

"No one can see the future, and you don't know anything for sure," Uncle Don said angrily. "I won't have you taking needless chances while you're on my spread and under my care."

"I'm eighteen. I can come and go whenever I want."

"You go and you'll break your aunt's heart." Uncle Don ran his hand through his close-cropped hair and released a heavy sigh, his anger spent. "I don't want to argue with you, son, but I have a ranch to run. It might be your ranch someday. I can't let my hands defy me—not even you, no matter if you are family. I have rules, and I expect them to be followed. If that's the horse you want, you've got him, but you break him right. Fair enough?"

Morgan shoved his hands into his pockets. "Fair enough," he agreed.

"I need you to ride out and check fencing today. Can you handle that?"

"I can handle it."

Anne sensed a thick tension coming from Morgan. She held her breath and hugged the wall tighter. If either of them caught her eavesdropping, she'd be embarrassed to death. She hadn't meant to listen but now that she had, she found Morgan more intriguing than ever.

She couldn't help wondering if one summer would be enough time for her to figure him out. One summer. It was all she had.

Seven

By the end of the day, Anne realized Maggie hadn't exaggerated about how tired she'd be. She stifled a yawn at the dinner table. "Maybe you're overdoing the outdoors routine," her father suggested anxiously. "Maybe you should take it easy, rest more."

Anne didn't bother to argue with him. "What do you know about the outdoors? While the rest of us went on a trail ride, you sat in the cabin with your eyes glued to your computer screen."

"I'm doing a paper for a journal on medieval lifestyles. I have a deadline to meet," he said. "I'm sure there'll be another ride tomorrow."

"Will you make that one?"

"Would you miss me if I skipped it?"

Anne hugged him to answer.

That night, when everyone settled around a large

campfire to hear a cowboy tell tall tales, Marti slipped in beside Anne. "Having fun?" she asked.

"Yes, but I ache all over."

"That's normal. After my first day on a horse, my buns were so sore, I could hardly stand."

Anne smiled. She didn't say that she'd ridden often in Central Park on horses she rented. Of course, at the time, she'd ridden hunt seat on English-style saddles, which was different from the wider western saddle style, but the same part of her anatomy was involved. "I enjoyed the trail ride," Anne said. "I wish you could have come along."

Marti picked up a stick and drew circles in the dirt. "Skip wants me to ride out somewhere with him and have a picnic."

"You don't sound very enthusiastic. I've seen Skip—he's cute."

"I don't think I should."

"Why not?"

"Actually, I think Skip's cute, too, and he's really nice to me. But if I really love Peter, then I shouldn't be attracted to Skip, should I?"

Anne watched Marti nibble nervously on her lower lip. "Why not? You're not engaged to Peter, and you think he might date other girls this summer. Why shouldn't you date Skip? Isn't this one of the reasons you're out here—to see if your relationship with Peter is the real thing? I mean, if he loves you, and you love him, then dating others shouldn't make a difference in your feelings toward each other, should it?"

Marti was looking at her, wide-eyed. "What you're saying makes sense. I like Skip as a companion. I'd like to get to have some fun. It's nothing serious. Plain fun." She perked up. "I have an idea. Why don't you come along on the picnic?"

"I'm certain Skip wants me as a chaperon!"

"No, no, silly. His friend, Morgan, can come too."

"Oh, I don't think—"

"You could do worse than Morgan." Marti batted her dark lashes as she pleaded with Anne. "As a favor for your *amiga*. That's me. Your friend. *Por favor*?"

Anne giggled. It was hard to say no to Marti. Anne couldn't deny that she was drawn to the idea of spending time with Morgan. She wanted so much to have a good time, but she felt as if she were trying to live two lives. One, as a regular sixteen-year-old. The other, as a sixteen-year-old stricken with HIV, who had nothing in front of her but a lingering death once full-blown AIDS hit. How could she make it with so much bottled up inside her? With no one to talk to? Is that what JWC had meant by saying, *"I hoped for a miracle, but most of all I hoped for someone to truly understand what I was going through."*

"Are you okay?" Marti asked. "You checked out on me for a minute."

"Sorry. All this talk about romance made me hyperventilate," she quipped, to hide what she couldn't reveal. "Don't worry. I've got it under control now."

Marti burst out laughing. "Anne, you're so funny! I'll bet you're the life of the party at your school."

"That's me—party girl."

"Then it's settled," Marti said. "I'll tell Skip you're coming on our picnic, and he'll tell Morgan. We're going to have so much fun, Anne. Wait and see. A real *fiesta*."

Anne figured that Morgan would probably nix the whole idea. Marti tossed the stick into the campfire, and Anne, deep in thought, watched the flames devour it.

At the end of the first week, Anne's father informed her, "I've made an appointment this coming Monday with Dr. Rinaldi, the specialist you're supposed to see here. I've asked Maggie Donaldson if I can use the station wagon to drive you into Denver."

"Dad, how could you? I don't want to see a doctor. Besides, Monday is another trail ride, and I don't want to miss it."

"Anne, this isn't up for debate. You have to be evaluated. You must stay on top of your medical condition as long as you're in Colorado."

"Well, I hate it, and I don't want to think about it."

"It's not going to go away."

"I, of all people, know it's not going away." The pain in his eyes made her sorry she'd lashed out at him. "All right," she said, feeling remorseful. "I'll go. But I don't have to like it."

They left the ranch right after breakfast and drove the hundred miles to Denver. The city, with traffic and noise and exhaust fumes everywhere, was a shock to her senses. The weather was dry and hot, made hotter by the sun's reflecting off concrete and glass buildings. The large hospital complex was surrounded by looping roads and expansive asphalt parking lots, packed with parked cars. Anne missed the quiet ranch.

She endured the blood test and physical, then sat with her dad in Dr. Rinaldi's office while the physician reviewed her records.

"How's Anne doing?" Her father craned his neck to see the chart the doctor held.

"Her lungs are clear. However, she's anemic, so I want her taking iron and B-12 to build up her red blood count."

"Maybe that's why I'm feeling tired," Anne offered.

"You've been bothered by fatigue?" her father asked. "You didn't tell me."

"It's no big deal, Dad."

"Yes, it is a big deal," Dr. Rinaldi countered. "Fortunately, your T4 cell count is still up around five hundred. If it falls below two hundred, you're going to be at serious risk for infections. That patch of dry, flaky skin on your back and upper legs is also a symptom of lowered T cells. I'll give you a cream for the rash."

Anne only nodded. The information about her T4 cells bothered her. While the number was still within acceptable limits, it was lower than when she left New York. She felt time and good health slipping away from her. "I'll do what you tell me," she promised.

"I've spoken with Dr. Becksworth in New York, Anne," Dr. Rinaldi said. "We both think it prudent that you start on AZT right away."

She still didn't want to. She didn't want to face the side effects. She'd made so many plans with

Marti and Morgan. "Please let me have three more weeks at the ranch. As soon as I get back home, I'll begin taking the drug."

"I don't think that's wise," Dr. Rinaldi replied.

"You don't understand," she insisted. "I need to live normally before I die." She felt waves of desperation.

"Anne, be reasonable," her father said. "It's your life."

"Don't force me to do this yet," she begged.

"I understand how you feel, but I disagree," Dr. Rinaldi said. "Nevertheless, I can't force you to start on AZT against your will. However, if you have any new symptoms—fever, shortness of breath, or persistent cough—I want you right back here to start the medication. Understand? The length of time from infection with HIV to the development of AIDS hasn't been adequately researched in women. All we kow for certain is that women face serious illnesses with AIDS that men don't, for instance, cervical cancer and pulmonary tuberculosis."

"If you're trying to scare me, Dr. Rinaldi, it's working," Anne said. Her hands felt cold and clammy, and she was getting queasy.

The doctor's gaze softened.

"I know you want me to begin treatment, and I'm being stubborn," Anne told him. "I'm not in denial. I know I have HIV. I've had to accept other things I couldn't control—like my mother dying. It's made me tough."

Dr. Rinaldi steepled his fingers. "Women with AIDS are dying six times faster than men with AIDS. Once a woman is diagnosed with AIDS, her life expectancy is less than thirty weeks. I simply want to delay that time for you as long as possible, Anne."

"Listen to the doctor," her dad pleaded. "Let's go back to New York or start on the AZT, Anne."

"People can beat odds," Anne said, lifting her trembling chin. "Dad, let me have a few more weeks to remember."

"All I can help you with is postponement of full-blown AIDS," the doctor replied. "AZT has the power to delay the onset."

"But not the inevitable," Anne remarked.

"No, not the inevitable."

She looked from Dr. Rinaldi to her father. She felt their anguish on her behalf, yet she couldn't forget why she'd come to Colorado. JWC had given her the Wish money without strings, to spend on anything she wanted. Anne knew what she wanted. "Then, if the outcome is exactly the same either way, I'd rather have a few weeks of freedom. I can't forget what's hanging over my head, and I know you're both only trying to help me. . . . Thank you for that. I have very few choices for my life. Please, let me make this one."

Morgan paused while walking the bay stallion around the training ring when he saw the station wagon coming up the long drive toward the main lodge. Anne and her father had been in Denver the whole day. *Probably shopping,* he thought. His mother used to shop continually. Even when there was no money.

He watched the car pull into its parking space and Anne and her father get out. Even from his distance,

Morgan could see how exhausted and defeated they appeared. Anne's father tucked her under his arm as they headed toward their cabin. To Morgan, the gesture appeared protective.

Morgan thought of Anne as beautiful and wealthy. What in the world could she have to be unhappy about? He pulled the tether and clicked to the horse. The horse obeyed, following Morgan docilely as he resumed walking in the ring.

"I need to stop thinking about that girl," he told the bay. Yet, even as he said it, Morgan knew it was becoming impossible to do so. Somehow, Anne and her sad eyes had gotten under his skin. Which was stupid—especially in his case, when he knew what his own future might hold. Exceedingly stupid.

Eight

MORGAN BEGAN TO watch Anne. He observed that although she joined in many of the group activities, every afternoon she saddled up Golden Star and rode off alone. One afternoon, curiosity got the better of him, and he followed her.

He allowed Anne plenty of distance. Since he was an expert tracker, he easily picked up her trail if she got too far ahead. He figured out that she was heading toward Platte City, a small town about ten miles north of the Broken Arrow. Many of the married ranch hands lived there with their families, and sometimes Morgan went to the town to relieve the monotony of ranch life. The main street offered residents only a few stores, a movie theater, an ice-cream parlor, and a pizzeria. He couldn't figure out what Anne found to do there every day.

He rode up on the outskirts and reined in his

horse. He saw Golden Star tied to a tree in the yard of the local church. The whitewashed wooden building was very old, but in good repair. Its tall steeple stabbed into the sky, and from the looks of the parking lot, the church appeared deserted. Morgan dismounted, tied his horse to the tree, and slowly climbed the front steps. As he reached for the door handle, he lost his nerve. What would she think if she saw him come inside?

"Just don't let her see you," he told himself, pulling open the door. Inside, sunlight slanted through a single stained-glass window, spilling a rainbow of colors over the altar. The wooden floor and pews gleamed, and a faint odor of lemon wax hung in the quiet air. He saw Anne sitting alone in the very last pew, her head hung low. Suddenly, he felt like a trespasser. He tried to ease out, but his boot scraped on the floor, and she turned.

Her eyes grew wide with recognition. "What are you doing here?" she asked, looking as if he'd caught her doing something sinful.

"I saw Golden Star tied outside, and I came in to investigate." He hoped the half-truth would be enough of an explanation for her. "You okay?"

"Sure. Fine. I was . . . um . . . just contemplating."

"Contemplating what?"

"Things." She gestured vaguely. "I asked permission from the minister. He said I could stay."

"I'm not prying," Morgan said hastily. Now that the mystery was solved, he felt foolish. "I was surprised to see one of the ranch's horses outside . . . that's all."

Anne stood. "I come here some afternoons to be

alone. Some days, I stop by the library and check out books. I'm real careful with the horse."

"I'm not worried. I've seen how well you take care of him." He fiddled with the hat he'd removed when he came inside. "You go to the library? Man, when I graduated, I swore I'd never read another book." Anne looked horrified, as if he'd blasphemed. He chuckled. "Let me guess. You're a bookworm."

"The worst kind. I can't imagine never reading another book. It would be like your never riding another horse." She started for the door, and he felt bad, sensing he had spoiled something special for her.

"I didn't mean to interrupt you."

"It's all right." She glanced at her watch. "I should be heading back, before Dad misses me."

He followed her outside, where they paused and blinked against the brightness of the sun. To one side of the church, there was an old cemetery. "Have you ever checked out the tombstones?" he asked, trying to make up for intruding on her. "Some of them date back a hundred years."

For a moment, her expression clouded, then her large brown eyes warmed. "Show me," she said.

He walked her through the old graveyard, pointing to various headstones. He stopped at one and said, "Here lies my Great-great-great Grandmother. She was a full-blooded Cheyenne who converted to Christianity." The stone looked ancient and sunbleached and bore the name Woman Who Wears a Cross.

"I didn't realize your family went back so far. Tell me about them."

Morgan was annoyed at himself for mentioning it. The last thing he wanted to discuss was his family. "Some other time," he said, stepping to the next marker.

Anne stooped and plucked a handful of wildflowers from around the old gravestone. "One of my favorite poets is Emily Dickinson. She wrote about death in many of her poems." Anne cradled the flowers against her cheek. "One of my favorites starts out, 'Because I could not stop for Death— / He kindly stopped for me— / The Carriage held but just Ourselves— / And Immortality.' "

Morgan felt a chill as he saw the image of black-robed Death pulling up for him in a horse-drawn carriage. "Emily was kind of depressing, don't you think?"

Anne looked thoughtful, and he was struck again by the fathomless sadness in her eyes. "She was very original, and her imagery is wonderful."

"You sound like a teacher."

Anne laughed. "Sorry. I've always wished I could write poetry, so sometimes I get overly enthusiastic."

Morgan saw pollen left by the flowers on her cheek. He reached down and smoothed his thumb across her silky skin, then wished he'd kept his hands to himself. Touching her made him want to touch her more. "Whatever happened to old Emily?" he asked.

"She died a recluse. It must be sad to die alone. Yet, I don't think she was afraid of death. In another poem, she wrote, 'I never spoke with God, / Nor visited in heaven; / Yet certain am I of the spot / As if the checks were given.' "

"Is that why you come to the church? To contemplate poetry?"

Anne looked over her shoulder toward the simple white frame building. "No. I come to find peace."

Morgan thought her answer baffling, but on one level, he understood it perfectly. "If you find it, share it," he said. "I've always wondered what peace would feel like." Her eyebrows knitted together, but before she could ask him a question, he took her elbow and said, "Come on. We'd better start back before Maggie rings the dinner bell. On the way, we can talk about the picnic Skip's planned for next week. You are coming, aren't you?"

Anne sorted through her closet in vain. "It's no use," she grumbled to the empty room. She didn't have a single thing to wear on a picnic.

"What's the big deal?" Marti had asked that morning. "You throw on some jeans and a T-shirt."

The "big deal" for Anne was spending all afternoon and evening with Morgan. Ever since he'd caught her at the church, ever since he'd touched her cheek, listened to her talk about poetry, ridden home with her, and studied her so solemnly with his blue eyes, she'd been unable to think of anything else.

She'd never known anyone like him. All the boys back home in her school were like children compared with Morgan. He was guarded and mysterious. She yearned to know what motivated him, what made him so secretive and distant. "Forget it," she told herself. "Just have fun with him." She attacked her closet again.

Anne was still trying on outfits when Marti arrived. "Aren't you ready yet?" Marti wailed.

"Almost. Which looks better—the blue shirt or the red one?"

"The blue. Now, let's go. The guys are waiting down by the corral, and we need to get saddled up."

Hurriedly, Anne changed shirts and tugged on her boots. At the corral, she slipped Golden Star a lump of sugar and tossed a saddle over the horse's back. She tightened the cinch and swung her leg over. "What's keeping you?" she asked Marti.

"I'm all thumbs with this saddle," she complained. "How do you do it so quickly?"

Anne didn't tell her that her speed came from wanting to be with Morgan. "Lots of practice."

They rode through the yard to the edge of the fenced property near the barn and corral. Blond-haired, blue-eyed Skip couldn't take his eyes off Marti as they rode up. Anne noticed that Morgan smiled at her, but there was no gleam of adoration in his eyes like the one in Skip's.

They fell into a slow pace, with Skip and Marti riding in the lead. The sun beat down on Anne's back, and the air smelled like newly mown hay. "I thought you might be riding the bay by now," Anne remarked, noticing that Morgan was astride his regular quarter horse. "I've seen you working with him, and he looks tame to me."

"I ride him, but my uncle's giving me grief. He says that the horse spooks too easily and that he'll never make a work horse."

"Isn't it all right to have the horse just because he's beautiful? Just because you like him?"

"A horse has to earn its feed. That's my uncle's philosophy. As for me—I agree with you. I'd like to get the bay to the point where he's show-worthy."

"Have you done that kind of thing before?"

"I ride the rodeo circuit in the late summer, before we have to bring the cattle into the winter grazing range. When rodeos hit the small towns around here, people turn out for the fun. I'd like to exhibit the bay, ride in the parades."

"You really ride in rodeos?"

Morgan grinned. "Bronc busting's my favorite event."

"You actually ride a horse that wants to throw you?" She remembered the time she saw him tossed around the corral by the bay. He'd hit the ground with such a thud, she'd actually ached herself.

"It's good money."

"Aren't you afraid of getting hurt?"

"It goes with the sport. You know, 'no pain, no gain.' "

"The parade part seems more my speed. Waving at people from the back of a beautiful horse—yes, that's more like it."

"You need fancy gear for that—expensive saddles, clothing—lots of flash. Tourists like to see movie-star cowboys. The real thing isn't very glamorous."

She thought the real thing was very glamorous. "I've never been to a rodeo. It sounds like fun."

"Platte City has its Pioneer Days celebration soon. As part of it, there's a rodeo. I'll be riding in it."

"Pioneer Days? Can I come?"

"Sure. The whole ranch attends. You'll have a good time." He looked sideways at her. "After I ride, we could do something together—if you want to, that is."

If I want to! Anne could hardly keep from shouting. "I'd like that," she said calmly.

Morgan clucked, and his horse quickened his pace. "Come on. Let's catch up to Skip and Marti. If we're not careful, Skip will eat all the food before we get a bite."

Anne urged Golden Star to keep up, all the while smiling to herself. She was with daredevil Morgan on a golden Colorado afternoon. He'd invited her to a rodeo. She wished she could bottle the afternoon. Life was beautiful. If only she could make it last.

Nine

THEY RODE ACROSS grassy fields, up rocky terrain, through narrow rocky inclines. The ground flattened out again, and they crossed through a creek that gurgled over sparkling stones. The sun was setting when they came to a lone tree in the middle of a flower-studded field.

"We're here," Skip announced, reining in and dismounting.

"Where's 'here'?" Marti asked.

"Heaven," Morgan replied, swinging down from his horse.

Anne swung off Golden Star and glanced in every direction. She wanted to race across the field. She wanted to embrace the sky. "You're right—this place is heaven," she told him.

They removed the saddles from the horses and allowed the animals to graze. Skip spread out a blanket, and they opened a picnic basket. "How long did you plan to stay, Skip—until the next Ice Age? There's so much to eat!" Anne exclaimed.

He plopped down on the blanket, across from Morgan, who'd already staked his claim. "I wasn't sure what everybody'd want to eat. I brought fried chicken, tortillas, burritos—do you like these things?" he asked.

Marti made a face. "Never touch the stuff. I prefer lobster."

Skip looked crestfallen, and Marti laughed playfully. "Everything looks delicious."

Anne placed the tip of a chili pepper on her tongue. Immediately, her mouth felt on fire and her eyes began to water. "No fair! They're too hot!"

"Everything Spanish is hot," Marti said with a flirtatious, sidelong glance toward Skip.

He flopped backward dramatically. "I'm in love."

By the time they'd finished eating, the sun nestled between two mountain peaks. Morgan pulled Anne to her feet. "Let's take a walk."

They crossed the field, walking toward the setting sun. "Do you suppose poets could write about this view?" Morgan asked, pointing to the hues of pink and lavender in the sky.

"The world is so beautiful sometimes that I can hardly stand it." Anne kept thinking about the generous, anonymous benefactor who had given her the means to be in Colorado. How she longed to thank JWC. How she wished she could meet and know this person. Anne bent and gathered a handful of colored blossoms.

"You really like flowers, don't you?"

"I always have. My father told me that he first fell in love with my mother because she reminded him of an English garden." Anne laughed. "When I was little and hated taking baths, he'd say, 'Anne, one can always distinguish a great lady—the air around her smells like flowers.'"

"Did it get you in the tub?"

"Every time." She smiled at him.

"Marti told me that your mother died when you were young."

"That's true. I miss her still."

"Do you remember much about her?"

"It's difficult to remember. I know from her photographs that she was beautiful. Mostly, I recall small things."

"Such as?"

"She laughed a lot. I remember how she and Daddy would sit on the front steps and laugh together. Mother was British. Daddy met her while he was studying at Oxford. And she truly did smell like flowers." Anne closed her eyes and inhaled, as if the Colorado air might somehow import that other fragrance from across time.

She opened her eyes to see Morgan staring at her. She wondered what it would feel like to rest her head against his chest, the way she'd seen her mother do with her father. "What about your mother?" she asked, hoping her feelings weren't written on her face. "Was she descended from the Cheyenne grandmother?"

Morgan had avoided discussing his family, but now he felt secure and talked. "The Cheyenne is on my father's side. My mother was a beautiful woman

too, but different from the way you described yours.
Mama loved a good time. She should never have
gotten married. And she and my dad should *never*
have had a kid."

Anne felt sorry for Morgan, for the hurt look that
surfaced on his face. Had his mother treated him
badly? "What about your father?" She expected
Morgan to say that his mother had run away with
another man and that his father was around somewhere.

"My dad's dead."

The matter-of-fact way he said it shocked Anne. "I
see," she said, without seeing at all. Did that mean
that his mother had abandoned Morgan—simply
walked out of his life? And how had his father died?
Morgan didn't add anything, although Anne gave
him plenty of time. "How long have you been living
with your aunt and uncle?" she asked after an awkward silence.

"Six years."

"Your aunt cares about you. I can tell."

"I know," Morgan said. "She's my dad's sister. We
have a lot in common." Talking about his parents
had depressed him. Recalling the look of love in
Anne's eyes when she spoke about her parents only
intensified his pain. He pitied the little girl whose
mother had died and left her behind. He ached for
the twelve-year-old boy he'd been when his father
had been taken away and his mother had packed
her things and left, even though he understood—
still understood—why she had. He honestly didn't
hold it against her.

His mother's words came back clearly, although it

had been almost seven years. *"I can't stay. I can't sit around year after year and wait for this to happen to either Maggie or you. No one should have to have this happen. No one. It's a living nightmare."*

"Has our conversation depressed you?" Anne's question pulled Morgan back into the present.

"No way," he replied, forcing a smile. Looking over her shoulder, he could see Skip and Marti kissing. He wanted to kiss Anne too. He wanted to take her in his arms and kiss her until the fear inside him went away. "I learned to live with it a long time ago."

Anne didn't want to challenge him, but she was certain he'd never learned to live with what had happened to him. She gazed skyward and saw that stars were beginning to appear. "I've never seen so many stars," she said, hoping to recapture their earlier mood. "In New York City, you have to go to an observatory to see this kind of star power."

Morgan looked up and studied the star-studded night. "Out here, you take some things for granted. Night skies full of stars is only one of them." Pretty, rich girls from big cities, whom he didn't want to become involved with, were another.

"Look!" Anne cried, pointing heavenward. "A shooting star!"

Morgan watched the star streak across the night. "Some nights, it seems like the whole universe is falling to earth."

Anne could only imagine. Still staring upward, she heard Morgan say, "We should head back. It's a long ride home." She followed him back to the blanket, disappointed. Marti was making repairs to her lipstick, and Skip looked thoroughly kissed. For a moment, Anne felt a sharp twinge of envy. If only Morgan felt that way about her.

"We need to saddle up," Morgan told Skip.

"So soon? Marti has the whole night off."

"Well, I don't," Morgan said, forcing Anne to believe that he was making up an excuse to be rid of her.

Skip touched Morgan's shoulder and whispered, "Is it because of what her old man said?"

Anne heard his words and whipped around in time to catch the warning glare Morgan shot to Skip. Skip shuffled self-consciously and began folding the blanket. Flabbergasted, she stood rooted to the ground. She felt shock, then humiliation. Had her father *dared* to go to Morgan behind her back? Had he actually said something to him about her condition?

Her fingers were stiff as she saddled her horse, but once they were all on the trail, she couldn't keep silent. Skip and Marti were lagging behind them this time, and once Anne was sure they were out of earshot, she said, "I heard what Skip said back there."

"I figured you did. He's got the tact of a skunk."

"Don't be mad at him. I'm glad I overheard. What did my dad say to you?"

"It's not important."

"It is to me." Her heart was pounding, and her hands trembled on the reins.

"He didn't threaten me or anything. I know he's only concerned about you."

In the dark, she couldn't make out his expression. "He didn't threaten you?"

"He asked me to leave you alone, that's all."

Her anger flared, but she bit it back. "I wasn't aware you were bothering me."

"All right. . . . he doesn't want us spending so much time together. He doesn't want me to get too involved."

"Why?"

"It's a fact of life, Anne—fathers who bring their daughters out to the Broken Arrow for a summer vacation don't want them to get sidetracked by some dumb cowboy who's got nothing to show for his life. I'm not well educated. I'm not wealthy. I'm not any of the things fathers want for their daughters. I understand his feelings."

"Well, I don't! He had no right—"

"He had every right."

"My dad and I don't have that kind of relationship." How could she explain it to Morgan, who had no father and who argued with his uncle about control of his life? "My father's always given me space to make my own choices. He's never imposed his will on mine. And he's always trusted me. It's just now that . . ."

"Let's just forget it," Morgan said. He clucked to his horse, urging it to a canter.

Anne balled the reins in her fist in total frustration. She broke out in a cold, clammy sweat. She dug her heels into Golden Star's side and rode in a slow gallop all the way back to the ranch.

Ten

⁓

"DIDN'T WE HAVE a ball?" Marti asked.

"Sure. A great time was had by all."

"Maybe you were right about my giving other guys a chance. Maybe I deserve to see what there is beside Peter. Maybe we can do this again soon."

"Maybe so. I'll catch you tomorrow."

"Sure . . ." Marti's voice trailed off as Anne hurried toward her cabin. She didn't want to be rude to Marti, but she had plenty to tell her father.

Her father was sitting outside on the steps when she arrived. "Did you have fun?" he asked.

Anne felt betrayed and didn't bother to hide it. "Waiting up for me? You haven't done that since I was thirteen."

"Whoa . . . wait a minute. I'm just breathing in all this wonderful fresh air you're always telling me about. What's the problem? You sound as if you're indicting me."

She crossed her arms and stood in front of him. "I know that you told Morgan to leave me alone."

"How do you know that?"

"It came out in conversation."

"It simply 'came out'? Did he tell you?"

Anne recognized her father's attempt to put her on the defensive. She figured it was a skill teachers must cultivate in order to deal with belligerent students. "Why did you do it, Dad? Why would you tell him such a thing when you know I want a normal life."

He sighed heavily and urged her to sit beside him on the steps. "All right, maybe I did question him about his motives toward you."

"His motives? What are you—a detective?"

"You're infatuated with him, Anne."

She felt her cheeks color. Were her feelings so obvious that her father could read them from a distance? "I've never known anyone like Morgan before."

"Anne, this type of attraction is a first for you. It's been a long time coming, but the time has arrived. I've never seen you interested in a boy before, and it's ... difficult for me."

She hated the way he made her special feelings for Morgan sound so common and ordinary, as if they made up some kind of phase *everybody* went through. "You must think I'm a real social reject."

"I think you're beautiful, talented, smart, and heads and hands above any of the overly hormone-infused teenage boys from high school. I knew none of them could ever hold your interest."

"You're my father—of course, you think I'm one of a kind."

"As your father," he said, "I've been both anticipating and dreading this day for years. The day when you'd meet a guy who saw you for the wonderful person you are. And wanted you in every way."

She was missing her mother again. "You make it sound like I'm some raw, throbbing hormone, waiting to be pounced upon by some guy." In spite of her irritation, Anne smiled. "You can't be worried that I might trip and fall into his bed. We both know why."

When her father answered, she knew he'd given his reply much thought. "Sometimes, when I look at you, I still see that gangly eleven-year-old with the bruised knees and scraped elbows. It's difficult accepting that you're a grown woman. That you're feeling all the emotions of a normal sixteen-year-old. I never wanted to think of you growing up and getting involved with any man ... not even the one you marry and now ..."

"Except we both know that I'll never marry, don't we?"

She saw that his eyes were damp. "Sometimes, when I think about what's happening to you, it's more than I can bare. Sometimes, I wake in the middle of the night, and I'm sweating and shaking, and I can't catch my breath. I can't believe all that's being taken away from you. It isn't right. It isn't fair.

I'd give anything to have the disease and see you free of it. But I can't."

First, he lost her mother; now, he was losing her. Not in a normal way of giving her away in marriage. But to premature death. Just for the moment, she caught the impact of his anguish. "Daddy, I've been trying to sort out answers for myself about what's happened to me. I've thought about little else. Not just 'why me?' but why people have to suffer in the first place. Maybe we're not supposed to understand. Maybe all we can do is accept what we can't change, and keep on going. I realized that after mom died or I couldn't have gone on."

"It sounds as if you've examined life's imponderables with far more maturity than I have given you credit for," her father commented.

"That's what I've been doing when I haven't been riding, or looking longingly at Morgan."

He gave a quiet, sad laugh. "I don't feel I'm doing enough to help you. Enough to protect you."

"I'll need you most when we go home. When I get really sick."

"I'll be there for you. I'll never desert you, Anne." He pulled her to his side and kissed the top of her head. "In the meantime, you be careful around Morgan. Don't do anything foolish. I don't want you to have a broken heart too. I can't fix that either."

Anne wondered how she could be anything but careful. She knew what was at stake. Perhaps her father was right. Perhaps it would be best to stay away from Morgan altogether. To completely shield him from harm's way. After all, if he ever knew she was exposing him to HIV, what would he do?

Perhaps it had been a mistake to come to the Broken Arrow. She thought about JWC and for the hundredth time wondered what had possessed a person she didn't know to give her so much money. Surely, JWC and the One Last Wish Foundation had made a mistake. In receiving the money before the onset of actual AIDS, Anne had squandered some of it foolishly and chosen a path that was leading to heartache.

And yet, she was glad she'd met Morgan, who had the power to make her heart skip a beat with a mere glance. If it hadn't been for the Wish money, she would have never met him. And if she'd been perfectly healthy, their relationship still would have come to nothing more than a summer fling, she reminded herself. After all, what could he possibly find exciting about a inexperienced girl who knew nothing about love, who picked wildflowers and loved poetry?

It didn't take a genius to figure it out. Anne was avoiding him. "Chalk one up for Daddy," Morgan told himself sourly as he pitched hay in the barn one afternoon. Why was he surprised? Snobby little rich girls were all alike.

He should have just gone ahead and had a good time with her physically when he'd had the opportunity. But, no . . . he'd backed off, kept his hands to himself, all because—

His thoughts were interrupted when he heard someone come into the barn. He looked over the edge of the loft and saw Anne wandering aimlessly around the quiet barn. She was hugging a book and looking for a place to sit. *Why does she have to come in here?* He didn't need the aggravation.

He watched her settle on a mound of hay and open her book. He wished he'd taken to books—maybe then the two of them would have more in common. He decided that he wasn't going to hide from her, ignore her the way she'd been ignoring him. Morgan began to whistle, tossed a forkful of hay down from the loft, and saw it land near Anne's feet.

A startled cry escaped from her, which gave Morgan some satisfaction. He shimmied down from the loft. "Sorry," he said. "I thought I was alone in here."

"Me too." Anne started to rise, but when she planted her hand in the hay to give herself a boost, she yelped in pain.

"What's wrong?" Morgan started toward her. She lifted her hand, and he saw a line of bright red blood across her palm. He felt a sickening sensation in his stomach. "There must be something sharp under the hay. Don't move." He knelt beside her.

Fearfully, she stared at her bleeding hand.

Morgan reached beneath her, lifted her, and placed her safely away from the hay and its invisible weapon. "Let me see how bad you're cut."

"It's nothing," Anne said, keeping her hand close to her body. "I'm fine."

"You're not fine. You're bleeding. You may need stitches. Let me wipe it off and examine it."

Her eyes widened, reminding him of a deer trapped in headlights. "No! Don't touch it!"

"Why? I want to help. I've seen blood before."

"Stay away! Please, don't touch me." She was shaking all over.

"At least let me wrap my handkerchief around it to try to stop the bleeding." He fumbled in his jeans pocket.

"No!" She darted backward. "My father and I'll take care of it."

"But—"

"Please—you don't understand. I-I can't explain. Just don't touch it." Wild-eyed, panicked, she spun, and clutching her hand to her side, she bolted from the barn.

Dumbfounded, Morgan watched her run back toward her cabin.

Eleven

~~~

"LET ME SEE your hand. Does it hurt?" Marti looked worried at the dinner table that night.

"It's nothing," Anne insisted. "The doctor in Platte City put a bandage on it and gave me a tetanus shot. Talk about something that hurt—" She rubbed her arm, hoping to distract Marti.

"Morgan acted impossible all afternoon. He felt it was his fault."

"He had nothing to do with it. I cut my hand, that's all." Her eyes met her father's over Marti's head. When it had happened, all she could think about was Morgan's touching her blood and somehow absorbing the HIV into himself. And when she had to face the doctor in Platte City, when she had to tell him to take extra precautions before treating her, the reality of her situation almost devastated her. "We should leave," she'd told her father in the car coming back to the ranch. "We should go home before I infect somebody."

"Nonsense," her father had said. "If we leave, it'll be because you truly want to go. You're not a threat to anybody. Do you want to leave?"

Anne felt she was a threat. She also felt dishonest because she wasn't telling people the truth about herself. Did her friends have a right to know? A right to choose whether or not to be around her? She felt like a coward because she couldn't bring herself to tell them. Or to see the horror on their faces once they knew.

"*Oya!* Listen to me, Anne," Marti was saying. "I want to know if we can go into Platte City for Pioneer Days on Friday. I have the whole day off, and I want to go have some fun."

"I thought you were going with Skip."

Marti glanced around, then leaned closer. "He'll meet me in the afternoon, after the rodeo. You and I can see the sights until Skip's free."

"I don't know . . ." She remembered when Morgan had suggested she come to the celebration with him. After the way she'd been acting, he would probably be keeping his distance from her.

"You can't tell me no," Marti said, with a quick smile.

Anne shook her finger at Marti, who giggled and called over her shoulder, "The van for Platte City leaves from the main lodge Friday morning, and you'd better be in it with me."

On Friday, a whole crowd of guests rode into the small city. A large banner hung over the main street, proclaiming Pioneer Days, and booths and stands selling food, arts and crafts items, and western memorabilia lined the thoroughfare. People jostled along the sidewalk, and set up chairs down the side of the street for the parade scheduled at high noon.

"Isn't this fun?" Marti asked. She and Anne strolled down the sidewalk, licking ice-cream cones.

"*Si,*" Anne replied in Spanish. "*Estoy muy—*" she struggled to remember the Spanish word for 'fun' and ended up saying, "—fun!"

Marti laughed gaily. "What an accent! Come on, let's grab a spot to watch the parade."

They sat on a curb, and when the parade started, Anne discovered they were in a perfect position to see everything. Marching bands, convertibles filled with pretty girls, clowns, and riders astride different breeds of horses passed directly in front of them. Anne identified groups of palominos, pintos, paso finos, quarter horses, and purebred Arabians, ridden by men, women, even children dressed in western and Mexican clothing.

"Look, there's Skip," Marti said. She waved to a clown dressed in baggy pants, an oversized shirt, and a flaming red wig. His face was painted white, except for exaggerated drawn-on red lips.

"How can you tell?" Anne teased. Skip stepped from the parade line and handed them both balloons. "You look adorable," Anne told him.

"Thanks. Are you both coming to the rodeo? I'll be working the ring, and Morgan's going to ride," he said.

"Clowns work in rodeos?" Anne asked.

"Important work. We distract the wild bulls when a rider gets thrown."

"How? Do the bulls fall down laughing?" Anne kidded, but the image of Morgan's being thrown from the back of a bucking horse flashed through her mind.

"Very funny," Skip said as Marti giggled.

"Don't you ride the broncos or bulls?" Anne asked.

"Do I look crazy? Not this boy. I participate in the roping events and the barrel races." He glanced at the passing parade. "I'd better catch up." He grabbed Marti's hand. "March with me."

"I can't."

"Sure you can. You and Anne can hook up in the stands at the rodeo."

Anne could see that Marti wanted to go with Skip. She gave her a nudge. "Go on. I'll shop and meet you in an hour."

Once Marti and Skip had joined the parade, Anne settled back onto the curb. A group of riders was coming down the street with a banner heralding the Broken Arrow. As they passed, she recognized many of the ranch's workers. Her breath caught when she saw Morgan riding the prancing bay range horse. He'd tamed him! Her heart swelled proudly, and she waved, but she wasn't sure Morgan saw her.

When the parade ended and the crowd broke up, Anne wandered through a few stores, buying souvenirs for friends back home. In so many ways, she felt like a normal tourist with nothing to do but have a good time. If only it were true. "No negative thoughts," she told herself sternly.

She entered a western-wear shop and browsed, admiring fringed, buttery-soft buckskin jackets, a pair of snakeskin boots, and elaborate western shirts, en-crusted with appliqués, sequins, and glittering jewels. On one wall, she saw ornate Stetson hats, chaps, and leather belts. But it was a saddle sitting atop a sawhorse that took away her breath.

The saddle was black leather, decorated with sterling silver. Anne fingered the saddle's rich, hand-carved depressions and ran her palm over the intricate silver design patterns. She'd never seen anything like it, never knew such a utilitarian piece of equipment could be made to look so beautiful.

In her mind's eye, she saw it across the back of Morgan's bay stallion. She remembered what Morgan had told her about wanting to show his horse and how expensive proper show gear was to buy. She lifted the price tag and raised her eyebrows. The saddle cost almost two thousand dollars. She chewed her bottom lip. How she'd like to buy it for him!

Her mind returned to the time in the hospital when she'd discovered the OLW envelope on her pillow, and to the sense of absolute awe she'd experienced when she'd seen the check, the enormous amount of money given to her by someone she didn't even know. Hadn't the letter said, ". . . *the true miracle is in giving, not receiving*"?

While Anne knew she couldn't keep the origin of such a gift as the saddle from Morgan, she certainly had money enough to buy it for him. Moreover, she *wanted* to buy it for him, wanted him to feel what she'd felt when JWC had unexpectedly blessed her life. Heart pounding, Anne made up her mind and found a clerk.

After she'd acquired the saddle, a matching bridle, and a handwoven saddle blanket, she made arrangements for her purchases to be delivered to the Broken Arrow the following day. Pleased with herself, she followed the crowds to the outdoor rodeo arena, where she found Marti already perched in the stands for the show.

"I thought you'd gotten lost," Marti said.

"Just sidetracked. Did you have a good time?"

"The best time. I like Skip so much. He's sweet and kind and treats me like I'm special."

"You are special," Anne said.

Marti dropped her gaze. "It makes me realize how badly Peter has treated me, and I've taken it like a fool."

Once the rodeo began, Anne lost herself completely in the atmosphere. The barrel race had several age categories, three won by cowgirls. Skip placed second in the men's group, and Marti cheered more loudly than anyone in the stands for him.

The sun was setting and the arena was lit by overhead stadium lights when it came time for the bronco-riding events. Anne felt jittery. The object was for the rider to stay on the horse for as long as possible. A buzzer would sound at the end of a specific time period, and any rider who was still mounted became a finalist. "What's the prize?" Anne asked.

"A hundred dollars," Marti told her.

Anne didn't think it sounded like enough money for such a brain-rattling, teeth-jarring event, but she kept quiet. The first rider out of the chute was tossed off like a rag doll. Anne winced as he thudded onto the ground. Yet, he got up, dusted himself off, and hurried out of the ring while other riders captured the bucking horse and led it back to the holding pen.

By the time she heard Morgan's name called, her jaw hurt from clenching her teeth. She watched as he swung from the side of the special chute onto the back of a horse called Loco. "A horse named Crazy," Marti remarked. "He must be some mean one."

Anne saw Morgan wrap a gloved hand around a rope tied to the horse and raise the other hand into the air above his head in the classic one-handed posture of bronco riders. A bell rang, the gate opened, and Loco exploded into the arena.

The horse gyrated and twisted itself into impossible contortions. He hit the ground stiff-legged, his head pulled low, his eyes white with wild fury. Morgan twisted with him, gripping the horse's heaving sides with his knees. To Anne, it seemed an eternity until the buzzer sounded. The audience erupted into cheers.

Morgan released his hold on the rope and kicked himself off the animal's back. As he dropped, his boot caught in the rope. Suddenly, he was hanging sideways from the horse, unable to get off. Morgan dangled helplessly from the furious animal as it continued its mad twisting and bucking, its deadly hooves lifting off the ground, inches from Morgan's head.

A cry raced through the crowd as the spectators grasped his deadly predicament. Anne froze, watching in horror. All at once, the arena filled with clowns and men on quarter horses chasing after the bronco. One clown waved a blanket, causing the horse to stop abruptly. Quickly, two mounted cowboys came alongside Loco, sandwiched the wild horse between them and snatched his headgear, forcing him to stand still.

Clowns helped loosen Morgan's trapped foot and lower him to the ground. Others baring a stretcher ran into the arena and lifted him on it. Through her daze, Anne heard Marti yell, "They're taking him to the hospital tent!"

Twelve

ANNE RACED OUT and turned down a path, made narrow by parked horse trailers. At the far end, she saw a large tent with a red cross painted on its side, and rushed toward it. Outside, a woman wearing an armband bearing the same red cross stopped her. "Can I help you?" she asked.

Flustered, Anne groped for words. "They brought in a rider from the arena . . . he'd been thrown, dragged. I need to see how he is. He's a friend."

The nurse offered a reassuring smile. "Calm down. The doctor's taping him up now. He's got a couple of cracked ribs, some bruises and contusions, but he's going to be fine."

Anne felt her knees buckle with relief. "He won't have to go to the hospital?"

"I think he refused to go."

"Do you suppose I could go in and see him?"

"You'll have to wait in line—his family's in with him now. They looked plenty scared—and hopping mad!"

"Are you positive he's all right?"

The nurse reached out, took her hand, and said, "Don't take it so hard, honey. These cowboys are a pretty tough bunch. I've seen men stomped on by bulls weighing a ton, and they still get up to ride another day."

The tent flap opened, and a man in a lab coat stepped outside. "The boy doing okay?" the nurse asked.

"Miraculously, yes. The X rays showed no breaks other than his ribs, but that ride wrenched several muscles. He's going to be sore for a while."

"See, I told you not to worry," the nurse said to Anne.

Anne still wanted to see Morgan. "Go on, honey. Go see for yourself," the nurse said.

Smiling gratefully, Anne entered the tent carefully. Morgan was shirtless, sitting up on an examining table, a thick swath of adhesive bandage wound around his torso. Standing directly in front of him were his aunt and uncle.

She heard his uncle's angry voice, ". . . can't believe the chance you took!"

"I've ridden in plenty of rodeos. I just had some back luck today."

"Bad luck! You almost got killed!"

"I *like* to ride," Morgan replied stubbornly.

"No one cares if you ride in rodeo events," Aunt Maggie interjected. "But what's wrong with the barrel races? Or the calf roping?"

Morgan snorted. "They're not my style."

"Almost getting yourself killed is more your style?" Uncle Don shook his finger in Morgan's face. "You know what your problem is? You've got a death wish, boy! You won't be happy until you *die* out there."

"Stop it," Aunt Maggie commanded, grabbing her husband's arm. "Carrying on here and now isn't helping anything." She stepped closer to Morgan and took his face between her hands. "Oh, Morgan, you scared us to death."

Morgan looked into her eyes. "Sorry, Aunt Maggie," he mumbled.

"You're all the family I have left, Morgan. I don't want to lose you. Please, please stop this crazy, reckless way of living. Why do you do it?"

Anne saw Morgan reach up and wipe a tear from his aunt's cheek. "You, of all people, understand *why*, Aunt Maggie. You know more than anyone what might lie ahead for either one—or both—of us. You and me . . . we're different from the others."

"That may be true, but I'm living with it without risking my life. Somehow, you've got to make your peace about it."

"I can't."

Anne felt like an eavesdropper. What in the world were they talking about? What was "different" about Morgan and his aunt? They looked normal. *So do you*, she reminded herself. Could anyone tell by simply *looking* at another person what lay in the darkness of his or her life?

Uncle Don cleared his throat. "I didn't mean to be so hard on you," he said gruffly. "Maggie and I are really glad they could patch you up." He put his arm around his wife's shoulders. "We'll load your horse up in the trailer and take him back to the ranch for you."

"Thanks."

"Come with us," Aunt Maggie said.

"I'll catch a ride with Skip. I'm fine. Stop worrying about me."

His aunt and uncle both hugged him, turned, and walked toward the tent's exit. Passing Anne, they gave her a brief nod of recognition. She felt out of place. Morgan saw her. "Why are you here?" he asked, registering surprise.

"I saw you get thrown. I was concerned." She came toward him.

He edged off the table, wincing with the movement. "No need to be. Besides, I look pretty awful— and I know how the sight of blood gets to you."

"Only my own," she said humorlessly.

He picked up his torn shirt and attempted to put it on.

"Let me help," Anne offered, taking it from him and easing it along his arms. She stepped in front of him and began to button it. His face was inches from hers, and he was looking down at hers. Her breath caught, and her heart began to hammer crazily. "All finished," she said, slightly breathless.

He caught both her hands with one of his and settled them at the base of his throat. She felt the warmth of his pulse. "Are you?" he asked.

Torn with a desire she could barely suppress, Anne gently tugged her hands loose and stepped backward. "We should be going."

Morgan eyed her patiently, then reached for his hat. "I should have accepted a ride home with Uncle Don," he admitted. "I really am pretty sore."

Anne felt the air still humming between them. "Maybe Skip's ready to go on back by now."

"Let's go find out."

They rode to the ranch in Skip's old pickup truck with Marti fussing over Morgan, half scolding him in Spanish, half rejoicing that he hadn't been killed. Anne rode in silence, cramped for space, trying not to lean against Morgan's taped ribs. In the darkness, her hands trembled. She was unable to forget how much she'd wanted to put her arms around him.

At the men's quarters, Skip helped Morgan from the truck. "I'll drive the girls around," Skip said.

"Drive Marti," Morgan told him, taking hold of Anne's hand. "Let Anne stay with me for a while."

"I shouldn't," Anne said, knowing she should climb up into the truck and get out of there quickly.

"I'll need some help," Morgan countered.

The row of housing looked empty and deserted, and Anne realized that everyone was probably still in Platte City. She gulped and, against her better judgment, agreed to help him to his room.

Morgan's room was small, sparsely furnished, but tidy. It contained a table and two chairs, a bureau, a single bed, a TV, and a stereo system. A small refrigerator, a microwave, and a sink for washing dishes lined one wall. She wondered why he chose to live alone with the hired hands rather than in the comfort of the main lodge with his aunt and uncle. She knew without question that they would have allowed him such a privilege.

"I like living here," he explained, as if reading her mind.

Anne's hands fluttered nervously. "You've done a nice job with the room."

"Probably not anything like what you're used to."

Puzzled, she didn't know how to answer. "Maybe I should get you settled before Skip comes back for me."

"He'll be a while."

"He does seem to like Marti, doesn't he? I think they make a cute couple. Don't you?" Anne felt as if she were babbling.

Morgan eased onto his bed, propping the pillow against the headboard, and snapped on the bedside lamp. "Turn off the overhead, will you? It's hurting my eyes." She flipped off the main light switch with shaking fingers. "Come here," he said.

She came, and he urged her to sit on the side of the bed. She felt like a moth drawn to a flame. "Don't your ribs hurt?" she asked.

"Like crazy." He reached up and ran his fingers through her long, dark hair.

She quivered. He turned off the lamp, and suddenly moonlight streamed through the window over his bed. Squares of white light stretched across the spread and dripped onto the floor. By now, Anne's heart was thudding so fast that she was certain her body couldn't contain it. Her bones felt like warm liquid.

He pulled her closer and kissed her forehead, her temple, her closed eyelids. "Stay with me, Anne," she heard Morgan whisper. "Please stay the night."

Thirteen

~∞~

STAY WITH ME. Anne heard the words echoing in her brain, felt the yearning they carved inside her heart. To stay with Morgan, to spend a night in his arms, to taste a world she'd only read about in books and poetry. . . . "Skip will be coming back for me soon," she said.

"Skip will pull up outside and honk. If you don't go out, he'll drive away." Morgan cupped her chin and stroked her hair. "You must know how much I want to be with you, Anne. I've tried to stay away from you, tried to pretend that I wasn't attracted to you, but for the life of me, I can't pretend anymore. You're very beautiful, and I want you very much."

For the life of me. The words fell like hammer blows into a core of cool logic inside her mind. What he was asking of her could cost him his life. She'd read about, heard about, and knew how to practice safe sex, but in one heartrending moment, she realized that such safety could be illusionary. And one chance, even one in a million, was one too many for her to risk his life, no matter how much she wanted to stay with him. "I can't stay." Dragging out the words was difficult.

"Why?"

"I just can't." She pulled away from his arms and stood, struggling to keep her voice steady.

"Anne—"

"I think I should wait outside for Skip. I think you should get some rest." She was trembling all over.

He looked up at her, and in the swath of moonlight, he looked wounded. "Sure. Whatever you want."

Anne felt tears jamming up behind her eyes. She fumbled for the doorknob. It felt cold and hard in her grip. Once she stepped out of the room, this part of her life would dissipate like smoke. She wanted to run back to him, throw herself in his arms, and beg him to hold her, kiss her. She knew in that moment that she loved him, but could never tell him.

"Good-bye," she whispered. And with more bravery than she ever dreamed she possessed, Anne stepped quickly into the night.

She arose early the next morning and went straight to the lodge. The aroma of fresh coffee, sizzling bacon, and baking biscuits filled the air, and a radio played country music in the background.

When she entered, Morgan struggled up from one

of the sofas and came toward her. "Morning," he said. His eyes looked guarded.

"You feeling all right?" she asked, her heart thudding.

"I ache all over. Uncle Don's relieved me of my duties for the next week; the doctor told us it'll take at least six weeks for the ribs to completely heal. Anyway, I'm supposed to be taking it easy."

"Then you should still be in bed, resting."

"I wanted to talk to you. I wanted to apologize for last night."

Anne nervously glanced down at the floor. "There's nothing to apologize for."

"I was out of line. I never should have asked you what I did."

She didn't want him taking it back. She wanted to think, even now, that he'd meant what he'd said. "It's okay. Forget it."

"I guess that bronco rattled my brain," Morgan said with a sincere smile. "I'm sorry if I insulted you."

"You didn't insult me."

"Then you're not angry at me?"

"I'm not."

Morgan tipped the brim of his hat to her, then limped painfully away.

Anne thought the matter was settled and that she and Morgan were finished, so when Maggie asked her to go see Morgan down in the barn, she was surprised and mystified. She hurried to the barn, eager to spend any time she could near him. When she came in out of the hot, bright sun, she saw Morgan leaning against the gate of a stall, the fancy leather-and-silver saddle thrown over it.

"It came!" Anne cried, hurrying over. She'd forgotten all about it. "Do you like it?"

"I thought my apology was enough." His voice sounded cool.

Anne felt her smile fade. "I don't know what you mean."

"Did you think you had to soothe my feelings with this?"

She was confused by his hostility. "I thought you'd like it. That you would use it on the bay, during parades. I thought you'd be pleased."

He shook his head and pushed stiffly away from the stall. "You little rich girls are all alike. You think that you can buy anybody's favor, purchase anything you want with Daddy's money."

"Rich?" She couldn't believe his assumption. "What makes you think I'm rich?"

"I know what that saddle cost. I've looked at it many times. Don't tell me you didn't spend a fortune on it."

Anne was speechless. She wanted to tell him she wasn't wealthy, hadn't been born into the lap of luxury. Yet, how could she explain? She clamped her lips tightly. There was no way, of course. It was far better to allow Morgan to cling to his false assumptions about her than for her to explain reality. "It's a gift, Morgan, with no strings, no hidden motives."

"I don't want it."

She held her head high. "It's yours anyway. If you really don't want it, you can throw it in the garbage, for all I care. Rich girls like me can buy others." She spun, kicking up dust and hay with her boots, and jogged quickly away from the barn and the gleaming saddle.

The next week dragged for Anne. She didn't feel well, either. Her glands were swollen, and a persistent cough plagued her. Sometimes she awoke in the night sweating profusely. Her appetite decreased, but she attributed that to the unhappiness she felt over her estrangement from Morgan.

One afternoon, a steady rain forced all activity on the ranch to a standstill. Anne confined herself to a game of solitaire in the main lodge, hardly noticing the guests who grouped around the TV set and board games. From the corner of her eye, she saw Morgan sitting on the hearth of the great stone fireplace. He was entertaining a group of kids with a length of rope, showing them how to tie different kinds of knots.

A violent clap of thunder shook the rafters. Anne started, and kids squealed, scampering toward their mothers like frightened kittens. "It's only a big boomer," Anne heard Maggie explain to everyone. "My mama used to say thunder was only the angels bowling up in heaven."

Laughter rippled through the room. "Fall's coming," Maggie added. "Summer rain means autumn's on its way."

Anne didn't want to think about autumn, because it meant she'd be back home, and if her health held, she'd be back in school. She'd miss the outdoors, Golden Star, Maggie, Marti, Skip, Morgan—most of all, Morgan.

Suddenly, the door of the lodge banged and Skip

stood framed in the open doorway. His yellow slicker streamed with water that puddled on the floor around his boots. "Morgan!" Skip shouted. "You'd better come quick. Your bay bolted, tried to jump the fence. He's hurt. Bad."

Fourteen

MORGAN GOT UP too fast, and a stabbing pain shot through his side. He clamped his hand over his taped, bruised ribs and limped toward Skip. "What happened?" he asked.

"The thunder must have spooked him. I was in the barn and looked out in time to see him try to jump the corral fence. There wasn't enough room for a running start, of course, and he went crashing through the poles."

Morgan felt a sickening sensation in the pit of his stomach. "Is he up?"

"Last I saw, he was thrashing on the ground. I came to find you, quick as I could."

Morgan didn't wait for further explanations. He shoved past Skip and hurried outside into the driving rain faster than his aching side wanted him to move. If his horse was still down, it meant only one thing—he was too hurt to get up. Horses instinctively sought to stay upright.

The rain was driving so hard, Morgan could barely navigate his way to the corral. He was drenched to the skin and trying to maneuver through the mud. He arrived at the corral, but the rain was so heavy, he couldn't see from one side to the other. Skip caught up with him. "This way," Skip yelled.

Gasping for breath, Morgan hobbled after him; his lungs felt on fire. The horse was lying on the ground, one of its legs twisted at an angle. The animal continued to thrash, but its movements looked weak. Morgan crouched by the bay's head. Its eyes were wide with fright. "Take it easy, fella," Morgan said, stroking the animal's neck.

Skip knelt beside him. "It's bad, isn't it?" He had to shout to be heard above the rain.

"The worst. Uncle Don always said the horse was spooky. I should have listened to him, should never have tried to make him my own."

"Don't blame yourself."

The horse was one more thing he'd loved and lost. Morgan rose painfully and steeled himself for what he knew he had to do. The horse would have to be put down. The ranch couldn't afford to nurse a horse that had value only to him and that would probably never be right even if he did heal. Feed and veterinarians cost money. "Dumb, hardheaded beast," Morgan said to himself, trying to distance himself emotionally.

"You want me to take over?" Skip asked.

"I can handle it." Morgan felt a coldness inside himself, similar to the one he'd felt when he'd learned about his father.

"You sure?"

Morgan nodded.

Skip went into the barn and emerged with Morgan's rifle. He handed it to him.

"What are you doing?" Anne's frantic question above the roar of the rain took Morgan and Skip by surprise.

Morgan turned, ignoring the pain in his side from too quick a movement. "Get out of here," he said.

"I won't! What are you going to do?" Her eyes looked wide and frightened. The rain had plastered her clothing to her body, and her hair hung in soaked ringlets.

She tried to march past Morgan and Skip, but Morgan caught her around the waist and pushed her toward Skip. "Take her back to the lodge," he ordered.

Anne struggled. "I won't go! You're going to shoot him, aren't you? You're going to kill your horse!"

"His leg is broken, and he's suffering. It's the humane thing to do."

"But there are doctors—vets . . . you could call someone . . ."

"Get her out of here, Skip."

Skip tried to pull her gently away. "Come on, Anne."

She broke from Skip and hurled herself at Morgan. "How can you do such a thing? I don't understand how you can be so heartless."

Morgan raised the rifle, cocked the firing mechanism. "Don't you know, Anne? Life's cruel."

She drew herself up tall and glared straight into his icy blue eyes. "Not life," she said. "People are cruel."

Anne shook off Skip's hold on her elbow, spun, and ran as hard and fast as she could. She shivered. She was so wet and cold that her teeth chattered. She didn't care. Nothing mattered, nothing except putting distance between Morgan and his shattered horse, and herself.

From far away, she heard the sharp, distinctive crack of a rifle. Anne covered her ears and cried out as if the bullet had hit her.

Anne stayed in bed all the following day. Her body ached, and she felt a pressure in her chest, as if weights were pressing against her, making it difficult to breathe.

"I've called Dr. Rinaldi in Denver," her father fumed. "How could you allow yourself to get drenched yesterday? You know your immune system can't handle this."

Anne was too weak, too ill to argue. Her father bundled her up, put her in the backseat of the ranch's station wagon, and drove much too fast all the way into the city. After Dr. Rinaldi examined her, he wrote several prescriptions. "You've got pneumonia. For an HIV-positive person, this is extremely dangerous. You'll need to be hospitalized immediately."

She tried to protest.

"You can't put off going onto the AZT any longer.

I believe that your blood work will show that your T4 cells have fallen drastically. Let me check you in to the hospital, start you on AZT, and get your infection under control."

She shook her head. "I want to go home, back to New York City." She looked to her father. "Can you get us a plane to New York tomorrow?" Anne felt surprisingly calm. "We can pack and be to the airport by morning," she said.

"I'll pack. You rest," her father said. "Doctor, can she manage the trip?"

The doctor spoke against it, but finally admitted it was their choice.

They arrived back at the ranch late, but Anne insisted on saying good-bye to Marti. They'd be leaving before dawn. Anne slipped into the cabin and shook Marti's shoulder.

"Is it time to get up already? I feel like I just went to bed." Marti rubbed her eyes. "Is that you, Anne? What are you doing here? Is something wrong?"

"My dad and I are going home," Anne whispered.

"What?"

"Right after we pack."

"But why?" Marti sat upright.

"I'm not feeling well, and Dad wants me home, near my own doctors."

"I thought you just had a cold."

For a moment, Anne was tempted to tell Marti the truth, then her courage failed. She wanted Marti to remember her fondly, not with fear or disgust. "I have to go."

"But what about Morgan? Have you told him?"

"You tell him for me."

Marti gripped Anne's hand. "There's something really wrong with you, isn't there?"

"Yes," Anne admitted.

Marti stifled a cry, then threw her arms around Anne. "I knew it. Morgan told me about your cut and how you acted. I decided not to ask you about it, but it's got something to do with your leaving, doesn't it? Anne, tell me."

"I can't," she said miserably.

"I'll miss you so much." Marti was starting to cry.

"I'll miss you too." Anne hugged her friend tightly.

"If it weren't for you, I'd never have realized Peter was bad for me."

"What did I do?"

"You told me to date Skip. I never would have if you hadn't encouraged me. He's the best thing that ever happened to me."

"Don't tell Peter when you're back in LA," Anne kidded. "He may come after me. You were a good friend to me too, Marti, especially when I needed one who didn't ask questions. I'll never forget you."

"Will you write me?"

"I'll write." Anne knew she'd probably have plenty of time, lying in a hospital bed. She rose, but Marti refused to release her hand. "What's wrong?"

"Oh, Anne, I just had the strangest feeling. I'm afraid I'll never see you again. I know that doesn't make any sense, but I'm scared. Promise me you'll come back next year, and I will too."

"If I'm able," Anne said, trying to sound cheerful.

"I have to go." Anne extricated her hand from Marti's and headed toward the door.

"I'll light candles for you in church every Sunday," Marti said with a quivery voice.

"*Gracias.*"

Marti began to cry. "*Vaya con Dios*, Anne. Go with God."

"I will, *te amiga*," Anne whispered, and shut the door softly behind her.

Fifteen

$\sim\!\mathcal{C}\heartsuit\mathcal{D}\!\sim$

Bᴀᴄᴋ ɪɴ ɴᴇᴡ ʏᴏʀᴋ, Anne was hospitalized immediately. Her recuperation from pneumonia was long and painful, her adjustment to AZT difficult. She had no energy and was nauseous and sick. She suffered with unbearable itching. Everything made her depressed. "I can't blame it all on the AZT," she told her father. "How else is a person supposed to feel when she knows she'll never get well?"

Her doctors were thorough. They tried her on different combinations of drugs, but her T-cell count continued to plunge. When Anne confronted the doctors, they told her she now had full-blown AIDS. She took the news as courageously as possible—mostly for her father's sake.

After her release from the hospital, her father took her home where she was too weak and ill to resume a normal life. Anne was lonely. She hadn't confided in any of her friends so no one visited or called.

"Let me talk to the kids you know," her father urged.

"It doesn't matter," Anne told him, even though, deep down it did matter. She figured none of them would know what to say to her, or how to act around someone who was terminally ill. As summer faded into fall, confined to her bed in their apartment, Anne fought to keep her spirits up by reliving her Colorado summer in her daydreams.

She gazed longingly out of the window in her bedroom, watching the bare branches of a tree bend in a raw, November wind. "Can I get you anything before I head out to class?" her father asked, entering her room.

"I'm fine. You go on." She knew he hated leaving her alone.

"Mrs. Hankins must have been delayed in traffic," he added. "I can call and have someone cover my classes for me."

"Dad, she'll be here. Stop worrying."

He bent and kissed Anne's cheek. She held her breath, knowing it was a silly thing to do. She knew AIDS wasn't contagious by kissing this way, but she was nervous anyway.

"There's a PBS special on tonight," her father said. "I thought we could watch it together."

"I'd like that."

"It's a date then. I'm off for now."

"Have mercy on your poor students."

From the doorway, his smile looked tight. "Mercy. I've forgotten about that concept."

Anne adjusted the pillows against her back and sighed heavily. If only the days weren't so long. She knew JWC, her secret benefactor, understood what she was experiencing. She knew the words in the letter by heart. *"Through no fault of our own we have endured pain and isolation and have spent many days in a hospital feeling lonely and scared."* Surely, Anne decided, JWC had endured AIDS, for no one who hadn't could possibly understand. However, "lonely and scared" didn't begin to define what Anne had feared most in the hospital.

After weeks of treatment, she'd grabbed her father's hand one night and sobbed, "Promise me, you won't let me die in this place."

"Honey, you're not going to die yet," her father managed to reply.

"It's not the dying. It's the thought of dying *here*. Take me home. Please. No matter how bad it gets, promise me, you won't make me come back to the hospital."

"I can't make such a promise. I couldn't save you at home."

"Don't try. Just let me go. Don't let them hook me up to machines and keep me alive just to endure more pain." She felt desperate. "I want to go home. I want to be in my home . . . my room when it happens, Daddy."

He tried to calm her. "Take it easy. Don't think about this now. Think about getting well. I'll find out all that I can about caring for someone with AIDS at home."

"You wouldn't mind taking care of me?"

"Oh, Anne ... I won't leave you in the care of strangers. I love you."

Anne smiled at her father's tenderness. She'd met AIDS patients in the hospital who'd been disowned and abandoned by their families after their diagnosis. She couldn't understand such misery. Her father had cared enough about her to undertake the chore of home care, and devoted all of his time to her.

"Anne, it's me, Mrs. Hankins." The older woman's voice floated down the hall into Anne's room.

"I'm in my room," Anne called.

Mrs. Hankins bustled into the room. "Sorry I'm late. Missed my bus." She set down her things and took off her coat. "All ready for that bath? I thought we could wash your hair today too."

Anne was more than ready. Ever since her skin had erupted in painful, itchy shingles, her relief came from the oatmeal bath soaks Mrs. Hankins helped her with three times a week. Her hair was a different matter. Most of it had fallen out because of the drugs. She'd cut it until it was no more than a few inches long all over her head.

"Joan of Arc was also closely cropped," her father had kidded. Yet, she'd seen sorrow in his eyes when he'd gathered up the handfuls of her once long, beautiful, brown hair.

Mrs. Hankins brought out a pale pink flannel nightgown from Anne's bureau. "This is pretty. I'll help you into it when we're finished."

As Anne soaked in the soothing tub of water, Mrs. Hankins changed the bed linen and put a bouquet of fresh flowers into a vase. Anne was grateful to this woman who came several times a week to help her.

She was from a group of volunteers called Good Samaritan. Their mission was to provide practical support for AIDS patients.

"Why would you want to help me? You don't even know me." Anne had said when the chaplain at the hospital had first introduced Anne to Mrs. Hankins.

The woman's blue eyes studied her tenderly. "I lost a son, Todd, to AIDS. His own father wanted nothing to do with him. I nursed Todd, trying to ease his physical and emotional pain.

"The Good Samaritan group showed us both how to accept what had happened. To accept God's love and to forgive ourselves, and others, for what we can't change. I promised that once Todd was gone, I would continue to live out the call to love and service. It seems the very least I can do."

In the two months Mrs. Hankins had been coming to her home, Anne had become deeply connected to the caring woman who helped with her most personal needs. Her presence gave Anne's father a break from the constant strain of caregiving. There were others who helped too—a social worker, a nurse, and her doctors—but Anne appreciated Mrs. Hankins the most.

"All through?" Mrs. Hankins asked, coming into the bathroom. "Let's blow dry your hair. Would you like to put on some makeup?"

"You know none of that will help the way I look," Anne replied, refusing to so much as glance at her reflection in the mirror.

"Trust me," Mrs. Hankins said with a gleam in her eye, "it will help you feel better."

When Anne was safely tucked between clean

sheets, Mrs. Hankins said, "I'll go tidy up the kitchen."

"You don't have to do that. Dad will—"

"Your dad's a fine man, and I'm sure he's a fine professor, but his kitchen skills are a bit lacking."

Anne smiled. She was familiar with her father's bad habits. Depression stole over her as she imagined him living alone, without her. Anne struggled against it. She leaned back against the pillows and, while Mrs. Hankins bustled about the apartment, Anne stared up at the solitary patch of grey sky.

She closed her eyes and pictured the rugged mountains of Colorado etched against the bright blue heavens. The image of Morgan astride his big bay stallion galloped across the canvas of her memory. It was Morgan she missed most of all. She told herself that just as there was no more bay horse, she had no hope of ever seeing Morgan again. Yet, like the bitter wind that surged outside her window, the memories persisted, filling her with both longing and despair for what could never be.

Sixteen

◆

"PEOPLE ARE CRUEL." Over the months, Anne's words returned to Morgan time and again. What he heard her *really* say was *"You're cruel."*

The look of horror in her brown eyes and the revulsion her face expressed when he shot the bay, hounded him. She hadn't understood, of course. She'd thought him cruel and heartless, when in reality he'd done the most humane thing possible. They had parted in anger, she had left for New York, and he'd never been able to tell her he was sorry.

When Marti had first told him that Anne had gone without so much as a good-bye to him, Morgan had been furious. He couldn't believe that she'd deserted him. Marti insisted that something had been wrong with Anne, something to do with her health. Angrily, he had brushed off Marti's explanation, but as summer turned into fall and he began to overcome the hurt of Anne's abandonment, he began to remember the wonderful times they'd shared. His anger dulled, while his good memories grew vivid.

Cold November wind blasted down from the mountains, bringing snow before Thanksgiving. Skip, who'd stayed on as a regular ranch hand, took off two weeks and went to L.A. to visit Marti. Morgan tried to keep himself busy with ranch chores and with the search for a horse he liked as much as the bay.

Skip called him over Thanksgiving. "You should come out here, Morgan. The sun shines every day."

"Don't get a sunburn."

"And Hollywood is something else!"

Morgan grinned, hearing the excitement in Skip's voice. "Don't go getting 'discovered'—we need you back here. How's Marti?"

"Great. She's already asked Maggie for a job next summer. I guess I'm irresistible."

"I won't tell her you said that. Has Marti heard anything from Anne?" he asked, more casually than he felt.

"The last letter she got, Anne wrote that she'd been in the hospital, but that she was home now."

"The hospital?" Morgan felt his heart constrict. "What was wrong with her?"

"Anne never says, but Marti believes it's something really serious. Why don't you write Anne?"

"I'll think about it." Morgan hung up and thought about little else. Why was life treating him so unfairly? First his father, now Anne, and eventually, maybe even himself and Aunt Maggie. Morgan hated the injustice of it all.

A week before Christmas, he went to talk to his aunt. "I've been thinking of taking some time off," he said.

Maggie put down her pen and closed the ledger book she was working with. "You're not a hired hand, Morgan. You're family. You work hard, and if you want to get away for a while, go on."

"You don't think Uncle Don will mind?"

"If you'd gone to college, you wouldn't be here at all. He won't mind. Where will you go?"

"East." His plan had been forming for weeks, and now it had taken on an urgency.

"How long?"

"I don't know."

"I wish I could help you be happier, Morgan. Maybe some time away from here will do you good."

"It's not just that," Morgan said haltingly. "There are a lot of things I need to figure out. I need some time to sort through them."

"You know I understand."

He knew that his aunt did. She might be facing the same horrifying future as he. "I'll let you know when I get where I'm going," Morgan promised.

"This is your home, so take a break, then come back." She hugged him tight.

"Thanks, Aunt Maggie." Morgan felt a knot lodge in his throat. It was difficult to think about leaving, but he knew he must. He had to find some answers, not only about Anne Wingate, but about Morgan Lancaster too.

Anne propped herself up in bed and tried to read. The type on the page of the book kept blurring. This new problem frightened her very much. She couldn't stand the thought of losing her eyesight and not being able to read. Her father had brought her a tape recorder and stacks of books on tape, but going blind was horrifying.

Exasperated, she tossed the book aside. Out the window, the sky promised snow. Maybe they'd have a white Christmas. She smelled the scent of gingerbread coming from the kitchen. Mrs. Hankins's work, Anne knew. Her father was out doing errands. Anne had asked him not to bother with presents for her this year, but he'd been so appalled that she'd not mentioned it a second time. Still, she knew that her time was running out and hadn't wanted him to waste time and money for a Christmas she might not live to see.

Every day, she was weaker, sicker. Her latest blood work had shown a very low platelet and white blood count. Right before Thanksgiving, she'd had to return to the hospital because of a persistent cough and high fever. Thankfully, she hadn't developed pneumonia again. She heard the door buzzer; Mrs. Hankins answered it.

Minutes later, Mrs. Hankins came to Anne's room. "There's someone to see you," she said.

"To see me? Who is it?"

"A very handsome young man. He wouldn't give his name."

"He must have the wrong Anne Wingate." She couldn't imagine that anyone from school would just drop by. "I really don't feel like having visitors anyway."

"He said I had to persuade you. I told him I'd try, but it's up to you, Anne."

Anne was mystified. "What does he look like?"

"A cowboy."

Anne's stomach lurched, and her heart wedged in her throat. It couldn't be. . . . "Please don't let him in."

"I'm in." Morgan stood at the doorway.

Anne covered her face and attempted to hunch down under the covers. "Don't look at me," she cried.

"You'd better wait by the entry door," Mrs. Hankins said.

Morgan stepped around Mrs. Hankins and moved close to Anne's bed. "Look at me," he said. She kept her hands over her face, but he noticed lesions along her neck and on one of her hands.

"Go away! Please! Don't look at me! Why are you here?"

"I had to see you."

"No!" The word sounded final and tortured. "I'm hideous, I'm sick. Go away!"

"Please, young man," Mrs. Hankins said. "You're upsetting her."

Morgan gently took hold of both Anne's wrists. Even though she tried to hide, he saw her face. She looked thin and gaunt. "I let you look at me when that bronc rearranged my face last summer."

Slowly, Anne raised her eyes to meet his. She could hardly keep from weeping. She wanted to run and hide, and yet she wanted to throw her arms around him. He looked so wonderful, so healthy.

"I've changed, haven't I?" Anne asked, her voice quivering.

She'd changed horribly, he thought, but he knew what courage it had taken for her to face him. "What's wrong, Anne? We're all worried about you."

"I'm ill." She held her head higher now, almost defiantly.

"Are you allowing him to stay?" Mrs. Hankins asked.

The damage was done. There was no use trying to hide the truth from Morgan any longer. "It's all right, Mrs. Hankins. He can stay here."

"Anne tires easily," Mrs. Hankins warned. "I'll be in the kitchen, Anne."

"I want to know what's wrong with you," Morgan insisted gently once he and Anne were alone. "Please tell me. Maybe I can help."

She gestured to one of the lesions. "This is Kaposi's sarcoma. A type of skin cancer."

His gaze barely brushed over the ugly lesions. "Skin cancer is the reason you left so suddenly last summer? I want to know why you went without even saying good-bye to me."

"You should have phoned. We could have discussed it over the phone."

"Too impersonal."

"You should have told me you were coming."

"I was afraid you wouldn't see me."

"You would have been right." She sighed and nervously brushed her hand through her wispy hair. If only she could look pretty again.

"You've changed the subject," he said. "Tell me what's going on."

She hated to, feared the look of revulsion that would cross his face. "I have AIDS." She stared straight at him, waiting for him to bolt toward the door.

He felt as if he'd been slammed on the ground from the back of a bucking horse. He didn't know a lot about AIDS, but he knew it was fatal. "Is that what you've been afraid to tell me?"

"Aren't *you* afraid?" She couldn't believe he was enlightened enough not to be fearful.

Morgan shook his head. "I'm one person who isn't afraid."

It was her turn to be surprised. "Do you know someone with AIDS? Do you have AIDS?"

"No."

"Then why—"

He folded his hands together and silenced her with an anguished look. Quietly, he asked, "Have you ever heard of the disease Huntington's chorea?"

Seventeen

"HUNTINGTON'S CHOREA?" ANNE searched her memory for the meaning of the name. "No, I haven't. Tell me about it."

"It's a genetic disorder. It gets passed along through families. The word 'chorea' comes from a word that means dance." Morgan gave a bitter chuckle. "It's a dance, all right. A victim has no control over his movements. For no reason, he jerks spasmodically. He gets worse and worse until he can't walk. Then his muscles get stiff and rigid. All the while, the mind is affected too, and the victim turns paranoid. Eventually, the person becomes totally disabled, no more than a living vegetable. And finally—sometimes after years of suffering—he dies of choking to death, or from pneumonia, or heart failure or a blood clot. The folk singer Woody Guthrie died of it."

Anne blinked, feeling the anguish of Morgan's description. "Why are you telling me this?"

"Do you remember when I told you that my father was dead?" Anne nodded. "That's not true," he said. "He's in an institution in St. Louis that specializes in caring for people with Huntington's."

"Oh, Morgan . . ." Anne felt tears well in her eyes.

"It's simpler to say he's dead. . . . I mean, he may as well be. He's totally disabled and out of it. I was eight when his symptoms first started, but I still remember what it was like—what he turned into. Up till then, my daddy was a big, fun-loving cowboy. One day, his body started making weird twitching motions. He started falling down while walking. At first, the doctor thought he'd had a seizure, so he put him on medicine. It didn't help.

"Then, gradually, Dad turned mean and crazy. He chased Mom with a butcher knife one time. Another time, he drove the car right through the side of the house. Finally, after five years of living with this wild, spastic lunatic, Mom and Aunt Maggie decided to lock him away. That's when another group of doctors realized he had Huntington's disease."

"Is that why your mom left?"

"When the diagnosis finally came in, she was burned out. Like I told you, Mom was once a pretty party girl. She never signed on for Huntington's."

"But she had you to care for."

"I was better off with Aunt Maggie and Uncle Don. I know it's hard to believe, but I understood why my mom left, and I didn't hold it against her. I still don't and I never will. I've made my peace with that."

Anne could hardly absorb why he wouldn't have resented her for leaving him. "But once your father was being cared for, the two of you could have made it."

"I'm not so sure." Morgan stared down at his hands. "Huntington's doesn't strike when people are real young—people get it when they're in their thirties, or even their fifties. A person—a blood relative, that is—has a fifty-fifty chance of getting it if the gene for it is already in the family."

His voice had dropped so low that Anne had to lean forward to catch the last. A silence fell in the room, and she waited for him to resume. He didn't, but in the lengthening silence, she caught the drift of what he'd left unsaid. The weight of it took the breath from her. "Your Aunt Maggie could get it," Anne said slowly. "Or you."

"That's right—either one of us. We're walking time bombs. I know Mom couldn't have faced it again. It was easier for her to walk away from the pain of the past and make sure she didn't have to face it again."

Anne couldn't understand such a solution, but she didn't say anything. She knew his aunt and uncle truly cared for him. "Isn't there any way to know if you'll get it or not?"

He shrugged and didn't answer. "When Aunt Maggie took my daddy to that nursing home, the doctors explained that it could take him upward of twenty years to die, because in other ways, he was in good health. Twenty years of existing in hell, while his brain slowly turns to jelly. Aunt Maggie and Mom got out of there as fast as they could."

"You haven't seen him in all these years?"

"No, and I don't want to." His tone sounded so final. Anne wanted to tell him that if she could see her mother again, even for a minute, she wouldn't care about the circumstances, but she let Morgan continue. "I was twelve when Dad was institutionalized, and I've lived these past six years knowing that it might happen to me . . . and that there's nothing medical science can do to stop it. There's no cure."

"I overheard your uncle say you had a death wish. At least, now I understand why."

"Maybe he's right. I guess it's easier to take chances with my life, to feel like I'm in control somehow, than to sit and wait for Huntington's chorea to drop in on me."

Anne comprehended his reasoning perfectly. Hadn't that been what she'd done by choosing not to begin AZT treatments when she could have, but instead going to the ranch? "It may not happen to you," Anne suggested. "You might not be doomed, and you should try not to ruin your life."

"I've got a possible twenty-year wait before I find out, and I don't want to be tested and know for sure. What kind of life is that? What kind of plans can a person make with that hanging over his head?"

"Oh, Morgan—"

"Don't feel sorry for me." He glanced at her sharply. His expression softened. "I guess I shouldn't complain so. You're the one who's worse off. Anne, you should have said something to me before you left—I care about you, about what's happening to you."

"I didn't know what to say," she replied. "Do you

think it's easy to tell someone such a dreadful thing? I wasn't sure how you'd take it. I didn't know about your problem. You didn't confide in me either."

"I guess you're right," he said. "We were both afraid."

"How did you get here anyway?" she asked, changing the subject.

"I sold the saddle." She nodded in understanding. "I never did find a horse I liked as well as the bay. Maybe something will come in off the range in the spring—a colt, something younger, easier to work with . . . not so spooky."

Anne remembered the beautiful Colorado mountains and longed for her lost summer. If only . . . "I hope so."

Morgan tried to hold on to his new feelings. He felt comfortable being with Anne. He'd never told anyone his secret until now. The intense empathy on her face touched him. Even in her pain, she could feel compassion and concern for him. He wanted to hold her, and yet, he wasn't sure she'd let him. He wasn't afraid of her AIDS. He didn't even care how she'd contracted it. All that mattered was being with her.

Feeling lost for words, he glanced around her room. It looked homey and peaceful, filled with books and posters, a stereo, and stacks of CDs. "I thought a rich girl like you would have all kinds of maids and servants," he remarked.

"You keep accusing me of being wealthy," Anne said, baffled. "Why is that? My dad and I aren't rolling in money."

"I know how much it costs to spend a whole summer at the Broken Arrow, and how much that saddle cost. I just assumed . . ."

"Let me show you something, cowboy," she said. "I've shared my one big secret, but I have another incredible one." She reached over to her bedside table, picked up a piece of folded paper, and handed it to him. "Believe it or not, this is the source of all my wealth."

Morgan could tell the letter had been folded and refolded many times. He read, growing more astonished with every word. "You mean somebody just handed you a check for one hundred thousand dollars?" he asked when he was finished.

"Yes."

"That's hard to believe."

"It was for me too. Dad didn't want to, but I used that money for us to go out West. Even though I don't know the identity of JWC, I've been grateful for what he or she did for me. I'm positive this JWC has had a similar experience. We're kindred spirits."

"What about the rest of the money?"

"It's going to care for me while I'm sick. The medications are expensive, and the hospitalizations too."

"The woman who opened the door?"

"Actually, she's a volunteer. She lost a son to AIDS, and now she wants to help others. I've made my dad promise not to let me die stuck in the hospital," Anne explained.

"But, what if—" Morgan blurted, wishing he'd thought before he'd spoken.

"What if I get so sick, I die at home?" Anne finished his question. "That's my goal. I want to die in

my own bed, with no machines or impersonal surroundings."

His eyes grew wide. "It's that control stuff again,
Morgan. I can't stop myself from dying, so I'm
choosing my place and my way. It was hard to convince my dad. It's not much, but it's all I have."

Morgan stayed for dinner that night. With effort,
Anne came to the dining room table, where she,
Morgan, and her father ate and made small talk. All
through the meal, Morgan sensed an undercurrent
of hostility coming from Anne's father. After Anne
was tucked into bed, he decided to talk to Dr.
Wingate before he left.

Morgan approached him in the living room. "Can
I speak to you, sir?"

"What is it?"

"I would like your permission to stay here in New
York and to visit Anne regularly.

Dr. Wingate tapped his fingers and gave Morgan a
skeptical, searching look. "Why?"

"I care about her."

"I care about her too. I don't want her hurt."

"I don't plan to hurt her."

"She's going to die, Morgan. We don't know how
much longer she has, but it could take months."

"I don't care how long it takes. I want to stay."

Dr. Wingate paused, thinking. "Look, I've attended classes about how to properly care for Anne
at home. We have a team of doctors involved, and
volunteers too. There are precautions that must be
taken every step of the way."

"I'm not afraid of catching AIDS."

"The precautions aren't for your sake. They're for hers. She's vulnerable to infections. Even a common cold could kill her, and we just made it by after her bout with pneumonia."

"I'll do whatever you want. I'd just like your permission."

"I know she likes having you here. She's shown more spirit, more spark today than she has in the last month. I won't lie to you—these past few months have been pretty hard on me. I attend a support group for parents." He adjusted his glasses and stared hard at Morgan. "If you want to stay, I won't stop you. If you can make my daughter's life better, I can make room for you here in the apartment."

"Look, I don't want to put you out. Maybe I can find a place—"

"This is New York City, Morgan, not Colorado. You don't want to be in some fleabag hotel. No . . . you'll be better off here—if you want to be."

Morgan thought his offer sounded almost like a challenge. "All right," Morgan said. "I'll move in. Thank you."

"You may not thank me for long, Morgan. I'm doing this for my daughter. Whatever time she's got left, I want her to be happy. You make her happy. Please, don't do anything to hurt her. She's suffering enough already. She got AIDS through a blood transfusion that we thought would save her life. Now, no one can save her."

Eighteen

MORGAN READ EVERYTHING Anne's father gave him about AIDS. The facts made him shudder. What a terrible way for a person to die, he thought. About as terrible as having Huntington's chorea. "The real enemy is death," Anne told him during one of their many long talks. "Sometimes when I hurt really bad, I think of death as a friend, but then I think about how wonderful it is to be alive, and I see death as terrible. I wish I could live. There's so much I wanted to do."

He reached over and took her hand. If death was her enemy, he wanted to hold it off for her. "I've been wanting to ask you something."

She clung to his hand. His skin was warm, and it felt so good to be touched. These days, few people touched her without wearing latex gloves. "Ask me

before the pain pill takes effect and I get spacey,"
she said.

"The night I asked you to stay with me . . . would
you have stayed if it hadn't been for HIV?"

She thought for a long time before answering. "I
know this is going to sound corny, but I'm going to
say it anyway. That night, I wanted to stay. But deep
down inside, I've always wanted to wear white at my
wedding and have it mean something. Not that I've
ever longed to get married," she added hastily. "I always wanted other things first. College, of course. A
career. But *if*—and this is a big if—I ever was to get
married, I'd want my husband to be the first man
and the only man."

"It doesn't sound corny."

"Knowing that I could have infected you with HIV
made me know to stop. Still, I want to believe that
even if I hadn't been HIV-positive, I would have said
no. It's nice to think that you can do something no-
ble, even when it goes against what you want to do."
She touched his cheek, "Morgan, I *was* tempted."

He smiled ruefully. "I wanted you to stay, but in
a way, I was glad you didn't. Even though the rejection hurt, it made you more special."

She fell asleep smiling. Morgan watched her, reliving the short time they'd shared in Colorado. The
night he'd held her, almost made love to her . . . the
afternoon in the old church and cemetery . . . the picnic in the field of flowers . . .

Looking at her now, he saw beyond the gauntness,
beyond the skin eruptions, the shorn hair, the pallor
of her flesh. What he saw was a girl he loved and
could never, ever have.

*   *   *

On Christmas Day, Anne's father carried her out to the tree in the living room. He settled her gently on the sofa and proceeded to heap her lap full of gifts. "Dad, you shouldn't have," she protested.

"Hey, it's Christmas. You know I couldn't let it pass without buying you my usual assortment of useless presents!"

She struggled with the wrappings. He knelt on the floor in front of her. He reminded Morgan of a little kid trying hard to please. "Here, let me help. I told that clerk not to use so much tape."

She opened boxes packed with sweaters, socks, a fleece bathrobe, sets of pajamas, and classical music CDs. "It's too much, Dad," she admonished.

"I saved the best for last," he said, pulling out one more small, flat box.

She opened it and let out a delighted cry. "Daddy, it's a first-edition Emily Dickinson! You shouldn't have! I love it. It's beautiful." She held up the book and flipped through it, eyes glowing. She leaned down and hugged him.

"I did a computer search and found it in an antiquarian bookstore in Boston."

Anne showed the book to Morgan. "Give my dad that box with the red paper, please" she said. "I've got something extra special for you too, Dad."

Morgan fetched it, and Anne's father shook it dutifully. "It's heavy."

"Be careful with that."

He undid the box. Inside lay a hinged photo frame, and when he swung it open, tears formed in his eyes. On one side was a photo of Anne's mother;

on the other, a photo of Anne. Morgan, looking over Dr. Wingate's shoulder, couldn't believe the resemblance between the two women. "Mrs. Hankins helped me," Anne said, seeing her father's reaction. "I slipped your favorite one of Mom—the one that got damaged years ago—from the album and had it restored and hand-colored. The one of me was my sophomore yearbook photo."

"You told me they weren't any good."

"Well, I changed my mind. I mean, considering the way I look now."

He looked up at her and held the photos to his chest. "You're beautiful," he whispered. "You're both beautiful, and I'll treasure this forever."

Morgan felt awkward, as if he was intruding. "I got you something too," Anne told Morgan. "Mrs. Hankins selected it, but I told her what to get."

Morgan ripped open the box to find a heavy sweater of dark navy blue, along with a framed photo of Anne on Golden Star.

"Marti took it this summer and sent me the negative. I had it enlarged."

He couldn't take his eyes from it. She looked lovely and perfectly healthy. "Thank you," was all he could manage.

"It was one of the best times of my life," she said. "I'll always be glad I went."

"Aunt Maggie shipped this to me for you." He fished around under the tree and dragged out the gift he had for Anne. He wanted Anne to like it, hoped she'd grasp what he really wanted to tell her, but couldn't put into words.

She removed the paper slowly, with effort, because her hands ached so badly. Inside the box lay a pale buckskin dress, adorned with beads and feathers. "Remember, I told you that my great-great-great grandmother was a full-blooded Cheyenne?" Morgan asked.

The afternoon in the cemetery by the church sprang vividly into Anne's mind. "I remember."

"That's a Cheyenne ceremonial wedding dress. I thought you might like to see what one looks like."

She placed the soft deerskin against her cheek. She understood what he meant through the gift, what he couldn't say in front of her father. A large lump swelled her throat shut as she gazed into the depths of his blue eyes. "The Cheyenne must have been wonderful people," she said softly, "to have dressed their brides in such splendor."

He wished he could tell her how special he thought she was. He wanted to thank her for allowing him into her life. He wanted to tell her that this was the best Christmas he'd known in years. "Cheyenne women are brave and beautiful," he replied. "And I should know."

Anne's father served turkey with all the trimmings. Morgan ate heartily, to make up in part for Anne's eating almost nothing. Afterward, he insisted she call Marti, who squealed with delight when she heard Anne's voice. "*Feliz Navidad*," Marti shouted.

Hearing Marti's voice triggered a flood of memories. "Morgan tells me you're going back to the ranch next summer," Anne said.

"Oh, Anne, if only you could come back too."

If only . . . "I'll be with you in spirit."

"I'm glad Morgan's with you," Marti said, her tone subdued. "I *told* you he liked you."

"Have a wonderful life, Marti."

"*Te amo*, Anne."

"I love you too." Anne hung up and wept softly. There were so many people she was going to miss.

"I didn't want you to be sad," Morgan said, apologetically.

"It's all right. I'm glad I talked to her. You make sure Skip treats her right. Her old boyfriend didn't. She deserves the best."

Toward nightfall, Morgan went for a long walk alone. Snow had fallen, fresh and white, but had turned dingy in the streets. Everywhere he turned, there was traffic, noise, and people hurrying along the sidewalks. He began to miss the solitude and beauty of Colorado. Yet, he'd promised himself he would stay for as long as Anne was alive. He thought about trying to find a job, something to help Anne's father with expenses. He wanted to contribute in some way.

By the time he returned to the apartment, it was late. Certain Anne was asleep, Morgan crept toward his sleeper sofa. A light coming from Dr. Wingate's study caught his eye. He wondered why Anne's father would be working on Christmas night, then decided to talk to him about getting work. Morgan tapped on the door, and entered after hearing a muffled, "Come in."

He saw Anne sitting in front of her father's computer. Surprised, Morgan blurted, "What are you doing up so late?"

She gave him a weary smile and gestured toward

an empty chair beside the desk. "I've been touring various libraries," she said.

"What?"

Anne tapped several computer keys, and the printer began clacking. "My father gave me the idea when he told me how he searched for the Emily Dickinson book. I don't know why I didn't think of it before."

"Think of what?"

"Doing a computer search about Huntington's chorea," she said. "Sit down. I've discovered some very interesting information for you."

Nineteen

MORGAN WENT HOT and cold all over. He wasn't sure he wanted any more information about Huntington's. "You should be resting," he told Anne. "It isn't good for you to be up this late."

"I'll have an eternity to rest," she said matter-of-factly. "I only have now to be alive."

"Don't talk that way."

"Sit down," she repeated. "There are some things you need to know." He sat. She tore off paper from the printer. "I researched medical magazines and newspaper articles. I've read and printed out the material for you. The interviews with people who are facing the prospect of Huntington's are interesting."

"Let me guess," Morgan said dourly. "It's tough to make plans."

"First of all, I think you shouldn't be afraid to take the test. The test wasn't in use until 1986. I guess it's like my AIDS problem. They started screening blood in eighty-five—too late for me." She shook her head. "Anyway, the test is a predictor. It requires blood samples from your relatives, like you and your Aunt Maggie and your father. Is there anyone else in your father's family?"

"I don't think so. My grandparents died years ago."

"The test looks for certain DNA markers on genes of groups of family members. If the marker's found in any one person's genes, it means the person will get Huntington's. If it isn't, he's home free."

"I know about the test. So what?"

Amazed by his lack of interest, Anne declared, "All it takes is a blood sample, and according to reports, the test is over ninety percent accurate." She shuffled through the papers in her hand. "The testing is expensive, up to five thousand dollars, but it would settle the matter once and for all for you and your aunt."

Morgan gave her a quizzical look. "And what if the test is positive? What if it tells me I'm going to get Huntington's? I'd get to trade worrying about *if* the disease will strike for worrying about *when*. What kind of comfort is that?"

Anne was at a loss for words. She'd thought he'd be overjoyed to know he could stop living with uncertainty. "I figured you might want to know. You could prepare—"

Morgan bolted out of the chair. "Well, I don't want to know. If it's going to happen to me, then I'll have years and years to think about ending up like my father. Plenty of time to contemplate turning into a maniac and living in an institution."

"But you'd also have time to plan for your life."

"What kind of plans does a person make when he knows he's going to die a horrible death?" She stiffened, and instantly, he wished he'd minded his tongue. "I'm sorry. I didn't mean to hurt you."

"Believe me, I know what it's like to live with an automatic death sentence, Morgan. I know what it's like to feel your life slipping away from you, and know that all the medical technology in the world can't save you. But even so, you have choices. I chose to spend the summer in Colorado instead of the hospital. What I'm telling you is that you may not have to live with a death sentence. You have the opportunity to know if you can live a normal life or not."

"What's the point?"

"You don't have to take such reckless chances with your life. You don't have to keep courting death, daring it by living dangerously."

"Now you sound like my aunt and uncle."

"You can make plans for a future," Anne pleaded.

"It isn't that simple," he insisted. "If the test is positive and people find out, how do you think they'll treat me?"

Morgan had begun pacing. Suddenly, he walked over to the chair where Anne sat. "What if Aunt Maggie and I took this test, and I found out she's going to get it but I'm not? How do you think that would make me feel? Or what if it's the other way around?"

"You'd let guilt stand in the way of knowing the

truth? Truth sets people free. Don't you want to be free?"

He avoided Anne's question. "My aunt's been good to me. I don't want to see her suffer."

"Doesn't she wonder if it's going to happen to her?"

"Sure she does. She told me that every time she drops something, or trips, she wonders if it's the start of Huntington's for her." He thought a moment, then asked, "Both of us would have to take it—isn't that what your research says?"

" 'The larger the genetic sample, the more accurate the results,' " Anne quoted from one of the pages.

Morgan rocked back on his heels. "Does any of your research say there's a cure yet for Huntington's?"

"No. It's like AIDS—no cure."

"Then we're back to square one, aren't we? What's the point?"

Anne felt frustrated. Why was he being so stubborn? He was allowing his irrational fears to direct the course of his life. "So, you don't want to know? You don't want to ever take the test?"

Morgan leaned down over her chair. "So long as I don't know, I have hope it won't strike me. Without hope, what else is there?"

"That's not hope—that's gambling, playing the odds." She reached up and touched his cheek. "I knew that I had no hope of living—of beating AIDS. But it didn't keep me from wanting to live every moment I had left. If I hadn't wanted that, I would never have met you."

Morgan felt a heaviness in his chest. He wanted to

hit something with his fist. He wanted to tear something apart with his bare hands. He looked down into Anne's upturned face and forced the anger down. He pulled her to her feet and gently wrapped her thin, frail body in his arms.

She lay her cheek against his chest and felt his lips move in her hair. She heard his voice come softly from above her. "Anne, I appreciate all you've tried to do for me, all the time and energy you spent on this project. I can't face it the way you have. I wish I could, but I can't. Please understand."

She clung to him fiercely. "I understand," she whispered sadly, knowing that she didn't.

Christmas was the last good day Anne remembered having. She ran a fever which rose steadily, and began to cough. The home-care nurse listened to her lungs. "She should be in the hospital," the nurse told Anne's father.

Racked with pain, Anne turned glazed eyes toward him. "No hospital," she wheezed. "You promised. It's my choice."

Her father's face looked ashen and tortured. "Isn't there anything we can do for her at home?"

"Oxygen, of course," the nurse said in resignation.

A portable tank was brought in, and a mask slipped over Anne's mouth and nose. More medications were ordered, and an IV was inserted into her arm to maintain proper nutrition. She slept propped up on a stack of pillows.

Morgan acted like a caged cat. He paced, went out on endless walks, but would suddenly panic, thinking that Anne had died and he hadn't been with her.

Then he'd turn and run down the sidewalk like a madman all the way back to the apartment. Heart pounding, he would rush inside and to her room; only when he saw her, heard her labored breathing, would he calm himself.

He felt that there was something left unfinished between them. He couldn't determine what. He only knew their differing viewpoints about the test for Huntington's had become some sort of wedge. Anne was too ill for them to discuss it again, but he thought about it constantly. He wanted to be at peace with her, wanted her to know how much he loved her and would miss her.

One afternoon, he stole quietly into her room. Her eyes were closed, and the book of poetry her father had given her for Christmas lay across her lap. He watched her chest heave, listened to the hiss of the oxygen tank. Her eyelids fluttered open. "Hi," he said.

She smiled weakly. "Hi, yourself. I was having a dream."

"About me?"

"You're so vain. I was dreaming about my mother. I was a little girl again, and we were together." Morgan swallowed against the thick knot in his throat. "I'll see her soon," Anne continued.

"Please, don't . . ."

"No tears in heaven, Morgan. Remember that."

He turned his head, not wanting her to see the tears in his eyes. He took a long, shuddering breath. "Were you reading?" he asked, pointing to the book.

"Trying to. My vision keeps blurring. Very annoying. I know most of her poems by heart anyway, so I guess it shouldn't matter."

He picked up the book and dragged a stool beside her bed. "Want me to read to you?"

"You told me you don't like to read."

"I don't mind." He leaned forward. "Just don't tell Skip!"

"Your secret's safe with me."

He thumbed through the slim volume of verses. "I forgot how depressing Emily was."

"A poet par excellence," Anne said. The effort cost her, but she felt a sense of peace come over her. How wonderful it was to have Morgan holding her book, doing this kindness for her that went against his rugged nature.

"Which poem?" he asked.

"You choose," she said.

He flipped a few more pages, then settled on the one he knew she liked best. In his deep, voice, he read, " 'Because I could not stop for Death— / He kindly stopped for me— / The Carriage held but just Ourselves— / And Immortality. . . . ' "

Twenty

"ANNE, ANNE!" MORGAN was awakened from a sound sleep by the voice of Anne's father shouting her name. Morgan rushed to Anne's room. Dr. Wingate was frantically trying to get her to respond, desperately trying to find a pulse. "Call nine-one-one!" he yelled at Morgan.

The emergency squad arrived in minutes, and although the team tried to resuscitate her, they couldn't. Morgan hung in the hall, feeling numb and cold. He couldn't see her body for all the people surrounding her bed. He didn't want to, really. He wanted to remember Anne as she'd been in life, with a smile on her lips, her eyes closed, listening to him read her favorite poetry. Death had come for Anne Wingate. Morgan hoped that her final journey had been painless.

Once the body had been taken away, Dr. Wingate

sat on the sofa and stared at the floor with red-rimmed eyes. Morgan called Mrs. Hankins and told her. "Oh, my poor, dear girl," she cried. "I'd come to love her like a daughter." The older woman sniffed and added, "It was a merciful way for her to die, you know ... to simply slip away into heaven in her sleep. I've seen AIDS patients die much more horribly."

Morgan took little comfort in her words. Anne was gone. Nothing could bring her back. "Dr. Wingate wants to have a memorial service here after Anne's funeral," Morgan said. "He wants all the people who cared for her to come here instead of to the cemetery."

"I'll make some calls," Mrs. Hankins offered. "You make sure the professor takes care of himself."

Over the next two days, Morgan and Anne's father worked silently, side by side, taking care of necessary arrangements. They dressed Anne in the Cheyenne wedding dress. She looked beautiful lying on a bed of white satin, in the soft buckskin decorated with feathers and beads. In the coffin with her, Dr. Wingate placed a photo of Anne's mother and the One Last Wish letter. "It gave her so much joy," he explained to Morgan.

"Did you ever learn who JWC is?"

"No. In a way, I don't want to know. I'd like to believe that this JWC is part of life's mystery—someone who is kind and good. He or she is probably somewhere in the world doing other generous things for good people like Anne right now. It helps balance out a world where someone gets AIDS and dies before her time."

At the memorial service, Morgan realized it was comforting to sit around with the people who had known and loved Anne and hear them share memories of her. When Marti called from Los Angeles he was grateful to hear her voice.

By the end of the week, Morgan started packing his things. He folded shirts and jeans, stuffing them along with his Christmas gifts into two duffel bags. Since he hated good-byes, he'd planned to be gone before Anne's father returned from teaching his morning classes. Morgan wrote him a note and thanked him for allowing him to be a part of Anne's final weeks.

Anne's father came in just as Morgan was finishing. "I didn't expect you back so early," Morgan said.

"Today was my last class till the fall," Dr. Wingate replied. "The head of my department told me to take my sabbatical early. Anne and I were planning to visit England next summer, you know." He struggled to keep his voice even. "Anyway, they told me to go on now, so I am. I'll be going to London."

Morgan felt sorry for him. "I'm sure the time off will be good for you," he said.

"Are you leaving now?"

"I don't want to wear out my welcome."

"You won't, Morgan." The tall man rested his hand on Morgan's shoulder. "I know I didn't exactly welcome you here with open arms when you first came, but I'm glad you've been here. I truly appreciate all you gave to my Anne."

"Thank you, sir."

"Anne was very fond of you. You made the time she had left special. I'll always be grateful."

Morgan swallowed against the thick lump in his throat. So far, he'd kept his tears private, and he didn't want to lose it now. "I'll never forget her."

"Are you going back to Colorado?"

"Not directly. I have a stopover to make in St. Louis. Someone I need to visit."

"Family?" Morgan nodded. "You're lucky," Dr. Wingate said with a sad smile. "I wish I had more family around me. I wish . . ." He shook his head and tried to collect himself. "I feel so lost, even though I tried to prepare myself for the inevitable!"

"You're entitled." Morgan picked up his bags.

"Wait." Anne's father said. "Anne gave me something to give to you." He patted his pockets. "It's here, I know. She wanted to be sure you got it. Here it is."

Morgan took the white envelope carefully.

Dr. Wingate explained, "I know that it's a check. Anne told me it was for some expensive test that you might want to take someday. A test you need to take. You know, Morgan, Anne's right—you should really think about going on to college. From what I know, you're a bright young man, and it's not as if I don't see plenty of freshmen entering college. Trust my judgment. Don't waste your life."

Morgan stared at the envelope and read what Anne had written: *The true miracle is in giving, not receiving.* He recognized the words from her One Last Wish letter. Of course, Anne's father had no way of knowing what test Anne was talking about, but for Morgan, knowing that she'd given him the means to explore his future left him dumbstruck.

"Thank you" was the best he could trust his voice to say as he tucked the envelope into his coat pocket.

He held out his hand, and Anne's father shook it. "Keep in touch, please," Dr. Wingate said. "You know where to find me."

Morgan agreed, then heaved his bags and started down the hall. As he passed Anne's room, he stopped and stood in the doorway. His gaze swept through it. The bed was neatly made; the sickroom paraphernalia, removed. A shaft of winter sunlight poured through the window. The room looked soft and shimmery, ready and waiting for someone who would never return.

He closed his eyes and recalled Anne's face, her smile. He realized that she had been like one of the shooting stars he'd seen so often in the Colorado night sky. Anne had streaked across his life and lit up its darkness.

He caught the scent of a garden drifting from her room, but wasn't surprised. *"Daddy says one can always distinguish a great lady. The air around her smells like flowers."* Morgan heard Anne's voice as clearly as he had on the golden summer afternoon only months before. He nodded in understanding, even though he saw no flowers in her room. Her presence would always linger in his life, no matter what his future held.

"I won't forget you, Anne," he vowed. Morgan turned and walked quickly toward the front door.

Dear Reader,

I hope you enjoyed these three novels. The One Last Wish books are close to my heart. Each character in each book faces life's challenges with courage and dignity. I hope you'll want to read the other One Last Wish books and the Jenny novels, which continue JWC's legacy:

Mourning Song
A Time to Die
Someone Dies, Someone Lives
The Legacy: Making Wishes Come True
Please Don't Die
She Died Too Young
All the Days of Her Life
A Season for Goodbye

I loved writing these books, and my wish is that you will feel inspired to face your challenges, whatever they might be, with courage and hope.

Best wishes,

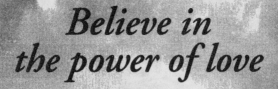

Be my angel . . . .

Special hardcover edition!

ISBN: 0-553-57145-1

*H*eather is unprepared to face the famine and misery she encounters when she joins a mission group. Only Ian, a medical volunteer, can help her see beyond the horror in this inspirational new novel from bestselling author Lurlene McDaniel.